Amoebic Simulacra

Stories

Christopher S. Peterson

Fomite

Burlington, VT

ISBN- 978-1-947917-15-6
Library of Congress Number- 2019940229

Fomite
58 Peru Street
Burlington, VT 05439
www.fomitepress.com

To Betty Jo Peterson, RIP

Amoebic Simulacra is a becrazed carnival ride, the varietal voices of these mind-altering stories uttering fiery satanic verses. In addition, the book is a psychedelic bottle rocket with a wackadoo genie inside, on a space-age acid-trip to a colorful Weirdsville. It is a literary hallucinogen capable of giving the reader insectean antennae.

Contents

Sea No Evil

Pissing in the wind: Californian dream of strange daze in high times. The place is the equivalent of a faded postcard, paperback, album cover, a funky haven with good vibes for misfits on the margins. Swinging (or hanging, depending on your situation) Seventies in an alternate dimension, a galaxy way far away. Dig: Smogswept sky with the glowing, garish hues of blown glass. Piano Tuna, a scrawny, pale-complected, goateed gumflipflop, a slacker/stoner, garrulous, garden-variety guy, second-string curator at the 'Leave it to Beaver' museum, 'Joie de Cleavre', a master of disaster, dull as ditchwater, who aims low and shoots his own toes off, is firmly ensconced in his favorite toffee-brown beanbag chair in his pistachio-ice-cream-green bungaloid bachelor pad (rent exorbitant, enough to bend one out of shape) adjacent to the rather posh Doiph Inn belonging to a Swedish gazillionaire, and blazes a bong in a Last

Supper-like party with his pals, Fillmore East fuckups, writer Salmon Rushdie, photographer Manta Ray, artist Keith Herring, rapper Busta Crabb, and twin Charlie, acid-tripping beach-bums, outcast kinfolks, freedom-fighters, admittedly cultural detritus, rallied against their foes, the squares, these forces promoting fear, the recovering fratboys chemically influenced and immersed with insane intensity in a dopehead gabfest, prosaic and poignant, on the Summer Of Love being a Big Bang Last Sigh, and Einsteinian theories of light, sharing StarKist out of the can. A 'Tom and Jerry' cartoon is on the crappy TV. PCP taken. The zomboid chums discuss the possibilities of Godzilla being a Korean or Vietnam vet in disguise. Hits off a fat-ass spliff. An 'Adam-12' re-run materializes magically on the boob tube. With his disheveled hippie appearance, old-fashioned (Victorian-era) mutton chop sideburns untrimmed, and unkempt Medusa moptop, Piano Tuna believes he blends in better when on the job sleuthing (usually nonlinearly) ... He is a laid-back, proud private dick, Jim Rockford through the Looking Glass of Dashiell Hammett, a relocated Bostonian who resembles a strung-out, real-life Shaggy from 'Scooby-Doo.' He's wearing a Meat Loaf 'Bat out of Hell' tee-shirt, hip-hugging bellbottom jeans, and Roman sandals. He knits his 'Kolchak' tube-socks that whistle the program's theme when you walk. LSD dipped into. Tide sounds like canned sitcom laughter. An 8-track tape of The Three Degrees' silky-smooth song, 'When Will I See You Again', plays. Minnellian-MGM-moving-picture-color-noirish city. The glaucous ocean has this rancid spoiled-Brussels-sprouts-mingled-with-damp-cheap-vinyl odor. Waves thump on sallow sand. Marmalade moon glares in the jujube-jet firmament which spits sleet-seeds; an infinitesimal meteor shower. Whisperous surf. Harbor hell ... moored, monstrous boats seesaw. Battlecries of seagulls. Wishing-aloud waters. Dolorous strains of Neil Young. Ships' horns in the misty distance sound as cows lowing. Stars with glow worm glimmer. Saliferous breezes bring on a spicy-stew aroma. Thunder has a Bali-gong-deep resonance. Lightning's profound fiery chariots only the prophets could have predicted. Buildings look like a bunch of edifices that play a town on television. Bees of citizenry hum in the hive of the metropolis. Here's a region where climate change can occur instantly, turning from hot to cold and vice versa. Stupefied scientists speculate global warming is simmering to a boil. Mutha turned out, blasting from a sunburned, skinny skateboarder's boombox: the searing 'Maggot Brain' tune from Parliament Funkadelic. Miniskirted knockouts sashay. Bikers fit and tanned mill around their Harleys. The chiaroscuro is a cosmic lantern show. A massive, modified barge, The Snark, a cross between a monastery and Disneyland, the vessel a rupture in the maritime universe, lurks predaciously. The Loan Shark, an alpha-ape with bingo-witch tits, a brutal, Brylcreemed brontosaurus, in proximity to cranes and containers on the pier, uses his cement-block fists, with a prize-fighter's precision, to seek out the soft spots in the solar plexus of a mulatto hip-hopper, pathetically pleading for a pardon. He made the mistake of borrowing money to jump-start his record-label and fell behind on the payments. Pummeling on an epic scale. Silver-and-gold falsies knocked out. Imagine a teenage girl's hazel, lachrymose, almond-shaped eyes: filmy, round windows looking out at identical grassy hills, illumination in its liquescent state, the flecks in her irides an incandescent storm, a retiform retinal rain. Holy hallelujah! Her name is Fabienne Frisbey-Francart, a surfer-gal/flower-child, a welly-wearing, lissome bombshell, gallinaceous, goofball giantess, duck-walking, an auricomous angel, a lostcause badapple babe who sure loves her poncho and swampers, with a Bride-of-Frankensteinian-noctambulistic gait stepping into Piano Tuna's Bleak House, a Day-Glo Golgotha, unannounced, befogged with pot and blowing in on her personal weather system, and promptly plopping on his lap. She's his semi-ex, an idiot-surfant with wavecraft superpowers. Hasn't seen the gorgeous gamine in many months. She disassembled their affiliation and skipped. Compute? She was not kicked. She set sail, canceled their series. She's the port in his storm, a ham in his sad sandwich. He is the squeaky wheel she greases. Howdies. Peaces. Rapping. Right on. It's material she perpetrated taking the exit ramp. Didn't use a stick shift. Accusations, abridged, of relationship dismantlement. She takes a toke and swig, in a fit of giggles, revealing adorable, snow-white snaggle-teeth. Her tawny, lengthy limbs. His hormonal homing device circles in on her. She tells him her fisherman father, Bastien, has gone missing. Back-of-milk-carton MIA. Herring calls her a "glorious goddess." The others gawk and gulp. "Dynamite," sez Rushdie. "Kiss my grits," Crabb. His bro-cooks aren't going to spoil this broth. She, a jailbait femme fatale, a clear and present danger, ready for prime time, rises, skips to the boiler-large keg, straight, stiffens, and the hula-hoop Saturn-rings those horsy hips. Her washboard-middle. MFSB's groovy hit 'TSOP' cranks from the stereo speakers. Pomegranate yogurt used as dip for Wise potato chips by Manta Ray. Levis commercial. Flat Pepsi imbibed by Busta Crabb. Salmon Rushdie ingests Eggo waffles marinated in melted butter and grocery store chili. Coca Cola-colored clouds. Longboards and rock-and-roll. Horrendous gridlock. Altered states and trash television. He's got quite a mystery to solve, a humdinger whodunnit, the humanoid Sherlock Holmes does. He's gonna catch it like a surfer a gigantic wave. He absorbs her as a wet towel does sand, really loves her from floor to ceiling. He never got over her. Not even close. He's got the serious munchies, craving Burger King. She slathers herself over him akin to an industrial-size trowel. Is she kicking his tire? She is a signal in the noise. Weed imposes order on chaos. Marijuana creates law and order. Parabolic flight of his missile-penis. The blonde glamazon ingenue orbits the dingy dump in a centripetal swirl. His pet hamsters suddenly transmogrify into cardboard cutouts of 'Gilligan's Island' cast members and quote Shakespearian dialogue in a Munchkinland Technicolor environment. Cannabis brume. M&Ms advertisement. Utopian L.A.. He is a PI in Paradise. He wants her to climb his Everest without gear. Significant suspense. Everything's hunky-dory because Andy Gibb's 'Shadow Dancing' plays on the radio artifact on the bookshelf, followed by Carly Simon's 'You're So Vain', the gravelly-voiced DJ, Wolfman Jack, and Billy Paul's 'Me and Mrs. Jones.' The penile light-house ejaculates semenoid lambency from its circumcised tiptop. Blood of night in its vast volume seeps into the swimming pool of day. Piano Tuna's Aquarius has come of Age. Abruptly he boots his buds and bro, a Geek chorus, so they won't poison his well. Effulgent blurry patterns bleared on the curb piebald with pigeon-poops. An insectival pickup is parked and idles, has definite engine deficiencies. A slender tomboy with a crewcut and in a halter and denim shorts nearly clips a near-naked thickset jogger in a Panama hat pushing a stroller with her scooter. Flies flitter, could easily pass for flicked ash. Fabienne sitting on the couch says the megapolis is a large-scale loony bin, basically. He sips herbal tea, seated on the sofa. Despite having lived here for a decade he still feels like a transplant. She fellates the hash-pipe. She explains she's in the process of setting up a dual-business, doing double-duty as an acupuncturist and chiropractor, her learning curve EKG-ing for reasons various, using a hitherto vacant doughnut shop for her practice. She soughs, fusses with a Rolodex, ashtray, turntable, as if she's inspecting the joint, on the lookout for inventorial irregularities. She is eye-catch-ingly cute, a Slim Jim-thin Wonder Woman sucking on a phallic symbolic Tootsie Roll. Heinous traffic. She suggests he attend a seminar for the perfect weight-gain program. Huh? She mentions the Snidely Whiplash-diabolical Cap'n Prawn, his busy 'Prawnsong' pawn-shop, and the infamous, flat-topped, Dudley Do-Right-esque cop, Stingray, his newspaper-front-page, high-profile busts, reportedly settling scores with his numerous enemies, and changes the subjects. The two strip, sedu-lously, simultaneously. Rollicking rumpus. Her faint flaxen mustache. She raises his flag. Heaven in its serenity and solitude (fast) food for thought. Rip-roaring rumpus. Illusory impression of nature's metamorphic anatomic improvisation. Carnal fire. Clockwork mecha-nisms of manipulation. Bluffing and baiting. It is as though both are attempting to find that fine line to cross when one threatens another ... how far do you go to convince that the threat has substance, before pulling back? To give the perception that one is willing to push it to the limit, perhaps past the point of no return, the aggression is authentic, the element of possibility enhancing the experience. You stand on one leg and give the impression of two. There is the inevitability of certainty, like you have a severe headache which has signs of an impending migraine. He's dead-beat. She's in it for the long haul. To be otherwise is kinda on par with preparing for a vacation and ultimately staying put. Her pudendal pings and pangs. Screwing on the level of combat sport. Somatic slapping during intercourse proving painful for her. They cuddle and kiss. He wraps round her not unlike a shroud. She has an ambiguous allegorical figure. She affects him as changes atmo-spheric. He analyzes her like a tailor would an expensive fabric; or as a set-designer interesting theatrical decor. She's rigid when she should be relaxed. He is sorta centrifugally self-conscious. Fondling, penetration. She sez he's a splitting image of Walerian Borowczyk's Mr. Hyde. Scenery is as a play production's stage. Bright festival of the vault. Prayer of foreplay, benediction of sex. They sleep together. When he wakes she is gone. No note, nothing. Later, snorting lines off a compact mirror and absintheanly crocked (Mike Hammered), in front of an episode of 'Woody Woodpecker,' he receives a phone call from her - washed-up actress, Rebecca DeMoray Eel (a statuesque, fair-skinned, sexy redhead), needs to have her vintage Steinway fixed. Ok. No problem.

Bootsy Collins-bass thunder. George Clinton-flashy leven. The small shrimp craft with a crew of a dozen swabbies is adrift, disabled. They are aware their hours are numbered. It's a foregone conclusion, a waiting game. There was a direct hit. The salts sob, slowly sinking, smoke cigarettes, drink liquor, write letters and put the notes in beer bottles for friends and family, eat clams and fries, shoot the shit. The titanic tanker, The Snark, a leviathanic mechanoid beast, a shop of horrors, moves in like a bull for the wounded toreador. It belongs to midget crime-lord Cap'n Prawn, this fiendish supremo "professor" of criminal sciences, a lascivious lowdown nutjob gnomic Phantom of the Opera, appearance recalling a fake photo of an alien in some stupid tabloid ragazine, with breath foul as goat cheese, self-satisfied smirk, voice an evil spirit Neil Sedaka warbling while gargling asphalt, peepers shot-glasses misted with condensation, the besuited mobster with a demented death-stare that would give you fucking fits of the vapors. His entourage: Miss Pike, catsuit-clad, off-her-rocker resident dominatrix, an Elvira-semblant slag with a modulation like Casey Kasem if he inhaled hellacious amounts of helium, meaty arms, paddle-mitts, beefy legs, flipper-feet, and perma-sneer, dentures razor-sharp; Doc Plankton, a schizoid, irredeemably insipid dweeb inventor articulate like an over-caffein-ated Count from 'Sesame Street' who reminds you of a PED-jacked penguin with a Cagney-esque simper and mugshot-mug who waddle-skulks as a mischievous school-kid, with a handlebar-mustache, chunk of chin-moss, and spray-painted comb-over, dressed in a creamy lab-coat and polyester slacks, his wonkish bifocals held by bat-ears; the Piranha, burly, monosyllabic goons, steroidic thugs, breast-beaters who lube their nerves with Red Bull and who suck adrenaline vampirically, mutant ruffians tough like sacks of anvils with phone book-sized hands and feet, pies lifeless as video cameras, dapper hoods with mangled, mushy, Munchian mouths, sauerkraut-beards, and shotgun-barrel nostrils, whining as wusses, head-hunting storm-troopers armed to the teeth in seersucker camouflage tuxes, bullet-proof life-vests, and orthopedic shoes, their submachine guns slung over broad shoulders, breathing sounding not unlike an air-conditioner's shushings, smack-laying, high-motor, big-hitter mashers shot-out-of-cannon-quick, rootin' and tootin' and cigar-chompin' ... Cap'n Prawn and his motley crew of creepy minions, with a monopoly on misconduct, are indeed individuals you wouldn't wanna mess with. They are currently employing increasingly innovative and insidious methods to eliminate the competition by any means necessary. Walls visually correspond to otherworldly backdrops in old movies. Alkaline air. Juvenile Jena, a trampy runaway, a vaguely Velasquezian Infanta, in a boisterous bathing-suit-and-pumps getup, moves mechanically, as if a toy wound up. Prawn croaks, assessing her as though this is a cast judgment, envisages himself a saint in a sanctuary, projects her on a prurient parallel plane. Her dull discomfiture sharpens his desire for her. He insists his intentions are innocent, his expression enigmatic, embracing her. Her incessant wiggling irritates him. He envisions her posing in his arid antechamber for a nude portrait, performing cunnilingus on her as he masturbates. She reluctantly hugs him. His bed - dolphins coupled in coital congress. He meekly confesses he's addicted to cough syrup and kiddie porn. The baroque bathroom consists of a vaginal sink, cuntal tub, scrotal bowl and penial toilet. He has a stench of urine and feces, the villainous son of a bitch scary enough to make your hair stand on end, tough like an interrogator torturer of a terrorist captive, impudent as an adolescent felon, possessed like a maniac, narrow-minded as a specialist applying his specialty, oddness pronounced, temper explosive, studying his little slut like a music teacher a student instrumentalist soloing and hitting the wrong notes; or as an art critic who prefers impressionist stuff surveying a cubist's creation, it incompatible with his taste and he is annoyed at the prospect of accurately appraising the painting. His cellophane-crinkled brow. Thoughts, for the nonce, under the cerebral seal of secrecy. Here's an awful abyss. His tiny whore beholds these yawning bank-vault quarters. Baboon-bottom-blue empyrean.

The cruel curmudgeon relishes sowing suffering, revels in the excitement as an entertainer devising his entertainments, seized by an atrocious audacity and thrill, in his particular case perverted strategies. He stares at the young, luscious cutie-pie and flies into a frenzy. With the li'l 'tween hooker he's Pan frightening a nymph. The pylon-sized gangster is a projectile, aim true. He is merciless, malicious, adept at inflicting agony, a derangoid death-dealer. Her anguish is palpable. His lust is conspicuous. He scrutinizes her supple, bared, stocky body. He's a devilish bully who unleashes his profound rage. Orgy of fury. And can he surprise-attack, like death can life, weakness strength, sickness health, vice virtue, and, heck, even Gabriel the Prophet to chitchat about the Messiah for Christ's sake. Ogling her exquisite breasts, charming bum, bulging belly, Hobbitoid feet. Her soda pop, straw-sipped, was sneakily spiked with a sedative. In her Gallicised slurry loquaciousness she rambles on full-bore about the twisted branches of her family tree. Prawn at this juncture thumbs her scallop-omphalos and rims her racemose rectus like Phidias etching an obscure nomenclature on Zeus's ring, his bent pinkie in her travestied tuchis as Plato in Canal. He's Pericles with Aspasia, grabbing her petite, pilose form, an excellent entirety. Raunchy, robust romping. She is a delicious dumpling, defiled, sodomized, and diligently. Muzak versions of musicals 'Annie' and 'Jesus Christ Superstar' in their entirety. He is a Lenin-ish authoritarian who thrives on razing a town to the ground, instinct a key turning in the lock of action. The behemothic Snark ploughs through the turbulent Black

Sea. His countenance crumbles, due to deliberation. He has a considerable quantity of bitterness at his disposal, and he imposes the surplus, venting on her. He has a horrible habit, impulsively destroying things beautiful. Devastating degradation. His tongue is a dragon's flame in her. She's a damsel in distress. He laps her pussy and prods her posterior. Colonel Crenna Troutman, an acneous, balding, spindly director of security, erection displayed, strokes himself, licks his lips. It dawns on the queer Quasimodo he must take the initiative and intersperse tender osculations and gentle tactions into the animalian humping. She's oily and salty with fat content. Nether regions molested. The smallfry's scarface whitewashed. He ravages her. Experimental skewering. His menacing moue. Malformed fingers drilling sacred orifices. Cessation. He scratches an itch on his glabrate dome. She glowers at him like a nun at obscene graffiti. He's a public awareness ad personified for symptoms of dementia. Precip pitter-patters. Brand-new walnut-floor. Cap'n Prawn, a rotten soft-boiled egg, manipulates the masses as religion.

It is hellaceously hot 'n' humid and Rebecca DeMoray Eel's mansion is an impressive residence, ostentatiously stunning, its exterior recollective of a hybrid of Moulin Rouge and an Italian palace, its interior, rambling for blocks, riotous with ornate furnishings. Air-con requires attention. Piano Tuna, fried on herb, disembowels the polished classic piano in the quaint and quirky room. His mind meanders off the cranial reservation. He's got butterflies in the basket. There is no shame in his game. Dusk gradually composes it. He sweats as a pig, has a wicked wedgie like you read about. Beach hustlin' and bustlin'. Saltant combers. Coruscation'd assimilated itself to the afternoon and alienated itself. Morning was a deadly bore. Saturated oxygen begins to dry; a baby's face after it had shed tears and a nurse caringly and calmly wiped it with a towelette. Rebecca is dressed to kill in a turquoise bikini and cerise high heels, to best beat the heat. She bends to better offer him a bowl of blow. Pro tuner that he is he positively declines. Slave-driver she ain't. She sniffs, saunters to and fro. Gosh, he daydreams of rising up into her as mercury in a thermometer in a scorcher, and of a mixture of saliva and sperm coagulant on her pallid, slightly flabby belly. The pimples on her flaccid lower back in the refulgence are peacock's eyes. Sinuous fulgent stream through blue heron-tinged curtains. His confidence is lacking, especially after Fabienne split most unexpectedly, and his hope to nail the sleek, carrot-maned thespian fades not unlike a mothball stink on worn clothing that was stored in a chest for eons. Her upper thighs somewhat cellulitic. The fine down on the planar plank of her tummy in the terra-cotta phosphorescence glistens as if irised algae on the surface of a lake. Her navel wide like a carnival lollipop. They listen to Cher's 'Gypsies, Tramps And Thieves.' Kools. Coke. Fuck. Avant-garde fudge omelette at the intellectual 'Fu Munchu' hash house. A quickie. Cadences rise, sound as though they're from a PA. He is a few fries short of a Happy Meal.

Dipstick ain't reachin the oil. Jibber-jabber. Parlor like a business-lounge liberated from an airport. Oinking her his cardiac organ has the sonancy of a Copelandic brass section, sounds as if its raring to go, dahlin. Oxygen as though a bulletproof barrier. They are tubeside. Fans not cooling. Her rock-bottom pays the price. He'd disregarded the imaginary 'Abandon All Hope' sign posted on her rump. Experimentally porking her he thinks they resemble 'The Thing With Two Heads.' Fortune-teller cards of flashes dealt before his very eyes (unlatched from hers) thanks to the augmented grass. She, in her power birthday suit, lets it, and him, ride. Her long skirt, longer jacket and serious shoes were jettisoned. It's all systems go. She sucks on his Popsicle, eats him alive, puts on lace-intensive lingerie and an Eric Carmen LP record choreographically. 'Barney Miller' in nice b&w on the screen. They converse on heretofore unsolved maritime mysteries and get baked. Radical roller coaster ride. He cannot believe this towering temptress is pushing fifty! For a moment he flips casually through a nifty worn copy of Thomas Pynchon's po mo tome, 'Gravity's Rainbow.' He is dressed in a pink bathrobe and matching fluffy slippers. She is diver-on-the-board poised. Visine-humectation. The megalopolis in the soaker is an ancient Atlantis. Her coconut rests on his shoulder like a parrot on a pirate's. Mentally he scans his list of debauchery to-do's. Making out as young lovers at the cinema. Her peaches-and-cream derrière reamed. She sucks on his nipple (stricken with thelitis) like a vampyre a jugular. His heart in his throat as if he ate an artichoke. She pauses for a second to partake of her home-brewed hooch. He submerses himself into her like a slumberer into R.E.M.. She's the center of attraction. Giving no quarter. No cavity spared. Iffy erotic enterprises. She is tempestuous as a tidal wave. He's denuded and defenseless; makes you think of the stoning of St. Stephen. Depravity bender. He's spreadeagled on the contemporary coffee (torture) table, his Cro-Magnon head lost in the snarls of curly hair. She springs like a grasshopper on him. He is rammed in the behind. He's testosterone redolent. Sphincterial exploration. And he spins, clings desperately to her; limpet on a hull. Her cronies, homo method (naturally) actors, amateurish as greenhorn hambones, anorexic dom Robert Kelp and roly-poly sub Rip Ride, manifest not unlike mirages and introduce themselves, conking him upside the cranium with cudgels, the thwacks sounding as baseball bats hitting a hardball, and he's out frigging cold. When he regains consciousness he is smack dab in the middle of a crime scene. His skull pounds and his vision is tripled. Rebecca was stabbed and strangled. He shrieks like an air-raid siren. Then he is cuffed, taken into custody by the hard-nosed Stingray and hauled away by his low-key partner, the huge Hammerhead, once a heavyweight champion wrestler, the Towering Inferno, the pair 'Dragnet'-serious, and is whisked off via police cruiser, a souped-up cardinal Chevy Malibu complete with sponsor-stickers, such as 'Feetena', 'Lifeservers', 'Oh Hairy', 'Quacker Oats', 'Wheez-It', 'Dums', 'Jerkens', 'Bit-O-Money', 'Slaytex', and so forth, in addition to racing stripes and number, to the Gothic station, with its barbed-wire entanglements, beside the

'Bagel Buster' and 'Seegar and Cereal Express' establishments, to be properly booked, charged with murder. He's interrogated in a spare room under harsh sapphire lava-lamp light, where he spills the pintos, explains he was "at the wrong place at the wrongest time," but they don't buy what he's selling. Hammerhead comments he is a "Furry Freak Brother." Stingray is stoic, doesn't get his meaning. Time crawls for Piano Tuna, languishing in a termitic, cramped cell, feeling totally setup, picturing Rebecca's ghastly corpse sprawled on the exotic rug, nicotine screaming at his nerves, and bond is posted. He's bailed by his representation, the tap-dancing, Mad Hatterish, high-powered, hotshot lawyer, Barry Cuda, who looks like an emaciated, choleric Chuck Barris in athletic attire, velour vestments cringe-worthy, and also wearing a bubble-wrap neck-brace, whose wrong-doings keep pace with his right-doings, admitting he's accepting his case "Pro Sonny Bono" solely for the publicity for his struggling rogue law firm. There isn't compelling forensic evidence against Piano Tuna, merely flimsy circumstantial shit.

AT A NEON-LIT, CLAMMY HASH HOUSE, busy as Grand Central, during a downpour, Barry Cuda, the loony adviser, speaking like he's delivering a sales pitch, informs Piano Tuna that a recent client, Bastien Francart, guilty as sin for being a poor parent to his daughter, Fabienne, has joined a culty church group, Mother of God!, run by senile priest Holy Mackerel, bolt-upright and buzz-cut, with his dog-collar and trip-over-long habit, and military retiree the Sturgeon General, hard-of-hearing and world-weary, an unapologetic alcoholic who is Popeye's Pappy-semblanced. Is this converse billable? Piano Tuna is ready for wheeling and dealing, over-susceptible to his party-animal ways, thinking of the shindig obligation this weekend at a dormitorium on a legendary campus. He has defaulted back to his childhood, infantilized himself, having blind faith he'll grow into maturity. He's got to buttress the nerdistocracy with his presence, hooked by its song, an epoch whose ending he cannot see coming through the pot-and-cig smoke, claimed by the celebration, the tapestry of dedication stitched by necessity. Nah. Perish the thought. Being stoned is an invariance in the parameters of being straight. Accepting gale force zen illumination. On a peak-period high his brain is a splitting seam in the fabric of his skull. His aftershave has a Downy detergent fragrance. Macy's Thanksgiving Parade in his head, crowd of coherent thoughts cordoned off. If his coconut was a funny farm his medulla oblongata would be in the paranoid ward. Sea and sky in cahoots and not unmodulated by the light Cracker Jack-colored. Medley of a miscellany of alarms. He is so confused ... if he were a cornerback he wouldn't have the capability of covering his shadow. Maxipad-cumuli commingled with Swedish Fish. Mist like it's made by a fog generator. Celebrants in rubberoid George Lucas masks and wrapped as Hershey Kisses in a retro eatery. Rainfall with the sonance of a running toilet. Cannonballing cloudlets. Eye-catching pop-up

Fabiennes, authenticity-challenged, in a metaphysical continuum of Mister Rogers's Camp Crystal Lake Neighborhood, nestled in a 'Jetsons'-ish city, wacky and jagged, in nauseating blears of sculptured neon, glowing in monster-movie radiation. Speech-balloon Goodyear blimp. A chirpy geezer's Munchkinetic verbosity. Foreign and domestic folks. Clouds karma-cyclical. Ambient digital air quotes of precipitation wash away chalk-drawn skull and bones (artistic anarchism) on a fragile synagogue. Muslim bagpipers and Norwegian choir perform 'Amazing Grace.' Hail sounds akin to bottles clanking against glasses. People as screen presences of departed souls. Midtown's shrink-wrapped. The universe expands, with a counterfactual smorgasbord of global graphics. Dogmess plentiful from a postmagical predawn dream. Overdesigned Hummus and Papaya joints with sublegal specialities. 'Progreaso,' 'Uncle Bums,' and 'Scary Janes' delivery trucks with dings and dirt not exempt from an unmerciful meter maid. Sun is a Hallowe'en jack-o'-lantern trick-or-treating in the cirri o'er haunted houses. The who-done-it ... he never saw it coming. How was he supposed to know? Is he being played? Is this game rigged? He thinks, pissily, he's pondscum. King Kong puffs on an Empire State Building-stogie. Uncle Sams in a block-bash creepfest at its zenith. A zillion vehicles are 'Battlestar Galactica' vessels, spaceships on a highway starscape. Piano Tuna vocally tiptoes. He won't get snookered in the schmoozathon. To him, if it looks like a duck, quacks like a duck, waddles like a duck, then it's Daffy Duck. Will bad turn to worse? He feels as vermin in Barry's wall. Or is the scatterbrained defender a mousetrap, verbiage spring-loaded? Where's The cheese? He has a liar's look. He's an idiot savant sans the necessitous savant portion. Seaport's Pearl Harbor. The pizza with elk-eye (zombie gazing) topping is nauseating. Ocean hyperventilates. Cuda's crocodile criticisms of the judicial system. His complaints come to a close. He takes the counsel of common sense. He goes with the flow of daily circumstances as ceremonial pomp, seems sincere as an atheist miraculously converting to a believer. He issues his words not unlike one reciting text from a holy tract, lines caption-leaden-ish, too swift to press the start button on the beat-down machine of criticism, flipping the switch on the kick-butt contraption. They essentially crash-land in an outrageous Thai-temple rathskeller in the vicinity of an Egyptian establishment of ill-repute. Area enveloped in an eerie, eidolic effluvium. Pelagic suspirations. Buddha buildings. Salmon Rushdie, the Bombay badboy of literary letters, Piano Tuna's closest compadre, strolls past the greasy window. Blubber-thick ale. Hillocks of pancakes. Piano Tuna visualizes Rebecca's scarabaean nombril, sanguiniferous DC comics' Joker-slash-second-smile carved in her throat quease-inducing. The cadaver was grossly, maybe comically contorted. They'd communicated as empty connected apartments. He was like a virgin she demeaned. She was a tantalizing tease, claimed she was his "protectress." Spotlight sunbeam. Burning breaths from his lungs. Manly lewdness. Janis Joplin's 'Me And Bobby McGee' and Jim Croce's 'Time In A Bottle' on the cathedran jukebox. Golly, does he yen for his nubile hippie-chickie, Fabienne. Absolutely. Her athletic build and ballerina grace. Her fanny, part of folklore ... She put ice cubes in his whiskey and whispered he was a bozo. Was she a snake-oil sales-girl taking advantage of a dumbfounded knucklehead with a hangover, a serial ganja-digger? She plunked on the filthy throne and peed, undies rolled at her ankles. Their lighthearted repartee. Those lithe arms and legs with their lady lanugo. Bummer. Did she deem him a pop-culture-riffing putz? Regardless, he could surveil her 24/7. He convinces himself he was her fastmouthed sidekick, Ah, to shorten his longing ... She could be an alluring arbitrix, and sound thoroughly psychotic. 'Welcome Back, Kotter' on the ol' aerial'd tube. The proprietor, a George the Animal Steele-hirsute-and-lardaceous-and-nuciform Asian, Hung Lo, with this Mr. Cleanish pate and nictitating earring, bends the antenna as a pretzel. Olive and violet vista looks radio-active, like out of a Japanese creature-feature flick. A stretch Rolls Royce limo pulls into a nubilous, unappeasable lot of a bilious health club with a helical fire-escape. Meanwhile Barry prattles on about crackers clientage. Goon squad of Piranhae march through the neighborhood with dead-serious Loan Shark, toupee lopsided, in the lead to shake down some stooges. Jive-arse mad dogs. Skyline borders the science-fictional. Gee, he yearns to bestow papal blessings upon geeky Fabienne's   Charmin-soft-and-white-and-squeezable buttocks. She's the crown jewel of honeybunches. Her garlic-breath. Perspiry armpits. Dirty feet. Runny nose. Multitude of personality disorders. He often fantasizes on her getting DPed by Cheech & Chong and/or gang-banged by the Partridge Family. Her fascination with roulette, stamps, Kleenex, and Caribbean cruises. Crepuscular coherence. Satanic-red welkin. Sprinkles with the sonancy of sizzling filament. Industrial shoreline diminished by the smaze. Air tastes as metallic grape. Piano Tuna's boatload of regrets. Mmm, would he surrender his soul to the Devil for a Fabienne sighting. He wonders if she's even in the same zip code. Reflections are intrinsically invitations for seeking out blunt and brew. She was kneeling on the grungy linoleum, in her purple panties (keester-cleft exhibiting) and yellow hooded sweatshirt, mindblowingly breathtaking, rummaging through the hand-me-down refrigerator (its door prime territory for varietal species of migratory magnets) for the Ziploc of wacky tobacky, babbling on getting "joint custody" of it. Ha. Without her he is a bar without the mitzvah, pre without the nup. Fish-shiny luster. Dominican and Haitian vendors. Beach-goers ooze out of the florid wallpaper. James Taylor's 'You've Got A Friend,' thence America's 'Horse With No Name.' Barry pigs out on egg rolls and rice and rum-sundae for dessert. Piano Tuna utters an upbeat version of Spock's "Live long and prosper" with a rhythm and bluesy intonation to say goodbye to Barry Cuda.

ANOTHER LEAD IN SEARCHING FOR BASTIEN, Oliver Hardy-shaped and Peter Lorre-faced, bites the dust. Piano Tuna, swivel-eyed, has been hunting them, chasing them into blind alleys. He'd put the word on the street to get the rumor mill spinning. His feelers are out there to find Fabienne's pops. Is there a more effective way of impressing a gal than locating her dear dada? Kaleidoscopic celestial sphere. His heart flutters like a parakeet in a cage, thinking of her healthy heinie, Tiepolo-carmine vaginal organ. His libido is an untamable beast. Tenderizing her butt, it with a dank-soil aroma. She is inscrutable as Rembrandt's Bathsheba, a beauteous butterfly stuck by his penis-pin. Yes! Mole marking her tailbone. Her clam a wound reopened digitally. He is a galavanting goober. Ideas on his grey matter not unlike cottages on a Scottish village. Her privates are cut fruit, the juice spilling. Peaceniks protesting at a dubious Korean massage parlor. Rubiginose sun. Opaline light blunt as a cafeteria knife. Black Panthers get wacked on smack at picnic tables in a park. Piano Tuna dredges up his nemesis, rule/ball-breaking Stingray, scowling and savage, square-jawed and lumbering, guardian of the galaxy, his stomping (and beating) grounds, running roughshod over him, bringing down his high, he who can cut to the bone and make the slicing artistic, a Bunyan-and-Babe two-in-one badass, the yin to his yang. Piano Tuna is cloudified, meandrous in a labyrinthine, mellow broccoli haze. This is a film 420 noir and he's on auto pilot where currents of comedy turn into rapids. Many weirdos encountered. Slapstick. Red herrings pile up in a bait bucket. He's a Shamus in Jesus sandals, a needle-using Philip Marlowe, a gonzo Elliot Gould in a surreal take on 'The Long Goodbye,' a slacker cat stumbling in some potboiler walkabout in the seedy city's underbelly, a jumbled jaunt in a time machine (the days, nights, weeks a veritable mishmash) and endeavoring to put the psychedelic pieces of the puzzle together. Pratfalls. He wants to get off the zany carousel, un-merry-go-round. Gin-and-tonic do the trick. Events have washed over him as psychotropics in a scuzzy opium den. With his mangy perm his appearance hints at a Harpo Marx shroomer. Fabienne's a Cali shamaness, a free-spirited mystic so existential Walt Whitman would've worshiped her. She orbits men like they're distant planets. He feels as Hackman desiring Melanie in 'Night Moves.' There was a threesome, Piano Tuna, Fabienne, and the brunette Valkyrie, Valerie, with her concave Lennon-esque spectacles, chiseled cheekbones, crooked canines, tie dye jersey, and flared jeans, and it was less a love triangle and more a lusty polygon, in his sun-soaked beach-shack, the trio inhaling and exhaling from Marlboros on the shag carpet cig-stained. He's a lower primate loser on angel dust, a sorry, slobbish Sam Spade flipping through Rolodex flashbacks. He muses thoroughly on free love, mulls over class warfare, ponders mortal enemies. Wasted, from pill-popping, to his bugged oculi a reformed junky family he is familiar with, in a reunion, transforms into an Art Nouveau Matisse rotoscope. To him this is all the roach-end of the flower-power era. Fabienne in her peekaboo Daisy Dukes ... In his Cecil B. DeMille pornutopia Fabienne writhes like she is an extra on speed. She's the wild young thing in 'The Big Sleep.' Her gnarly gnashers, copper tan. Her flat tummy. He is garbed in his undertaker finery. His doper's what-me-worry grin. Faith-healers and dream-peddlers. He plummets into bottomless rabbit holes, in his damaged Dodge Dart. Suspects are stepping-stones in a shape-shifting odyssey of a complex web. He isn't sure who or what he's pursuing. He clips his Wolverine-sideburns with scissors using the rearview mirror. In spite of his paranoid frenzy he completely pines for his lady. She is an unpriceable (even to Bob Barker) commodity. She's a looker with a husky inflection he's got a crush on. Life without her is a continual surfboard wipeout, is like scaling the Himalayas barefoot. He was rough with her, squishing her as a tube of toothpaste. She let him off with a verbal warning. He was a bundle of energy after the soirée with those snobby schmoozers at her sister's spacious gallery in town. Contemplating hippicide. A melodramatic, scene-stealing overdose. They, uh, pinkie-swore they'd never part. "It's not the destination," she purred, "it's the trip that matters mostest." Insectile helicopter. He receives invaluable information on Mother of God! and its ecclesiastical guru from the flagpole-like, swaggering, peacockish Huggy Boar, in Elton-esque shades, leisure suit and platform-shoes, from the hood, with his slick slanguage. He came through with flying colors. Closing credits for 'Kojak'. He missed 'Baretta'! 'War of the Gargantuas' is being broadcast. Great timing! No, he's got to tune into the 'Lawrence Welk' marathon. Right on! He sparks a doob; a salute to his independence. He scarfs fresh produce. His digestive tract feels rerouted though, detoured to ... Was it the Cheetos in the Cheerios, buried alive in the saccharoid sugar (freebie packets found in the mailbox) and irrigated in diet soda? What about 'Brady Bunch' and 'Superfriends'? Ya gots to prioritize. Crib's a toxic mess. Is he an incompetent clown when it comes to detecting? Who cares! Electric cattle-prod of a vibrator. Dust from demolition. Elvis picture Muzak. Showers vaporized. A mohawked black brother with prison tats pimpmobiling away from the curb, the mayo-white auto with dent-and-scratch stigmata, perhaps leaving a shagadelic situation, a soulful Peaches & Herb lovey-dovey/soulful ballad high-decibeled. Waterscape with tons of trees with lotsa leaves in the draining rays. Lipstick shades of an arcing rainbow, texturing the waxed paper sky. On his answering machine - a message from Annie Moan, a phone-sex operator: Marlin Gaye, her African-American husband (a fro-bro permanently contained in Shaft-duds, a handsome stud who is a soul-singing rising star), has vanished.

Annie Moan, an intermittent employee (receptionist) at the Oy! Store, operated by an avoirdupois Australian, is an elfin broad with a raven pageboy haircut, once a stripper/hooker now with meth-mouth and woodchip-chompers, kept in Native-Indian pajamas and moccasins, anticipating Piano Tuna's arrival. She is on a swing-seat on the porch of a pigsty roost. She welcomes him pleasantly with a slantwise smirk and they split a pepperoni pizza prior to playing billiards and knocking back a six-pack of Budweiser in her muggy cellar mural'd with Kiss, Led Zeppelin and Aerosmith posters. She stretches and yawns, and he gets a glimpse of her mussel-bellybutton and becomes an erectile effigy. She opens up on her hubby, Marlin Gaye, and puts on a cassette of a demo he'd been working on, a jazz-fusion opus, 'It Don't Mean Squiddly Diddly.' Piano Tuna jots down some notes in his pad. The lyrics are ridiculous and yet the music itself is ripping. The singing soars. Marlin can belt as Sly. His management has been ringing off the hook. The producer thinks it will be a giant hit, could skyrocket up the charts. He needs to tour, promote the single. Annie sez prepuce-snippers cut-work for tips, makes amorous advances and her lousy onion ring-breath propels him as an invisible force-field in sci-fi out into the main depopulated boulevard where he bumps into Miss Pike (they had a fling a while back), who is coincidentally headed towards the Mother of God! parish. The service, conducted by Holy Mackerel, is a real yawner, and downer, and there are mayhaps twenty followers in attendance. One of 'em is Bastien, in the third row pew, a dumpy doughboy of a sadsack with countable wispy strands on his flaky scalp, khaki chinos yanked up to his man-boobs. The Sturgeon General, suffering with dementia, shuffles with his cane, murmuring inaudibly on the altar. The basilica has matte-painting wainscot, full-service bar, greenhouse, steambath, Olympic pool, state-of-the-art gym, tennis court, rock-climbing wall, and a zillion convolutions of corridors, passages patrolled by overarmed Piranha, in their camo-fatigues, berets, flak-jackets and combat boots, presently wolfing guaca-mole burritos, nachos, cheese-fries, and quaffing smoothies. They move comparable to magicians' capes, the mountainous mashers pulled into catacombs like by the influence of gravity. Acid-rock-paisley, soundproofed grotto-flops. Surfedelic clambake. Doily clouds. An ambulance is a UFO. Briny deep is that wizened American Indian's face from the anti-pollution advert. Trim, teasy juniors in risqué raiment. Premature moon. Congregation beguiled. The sermon concludes and a ping pong tournament is held, the participants stepping on hot coals. Piano Tuna ambles on over to Bastien on the sidelines. He's catatonic, on quaaludes, drooling, dome a cranial arcade, mumbling he's "cured, won't diddle no more." And that's the scoop. He is psychologically torqued by a trauma. Piano Tuna tags Miss Pike in the capacious linen closet. He learns important info concerning drug-lord Cap'n Prawn and his cocaine-and-heroin smuggling operation, that Marlin was a small-time dealer who tried to get out of the business to focus on his music career but Prawn refused to release him from the contract and thus he and his group are relegated to being the house band on Prawn's Snark. She's a tub he thumps in, a gangster's moll, natural scent punished by pungent perfume, absented in rumination, a reed leaning, succumbing to a stream's course, more 'n a sight for sore eyes. She mentions off the cuff he's a hoot. His aggression creates her anxiety. She weathers the storm. They float as toothpicks downstream. Is she a vixenly booby-trap? He's erring on the side of selfishness, riding her hard. She has definition and depth. "Shiver me timbers," he whines. His bell bongs, bonking her. She responds, "Loose lips sink ships." Her hind in lockdown mode. Her stomach in upheaval. No rearend rushhour. Unsnortable crack crystals left on her bosoms. He bleats not unlike an automobile's horn at a jaywalker. Her integument winks as tinsel at Yuletide. High-voltage frenetic coition. They roil like steam from a radiator after a car accident. The diaphoresis drops on her satin derma layer are reminiscent of flying blades in a Kung Fu film, the frame frozen. He imposes himself 'pon her, conducts an improvised physical diagnostic on her. Mows on her muff. Therapeutic discourse. Joints creak as a drawbridge. Is she a manipulatrix? Her axillae tuftage. His heart sounds like pooch pads on wooden flooring. He's a chowhound on her crotch. Her parentheses of crow's feet. She mentions James J. Haddock, Prawn's numero uno de facto bodyguard, his pride and joy, a renowned pugilist, a kingly boxer once upon a time, scar-tissued, cauliflower-eared, with a bowlcut hairdo and Jimmy Durantesque schnoz, a scum-of-the-earth tower-of-power bully-for-hire, in Prawn's notherworld, who accosted her on an electric golf cart. Her routine on the trampoline was stimulating for Prawn, a "spastical, sociopathic shortstuff," his temper tantrums tending to have the sonance of a kennelful of canines. He said to her, bending her (crammed into an X-rated boykini and studded suede tank top, the outfit leftovers from her heyday as a club-hopping party-girl) backwards on the balance beam, he wanted to be a folk hero, living legend, Robin Hood, who stole from the rich but (conveniently) forgot to give to the poor. He had the emotional maturity of a maladjusted spoiled brat, she felt, was a virile supernova, Big Kahuna whip-cracking loose-cannon. She was an animal on his Ark, in his line of fire. They tumbled on the taupe ruglet. It sounded as a high-decibel domestic disturbance. His virgulate dong, baccate asshole. Piano Tuna does a Vulcan mind-meld on her temple and witnesses ... Her negligee of negligible length. Decor like it was taken from a forgotten sitcom set. Police-presence-ish Piranha. She sampled the corn chowder made by sedate chefs, licked her wounds in a kitschy-chintzy den Superfly would have dug. Gaggle of goosey ingenues, supple, hula-hon-hipped, with high-wattage and low-sincerity, speed-reading papers and guzzling heavy-duty joe, the gamines stewardi, robotic and red-eyed, not of earthy order, recruited from a stripjoint airline. Piranha jabbered as crack addicts needing fixes imme-diate. Oxygen laminated like a restaurant's menu. Breakneck bacchanalian venture. Revelations and reper-cussions. Her body language: ingredients mixed up. Fun-seekers, clingy leeches, court-certified delinquents, dungaree'd. Ocular sky with exploded capillary-cumuli. Planes purring. Bitches liquored/junked-up, honky-tonk habitues, made an orgiastic whoop-de-do. Chartreuse heavens. An island's expanse of luminous sand as diamond dust. Striking birds waltzed like street-walkers. Indigoid waters. Wallpaper achromatized as a Polaroid. A soulsister, sassy and sarcousy, was a Prawn pickup, her adorability an affront to the norm, in her scrimpy skivvies, tinkled like a telephone. Prawn defined his dedication to her by calling her a "negritic ho." She'd drawn her hurdies like drapes, blocking out her anal sun, and his indexer went through as a lightbeam. He descended into her, she ascended into him. He expired

on her like surf onto the shore. They were separate entities married in a vaster, solid substance. Perspiration
turned into wine. She was inspiring and indispensable.
He was formidable like atmospheric pressure. Did
someone ever scramble his brain with an egg-beater?
She was the bulging-at-the-seams nigga-object of his
desire, a black beauty with a guppy's physog. Their facets
as the two masks of Comedy and Tragedy on a Broadway
pamphlet. Behind a bamboo curtain the ghoulish,
twiggy, tallowy counterfeiter, Al G., with an Amish
beard, face flat like a gecko's, did his thang at the faux
fireplace. Prawn was a shrimpy Skeletor in senectitude,
a shriveled Crypt Keeper who gave out merits as a
teacher to prized pupils, and demerits to failures. He,
head-and-shoulders shorter than everybody else, looked
like a gruesome Dickensian newsboy, trap a livid lacera-
tion nevermending, with vaccination track-marks on his
pasty forearms, maroon sniffer visually corresponding to
an apple on the verge of falling off a branch. Network of
lines in his lineaments. Rumpy-pumpy on the
Bauhausian chair, a special edition. She was a narcotic in
his bloodstream. Trial-and-error of strenuous shagging.
His limbs tied around her as ivy a tree. Her haunches a
hideaway for his paws. He held her breasts like bombs,
appreciated her as an eye would art, an ear would music.
Her nicked-up kneecaps. His thumb was a point in
space and time in her lanuginose twat. The dose of
romantic remedy procured relief from his intolerable
solitude. Barrier of her keister was once unsurpassable.
Her dusky thighs were bifurcated leaves of a plant. Her
snatch stung. She was as essential to him like light to

life, darkness to death. His mangled maw, cadaverous shakers. He closed on her as an operculum on an oculus. Conga-line of carnality with his frenemies. He spewed Anaxagorean philosophies and spermic spumante on her sealing-wax-excrementitious bunghole. He got bang for his buck. Her complaints relayed as recitatives. Refrains of rain. Her planetoid posterior underwent a period of evolution. The pipsqueak's stiffy shrank. He found equilibrium in dissoluteness, not unlike a parachutist's feet reuniting with the ground from a great height, re-familiarizing himself with the terra firma. The flop was a disaster area, as a fallout shelter. She was unable to distinguish what exactly was happening, like occurrences in a deep sleep blending together. Was she encouraging or discouraging? Was she satisfied or dissatisfied? There was a distinct indistinction between reality and irreality. Unreason was the disturbance of reason. Rationality was denatured by irrationality. Reality was a restoration of unreality. She was a thesp ruled by her role. There was a Q&A. Cirri evaporated like vapor. Marvel of the tumescent bounding main, its succession of whitecaps. Ragamuffin runaways. Lurid lair out of some Kafka-esque Castle. Feudal flies. Sonata of sprinkles, with drizzly motifs and susurrant themes. Viridian ocean. The environment had its altered states. Roach-clip stars. He was a savage Svengali, a Tasmanian devil drill sergeant. Accommodation alcoves flickered with puce illumination as pumpkins. Silhouettes were skulking like ninja assassins in a chop-suey pic. Sard sea. His shower was the sprinkles. He was a New Age Lawrence in Arabia, Dots in Oz. Redolence of anal gas, floral bouquet, feet, vomit, and bad breath. The Marx Brothers rode a three-seater bicycle, Groucho at the helm, Harpo honking a horn, Chico picking a harp, their fast-yammering lip-synced. He was starstruck. Soundscape of the street - sirens, screams, breakage, tunes, motors, laughter. Empyrean was a black river, the cumuli, semiexploded kernels of popcorn, carried along. Buttermilk-yellow effulgence. He was Omar Sharif out of his mirage-mind. He paced hither and yon as a dipso-maniac anticipating a cocktail lounge opening its doors. He voided his bladder and bowels, the commode whale-configured. Nino Rota's 'Godfather' theme was in his noodle.

THE HOUR BEWITCHING, THE HEAT HIDEOUS, Piano Tuna, burned out, with an abdominal ache, schleps along the sodden shore, strewn with seaweed, a Sam who was Spade, in Roy Orbison shades, hitchhiking, thumb up (Fonzie scheme) the goober galumphing, praying he hooks a ride with partner-in-crime, a hard-core seafaring adventurer, Lancelot Rufino, a blind (terrible fireworks mishap), hunky, lean, sotto voce Argentine deep-sea diver who resembles a youthful, babyfaced Dean Martin at last call with Davy Jones bangs who could talk a cat off a fish-truck, never confusing hope and a plan, and who lives on a renovated WW2 submarine with his German Shepherd seeing-eye dog, Torsten. Lancelot was the proprietor of the 'See No Evel' (as in Knievel) place, opening and closing in a trice 'cause the patronage didn't possess Braille IDs. Piranha, technically Anglo, ginormous goombas, packing assault rifles and ammo belts, attack dogs with Gestapo tactics, mingle at a 7-Eleven. Winos on a scavenger hunt in a dumpster. He got tanked at 'Pier Pressure,' the preferred haunt he ghosts, usually sardined with longhaired lowlifes, dispensing their bumper-sticker bunkum, sucking righteous gonads. His uncertainty has a side effect of messing with his common sense. Even his red-alert gotta-go sensor is malfunctioning. Travel-brochure firmament has a pigment on the map of the human genome. Cheese danish is delish. His insecurity is a chord struck and suspended. Foot traffic in a self-centered sphere with emotional outbursts. Denizenry wearing wires. A rotund rabbi's Porta Potty rental in a shopping archipelago is called 'Holy Shit.' He rendez-vouses down the leafy lane with a summery shimmer. Annie Moan, the stumpy-leggy dame, a pixie flighty and unforgettable ... he'd like to acquire more intel on her, connect some dots, only it's not feasible, for he's racing against the clock and not motivated to navigate those murky waters. He was willing to jump in feet-first for her. He couldn't deafen himself to that siren's song. How could he refuse her request? Her case is a head-scratcher. She's at the center of his anesthetized attention. He'll get her out of the jam, a sticky situation. He expected seismic sexual sensations and has settled for tremors of titillation. Was he sent on a fool's errand? Is his ass grass? He shifts clutchlessly into high gear. He's a small-potatoes private-investigator, a junkie with a set of brand-spanking-new problems, serving two masters, or mistresses, spinning in off-kilter escapades, embroiled in these nesting-doll-like capers, scenarios soaked in splashes of color, unique and oblique, feeling as if he's flying and landing concurringly in the maritime mayhem, strung along by sundry puppeteers. This racket isn't everybody's bag. He sleepwalks in slumberland, fast-and-furious Chinatown, laser-focused (by his standards), with a peace-and-love mindset, avoiding straight-arrow, tight-assed, chip-shouldered copper Stingray, raining on his parade, crashing his bash, harshing his buzz. Is he in the crosshairs? He's fed up with corporate control, government power, the corruptions and conspiracies, Caucasian privilege. Confident his moral compass will point him in the right direction. Sun's a lemony smutch. A series of syringes and chrysalises of condoms. He fumbles on, ill-equipped, called into duty, interacting with unstable human beings, hustlers, dopers, land-developers, prosties, gangs, rockers, guerrilla radicals, upper crust jerks on downers, real-estate agents, skidding his wheels, losing himself chasing down clues, sometimes intersecting, crisscrossing double-and-triple crosses, ducking and weaving and twisting and turning as he walks the straight line. If he buckles, Fabienne and Annie collapse. For a threesome throwdown ... he would make them an offer they could refuse ... On mescaline he attempts to grasp, with nonchalant gusto, the dangling threads. His facial tics and slurry vocalisms. Intoxication papers over the cracks of inhibition. As for the Rebecca deal, he has to dig deeper. If he's going to be framed, he should get a clearer picture. And is Holy Mackerel some L. Ron Hubbardly fanatical charlatan? Piano Tuna is flare-panted and disco-fueled, the apogee of the antihero archetype, with a potpourri of proclivities, who is commendably committed to his clientry. Manifold magic carpet rides, dead ends, springboards, MacGuffins. Barry Cuda, the renegade attorney, a constitutional hunter always game for action, what's his roll in this farce? Yesterday's dream is tomorrow's nightmare. His past is the sun setting, his future a dawn rising. His present is a turning tide of changing times. 'The Wiz' soundtrack loops in his head. White supremacists discuss a mathematical system, disenfranchised youth, exchange fart gags ... whirlwind wavelengths he can't pick up on. Fabulous Fabienne fessed she was afraid of the Piranha, carried an aerosol can of Pam (she couldn't afford mace) in her purse. "Just shake and spray," she said. If all else failed, um, she'd be a whistle-blower. Is he a noob deep in dung? Is this a chess game, with the offensive and defensive maneuvering? Is it an entrance exam ... into what, exactly? A retarded doo-wopper of 'Cats,' the doozy courtesy of a soap-opera cast, in a sweatshop workstation in a spectrum of rarefied jellies. Could he go for an enchilada, pasta fazool, chased by a Fanta? He hoofs, hallucinates. Fantastic Fabienne was arctically cold, her air central'd, a life sized Barbie action figure in glow-in-the-dark briefs, a train wreck with a semimpish smile. He was deadpan. Her scungilli shell umbilicus. Her shoplifting biz was widespread. In her trendy flat, parentally paid for, they watched the Rams against the Saints at the Big Uneasy on the Magnavox, sacked out in a sleeping bag. She asked what her position would be if she played and he answered "tight end." His pulse sounds like type-writer keys tapping. A cappellan 'Miss Saigon.' Truly tasteless. He feels as a puck on Bobby Orr's hockey-stick. Frankly. Is he past his sell-by date? With his sedulous snooping he's wondering what he's getting himself into. Waggling like a prick. He has a lunchmeat odor. He reads a Mother of God! flyer, autographed by that senescent, solitaire-addicted Christer, Holy Mackerel, with his myth-making self-helping rug-pulling, hops over the occasional obstacle of sunbather. He was emphatically instructed by Barry Cuda to lay low during the investigation, to "chill as a fudgesicle." Is he the butt of a practical joke? His starbursting daydreams get real-world. He is flying high, bonkers from the emergency-vehicle's exhaust-fumes, and is horny as a frog in Spring. Convergence of ideas. He's shaken 'n' stirred. 'West Side Story' elevator-music emanating from an inflatable unmarked van's esoteric equipment. The persons making this racket (miserable enough to curdle cream) are corrupted. Who in Hades has the chutzpah to devalue Leonard Bernstein? Who has the cojones? Holy Fourth of July! The ivory sub, without warning, surfaces not unlike Moby Dick! From the dock of the bay he hops on board. The old friends high-five, Torsten barking excitedly, panting lecherously, and dry-humping Piano Tuna. Lancelot commands respect, is a born leader, has adaptability abilities, set apart from the rest, an only child of status-and-career-possessed parents. His existence was starved for familial nourish-ment. He should've sued for nonsupport. He's satisfied with the sustenance of Torsten and the sub, to Piano

Tuna a church weighted down by God, The Man Upstairs leaning on it. Arcade-game control-paneling. Hatches battened down, nightlights on, bulkheads secured. They submerge into the absinthian oceanic depths. It is imperative they pinpoint the whereabouts of The Snark, and pronto. His guest quarters are wicked comfy, as a yup's loft. The cot is peachy keen. Aquatic creatures, chimerical, flash akin to cards at the round panes with roseate drapes. Barrier reef. Sunken scow. A mako smooths along. He swills novelty java by the styrofoam cupload and gobbles a banana cream pie from its disposable plate. He mimes mouthing a hookah, and, apologies to The Rolling Stones, believes time ain't on their side. He has the nagging sensation of being a fish in a barrel. Is Cap'n Prawn a phony? The Snark a fake? The shebang bogus? These tales of an evil empire camp-fire stories? It's like the brainiacs vs. the jocks in high school, but infinitely more dangerous. His nerditude will serve him well. Perusing tabloids his optimism breaks down as an enzyme. He swigs designer alcopop with plenty of fizz and plays pinball. To be born-again, a schmuck in the burbs ... Row of snack machines proximal to an ovaloid officescape, dusty and littered. Ahab's whale. A Harryhausen octopus. A Spielbergian shark. In the commodious NASA mission control room with its archaic instrumentation, steampunky gadgets, outlandish doohickeys, Torsten monitors the antediluvian monitor screens, the blips bones. He was given a "visual scent," so he knows what to smell, erm, look for. Fathom the periscope-and-pulley system they've got rigged up. Lancelot snoozes, snores loud, at a booth in a capacious cubicle. Greenpeace rafts trigger false (close-but-no-cigar) alarms. Beach-babe Fabienne. They'd primal-screamed through sex. Her pleasure fell short. They recreated, zenlike, on a spaceship-chair near the spiral stairs, scarfing pastry and ginger-ale, warpspeed-freak smartcookies, of the Keebler variant, looking into subliminal messages on record albums, enjoying a joint epiphany, the coop carpentered into pseudorandom chaos, in a cosmopolitan nutward in its daily toiletward plunge. He gazed at her complex custom incisors within her intricate, curvaceous grin, Nosferatoid fangs installed by a Willy Wonkan dentist in Palo Alto. They used his Etch A Sketch and her Slinky, getting construc-tively stoned, before a Tequila Sunrise. Her festively colored (tropical fruit) clothes. Party Mix in a brighter world. His mitts on her were leaves feeling their way for light as she stared at a stapler. Like Dorothy she clicked her callused heels three times ... She gave him a draw-ers-tent. He did her to KC & The Sunshine Band's 'That's The Way (I Like It)' and Chicago's 'Feelin' Stronger Every Day.' Their mutual mystery had melo-dies and lyrics. He wallowed in the lukewarm bathtub of uncertitude. Ukrainian bistro next to an A-rab club domed as a sports arena. Bluejays made ee-ee-ee sounds similar to ones in the shower scene in 'Psycho.' She wore kiddy trunks, her howitzers mooshed as she rooted through the freezer for strudel and/or Creamsicle, settled for chocolate mousse cake, dummied up, pouting because she wanted to see the 'Space Ghost' musical performance at the Met and he didn't. She said he was a cheapskate. He felt like a sleazebag with a hardon. She surveyed him as Klaatu the boardful of equations in 'The Day The Earth Stood Still.' Scaffolding on the Leviticus cafe. Asparagus-green brine. Foam on rocks - creamed carrots. Dr. Pepper-froth cloudlets. She moved with that scalpel-precision body. His vascular organ was a jackhammer. Openmouth and backdoor options were nonnegotiable. Her nautilus-navel, pylonic nipples (projecting from her bazoongas as mini-muskets from round ramparts), rhapsodic respirations. Sweaty, she was a waxed bean doused in vinegar. Her yin yang was an eternal spring, limbs streaks of levin. Her jugs in his hands were souls scaled on the Day of Judgment. He sculpted her, carving her with caresses, informing her features, her curves with licks, chiseling the statue of her with strokes, defining her, bringing her into being with kisses, the threshold pushed to its limits. The mole on her chest was like a marker an ornithologist puts on a bird's breast to track its migration patterns. Her chortle, popping Chuckles candies, had the sonancy of cracked knuckles, asserting his appetition was a blindfold on his brain, permitting him to see things he'd only discover in the dark, their relationship was a recurring tribulation, as that of Ixion, and it was like Alcatraz: you arrived but didn't leave. He claimed in love sacrifice is neces- sary, a compliance that is crucial and she interrupted it was a necessary evil. Bars of lines on her bronze brow scored with note-beads of perspiration. Her crotch's cabbage was wet after her tinkle. She was meditative and modest when she went, with a medley of moans and groans. She swept the drops from her forehead it as a goddess would stars from the welkin. Piranha, with Jack Lordy-squeegee-pieces, Herculean power-houses with NFL linemen dimensions and V-8 voxes, in correctional system clothing, swimmingly stomped. Nanduti-clouds. She peeled the scab on her elbow like it was lettuce, snapped he was a tone-setter, had a kitchen-sink MO, cornered the market of her existence, snorted he honed in on her life as an MD on a patient's malady, he insisted and persisted, required and conspired. He was jolted, as if by shock treatment. An escalating rowdy-dowdy. Breakers on the sea - an Emerald City. His Byrdsian bob was off a bit. She was a trogonoid trollop with underwater-plant movements trill-talking, a hussy tra-la-laing. Platinoid sky. Window washer was a haruspex's grey beard. Her waterbottle-funbags. She plucked the vibrissae above her upper lip like a cherub a lute's strings, announced she was a battle-tested Joan of Arc. Argument subsided as a waning narrative. He had on a 'Six Million Dollar Man' tracksuit, had no fashion sense whatsoever. Her beauty was the foundation for the construction of his appetite. She was fanned like a deck of cards. He entered and exited her as the Devil did Regan in 'The Exorcist.' She was tusk-toothed. He was jonesing, had a monkey on his back. He looked not unlike an OD subject waiting impatiently for his next overdose. His straight baloney followed by a smug chaser. He was fierce-flushed, had a radio-announcer's voice, a jive-smart-ass. He was predatory and she was prey. He stank as a garbage truck, had dreads then, a Flying Dutchman on her, a sybaritic Speedy Gonzalez, wishing instant-gratification would last forever. She was Bambi, he was Thumper. She punched her karmic ticket.

Lid-flipped on blotter, he thought he was James Bond living in Smurf Village, that he was an entry-level foot soldier field operative controlling a noncompliant subject in a Mayan ritual in a local refinery adjoining an electric green power grid and turnip-tinted recycling center, he had no Choice, considering the Zermeloid Axiom n. More than just his suspicion was aroused. Their list of issues longer than his rap sheet. The portfolios of their problems was expanded. It was the beginning of their end. She didn't cut him any slack. She stole his happiness like a cookie from its jar. He was an ardent washing machine set for a second cycle. They exchanged opinions on space aliens in secret labs and time travel. Volume of Aesop's fables. Special K soggified in a bowl. Tenors and tones spiked. Her caterpillar-mustache. She blushed, a sarcastic moue tugging at the corners of her lips. He could ID that expression a mile out in mist. She ate at him as Mrs Pacman. Their tongues played hide-and-seek. Fuck-fling with gale-force. Crickety chorale. Her pachydermic sneezes, trucker's vocab with a scorpion sting, a pudding overegged, bellows-backside, schizoid sense of humor, much like her mother's, Solange, a proletariat warrioress who went through guys as automatic doors and who died of pancreatic cancer in a squalid sanatorium. She was rangy, lardy-dardy, had ranid-eyes, Streisand-sniffer, marigold-mouth, bazoo-ka-breasts, tumbly tress a petrified thicket, integument arboreal-animal soft, imbittered and imbalanced, breathing with the sound of a machete hacking at skeins of vegetation, a permanently PMSing dig-doler who was so self-important it was like she was organizing a

United Nations meeting where World Peace was at stake on a daily basis. Fabienne was a pinup centerfold. And she said his unimpressive unit was a pathetic package. Her arousal went AWOL. He felt as a sugar-cube dissolving in the piping-hot tea of her. His brainwaves were circuits rewiring themselves. Trailerpark castaways strapped for cash rode repining mopeds. Their R-rated F-bombs. Clouds were pompons shaken in slo-mo. Her lifeboat-lips. He chased her like an ambulance. His reverb-respirings. She was at the apogee of her adorability. His serpent in her pit. The apricot luminosity was hesitant, as a visitor in a new neighbor's home, wondering if he/she is welcome. His knuckle brushed her aureole like it would've the beak of his pet canary. They roared as airliners. Glistering orbicular sun nictitated like an aeroplane-warning beacon. She was a gork on gorp. Her boiled-pink bumsy-wumsy. She was an iron maiden, a maturing madonna. Varicose veins on her muscled thighs were like vines on tree trunks. Flies bombinated as transformers. A shopping centre was an El Dorado of damage. Wind was a Wurlitzer. Lightning sketched the skyline. Babel of thunder. His ringlets like dried banana peels, or baked palms. Perceiving her as being a member of the feminine syndicate, the Muffia. He went to town on her, gave her oral and optical attention. He had wooed, not wowed her. She skunk-sprayed, went to the show with precious cousins Aqua and Marine (who stuck out as two sore thumbs at a hitchhiker convention), attitudes like they were seraphs who'd fallen from Heaven into Hell, complaisant and conceited, fanatics for Pepto-Dismal, Mountain Goo,

Badzooka gugglebum, Hopeless Snowballs, and Killy Putty, weaving their way through the apartment like pickpockets a marketplace, and he ruh-rohed as Scoob, flopped on the floor as though electrocuted, gripped his yeabig schlong, had slicing sensations in his gullet, like inside incisions, wrist-slashingly depressed over this romanticide ... The sub chances upon the barge many nautical miles out at sea. Lancelot suggests they "torpedo the tanker" and Piano Tuna nods no. The pards shake hands, exchange farewells. Torsten tries to mount Piano Tuna. Lancelot, having "bigger fish to fry," drops Piano Tuna off on board as casually as a cab-driver would a passenger at a street-corner.

On Cap'n Prawn's good ship lollipop, hearing Olivia Newton-John's 'Magic' over the intercom, Piano Tuna, scouring for Marlin Gaye, is thinking Mutiny on the Bounty. He'll put a tent over this circus. His brain's a Mardi Gras. Unreality ramrods his reality. Boo hoo. His snail's progress, and he feels like he's ping ponging here and there, crab-stepping, ricocheting everywhere. Cadmium sun beats as if it is trying to communicate. Jedi talk in his noggin. No greenbacks = no mai tais. He struts, elicits Fabienne, thonged and flipflopped, sucking down Bloody Mary's, after a trippy Tupperware party (she spozed the place was cozy schmozy), in the flat, on a co-opted block, in her movie musical dressing room quarters, with its copious code violations (forget the contractors and inspectors), range of rodential tenants, tobacco smoke, roaches ignitable and insectival on an ill-advised armoire, Payless footwear, and fast-food packaging. She was junior-model-doll-faced and accessorized in charm-bracelets, semistoned and in pantyhose, utilizing the coat rack for a dancing pole, Piano Tuna, on the barstool, so cocked he had alcohol poisoning, feeling like a creepazoid in a privacy booth. R&B instrumental. Copies of fashion magazines and clothing catalogs. Coffeemaker and microwave innocent of logos. He was on the line with her. The connection wouldn't go dead. Irreality had slopped over into reality. Fact had no extradition treaty with fact. His actuality had a Santa Clause with fantasy in a loco North Pole. It was an ok quickie. His nerve receptors responded well enough. Mistrals riffled the pre-autumnal leafage. Tourists were terrorists. Redevelopment in vogue. Din of garbage collection. Downtown brickwork. Helluva halvah. His eyeballs rolled in different directions, he in a prone position. He was CIA and she was Al Jolson in blackface yodeling the opening 'Jaws,' frowning and fidgeting. Soaring high-rises. Steamy evening. Spritz had a scent of pencil shavings. With her prehensile toes she picked up pairs of panties. He popped a pill he thought was a mint and she changed into Mothra with perfume-flask hands and Pringle-chip fingernails. He shat himself, went all stinko. 'Swat' was on. No A/C. The zhlub was fugued. Her mane was pinned up, maquillage underdone, redeyed from a joyride, subteen-pert, half-subvocalizing, saccharimeter readings conveying him into a diabetic coma. She was sitcomically perky. Street below clamorous. Virdigris splendor admitted through wintry grey clouds. Her optically perfect physique, unnaturally smooth and sunbaked, back from the Comic-Con in Las Vegas, Baroquely beautified. She directed her negative energies in a positive way, datably inveigling, behavior in the realm of buttholery. Histing waters. Her Rock of Gibraltar bod. He wore a Speedo and was starry-eyed, cracking open a fortune-cookie, surviving an identity crisis from the hallucinogens. She had a floral aroma and turned him into a foot fetishist. The lovebirds took a dinner (casserole) break. She played a paradiddle on the sink with Sporks. A cop-show was on in the Petri dish pad. His retrospections vanish as prints in the sand ... Beach Boys-ish band segueing into a 'Wipe Out' number in a Swiss spa with a plenitude of cray cray props. A hirtellous Hindu's mouth movements have a sexual subtext, drawing in nitrous oxide. He, mentally ranging out of the perimeters of lucidity, with prosthetic teeth, makes goo-goo eyes at some wenches not health conscious. He, with a Tiny Tim intonation, explains Prawn's diesel-powered craft, wending through spinach-greenish aqua pura with disquieting cunning, has no radio traffic or running lights, it a ghost ship with high seas capabilities, mighty and fast enough to qualify as utterly scary, as if under the influence of occult forces, with an element of eeriness thrown in for good measure, that Prawn is infamous for latitude and longitude fixes with his vision. Gulls mewl. Guido musclemen, these hiredgun bodybuilders, are hoses of 93 octane spraying the bonfire of the commonality, act like they were raised by wolves, glaring pathologically. A Harlem negress. Blinking buoys look as though they're lit J's, dragged on in intervals. Surf-folk, early-risers, roll numbers on the salmony sand, pelagic curls crepitant, begging to be board-mounted. Hippies in their bathing suits at a cutout coastal diner slurp sauce, cram clams, burn peyote, and listen to rock 'n' roll music, records spinning on turntables like the flying saucers in an Ed Wood picture. Surly surf. Such a fake ocean and heaven. Crude-gooey tar-pit. Littoral crests so gnarlacious you'd have a disagreeable time on 'em if you're inexperienced at riding waves. Kareem-tall trees. Cumuli with menagerie motifs. Piano Tuna's heartbeats as Motown backbeats, shivers not unlike a junker's loose exhaust-pipe. He has on X-Ray specs, ears phone-jingling, gliding as if he's skating on an ice-rink, gormandizing a burger and frankfurter, having pulled a dine-and-dash, and fitting in splendidly, threading a maze of passages onto a vertiginous catwalk where weathered wrong-doers seeking sensations and good vibrations introduce their verbiage into the monkey business. What foods these morsels be ... Prawn to the blue abundance is what leprosy was to Molokai. Gaylords and gothtards. Cosmetic reef. Zombie insomniacs, undead and unwashed, a puzzled posse, in la la land, nadaville, with gaper-yaps, gangrel gangbangers all, divagate as though tykes searching for parents at a funfair, drift-netting the familial familiar. Swells sound like cicadas. Luminescence explodes as cans of brew shook and popped. Shredded-coconut cirri. The hockey-puck-sized hickeys Miss Pike put on his neck. He perambulates, has a gas station-re-stroom body-odor, behaving like a roadhouse chucklehead sloshed to the gills, fingers long as Zubin

Mehta's conducting batons. He cannot distinguish the details of the briny deep and the horizon because of the fog. What of Barry Cuda, the illegal eagle, misbehaving mouthpiece, the daredevil dramatist in the independent theater of his head? He was apparently extraterrestrialized, with a helmety hairdo, elastic countenance, and stroke-victim's speech, favored words over deeds, wore his heart on the sleeve of his zootsuit, the cables of habit difficult to snap, a passing cloud in civilization's sky, the crockpot counselor's complexion comparable to stormshine. He built his business like a bird its nest, collecting twigs, sticks and scraps here and there along the way, until the winds of change, competition, blew in to tear it apart. He was so irrelevant a non-appearance made a favorable impression. His shadow followed him as a bodyguard. Licorice Crow-black walls and lost-highway Yellow Brick Road-flooring. Moon's an infantile head, cloud a parental digit giving it a chin-up. Duct-tape-gray vault. Eucalyptus lozenge is tasty. Fabybaby … he doesn't have the heart to tell her that her dad is vegetabled in a sacristy and in the care of a glorified evangelist and his cult of impersonality, a barrel full of monkeys … Pastel-hued ceiling. Contrasting bands of chiaroscuro. He feels as if he's growing up quickly; his life late for a bus. Hoodlums, in Stetsons and trench-coats, with grim-reaper stares, racy ladies in glassy passivity, hapless Johns, cowpoke gunslingers, sweary, giggly teenyboppers, surfers, skaters and a mucid night-club which is an architectural amalgamation of the Addams Family house and a science bunker. Muciparous spate. Piano Tuna micturates in a porcelain-manatee urinal. Crumbs of cloudlets. Metropolis is a Tokyo-ish mental disco with a willion people right out of a Soviet expressionist pop-up storybook, under Prawn's thumb. He oppresses the rat-race, subjugates the masses, pays off the authorities. There's trouble with trade. Commerce is getting killed. Civil disturbance. Handshaking, baby-kissing, grandstanding politicians. Class conflict. Passé politics. Law enforcement corruption. Union problems. Illegal immigration. Unemployment up the wazoo. It's healthcareless here. Existence is a red cape to a bullish populace. Mucedinous condensation. Air like modeling clay. Crustose moon. Advertisement blimps as comic-book thought-balloons. Alpinic ATM machines. A defunct carnival plot unfolds in the smog. Piano Tuna roams. Starsky and Hutch lap battery-coolant out of an Alpo-labeled bowl. Hail like sequins shedding from prom gowns. His investigatory gadding. Elmer Fudd and Bette Davis share a knish and shine a TIE fighter rendered in optical brunet in a classic Proustian tearoom furnished with all the amenities. Larry Talbot as 'The Wolf Man' (as if a Sat morn low-budget cartoon character) practices kung fu and a ukulele. Spray-painted Baby Jesus and unreadable writing. Piano Tuna feels like his medulla oblongata is located between sanity and insanity. Game-show buzzing in his cranium. A hornet-hipped girlie galah with a marmoset-mug is au natural (except for a pork-pie hat) and has ponceau pomelos for tits and hums like tires on pavement behind this oxygen-tentish fly-screen. Her falcate toenails. She sounds as if she's auditioning for a glee club. He plods. Pert Fabienne ... her Pomeranian-proboscis ... in her cami-top and ankle-socks ... the bubbly, aureate Amazon front and center ... skin soft as a sigh ... rich like angel food cake ... the goofy-toothed nymphet breathing as steam coming from a burst pipe, flamingo'd (balanced on one amber leg) on the futon, her bunkum trampling him as though the bulls at Pamplona ... her skill-set in hell-raising ... she's no slouch ... her croaky inflection ... javelin shoulder-blades ... vermiform appendectomy-scar and Betty Boopalike peepers ... she spoke like a walk-on bit-player practice-reading from a script, reciting the lines, preparation praiseworthy ... he was a harried Houdini, his disappearing acts David Copperfield would admire ... she put him through the wringer ... her pit-a-pat strides, rat-a-tat delivery ... he was indifferent as a contracted killer ... He trudges through the Snarky phantasmagorium, has a reused teabag taste in his oral cavity, looks like a clue-free doofus in tight loafers who pulled an all-nighter in a nuked think tank. His cardiac organ knocks as a faulty generator, negotiating through adolescent automata, gazing frostily, making wisecracks, like a salmon struggling upstream. Klaxon fart. Salvo of snickers. Sonances of slapped flesh. Somebody's sentence gets amputated by an interruption, is left a stump. Rodgers & Hammerstein playing in a Guggenheim museum with a cross-pied Blacula curator with stainless-steel braces. This tub has more travelers than JFK. Rastafarian Rocky Balboan deejay and androgynous, battle-scarred Desi Arnaz beatboxing. A Bionic Womanly Shirley Temple impersonator in ruby slippers sells Slushes. She sounds as one of those cartoony chipmunks. Stingray and Hammerhead "develop," working undercover in Hawaiian-print toggery and straw-hats, stop and frisk him on the parquetry, in the queasy coruscation, swooping down buzzardly on his carcass, both hiccups in the continuity of his high, patting him down insensitively, acting like they are superheroes and he is the badguy, putting the kibosh on his investigation. The pigs have hooked and reeled him in. Stingray gives him the okey-doke, and whales on him. He gets plastered, laid out by Hammerhead, who goes through him as a knife through butter, a fire through bushes. Piano Tuna lit up like a Christmas tree. Stingray yanks him up. They're on what seems to be a death-march. They mosey as real estate agents and potential buyer. Stingray says he's a "condition with no cure," a habit he, Stingray, can't kick, an "authority flouter." Topless bimbos blow on tenor saxes. There is a claws-out conflict between a couple of Brazilian beauts, one with an argil aspect, the other with argillaceous integument. His memories are vivid, like he's seeing them through a viewfinder. A jocose sylph, so willowy the pickings would be slim, a mamzelle with water-balloon titties and kudu-limbs, joshes, in jockeys, wiggle-waggles. He feels as if he's on the hot seat, his edge dulled. Vapor is as though it is distributed from a defective gasket. Colombo clones on a pilgrimage. Vista is pink-slip-pigmented. Dziggetal-braying gales. Meanwhile, Marlin Gaye, in a warlock cloak, tears it up on stage in the gymnasium filled to the rafters, with his quartet of 'Heavenly Hosebags' backup singers, starlet-slender, in doubtful leather jackets, spandex sportsbras and shortshorts, bling catchpenny, vocally firing on all cylinders and Picassofied by the flickering fluorescent lights, the group consisting of a guitarist, bassist, drummer and organist, sledgehammering a muso-oriented, odd-metered, prog-metal version of Stevie Wonder's 'Higher Ground.' It is an incendiary concert. The band works up a sweat during the set and Piano Tuna wants to be showered in it. The music isn't chartbusting material, a product that would sell, only it is envelope-pushing. Imposing roadies keep the peace. Crowd in coarse camaraderie. Barry Cuda in his Coburn-as-Flint finery grapples with a Doberman Pinscher ... mano-a-fido ... Piano Tuna misses his therapeutic television. Viewing is a form of meditation. Monster mash in a blizzard of bullets - Piranha open fire. Muthafuckers with matryoshka-nested issues ... Hammerhead gets injured in the crossfire, plugged in the side, and Stingray finishes him off by capping him in the temple. It's as a filmed gunfight. More Piranha join the fray. It is like they heard some ultrasonic whistle. Piano Tuna goes "yoiks," his mazard lolling. What are his options? He weighs them. Stingray creates a yurt with his fingers. Prawn, as a Scooby villain, bitter-coldly curses, with an economical dismissive gesture, "I would've gotten away with this if it weren't for you meddling kids!" and escapes on a jet ski; a yardbird on a jailbreak. Lull in the shooting. Piranha skedaddle; a Dunkirk evacuation. No last hurrah, blaze of glory. They frickin' bailed! Piano Tuna, sprawled, makes a peace-sign to Stingray he's fine and dandy. Turns out, Stingray is a narcotics kingpin, wanting Prawn's "water territory," and was being investigated by Hammerhead. Piano Tuna and Stingray split the cargo.

Piano Tuna troops through rainbowed pools, making butterfly wings with every step, past a piceous El Camino, motor sounding like a Jaco Pastorius bass line, Glen Campbell resounding from within, he, Piano Tuna, having withstood an insomniac night, his drops of diaphoresis in the radiance rhinestony, taking in a tamale and salsa (there could be digestive repercussions), trades his half of the stash back to Prawn, scaring the bejeepers out of him, at the Prawnshop (alongside a death row of housing units and lowest-end motel, exterior with its trapeziform parking lot, interior filled with merchandise), a postmodern cabana with a radar antenna on the sheet-metal roof with a nexus of razor-wire, preserved as a constructional archive, dead-ending against a chain-link fence on a residential avenue amid suburban arterials, narrowing Piano Tuna's options, with a sawdust and bleach malodor, in exchange for a promise to take Marlin off the payroll. Prawn, so bantam he could tread water in a test tube, in a flashback freakout, following a scag-tag debauch, harboring a grudge, rips him a new one, says (about Marlin) that it's a reverse Don Corleone situation: "Just when they think he's out, he pulls himself back in." Herky-jerky runaround. His pilot-light blinders bouncing as busied bumblebees, with chilopodous digits, snigger clanking like a malfunctioning conveyor belt. He scoffs lobster, crab and squid at a Formica table with folding chairs. Flatulency vaporing. Marlin to him is "lost in loserdom," his wife Annie a "tragicomic cliché." His balderdash holds less water than a fishnet stocking. He has a 'Dirty Dozen' personalities, a melting pot mind. He talks like a monotone Kermit the frog, a lover of seaweed smoothies evidently. If the discussion were a basketball game Prawn is committing flagrant fouls (verging on fatal) and deserves a technical. He is as abnormal as a zit on an infant. His inflection sounds like a synthesized Ricky Ricardo on fizzies and a Tammy Wynette intonation. He's squat as a hedgehog, patience-challenged, master of the universe, with a Stalin-stare, head a geographer's globe of the world, take-out menu tongue, chompers the color of concrete corroded by car emissions, and pickle-built body with snapped-toothpick limbs. Piano Tuna feels like a sitting duck, he is at an Olympic event, experiencing a UFO sighting, showbiz highlights, his future apocalyptically blackened. Retail rhythms he ain't tuned to. His mental board is way out and overlooked in the waves. His itty-bitty receptor receives Prawn's message: he's toast. His heart beatboxes. He goes saline, the sob story on Marlin, he's a newlywed and all, should get a break, a second chance. Leftover meal of coleslaw, jalapeño Jell-O, alfalfa sprouts and mashed potatoes. Daytime TV. Kitchen appliance infomercial. Structures Trade Centerish and illumination-inundated look as snack machines in the sweeping eventide, edgeless and ephemeral. Money laundering in a GE washer and dryer, Count Chocula-brown. Sponge mop. Vinyl LPs. Infrared twilight. Tomb tenements Boo Berry-blue. Fuel gobbler at a meter in the fringe slum. Distressed amphitheater in a sorrowful sepia. Shameless product placements everywhere in Cap'n Prawn's business. To wit, 'Cheapios' Cereal, 'Log Cave In' syrup, 'Crakola' crayons, 'Blisterine' mouthwash, 'Sicken of the Sea' seasick pills,

'Muleburro' cigarettes, 'Taster's Choke' coffee, 'Raw Goo' spaghetti sauce, 'Rinkled Wrap' aluminum foil, 'Dull' canned pineapple, 'Ditch Masters' cigars, et cetera. An edentulous Korean cabbie with a Wyatt Earp-'stache making a schlumpy fashion statement gives a furtive glance at his puke-pigmented shitkicker's chromy bumper. Dilapidated deli looks not unlike the aftermath of a Third World conflict. Drencher sloshes. Obstacle course intersection. Sno-Kone dinghies. Murderous commuters round the rotary. Starless overcast. James J. Haddock, the racketeer with totally mangled mitts and impulse-control issues, seething as trashcan flames in a soaker, looms large, visage crumbled like old plaster, actuating as mall security in a martial-arts movie. He is a pustular crusher of Sasquatchian proportions, junk-yard dog aggressive, has a substance-avoidance personal policy, behaves around people as a lion does around zebras. His skin like Wonder Bread dunked in olive oil. Neo-country rendition of Abba's 'Dancing Queen' on the teeny-weeny transistor set on the counter. Peninsula panorama with wombat kaleidoscopes. A zaftig cowgirl space oddity, stout and discalced, a disgruntled employee, on an off-the-wall sci-fi geek-out riff, with nectarean perspiration, butane lighter and bulb of garlic as in a vaudevillian improv. Her vociferance of an ice cream headache. She has a murderous-moppet modulation and nonnuclear personality, holds the spoon Statue of Liberty-like. Her underpants should be banned for brevity. Abdominous murex mark from an emergency procedure when her appendix pipe-burst when she was eleven. Her voluptuous volume increases and decreases incrementally in the neon lights. She flips patties on the grill, blotches on her chest burgundy jigsaw pieces. Haddock's glower is a species of physical contact. Her lips overtaken by his. Her being a wire in winds. She packs a punch if you get her riled. He stares at her as a quitting smoker at a Virginia Slim. An anklet on the bureau anticipates her ankle. She's felt within an inch of her life. He is dedicated to his sordid instincts like an author is to his muse, traces the veins on her neck, drafting their future plans, as a draughtsman drawing a design which may never be built. She wants to deny him his exploits, deprive him of his satisfaction, to scurry like a mouse for the shelter of its hole. Her underwear reconfigured. Does her sphincterial fire require his wood? He is Apollo and she is his Chariot. Stuffed koala. Ol' Cap'n Prawn whistles the 'Green Acres' intro, jumpcut-moves, fluctuates as an an anchor's cable in changing currents, short as Dr. Ruth Westheimer, expressively suspires, bent out of shape, confidence smoke covering uncertainty that his company in the scumscape is soon to be defunct. His subwoofer flatus, turkey gobbling, vox sounding on the grindstone. He has no facial features, only a cartilaginous cast. He hee-haws and tee-hees. Piano Tuna sends out distress signals in a code of blinks and twitches, his alarm silently triggered, handling this predicament with the skill the situation demands, his apprehension in proportion to his determination. When will the boom be lowered on him? He's shaken to his core. His lank locks with pie-crust-crumb dandruff overdue for a shampoo. He has a jet laggy fatigue. His fate is in Prawn's hands. His unrealness resorts to retaining reality's services. He feels like a feather trapped in Prawn's pillow. Hearing Prawn, gouging seeds out of a watermelon as eyes from a monster, explicating Sprite is the Rolls Royce of carbonated beverages, is like to listening to different tracks on a warped, broken record. Vocoid gusts. Time-battered barbershop. An inked-up stick-figure. A walnut door has a 'Powder Room' typed tag on it. Ed Sullivan sings 'Oklahoma!' (in vibrato) in its entirety in there. Fancy schmancy furniture. Piano Tuna is serious as a poker-player, resists retaliation, for there would be ramifications. He fulfills his function of maintaining decent social standards. His head feels like it's going to explode, as a mosquito after biting Dracula. Periphrastic hooey. Phony angora sweater shawling a sickly armchair in an ambery afterglow. He's compassless, rudderless, in expectancy of Haddock opening a can of whup-arse on him, rain blows down in Chuck Jones Acme-anvil-dropping style. His heart races like a midnight express train. Is Prawn Xerxes, Piano Tuna the ocean, ordering it/him to be lashed for claiming his Snark? Boston's 'More Than A Feeling' is written in his DNA. His inner clock-alarm beeps. He has a hankering for Michael McDonald. Temps flatline. Lunchtime lineup. Ambeer puddles. Symphonic, breezy Steely Dan in his skull. He explains he's an anti-conformity individualist on a universal quest for independence against institutions endeavoring to co-opt his tuchis, belonging to a long-dead-gone generation, life is a wave he rides, he's chillaxin', goin' to keep on truckin', won't fasten his seat-belt, it's cool-a-roonie, his investigation is a riddle of cheeba paper-rolled up in the enigma of a bammer and blazed to a bud. He is strangled by loose ends. He grows balls. It's game time. Wet stuff's grainy celluloid stock, the light cig-burned cue-marks on the print. Long-ago-left construction site. He is a loopy Jake Gittes on opiates and coasting on a cloud of kief. Things have been hairily tranquilized. His livery out of a Lennon yard sale. He feels like he's plunging over the Niagara Falls in a barrel in the slowest motion. Skanks, cuddly as cacti, kitschified in charmy chokers and in concert-shirts and hipsters, get into a tractor-pullish spat. Cars cruising are schools of fish. Crow excursions. Huey, Dewey and Louie woodcarvings with Florsheims. Mello Yello fulgor. Sham-Arabian carpeting. An elliptical estuary is toxicity central. Tophats of smokestacks. Onkus orientoid orca. Hell's Kitchen is Heaven in comparison to this district. Boilerplate bohunk. Mundungus mephitis. An under-aged caucasoid cupcake, mighty fine, with a twangly tone, feather-duster eyelashes, and wearing a dress briefer than a burnout's short-term memory, is more a drug saunterer than runner, shameless in her circulation. Heavy-duty drama. Lincoln-esque Tunnel. Plants like drink-um-brellas. Mosquitoes snivel. Flinching luster. 'Flounders Keepers' pub. Double-decker automat. Masa-pollen. Density of ethnicity. Differing languages clash. Sluggish parking lot's concussive blasts. Crinal clouds drake-gray. An ebon Mustang with mags barrelasses. Giocoso zephyrs. Brakes sheep-bleat. Hunky himbo fudge-packer copper-toned and with a Robocop-rigid bearing birdily scritches. Riverside derelict shopping plaza. Yellow plum sun. Autos in alignment. Postapocalyptic macromall hangout where kiddies kibitz. Han Solo and Scrooge McDuck futz with a barbecue's propane tank. Piano Tuna is on more than a sugar-high. Windswept waterscape. Helix of humanity. Rain crackles as walkie-talkies. A nerdal stringbean semistunned by Gaddis. Go figure. An ellipsoidal Japanese hussy in Ray-Bans, past her sell-by date, dress dramatized, is perspiry and jittery, unblinking and unsteady, tilted at a precarious angle, with a stoner's smile, in a piazza-size, limestone maw with maple-leaf motifs. Matrixes of schoolchildren. Wavelets repelled by a wall. A ferry whoops it up. Garage disgorges a Gremlin bombing on a ramp and agitating into the unknown. Ribby radiator. Smoldering Puerto Rican prettified in callgirl caparison and with a curlew cast and currawong modulation bags reefer and cranches on Apple Jerks, not the brightest bulb in Prawn's treasure chest. Beagle-faced histrionic harlot in a gown strapless. Ravens with pennant-wings. The sky shows blue as grass does green after rain. Musical staffs of sleet. Streetsweeper in a no-parking zone of an Art Deco marina reminding you of a sizable oil-storage tank. Methane reek. Studio-audience-laughter karaoke in an intercultural rehab-clinic-back-room. Pen-and-ink lines of the pour. Screaming match of the Bi-Valves, these ribald, bisexual, cookie-cutter mollusk-men, nodose-noddled, manga-lamped, open-piano-mushed, candle-stub-eared, and noctuous-fluffy, wackazoid wrong 'uns. Commotion is king. Neither side prevails. Bardish 'Tempest' of testosterone in the cryptish cellar. Niggas, individuated in sameness, are sample-sounding, argot cut-and-pasted, swapping suggestions. One yo score-settles with a stealth-strike to another mope, who says he's got to ax his mudda sonethin. Ruckus raised. 'Ooh-La-L.A.' tavern. Homicidal drivers. Avian dialogue. Nondisclosure agreements made, documents signed. Stingray shows, says, "we're on different ships, not on the same boat," pops up not unlike a cork, rising as with wings in a void, and executes Prawn with a Glock, blowing his brains out, changing the boiserie into a canvas for a Pollock spatter-painting, and dispatches Haddock, reaching for his Beretta with lethal finesse, respirations jangling like a timer, sending him to Palookaville with promptitude. He'd been tailing Piano Tuna and knew he'd lead him to Prawn. Piano Tuna gasps, does a header, and faints ...

MARLIN RETURNS TO ANNIE. At the popular club, Studio 45, weavings of dancers en-and-disentangling themselves, Piano Tuna, grinding his gnashers, ripping up the floor with a boogieing flaky fille, cooler-than-thou, with a maize mop, trolley-bell voce, strobilaceous nipples, mouth calling for kisses, neck beckoning for bites, dermalayer smooth as a tablecloth, countenance glowing like a paper lantern, modulating in a cornball romcom way, enunciating her knowledge of her existential ennui, cutting a rug at a rate of knots to the filling-rattling racket, inebriating as a shot of sambuca, in tarty togs, is arrested by Stingray for the murder of Rebecca. Busted, hoary cord/mungo threads crinkled not unlike frost, his spirit is resonant as an empty expanse, heart clicking as a camera's shutter. His spine-snapping sobs, discarded chili dog hemorrhaging its contents. His complexion exhaust-bluish. We learn that Fabienne and Bastien have an incestuous relationship, Rebecca was in love with Bastien, who didn't reciprocate, and she threatened to blackmail him with what she knew of their relations, and Fabienne killed her and set up Piano Tuna to take the fall for her demise. And The Snark? It sank, of a sudden, off the coast. Do ya imagine Lancelot Rufino, a solo special ops force, had anything to do with it, using those tomahawk cruise missiles he cherishes? Righty then ...

Epilogue

You'll be spared the Oedipal details, but at a nudist resort on an tropical island, a profusion of paradise, weather enforcing its own protocol, with its orange crush celestial sphere, fruit trees and flowerbeds, Bastien, naked save for Confederate flag socks, a Michelin Man blondly and balding, living dangerously, basks like a seal on rocks bitch-smacked by surf, the nubbly nudnik slumped as a sack of rice, with a wan wapperjaw, Dick Tracy squint, Smeagol simper, and arctic-whitish chiclets, slow on the uptake and comical as a house comedian bourbon-bladdered, vascular organ pounding like cannon rounds on a metal hull, wanking, with Fabienne's feet, cute as bugs' ears, warm like sunned water, and with a vitamine odor, in lemon-juicy light, smothering his face, a chafed sole scoring a strike on his dewlap. Uh-oh. Her firstpass flyby puts him into flight. Her hair a bonfire unmessed-with. She's a vertical hypnotized snake, her lunch an edible Kandinsky. He is a rotund Reaper who hasn't missed a meal, one with the universe, cramming Nabisco ginger-snaps, comments there's no dress-code here. Sand flies like it was salt thrown by WWF's Mr. Fuji. She stork-stands, whines as a turbine engine, silhouette in support of its maker, does her better impression of a floozy. From his perspective her virescent blinkers glint, cuspidate cheeks three-ball redden. His tremors like earthquake aftershocks. Her ocherous muliebral mustachio, cormoid belly-button and mascle-cornhole. His eyes peeled, glued on her. She, reserved and radiant, affords him her company, waltzes as a lady of the evening, and washes over him not unlike the tide a shore. A preternatural enfant terrible, she'd skinnydipped, swum carvingly. He evaluated her as a prospector a mine. Her infectious personality an undertow dragging him in. She's Magdalene-magnifical, has a charred-wood body-odor. To her natation is a form of flying. Crests scroll on the beach gravy-browny. She's a line you don't cross, even though it's moving. She is not an engine to tinker with. Her cantaloupe-breasts, cherry-tomato nipples, pie-plate nates. She drops hints which he picks up. Her arms and legs tighten and loosen like a guitar's strings according to the temperature. Sherbet-cirri. It's hothouse-stifling. She's a masterpiece made available for his appraisal, awakening his senses for appreciation. Her aurous tresses poodle-permed. His hams reconcile with her haunches. Her being is Ground Zero. He is

ignorant, she is intelligent. She's stuck by him: a toothpick in a sandwich. She goes with his flow. Her rear-cleft
is a crack in space. He rides her into the sunset. They
copulate as tugboats chugging upriver, fornicate like
spaceships crashing, honeymoon-happy. She has him
beat five ways to Sunday, squeaks as a housekeeping cart
rolling in a hotel's hall. Money shot. Beat. "Klaatu barada
nicto," he says. Rubber meets the road. Remembrances
of them misbehaving on misadventures (epicurean escapades) for him are ice-floes breaking apart and drifting.
He's Orpheus aberrating into Elysian Fields. Lucid
loquacity of her lingo. She is handy with his prick like
a seamstress is with scissors. Youngsters hang ten. The
glazed donut of sun asserts itself. Seagulls caw. Corse-
colored, claviform scintillation. Youths are dolphining
through the royal drink. Summer-in-Sicily-sweltering.
Water-skiers leave counterpart mother-of-pearl ropes
in their wake. Omnific light. Naturalists of all persua-
sions, intoxicated gay blades Rip Tide and Robert Kelp
among them, pomped and circumcised, the tag-team
getting into ketchup-and-mustard squeeze-bottle
horseplay, clownly cosmeticized, weekend warriors
chop-sockying, jet-fighter loud, kamikaze-crazy, panto-
mimic as in a puerile playlet, middles with jiggle,
hurdies with wiggle, out of the contempo commodes,
horsily trot, cavalry-charge, converge and carouse under
a vibrant vault. So forth.

ADIOS.

Heathen Rage

Bakeoven bloodlands without bounds, stenciled by an autonomous alienraceauthorship rebated by a nother dimension mayhaps, devroid of mankind's reference, life and death of humanity graven pictographic on arcane rock. Crude recitals of croaks from ravens as satanic doves elevated on a ledge with abundant yuccas. Broad, hostile country under verdant capes in niggard rumors of bristling rain with its redundancy like it's kept in an ancient curse surmised by some remorseless sorceress. On the rim of flanks of a valley floor with its loose sand is a fabled compound out of some storybook with its clear water and good grass, beneath the peccary squinch of sun dyed beatred. In his desolate and cluttered ranch house, a camaraderie of cows a laggard coterie in the pasturage with its profoundest narration, Sloat, porcine, drinking cold coffee and eating warm beans, hears quite a commotion in the courtyard

through the varnished wainscoting. He is shaven and
shorn and sitting in this defecatory posture in the creaky
antique chair with its shabby deshabille, his mercenary's
eyes paganized, expression a theatrical tragedy mask.
Lonely, confused birdsong. He runs a silver coin back
and forth in a drunken dance on his villose knuckles.
His vile unionsuit looks certainly slept in. Its sleeves
tied around his waist. There are pink centipedal scars
and an inventory of sutures on his pallid potbelly, inau-
gurated by psychotic surgeons of besoused Spaniards in
a barbrawl backwhen, his side stamped with a rebusoid
brand. His bloated, mottled corpus is comparable to that
of a beached, ivorine manatee out of myth. He's smoking
a carven pipe, a nomenclatureless, gigantesque gorgon,
made vacant by terrible experiences, at a remove from
and provoked out of ravenous wastes of a doomed land.
He has an aspect of ennui in a lugubrious atmosphere.
Pouring himself a glass of sherry, putting on a Panama
hat, silent and still as a tailor's dummy. An unclaimed
dish of tuna casserole on a walnut desk in conflicting
umbrae. Furniture disassembled, results of a temper
tantrum. His new leather boots pigeon-toed on the
dusty wooden plank, his haberdashery bedspread. He is
the Sorcerer and the Apprentice at once, powerful and
unable to control himself, an ordained agent of affluence
deployed to this clime, a bulging spectre scraping away
his etched name on a shale plate bespoken gray as if his
fate is prefigured in it, wrote there. Coruscation cascades
through those muslin curtains, with a cadaverous color.
He holds a corncob like an artifact. The room's the size of
a jail cell you'd reckon, a peaceful place as any to ponder

the state of man. Glaucous, wavering illumination apparently seen from watery depths. He pauses to listen very carefully. Gunslinger-walking-into-a-saloon-type quiet. His aged bones feel as though busted glass. He has an abstract love for Helen, alternately viperine and a tigress, take your pick here, his tenant and neighbor who is deep in debt to him. He possesses an inborn, indwelling, undying faith in the Lord Almighty his savior. Shuffling a deck of cards. He's contemplative and spiritual. Clouds are patches of necrotic rot on a hellish horizon. A brouhaha, substantial and vehement, spontaneously combusts. He hears Helen goat-blatting and he rises in a bullwhip-motion and staggers outdoors. Her older son, the hulking Hodges, an elephantoid, scuzzy, stupid scoundrel, silt at the bottom of a pond, fat face appearingly ground chuck, is near-naked on a horse, thick, hairy legs curved parenthesized, a guyrope around his stumpy neck, about to be lynched. He gets sick over hisself. The moon full of itself climbs and whitens. He remembers the sun mean and yellowing. Helen sheep-bleats. A Mississippi nigger, originally from Californy, a greasy, monstrous raggedyman, grabs her from behind. To her he's a powerful African voodoo doll blackmagically alive. She balls her fist and lambastes his muscled forearm, futilely. Whereupon he releases her. Wretched, balding mules tethered to a hitchingrail snuffle and stomp. Diggs, Sloat's serpentine foreman, instructs his subordinates, clothed in overalls and flannel shirts. Fowler, Sloat's vulturous brother and assistant to Diggs, nods. In the tearing torchlight they're spidered by branches' shadows. Hodges hangs, dangles and kicks, gasping like he's drowning and desperately wanting oxygen. He thrashes helpless. Sloat's heart throbs with the pulse of Helen's screams. Her pitch runs higher. She sounds verily psychotic, brought to her knees, pleading for her boy's life. She struggles, shrieks, held tight by an ursine feller. She begs for his preservation. Hodges swings in his underwear til he's still at last. The dumb galoot attempted to steal some branded cattle and got caught red-handed by Diggs. Helen finally vomits chunkily. Human beings causing a ruckus. Sloat's ham-hands reach heliotropically, explains Diggs has the proper authority to make such decisions of import. Justice was served. Hodges was tried and convicted and punished fair and square. He was a transgressor, hungry and thirsty or no. The devil tended to him. Jesus Christ.

CREATURAL STARS INCUBATE IN THE MATERNAL, darker firmament. An unwashed, towering Tennesseean appareled in a soiled slicker and queer trousers and widebrim hat grunts as an ape and watches. His shoulders set in slouch. He considers the world's mindless history, nature and nurture and vice-versy. See the reddening dawn soaked in blood and time. Hear the crazed wilds, auscultate the confused tongues of unknowed fairytale beasts. Negritic migrants slogging coastwise upon a pastoral countryside, hands all arachnidan. Vault's vast visage a sanguiniferous agony. Tooting steamboats trundle on the river black not unlike lit birthdaycakes afloat. The clay of barbarous terrene shaped by Creation.

Papery pelicans in flight, their pilgrimage swimming in the haze. Smell of logs newsawn. Wraiths of whores in cheap attire, candle-white, wall-eyed and bathless, with an edge to their essence, latterday martyrs, seam the showers. Pasts and presents foller them. They cannot get shed of them, cain't chase the shame away. Nomadic nymphs, a pretty posse of primitives, are divine intervention's improvisations, sally forth into an earthen swamp, their slender forms connoting filmic unholy bog-figures exhumed and animated inexplicable. Canvas tents of workers. A hobbled hermit trudges as a grounded sloth, smokin bacca, crost a prairie sprent with withered flowers, passes a defunct fort and abandoned church, hikes where there journeys no fellow save he. A brown osprey soars oblique. Serene settlements. Decrepit sawmill. Barren farms. An empty lot. Crows' caw-chants. Reeds gnash. Lightning flares. Thunderclaps deafen. Steel-hued welkin is a cage with levin-bars, moon its piteous prisoner. The pitiful hobo sniffs, stamps. Quarrelsome Tiguas to their tasks tender their voices to the void. Cookfires' woodsmoke in the scrub. Scalloped eskers. Random falcons in crucifixions of flight. A tepid breeze blows through a depauperated mead to quit it of pollen. A couple hares hop on. Herders' camp. A brumal phantom hunkers. Vista electrified. Coyotes yip. A cave-countenanced Indian crouches tailorwise to inspect a steer, its ribcage visually correspondent to fishbones. A haggard drover whittles a stick with a bowie knife. Sandy trail with faint miasma. Pair of bloodred nighthawks arc like winged gulch-revenant refugees ... Witnessed by Diggs's antelopean daughter,

Felicity, who is to wed Sloat next week. An arranged marriage. Meanwhile, she is eagerly awaiting the arrival of anguilliform laborer, young Cobb, her lover and friend. On the shingled roof he taps on her window and she excitedly opens it and he crawls as a baby on in and they embrace and strip and kiss and fuck on the broken bed. Then they pack their bags and elope. Disappear into a crepuscular universe. When Felicity doesn't show up for the bacon and eggs breakfast Diggs knocks on her oaken door which opens on its own. She's gone and he knows it. He tells Sloat, who seems stunned, and with the afternoon off he goes into the studio to paint, however, not before assisting his leonine son, Prewitt, in loading bales of hay into the barn.

Weakened by Felicity's betrayal and strong yet, humbled by that treachery and not humiliated, Sloat rides over to Helen's adobe house determined to make amends. They talk on the porch with its guano droppings and rotspots. He stares at her gorgeous grungy discalceated feet in their arthritic torment, sadly says he's sorry shit happened, it was out of his hands, it was Diggs' call, not his to make. She replies sorrowfully she understands, but is hurt, and healing. Animalic corpse fly-choked in the swales of dying grass. A few chicks chitter in the noon blaze. Several strapping burros graze in the healthful purlieu. Yardfowls shuffle. She is surprised when he proposes to her. He expresses his affection hesitantly, like a meek greenhorn adolescent unused to

making overtures. She's shocked, has to think on matters.
He leaves and she has a powwow with her gorillian
servant, Muamba, who convinces her that connubially
connecting with Sloat will put her in a prime position to
get revenge on Diggs. She agrees. He's her adviser, her
protector, reminds her of the fact he's a moneyed landowner. It'll be a conjugality of convenience. The massive
blackman rubs her upper arms and she gazes at him for
a spell. I got to get, she says of a sudden.

GEATHERS, HELEN'S YOUNGER EQUINE BOY, performs
his daily tasks, a real grind, doing the chores diligently.
He is feeding the livestock after gathering crops for sell
when Muamba gives him the scoop entire on everthing,
firmly suggests he, Geathers, find the lovers soon as
possible. Muamba gets a glimpse at the arrow-pierced
heart tattoo on his sinewy arm. Beyond Sloat's iron gate,
in proximity to a stand of pecans and willows, Geathers
locates Felicity and Cobb's tracks: there are hoof distur-
bances in the dirt. Easy pickens, he thinks. The sullen
celestial sphere with colorful clouds reminiscent of a
fading fresco. He sets out after 'em. Traveling afar, he
manages while on horseback, a spotcoated, whites-
tockinged, compact Appaloosa his cowpoke daddy
gave him a year ago for he perished unexpected, to
avoid cutthroat degenerates, a heathen horde on troubled territory, painted savages, outlandish presences
searching for gold and silver, a primate army advancing
in a swaggering column elongate, by ducking into

clumps of buckbrush and scarves of shrubs. Pack of truculent ponies in a corral. Harsh territory. Band music from an enshadowed cantina. Aroma of burning coal. Shifty gamecocks grandstand. Dogies sulk. Plaza thronged with folks immigrant. Madman's forgefire in a garage as the wizened yokel beats metal. Gusts snap not unlike turtles. Alien desert. Golden eagles. Phallus of cliff a cosmic obscenity. These pigs grinning, jostling, snouts stuffed in a trough in the stifling swelter. Immensity of a foreign region. Skyline wilder yet. He takes the reins and leads the horse to a mineral well where they help themselves. Injin morts enhearsed in a carriage. The improbable stench is enough to stave off the flies and birds. He wafts his hat and waves his hand at the formidable stink in the shaley, hallucinatory clearing. A gyrfalcon makes a foray into the cobalt firmament, about a terracotta watchtower overlooking bleak country, changes into a mere mote in the delusional murk of morn. Bonewhite arroyo. Ore, rubble. Looted compound. Freightwagons of precious metals. Remnants the works as an ideational memorial of a legendary battle, with its merits and virtues, the chaos ordered up by the factions involved, presented, one supposes, to potentially eons of speculation, the combatants dead to this world, proselytes of an apostate consideration, the aftermath in scintillating, slanting shafts. Must've been some skirmish, he thinks. Bands of brilliancy. Revelations of tatterdemalion halfbreed young 'uns analogous to anomalous angels in the pristine keep of a cerulean day. Night beclamored with mistrusting menagerie's racket. He's composed. Vinage

like tentacles bound to treetrunks. Lobos dig up the
dead on a shimmering, heated aft. They trot, pick at
remains, drag bodies, yammer. A lean, austere, auburn-
furred one studies him with flax, winking eyes, snarling,
pawing at its long nose. Halfburied skeletons on a
pumice portion, the section seemingly chalkdrawn by a
child and a part of it erased on a board in its vastitude.
Cratered, whitehot void of terrain during a blistering
day of namelessness. His silhouette an untrue corrobo-
rate of his reflection in aquapura. A frockless turkey
vulture, a pitiable, featherless thing, pecked at by a skein
of edacious kestrels. The stark, semiarid parcel with its
geology of uncertainty, a changeling kingdom summoned
out of a demon's deranged dream. Barks sourceless.
Cooper's hawk installed on sootysoil probing for critters
that crawl. Godforsook wilderness. Lady aborigines as
packanimals assault this coach in a culdesac. Caucasian
victims spread willy-nilly. It was butchery. Geathers,
anxious, swigs out of his canteen. His horse has the
fidgets. They step on eggshells. Landscape with lethal in
it. The males collect wood and water. The females like
lunatical chimps gather an assortment of accouterments.
No short supply of them; there are a hunnerd of the
fiends. Botanized wooded draw has no equal to it, visually
speaking. He fantasizes strangulating and simultaneously
sodomising an enchanting fatgal, bareassed, lipmawed,
bosomy, hippy, and discalced, not a filament to that
bulky, tatted body, comically corpulent, filthy as cavedirt.
She seems to be expecting him, there on the flinty pan.
She recruits suitcases. He fiddles with his pizzle, ogling
the pygmoid baboon, troweling his member, kneading it

like a perverted pastryman would dough, with freemason mitts, and creates in a minute the semen matrix on his denim'd crotch and flap of his linen shirt, the glue akin to chaff oozing down a hopper. Wheeling northern harriers. Maze of malpais. A volcano delivers itself of lava. Five newkilled lads strung up an skinned adjacent to a hazardous cauldron. Crooked spine of a crippled crag. Bestial barbarians bold as brass, quiet like smoke, disciples of a questionable faith, sinners in defiance of the scripture. Merlins make for the terminus of a solid, stoned flue, encircle it as communicants. He cannot abide the sight of those flayed buggers. Inkblack nighttime with a myriad of veering and spouting bats. Moon unaccountably altered of its location, an ovaline, luminous ignis fatuus belated on an uncivilized earth and pieced in yawing clouds. Ciboleros parley and in pursuance of their peregrination, posted to their haven, pulling to their end entire, their proper place. Sheetwise levin. Gnarling thunderclaps. Parkland evergreens and redwoods enclose about Geathers, his Appaloosa. Eventually he chances pon Felicity and Cobb seminude and wading into a bluegreen lagune like beautiful baptismal entrants, infatuated with each other, laughing and splashing. They spot him simultaneously, lunging as a famished jackal on fresh meat, whinnying like a hyena, slicing and gutting Cobb and subsequently raping and scalping Felicity. She was sobbing, endeavoring to dress. The slaughter finished, the calm, clean water is inviting. He spits a glob of tobacco juice, peels, goes plumb under, and rises as a lowdown Lazarus. He visualizes deftly carving Cobb's exposed throat and the identic serpentiform, sanguined, slim streamlets springing and sissing forth, columnar snakes arching in the air, Geathers adroitly avoiding them, Cobb's facial expression aghast, limbs gone ropy, trunk a steamy stump. He withdrew his other skinning knife from his equipage, took Felicity's mane, ringlets wrapped round his wrist, holding her head as a mephitic outland doc, and used the blade to cut along her skull as casually as a facial shave, ripping away her scalp like an animalian pelt. He leered and she bobbed. They were whirling dervishes entrained on the pale shore, in dustspouts of their own making, by the saltbush, in the calamity of calescence. She dropped as a released marionette in a gory gallery. Grove of cottonwoods and aspens. Avians aligned like reluctant witnesses, allowing no affinity whatsoever. Squalid huts in the vicinity. Clusters of carts and wagons. Buzzards, congregation of them, are bizarre bishops. Berserker ones aggravate him. He unsheathes his rifle from its scabbard, balances it on his elbow's crook, fires a round, hitting the target, and it plummets as a torn kite. Ramrod upright he shoots down its brother. It pitches sideways in a havoc of feathers, blood and guts. His piece touches off again. He misses. His calvary-sword clanks against his gear. Warp of humectation. Mounts like temples. Drencher abates. Unique liaison of light and shadow. Structures of saplings on a stony heath. A rapid wind absolves him from the hot air in an adamantine abyss. An osprey's oration. Gazebo and benches. Shoeless youngsters honeyhued and rootyredolent slalom the shingled disclets of dung pats, and Geathers on horseback makes a gun out of his hand and

calls them unrepentants and playfully picks them off
one at a time. Jays rocket in amazed articulations as if
defiant defectors in a bedlam of coos to the east above
them all. A tarred and feathered midget on the roadside
in primrose plenty. As a livingthing he was a harness-
maker and minstreldancer who wished to quit these
parts, with its higher and lower orders, entombed in a
stonewall of degeneracy in its ubiquity made of preda-
cious peoples, the rage as though a resinous residue,
until revered marauders ambushed him. Fear had leaked
from his very pores. Lucent egg of sun. Quake of heat.
Wrack of cirrus. Sorrel goshawk on its reconnaissance.
Impoverished villagers knelt not unlike for mercy in a
sorted syndicate of remuda, the speculants armatured
with skeletons in stretched flesh, murmurous to chords
of misery, attentive as owls in a convergence of chiaroscuro, the congruence of luster and shade not lost on
him. Empyrean in its circus with its plague of soaker
and stitches of lightning contested by loud thunder.
Rain like it is concocted alchemically. A russety, massive
grizzly rises from the reeds with meat in its mouth,
charges at Geathers and swings its clawedpaw at him,
blindsiding him, raking his biceps, shredding the skin in
a single swipe. The horse hinnies and rears up, baring its
yellow teeth, kicking crazy, the bear in onefellswoop
yanking the man from the saddle as a strawdoll, lifting
him clear of terra firma. He sees a gobbet of flesh in its
jaws, its turbid eyes, brownblack muzzle, the brute
taking him hostage, surpassing ransom, lifting him up.
By instinct alone he pulls the pistol out of its holster in
mid-air in a fluid, swift motion. He is slammed jarringly

backfirst onto the esparto. The horse bucks, galopades off. The ursine creature roars and charges and Geathers, slot-oculus asquint, cocks, aims and fires. In squeezing the trigger he vies to expunge the wild animal from the history of existence's uttermost memory, the whole affair signaling the potential of achievement. He is acquainted with the conviction apprising him of what to do next, the intuitional counsel in an abstract amnesty. The shot strikes the grizzly in the middle and it groans low, thick fur bloodying quick in a menstrual damage to its groin, slathered in sanguine. Then it lopes moaning into the thin copse. He instantaneously tourniquets his arm with a spare bandagecloth at a weave of a brook braiding a bed and defecates in the acacias and felinely buries the stool. He finds the Appaloosa a quartermile away calmly feeding in the high weeds. He pets its hindquarters, whispers in its ear, and clambers onto it, obliged to chuck it up. He scrutinates the forest in looms of mist yond reprieve. Dwarf oaks. He learnt about survival by surviving. Geathers on the panicgrass holds his ochre cigarello like an instrument of sacred ceremony. He has a sore shoulder and crick in his neck. His anatomic aspect acquires an umbrageous presence, his progression as if he is engaged in a rash enterprise, with an imperative investment, the importance of determination antecedent to him. Encampment of yahoos stoic on scourged shoreline in a shambles of a row of smoldering shanties. Spidery shadows skate. He takes off his chaqueta in a befogged chaparral where he halts to dismount and see to his wound, it in probability carrying infection. Trees as though churchspires. Fantasy of sky.

At a stagnant pothole he builds a haggard fire, hazing the quacktalking ducks outa there. Thence he bites on a belt, seizes the pommel of saddle and grips his injured arm stout, hissing, tendons on his neck ropy, and doctorfies himself by cauterizing. He yells and quails flare from this phantasmagoria of sotol and secular spruces. He envisages the grizzlybear's berryeyes. Damn ye then, he wheezes. Halfwild feverland whitened akin to sunbleached corn, the scene in the distance like seen in a diorama defiling in his view. Patrolling pandemonium of these depilated mongrels. He mounts to move on again, his hounding silhouette reeling, its frail figure catchin him up. Quivering strobes of leven mark the constant sierras. A snowblue polarmoon. Arcatures of stars. Churlish dames luridlooking and longlegged and wearing variegated wardrobes debouch as celebrants into a bordello shack, infiltrating it, in continued conference, screaming like harpies, ushering each other. Geathers, ever gallant, contemplates on whether or not to join the revelers, squiring one or two with niceness into the sack. Should he invest the joint? A toss in the hay? How can it hurt? No. A quadrille ensues. Crenellated mugginess. An argosy of aboriginals on cottoncountry with an afterimage tainture as ardent acolytes. Pandemoniac pavilions trestled up. A juggler and fiddler perform. He doffs his hat outta respect, dons his vest. Battery of gunfire impels his hand to his weapon like a duelist. Hoofclops in a cadence. He loads the pistol's empty chambers with conoid bullets. The mutant millipedes of clawcuts smart somethin else. He rowels the horse onward. Natural cistern. Rolling peppercorn hills swelling gently with birds, in their deputation taken it, hemmed about by a clamoring multitude of anonymous oldmen on muleback; the geriatric vanguard of an amiable and altogether ambiguous revolution, their arrival heralded by the turtleish clacks of equipment. Apparitions of Apaches. Torrential downpour makes tidepools morninglory-blue, floods the flowery carpet of the steppe. In the driving rain he's as a representative of a necromantic pietistic sect, motivated by an ecclesiastical warden and motivated into the highlands with its signs and wonders and urged to convert the atheists. Into the unearthly foothills. Drizzle in a gorge hewn in rock, the passage carved by nature's chisel. Raggletaggle consecution of the rancid vaudevillian, mediaeval bedlamites from a stytown with their embellishments of mammalian parts maken them look unvaguely cannibalist, a voluptuous, strawberryblond, drabbled temptress violinist bow-sawing a tune. Geathers uses his goathorn eartrumpet to hear her superb playing, but he disdains saluting the disbelieving, draggled funsters in a fairy-book forenoon. They move like hunted game, their destiny havin 'em doubtless dragooned into an obscene oblivion. He's cowled in his slicker. Mammoth grottoes. Holly assassinated. Clangorous weather pronounces the hardwood brake. Stupid scavengers are spectral spastics, supernumeraries in a febrile nightmare. Wide-eyed and mutened, feeling threatened, he woodenly unhorses and shoots one in the forehead and slashes his sister's throat. There's a disbursement in the sulphuric shroud. His horse, newly caparisoned, prances in place and accidentally tramples a chubby toddler. He levels his Colt and murders three more in the space of seconds. Devonian slaughter. In the perilous mist he kills two more. Evilthings moronical. They flee in riflesmoke-fog. Bandsmen slovenly scatter forthwith, skelter up the dirt street. Geathers recommences his odyssey and camps on a butte at an arrant balefire, flamy tendrils shaping out shadows on the prairie in its tragic dissolution. Horrific stench as from a common grave. Fireflies not unlike unanimous flintstrikings in the diurnal course's demise. Cumulus plume as breath in cold. Shirtless, his sundry scars make him apparently a subject of operational experimentation. And he imagines the grisly hematic toupee-trophy stripped from Felicity, grueling a puddle, he a barbaric barber admiring his gruesome dirtywork, her naked, ghastly skull an awful bathing cap. He pictures her domical polyp, bloodslaked coconut, peeled thusly. So he mounts, gets an erection, pursues his penis in his pants, wields the prick like an implement in a pertinent, depraved equestrian competition.

Left tonsured, a gibbering monk, Felicity, singular survivor of a massacre, fetal on the ensanguined soil, touching it with her parched lips like the devout to a shrine, evacuates her bowels and bladder. Gingerly, wondrously, she stands tall and totters, a redolent, maimed miracle incarnate of an authentic killing-field. Cobb is sprawled, slain. She does not look at her bloody wig. Jerky-dried eternal lane taken. She's apparently aimless, as if with dementia, left with a boiled appearing baldpate. Rudimentary hut. Stable, smoldering. Death rules this realm of dust, rock and bone. Bister province porcelain-cracked. Vigilant vultures on a jagged pinnacle. Corrugated vastity about. A freakish, rangy Mexican lay prostrate on a berth of loam, has a rolled cloth to his chest as though it's a crucifix, babbles like a halfwit, close to particolored traprock/dyke. He mumbles in delirium. His malletshaped, Mongol head is split as a cantaloupe. She turns away in disgust. Razorous crimson horizon and islets of cloudlets with rebates of radiance. Parcels of boars an billies. Palls of cirri. Shiny stones glint like shards of mirrorglass. Legion of buffalo. Bloodstained cranefeathers. Heaven and Earth spliced up from her perspective. Weddingveil of sprinkles. Bulls tended by Native Americans wardrobed in costumes and madeup in cosmetics, gaudy grotesques with demented daubings, unfamiliar funhouse forms, a retinue of hellaceous harlequins out of a fire and brimstone carnival, a clan of becrazed clowns from a circus in Hades, worser than a Catholic reckoning, biblical wrath. Pneumatic sighs of winds. In pain, Felicity, bandylegged, bends, as in prayer. Whited sun's blind eye to her. She heads westward afoot. The forestal gloom transmogrifies into many shapes, makes many sounds. She pictures Cobb's dead body. The slaughter is behind her. She traverses a ridge. Waning moon. Scalloped canyon. She negotiates an outcropping, traipses over a talus, persistently picks her way thru the harsh coppice. The rippling air is folded translucent drapes. Perilous temperatures. A redskinned warparty disregarding her, a hobbled, disfigured castaway, balded and bleeding. A weird witch, strange and swollen, a wizened horrible in a feculent robe, provides a meal of tortillas and onion soup in a rancid hovel's earthy room. Felicity sits on a pallet and leans on a beam with a plate and bowl when she notices in buttresses of brilliance falling through the thatched roof a grossly tumid papoose, peepers sunken in its sockets, shriveled integument like curd, in snarls of insects, on excrementitious pudding and urinose tongue, propped by gourds and decorated with flowers, as some rude newborn saint, in a niche in the mud wall. The crone murmurs to herself and Felicity, whining quietly, scrambles on the floor dried to ceramic and out the rawhide door of a sagging portal. The shriveled succubus chuckles. The hag is a conducta into Abaddon. Unassuming townspeople travel as determined plague personified. Felicity's glabrate, hemic head circumscribed by raven, vermicule locks. A viciouslooking, thoroughly colossal Comanche with figblack pies on his imposing mustang has on a necklace of decaying human noses and ears. He glares and snorts at her and kicks her like in a loony ritual into a gutter with cusps of glass and conical balls of bullets as grounded suns. He cruelly croons in a warbled singsong. Shadows bearing their figures shade her for a moment and they mutely dissipate. She drifts like a diminutive djinn, her transit as if she's sucked by a harmless maelstrom, feeling a part of the environment, a native to nature. Children as though runaway sprites from limbo. They clutch at butcherpaper. Vault held for humanity's validation. Her vexed physiognomy. Her essentia the expansiveness of the extant. Seagreen tract weathered and sloughing into heartsink without remedy. Ruinous presidio. A tallow-candle of a golliwog with uncanny posturing in the lapsing lambency mills with loutish citizenship outside a tawney tavern chambering the disreputable. Refulgent elements of glowflies. A roehawk's wings whoop and a jackhare shies away. She's sceptic of her surrounds, the city, shimmering not unlike the sea, and its citizenry. A door slams. Palisades are behemothic backs. Clouds under consignment to the pipeclay-pigmented sky. The advent of her personage causes curs to curse. Gypsies as a lost tribe of the Israelites, their isolation attributed to the cataclysmic agencies of famine and disease out of the Old Testament, laboriously denying their destiny in the repository of this locale. They offer her lamb stew and she gladly accepts. At an aqueduct are halfnaked whip-persnappers like feral pups, ruddy, grimy, and brutal. A snake is a hissing fuse. Mesa's penumbral replicas. Whinnies. A company of outriders cameo and dismount for a siesta in sparse grass dewsoaked. Asthmatoid cach-innations. A large blackie is stuck to a treelimb, unclad torso skewered, oculi simious, nostrils gunbores, mouth agape, in the aloe and artemesia, as a sacrifice at the fernskirts of a wrothful goddess. Neighs. Redhot sun. Apache adventurers, oafish heretics, squat and roast a spitting swine at a roaring watchfire in the conjectural crepuscle. She actuates without incident, a shambling monstress. Emberous chains. Globy moon at its malev-olent meridian glowers whitely in the ashen welkin, an area of vantage. Wanderrabble on the gravelly road with its ossatures of oaks and scrawny rill. Heavens irate with storm. Aralia spinosas stand arraigned. Misshapen raptoroid soothsayer. Bland land looks like an immeasurable stranded dolphin. Sable soil. She crosses a square near to fainting, splits a universal stitching mis-sewn and weaves a new world, serried with tremendous windless heat and coils of dirt, with her person. Hemoid, crustal chevrons of scrape-marks etched on her scalp where her tress-strands were scythed as wheat. They are referents of her traumatic ordeal, her terrible suffering. She's a worm working her way in the suppurate sore of the cosmos. Putting on the broadbrimmed hat she found and vanishing into the purgatorial plains. Carrion birds like peculiar pontiffs with bearings of beseeching on a dehydrated knoll as an altarless, tabernacleless, pewless goddamned chapel. Eddies of showers.

LARGE HEART OF THE COUNTRYSIDE RACES wildly. Dew sparkles on fallen leaves. Geathers leads and follers his wearing appaloosa. A garish macaw sneers and caws from an emaciated branchlet. Trout hazed in the seething cataract by a sizable gunsoot-blackbear, swatting at them, the cascade hanging down over those great boulders. A wizened, grizzled gnome strokes his burro. Family of deer feed in bamboo by a muddy river in the tangled jungle. Their chewing has the sonance of a quill scratching on vellum. Creation beneath yon azure out of humanity's knowing, with godamighty's consent. He threads thru the tapestry of this wilderness, dictating the terms of his progress. Sunflowers and tamarinds.

Loinclothed Yaquis. He envisions Sloat dragging himself as a sexualized seal over Helen and he is filled with jealousy, wants to clove his cranium with an ax. Mob of importunates. Gaudy prosties of every age and shape and nationality gotten up in grease are like screwy transvestic patients emancipated from a mental asylum. He shoos and slaps them away. Cauterized desert with its heatlines fading in the dusk as a vanishing evil vision where raider-Spaniards were slain. Crows racket off a gametrail and zip along rimrock and over the firs and conifers. Fog not unlike steamengine smoke. Migrant gritbits sting his face in the zephyrs unabating. Moon hatches out of an egg of cloud. A stripling ganders impartial at a madman backing into a mineshaft like a rabbit shrinking into its hole, befrighted by a predator. They're dressed in polluted raiment. Geathers goads the horse into shrubs, making a circuit of them, to urinate proper. Bloom of his piss blossoms into a puddle on stale soil. A burdened moose breathing uneasily wanders. A shot rings out in the damp air and the buck is stone-dead, having sedately sunk heavily with sound on the rocky strait, leadslag lodged in its brain. Thereupon Geathers picks off a stocky, mustached, Mexican mule-teer mistreating mules by way of caning. And he pitches as a crippled martyr off a peak and explodes below in a burst of blood, strewn on the sharpstone. The animals struggling on a slope, plodding as if harried, the sections of the train separating and scrabbling, panic-stricken, scrappling the shale. His imbreachment of bushes pres-ents an unexpected encounter with fugitives eel-slippery. He nods, outnumbered, and they glare. He glowers.

Nothin transpires of it. The precipice is negotiable. Calamitous gulf secretive and unsympathetic. He blacks himself with the gloom, on the open territory, arms at the ready, every resonance kept in his cognizance, vigilance continuing. Gloaming unclaimed. Promised moon. Midmorning, condensation singing from the terrene, he digitally calibrates his hardon near these hale paloverdes, woolgathering he's putting his fingers in his mother's bodily orifices like a puzzle being connected, its completion predicated on the precise placement of each piece. Her corporeal construction sturdy. He is aggravated because a burly brunette host who wore overalls and moccasins docked him of his coins earlier on after they had sloppy intercourse in a Papago cabana. Foliage defers to him, he a whippingpost-built specie of journeyman extricating hisself from bramble and briar, turning the perturbed horse quarterwise. Vultures ostensibly cloaked and congregate on claywalls of a deserted compound, stationed as though an unfortunate forfeit is inevitable. Vagrants reposing, idlers forgot, wastrels at a wrecked wagon in a tarp. A pre-teen carrot-topped toothless imbecile in bra and panties giggles and stammers she is from Californy. Geathers wants her to fellate him while he rides only she slinks into the torn enclosure, a besmirched psuedosolarium with trash and trodden turds. A giant gentleman of color, bent like in grace, makes this gesticulate of hospice and says we gots beefribs, to which Geathers replies well I have me tiswin. 'Sides, I don't ingest nor imbibe with no niggers. Set somewheres else, the negro responds and puts a dipper in the pail. Aim to, adds Geathers, staring, and steers the appaloosa past the hardbit cavefolk. Wigwams untenanted. Indigents lug a keg of whiskey out of a jerrybuilt grogshop. A motley of miscellaneous denizenry rubberneck him and he warns them away, in a foul mood, haven hoped to be blown by the retarded tomboy, and currently on the lookout for provocation. Smoke from a barbycue rises as souls. Contrived civilities exchanged. Feral dogs snatch scraps of pork he thows 'em. Vista ventilates its anger upon everthin. Cholla and jornadas. He's a sojourner with substance, assesses a promontory as if there are portents held in it, a nation's history seen there, the urstone of a kingdom he usurps, the phosphorus endarkments of its ages, his origin contained within, and the cosmos becomes him entire. Hung travelworn coons in frugal clothes like dreadful effigies in the graying spate at a slapdash cairn with mesquite trees, several of their junglebunny kin hacked, a few mutilated beyond recognize, colorized countrypeople in all attitudes and years dismembered and or decapitated, these teams of wolves, growls and yaps relayed, wallowing in the unspeakably tragedy. Shells are medallions in the refulgence. Domain sere and haunted by sunchalked skeletons. Geathers spare like a jockeystick. Calcined architectural arc of ruminant ribcage. Muttersome ocean with surfacing seabeasts of waves. Riding at a canter. Cinderland's burnedout lakebed. Albino archipelagos. Crusty lava as though dried blood. Acreage alters in the effulgence, calefaction a malefic transient. Gulping water like to outwit the heat oppressive. A nubile, stobby and tattooed Yuma Indian beauty in willowbark regalia and wasting from cholera crepitates on her belly, whining, chin on a driftlog, at a sorry runlet. Geathers jumps down, simian stepping pegging him as an apen archimandrite in a skein of precipitation. The horse jerks and bucks because of the galled eagles with widest of wingspans shrieking in their soaring. He scrubs his planate abdomen, attitudinal not unlike a champion of a mime troupe, with a penumbral prefiguration, unzips and unbuckles, a petrified pillar over her, mungy trousers sustained about his twiggy hips, his dreggy shaker ravaging in them, as a debauched hambone thaumaturge in a sleazy sideshow mid ceremonious wands of boughs, and penetrates her from behind, committed to her cunt. Beset by him, she wriggles on the talc-sand like she's beleaguered by bees, her whimpers of protest muffled by his perspiry palm. He wiggles, thrusts, shoves her facefirst into the fish-hued beck with his elbow, drowning her at the same time he drills her. She anguishes 'neath her assailant. He calls her a ruby negrite. Her flowing jet hair floats, flimsy, incompetent skirt balloons. Her mewls nigh unto agony and into a soprano hullabaloo. He's crammed into her, clamped onto her. His Nubian injun. They churn on the clerical-black packed dirt. Carbonized skull of sun. He yawps' writhes. She thrashes, bubbles, ceases struggling. An assembly of aborigines squat in the cane while he plunges into her as if a malicious magician plummeting repeatedly into a trapdoor. The designed, irreligious swarm go to and fro like Neolithic reconnoitres and skulk into the shimmering and swimming mural of the pan, jabbering in their stoneage language, the savages shambling and slobbering, communicants in an extinct tongue, and deliquesce into the plateland at large. He, a man in a mode of monstrosity, skewers her. Immigrants traversing the dunes and wooded littoral tolerate this travesty. He keeps his composure with aplomb. The incident is as some corrupt birth scene not notarized by any canon. To him the outrage is a kid's conception of a crime, unaccountable to societal courts. He train-chugs-and-lopes and she puts forth raucous squalls in the saturated, destitute oxygen. He's a lecherous gymnast routined on her in the glassine jigsaws of pools. Her bosoms like teeninecy turnips. She is ripened, stiff as a department store manikin. Afire, his lungs sound seared. It is a holograph of humiliation quenched in the aqua-pura benastied with crud as he worries her vagina, husbands her bottom, to render her ruint, putting her in perdition. Dusk suffuses the glade overhung by a mantle of cirri. Her noise issuances like rabid rodentine feeding. She is deeply cherryred. He pulses as a boil of flame. His chest shawls her shoulders. He hoots when he orgasms and leaves her, bare of body, life leached from her. He cuts off the ears, scalps her, and partakes of tea and dates on a plankboard walkway. During an ecliptic event he examines himself. Signs of syphilis are showing. A mastiff goes after a crane. Its Gruidae brethren consult among theirselves. Without a stitch he takes stock of his weaponry in a satchel congruent to a scurrilous feudal lord his belongings. Leech of a scar on his fuzzy sternum. The horse's tail whisks. He is bedraped with a blanket now, a morbid manciple of the earth with the agility of a lemur, eyes larval in the luminosity, matted, stringy locks cleaved to his head. He shovels fried steaks, scrambled eggs, sausages and biscuits. He utilizes his rucksack as a pillow, restores himself in the cedar shade. He prods the Yuma with his chafed heel, pokes her with a stick like a malevolent, licentious dowser. Asteroids of boulders. Ram cadaver. Brigade of ants bearing parts of what might be a viper. Uncanny congress of garbled canines aprowl on a flat quadrant where oxen meander. Joshua jumble. Hornetnest on newspaper and cardboard. Perished elk. Stealthy heathens muster along the granite ridge congruous to bizarre sprites, beggarly beings as if anticipating with a curious equanimity a pestilence evolving out of its incubation. Reefs of vapor. Delegations of sycamores detailed by limning light. Night advances. A weedy wrack. Orion overhead evokes in him recognition. A cretin's antics distract him, the fool flailing, cranking a barrel organ, unprotected like a newborn, foundering as though to cast a spirit out, a mutant corporal unraveling in a primeval millennia, a cuckoo from the wildness of the country, abutting the hammered hind of a crag. Blam! Geathers executes him with a bullet in the back like an expert marksman at a county fair shooting gallery, as if he's been commissioned to initiate the coldblooded act in a passably artful way. Bang! Cruelty is his jurisdiction. He's a hut housing an evil spirit. He considers that moneyer Sloat and his tonnage of coinage. Silica siss of salmon sand where this colt cavorts. Serene heath. He finishes polishing his derringer, and, libidinous, contemplates eventuating the enterprise of coupling with the injun girlie once more, and grabs his scrotum, an ossified egg, and violates her corpse, moving with the weight of water sloshing in the stomach, and cries like a jackal when he climaxes. He withdraws himself and nibbles on sweets, still lusty, shotgun barrel-nares flared. Yonder she lay, silentious as though stone, in a sheet of spume. Her liquorcrazed, bulbous father bumbles like a storied hero marching through depleting military ranks for the battlefront when Geathers assails him, beating the owlheaded sadsack senseless, the sumbuck fallen from the salt and battery as meat cut down by a skinner, Geathers binding and gagging him and dumping him into the booming surf. I'm plumb full of sin an meanness, he tells himself, and snarls. The ovalshaped booger is unconscious. Geathers has the urge to fuck him royally but a foreboding gives him pause and he don't. He looks like a sallow scarecrow, a gangling sentinel, engulfing a baloney sandwich, cheese and crackers, and cake, with a chaser of sour sweetmilk. He swats at mayflies, seemingly waving farewell to a dear lover lost to him. Glomming his grub. Mountains are marvelous. Gaggle of cirri.

Tent show's hat tricks at a weird carny bepopulate with local rabble in a mudded mead, the droning crowd compassing it. A destitute meg barefoot and white as bone with an auburn mop and miceteeth waves at Geathers and he licks his reptilian lips and parodies puckering up. He debates if it'd be wise to abduct her ... Mummied cow carrion like a strange shipwreck, bony frame on a beachless vastness. Death had bled it of its life. Resonately he rolls onward, milling the neuter ground bequeathing a precedence of harmony and unguessed democracy and alien austerity. Claycolored empyrean. Cotton candy cloudlets. Lank, bland, niggerized progeny, these longlimbed, dispossessed, Aframerican gamines convened, with cabbages for tits and pumpkins for buttocks, pick through refuse in a dump, cussing and carrying on in unreckoned vaporized ghostings. He'd bet they've got reekyfishy loins in themthere dungydrawers. He could melt into 'em like butter in the mouth. He grips his peter. In the foetid kudzu, a rancidic amphitheatre, he, narroweyed, squirts his load of jissom. His fist is gorged with his gunk. An oldtimey churchgoer, leprose-gargoyle-semblant, gives them jellybeans. He has burrs stuck to his pressed chinos. His carriage comparable to a mechanical duck. He's got a teddybear physique and the verbal verve of a barker. Their gab is blackbook-related. Hellatious hot. Candyapple moon. Carousel of cats in heat. Balsams and sedge. A woodpecker raps. Demoniacal yodeling of yotes. Crateful of pigeonry. Prevalence of hens. The world waits for him, hungered, and he, put at hazard, a flatshanked, rangy reprobate, swaggers onto its sediment of sentience, bowing as a godserver on the accursed amberine badlands. He remembers that idiotic spitfire in her undergarments. Possum crap in rheumy rays. Mockingbird intones in the nightshade. Sun swoll up. Braying foxhounds. Crickets ever strident in midsummer. Squadron of sashaying and elements-exposed wantons hurry like refugees following a natural disaster; or they're rotating on a makebelieve dancefloor, creamy young countenances composed in esoteric portraitures in a vectored myriad. Traffic of godgiven badgals plying trade. Water gutters in a sink in the dogyard. A barechested, pantalooned, dirtyblond jailbait relieves herself, musically clapping a pair of spoons between her knees. Geathers' oculuses out on stems as a crawfish's. Cliff monolithic and sheer. He is a slaverous, straddle-legged, not threatless incubus. She pops the cork of a champagne bottle and it straybullet-flies. She releases a lively sigh while she shits in a visible continuance, looking reflectively retrained. She wipes with plantleafage and nimbly pirouettes to rejoin her colleagues jus before Geathers can snatch her. In the honeysuckle he sneezes a gout of green snot. Mutations of virid moss on a ramshackle outhouse mong bracken and jimson. In there, Geathers does his business, the laddered luminescence veinblue and runged by slats. In the sanctuary of the eve doltish cannibals inanely armed are composed on a dripping, bonestrewn knoll, the aggregate of their denuded bodies making a false gargantua, a scion of a polypheme pedigree, its oldworld shadow constructed pon the parcel, in the wake of a legendary campaign. Makeshift levee in a dike. Bows of bovine ribs in layered nebula. Ten miles from home the horse lames, snorts, limps, hobbled thus. It stands on three legs. It stamps and snuffles with a watchful eye. It paces clumsily, his nervousness the reason for its unrest. It snuffs, nickers. Devastated, Geathers dismounts and touches its eyelashes and cheek with his palm. Its shoulder shivers. Out of ammunition he resorts to wrestling a club from its bag to dispatch it humanely, swings and crushes its skull in two strikes. The beast screams and falls, hits the ground in a heap, anatomical assembly collapsed whole in the scraggly acacia and shakes. Blood gushes from the destruction of its head and it spasms, Geathers, body in a seizure of stress, holding it as if a pathetic and insane faith healer, feeling its indiscrete pulmonary pulse, the animal accommodating him, and it is still, froth foaming on and alas caking its mouth. He kneels not unlike one to mock prayer, shuddering violently with sobs, mind senseless, being palsied, with his fingers combing its mane, syrup-sticky with sanguine. He crabs sideways, brushes its palpable ribs. I could've coaxed it, he thinks uselessly. Nacre firmament. Sun coalred and bloodbeating. It surveys with a lidless fixity. Sky brooded in the overcast. Constellations of lightingbugs create precarious parallelograms, without designation. Charred coagulum of campfire remaints, it as though a dynamited crater, a circular cremation site. Tandem of rail and bunting in their chartless migrations above a quilted coulee. He walks the rest of the way primarily on rubble and gravel of bench-land, his frayedwiry figure trudging and defined on the terminal of the prairie, fetched into the incinerated welkin attending the inordinate aft. He has learnt to live by living. Leven fuses out of the celestial sphere. A hermit, wits gone total, chases a doe. Malodor of manure. Mallards mutter in a pomegranate orchard propagate with audible specks of insects. Rocks like landed meteors. Militia on the move through a barn-yard in lastlight. A falstaffian fellow fishes, ransacks a riverbed. His mare sniffs. Embers as sparks from a forge. Wigeons flap up. Alternates of avian auxiliaries. Geathers is an unredeemed mortalman, failing, ill for want of sustenance, a righteous initiate not altogether sane, surrendered to survival, schlepping on a dry estuary much reduced from its former estate, deliberates on the cerebral blueprint of the architecture of Muamba's laidout plot, a plan ... A jaguar devours a bison. Vault's puzzled by clouds. Weather made by grievous gods. Aw naw ... Kiss my ass ... His body unmeated by eatables deprivation, day spalding him from night, in a spungging spritz. He ort to keep going, only it ain't like he's got a mizzes to return to. Span of starlings sort the cumulus. For a pint! Hobbling through honeysuckle. Trapezoid of illumination. Waisthigh chickenwire. Clotheslines and cinderblocks. Belongings arranged in the mire where chance devised. The Yuma's bellshaped bum with its scabrous scallops and carmine bunghole visualized. Newfell obscurity. Ironrust skyline. Palimpsest of panorama. Spray of finches. His legs bowed akimbo. He strikes one as a beanpole troll in illfit toggery. Hurtle of herons. Heaven winks with stars. Moon peeps like a ghast, ridiculose, cyclopean groundhog. Cirrus in their configurations and delineated. Decaying sow in a stand of sedge. Batwings of leaves. Kneedeep in a creekbed he fills his flask. Vitriolic hirtellous hillbilly without relent implements his invocations, hailing up from calescent clefts of stygian Hades. He's a bedraggled manly metronome aswamp in a muddy meniscus. Blue yonder limitless and mutant, thunder rifling thew it. Mossbacked rocks. Moldcrept apples. Geathers bareflank and in a

humanscalp frightwig and armyshirt in medallions of
moonlight. Gong of thunder ringing, lightning with
dire intent, nictate slashes the product of a capable
filmcutter, a cosmic contrivance in the distance darken
to blackness in swathings of clouds. He's a false, part-
time ghoul on territory swaddled in miss lemon abelia
and solar flare azalea and baby gem boxwood. Cloudlets
closin ranks and motioning the moon in. Sparrows hove
into view and sprocket o'er a starlit sawmill. Lightnin
licks a rabbitsnare in a shadowshow in the sightless
gloom. He shinnies up the scarp and rodently scrab-
bles in the stratified, sparring scintillation. Follerin the
footholds in the stonefloor. Fieldgrass garlanded with
fantasies of florets and webbed with microscopic grains.
His flesh puttied by malnutrition. He is a dust-covered,
reed-formed anthropoid with a case of the fidgets.

MUAMBA SURREPTITIOUSLY SLITHERS into Geathers'
rathole room in the gloom. He's in a drunken stupor,
Geathers is. Muamba comes across the twinehandled
blade with the victims' blood caked on it. Ultimately
he plants the murder weapon under Prewitt's mattress.
Prewitt's given a necktie party by Sheriff Grady, the
lumpen law, and his jackass Deputy, Barksdale. The
evidence gainst him was not only overwhelmingly
obvious but he also had motive - he was accused at
various instances of having impure intimate relations
with his sister. This was confirmed by an eyewitness,
Geathers, who claims he saw them screwing on the

shore, as a devout Christian would swear on a stack of bibles. Anybody with a quarter brain in their cranium can put the pieces together at this point. He had mercilessly butchered them. Helen, Sloat's wife now, assessed Diggs' anguish. He's hollow, a husk, devastated. He'd put up a stink, all for naught. Helen reveals she is pregnant.

Roaming the Sloat ranch's perimeter early evening, on roving duty, Diggs sees Felicity curled in the enbrowned grass. He weeps, gathers her up in his arms as a bride, or an ogre scooping up a fallen maiden. It was Geathers, she says, soughs. His convulsed cries make him sound craziern a coot with the diarrheal drizzles. A rooster describes the bedimmed dawn, phosphorescent rays accruing. A squaw, genderless, deceased, is draped over shabby fencing not unlike a long strip of ruddled laundry in the lightglazed soapweed and scruboak. Felicity is malformed and disheveled and guzzles water from her father's flask. She is taken to an unused shed to be cared for. Sleeping soundly in a cot and enwrapped in wool blankets he impulsively pulls out his pad and sketches her. It's an inept rendering, he opines. And he kills Geathers by attacking him as he slumbers on a hammock, clubbing him to incapacitate him, flaying the soles of his feet with the business-end of a bust bottle, and strangling him with a cord. He's a revengeful deity, a barmy archangel, gets up, blood-sodden, like a distinguished honoree. He never took out his revolver. His American Cream Draft mare canters on the terra damnata of cinderland and they dissolve in the roiling fog. Limegreen, leathery lizards sleared in the sunshafts and with sly smirks and driedraisin eyes pressed to the molten boulders with elbows cocked. Lashing branches. A whale of a woman washes in the polluted ford, fends fellas off with her deformity. Retinal spectra race out of her hazel irises. Poplars are prophets in attitudes of exhortation. Pricklypear. Mist as smokin slag. Moonrind overhead. Scavengers scuttle like wingless flies through a spoiled village. Inflamed hole of the sun. He forsakes the pinchedpugfaced, mouse-eyed gnomes guffawing in the ocotillo. Cocks call. Grubby, grim soldiers from a nother capital assemble in a mudwalled courtyard as patients in an institution from a farfetched latitude talking among themselves and smoking cigars and grasping their muskets like talismans. Some laugh an drink. Diggs' saliva as venom. He's debating whether or not to shoot his daughter when he returns ... His head lolls, his body slumps inebriatedly. Thunderboom like fanfare for the commonman. Dreamless seaforms of clouds. A seamy leper profoundly sickern a mutt vending his wares and intoxicatedly wobbly. A mendicant jabbers. Timeworn, sunblackened populace in a putrid pueblo, such poignant peons. Carven gantlets of scarps. Apostles of albatrosses in benevolent postures and habited in feathery vestments perched on entablatures of rock. Suddenly Diggs is swallowed up, his silhouette seeking him, crafting his shape on the wasteland, scanning the ground for guidance, staying the light; a melanoid caesura in the rhythm of a harmonic universe. Trees appearing completely composed of bone on harrowed, anonymous terra firma. Anklebiters acting as disturbed dwarfs. A retard flails akin to a mannequin brought to life by strings. Foundlings absolutely darkened by damselflies and whiffing of wax. Mizzle like poltergeists of patriots. Beyond a sallygate at a doorsill are racks of beef and viscera. Hoofclops and hammerclanks and cartrattles in the jackpot metropolis where the chary coruscation finds orphans abroad, tadpole argonauts in their briefs, kids crouching as reticent monkeys and without curiosity, compunction. Gaunted, goldtoothed fortune-teller saunters, nagged by failing health. A buff eagle cruciate in the faultless welkin squawking oaths, coalbit eyes unblinking, in the covenant of space, its empyreal encounter unrecorded, ferrying itself in flight over the unrectified quinta, after the fled fulgor and into the problematic pitch providence of night with no real tacit rules. Whereupon boys and girls as felons from a juvenescent state penitentiary, amiable adolescent infidels conglomerate, cherubim much reduced, hellions substantiating hearsay, after their committed crimes have evaporated like liquid. Squatters, ardent anchorites, on the flyspecked playa in its desolation. Frieze of a flock of geese slurred together, lofting up, threw fantasms of cirri and over a luridine loch, augmenting it with their avatars of reflections, those floating ranks in the spumescent cumuli, chimeric, coalescing and separating. Holocaust of horizon in firmamentfold.

It's been a heretofore problematic pregnancy for Helen, fraught with difficulties, numerous complications. Giving birth presents more complexities, but she delivers a baby boy. A mulatto. It takes four stocky nurses to prevent Sloat from killing it. He orders the Tennesseean to get Muamba. He's gone missing. Sloat vows once Helen is healthy enough every employee is to line up to violate her. The nurses smuggle the baby, named Morgan by Helen, out in the laundry basket. On the outskirts he is handed over to Muamba, who osculates his brow, tactions his thumb.

As a nice gesture, a peace offering, Diggs has Sloat and Helen over to his private quarters to see his completed artwork. It is a portrait of Helen, divested, in a sylvan setting, and beside her is an arrow-pierced heart, rather clashing within the painting. It is an exact replica of Geathers' tattoo. The canvas is curious, Helen says, touching it. The material is interesting. It is Geathers' flesh. Helen and Sloat are horrified. Felicity materializes and slashes Helen's throat and Diggs stabs Sloat in the stomach with his dagger, only not before Sloat brandishes his pistol and shoots them both. It is as a scene out of some farcical tragedy for the stage.

Fowler's corpse crumpled in the corner. Tiny Morgan in his wickerbasket wailing. Muamba takes the bags of bills from the safe at Sloat's house. Helen had given him the combination. He holds his son up and hugs him. He bows his head, raises it, smelling the scented air, the fragrant grass, looking at that long road of the land, those countless trees, godmade, his eyes these annular, atramentous maps of man, his country of this world. How black the night is. How white the stars are. Then again.

THE END

Pinocchia: Hard To Be A Puppet

THE SILENCE IS A CHILD'S CRY CAUGHT in the throat. Pinocchia, this pinewood doll, wearing a nice cardinal dress, matching cerise slippers, and striped stockings, with yellow yarn-hair, marble-eyes, button-nose and carved asymmetrical mouth, is an imperfect pearl in a shell of the labyrinthine city. Soot drifts as in some sacred, solemn ceremony. Snow falls like ash from crematoriums. A gibbose, alabastrine moon in the sky black as well's water. Stalactiform stars. Seething light strikes dewdrops on a laced leaf, thus making a new species of varicolored beetle. Here, in Germany, during a World War, insanity rounds the edges of sanity. One catches craziness as you might malaria from cold air. There is so much unconquerable sorrow, atrocity, bloodshed, hardship, misery, grief and starvation. Decency has disappeared as if it'd never existed. Clouds eddy like currents behind a dam. SS Obersturmführer

Wolfram Off, a Nazi scientist, is a tall, wiry, stoop-shouldered, acneously complected, melancholic man pushing fifty, with a fish-eye-lens face and habitual lordly attitude, analytic avian's peepers, fleshly mini-violins for ears, harelip, cleftchin, hooked proboscis, slick eels of strands plastered on an onion-skin of scalp, corroded, crooked teeth the exact hue of turned apple, protuberant lips, drooping mustache, and has a cracked, muculent pince-nez see-sawing on his honker. His utterly unique, if creepy, countenance is comparable to that of a goat's. In the past he was married and owned a thriving timber business. He was very successful, had planted the seeds rather strategically. In the present he's a devil-thing, an evil creature, a brutish bastard chummy with that Mengele monstrosity and his ilk. But he is still brilliant. His wife died years ago from tuberculosis. They never had kids. Currently he's determined to conceive one. His faith and self-confidence are powerful like famine. Meemie-screaming air-raid siren. Embittered and enraged citizens flow as shadows. Madness everywhere. Hungry stray dogs roam and growl and bark not quite in unison, in packs, behaving not unlike wolves. Off now feels as a grain of wheat on the millstone of warfare; or a wick soaking in a bowl of olive oil. He considers the rampant upheaval, pain, suffering, cruelty, unreason, indecency. Thinking of this: he who flogs his back shouldn't complain of the stinging. With a delivery-doctor's precision he snips these numerous umbilical cords of strings from Pinocchia. He pictures her resembling his deceased beloved - a big-boned, pig-tailed, bosomy beauty with a big belly and bottom, meaty legs and beefy arms, fat feet and spatulate hands. Diligently he sets up the extravagant futuristic contraption he alone designed and constructed, in a narrow, dirty alley, bent like in a parody of penitence, those curious people fanning out as ripples in a pond from a tossed pebble. Spilled coffee and tobacco on the icy street where a gigantic soldier beat a bald, roly-poly octogenarian for a nebulous transgression. Collegial bookworms, wondrously attractive, swap elaborate, erudite literary opinions in the debris of a cafe. Showers tinkle. His incisiveness, investment. Gulls' wings flutter like surrender flags in the steel-grey empyrean. Severe stench of decay in the wintry thaw could be the main cause of insectival attentions. Rotten malodor in stirring breezes. He mutters to himself, twisting the dials, mumbles, turning the knobs, then curses, flipping switches. He knows his voice is on par with an inane, irritating sheep's bleat. Serious stink of garbage and human decomposition blends, no, clashes with the rich scent resin, fragrance of bark. Mountains miraculous. Beach's sand as salt. Off gets a glimpse of his solid, fortified headquarters, a courtyarded structure, the gothic, moss-smothered mansion with iron-barred windows and surrounded by really high brick walls. He chose the place himself, not a mean feat, looking at the carnage. Her birth will be the advent of a living, breathing marionette! She will have an aurulent allure, an angel unmolested by life, with plentiful saffron tresses and porcelain skin. He envisages her as a butterfly bursting forth from her chrysalis, so charming, out of the cocoon, prettiness personified, charging gingerly and recklessly, gallopading through a gentle gambogian pasture, cattle-grazed, and where peasants cultivate their land. She'll cartwheel, handstand and somersault near a livid lagoon. The russet blemish on his scarred, chiseled cheek. Haunted ghosts of citizenry forage. Spectral figures gracefully glissade. Grungy tribal orphans on the prowl. An awkward stork nests on a flat roof. Monumental alps. Filthy foundlings swim in a sea of dust, play hopscotch, leapfrog and jumprope, carrying on. And animals find shelter in bomb-blasted buildings. An androgynous juvenile with mousy pies, fair integument and unruly mop, frowning in deep concentration, roots through his pockets for ID papers in an impromptu interrogation courtesy of a scrawny Unterfeldwebel with a bandaged sneezer. Lothar, a mechanical, metalloid German Shepherd of Off's creation, whines, laps itself, and drools salivary oil. Waiting on the weather. Thunder roars like tidal waves and lightning flashes as press cameras. Off's ingenious, albeit cumbrous, boxy mechanism coordinates the levin to directly zap the puppet and she comes to, twitching and spasming, in a seizure, looking as an electrified toad in biology class; or like she is enduring an epileptic episode. He almost expects her to clench her fists and ball her toes, and orally foam. Christ's sake ... Incredible ... The furless dog yawns, squeaks, licks itself. Without any warning whatsoever, a torrent of enemy shells pelting in the pitch. Off ducks, remains focused on her. She gasps as a drowner suddenly resuscitated, apparently emerging from the icy pavement, and manages to gain her balance. She giggles, has an intoxicated veering to her gait. She is jerky, jouncy, unintentionally comical, with an uneven, exaggerated waddle, teeter-tottering like a toddler, at an unusual, clumsy pace, propelling herself along, humorously wobbling, Lothar scampering, yipping, following, sniffing. Off claps and cheers. She stops and stares blankly. She robotically blinks at her audience. He has made her to lure Jewish youngsters out of hiding. He resumes his applause. Lothar yaps, tongue wagging, and rolls. She neighs with laughter and does a slapstick pratfall to please him. She strains to read the words on a propaganda poster nailed to a telephone pole. "Gestapo," she calls him. He smiles in approval. She speaks as a student translator articulating a difficult language, feeling not unlike her brain is a bright balloon floating high up. A seltzerish spate has the tang of cinnamon. An antagonistic atmosphere. She is satisfied with the euphonic name he has conferred on her: Pinocchia.

SLUMBER FOR PINOCCHIA WAS NOT AN OPTION, an unattainable goal. She'd tossed and turned restlessly all night long on the plain pallet in Off's outlandish, disorganized, cold laboratory with its crepitant chiaroscuro. What didn't help her cause was the ghastly, deformed fetus, Benedikt Bismarck, a hardened hoodwinker, pesky bamboozler, a Hungarian in rank raiment (tailcoat and trousers, kept up with his tacky umbilical cord), bobbing in the formaldehyde in a jar on the metalline shelf, beside the mementos exhibited in a glassy showcase, many of them outrageous appliances, these apparatuses you wouldn't believe. He nasally, gutturally discoursed with himself. This impulsive homunculus was sickening and annoying in equal measures. Dawn was a glaring dream. She felt comfort, peace and tranquility. Morning was a majestic mystery, with its fierce fulgor ... implausible, intense, perplexing lambency! Her heart was warm with great pleasure. Off, his sharp jaw stubbled, beady blinders wearied, shares an incandescent hour with her, the two together during breakfast, at a beaming daybreak, engaged in a chess match. Eating his awful omelet and drinking extra-sweetened herbal tea at the little lopsided table, he feels as if he's prodding a turtle with a stick to get it to poke its head out. Angular laurels. A flock of tiny goldfinches in the curvature of a distorted distance swim as though a school of shoal over an orchard where mist rises from frozen earth like smoke from a heated frying pan when doused with water. Resolute, rodentine kids with pallor unhealthy balanced on boulders while a brown bear rummages through a wrecked, elements-exposed, empty, pastel pantry. Demolished post office, bordello and lingerie store. Haydn playing in an obliterated grocery store. A crater filled with pamphlets proclaiming the merger of societal soul and Germanic spirit. In conflict culture succumbs to its basest instincts. Frosted elms. A neat, abdominous, pimply fellow has a baritone delivery, busy with his trivia, totally absorbed in it. Din of gunfire ... a disturbing racket. Disconsolate livestock meander in the remnants of an ancient terra-cotta church. Solitude in squalor. A septuagenarian crone catches these leeches in the river with a bucket. An ugly, skinny merchant pants, worn out, his mangy donkey dragging a rickety cart with its wares, the warped wheels making creaking sounds. Hibiscus shrubbery. Off suspires, "God is strange." Then he explains in explicit detail what Pinocchia has to do, what is expected of her. He actuates with a subtle, elegant rhythm, enunciates with a certain eloquence, which fascinates her to no end. Odor of urine and feces. She talks not unlike a deaf girl learning to speak clearly. A bulbous ogress sweeps a doorway with a thinning broom, chatting with a warty hag. Material clings to their crotches, so there's a hint of genitals. Crisp gusts sigh. Pinocchia's flimsy, floral clothing preserves her privates.

PREPUBESCENT SIBLINGS IN TATTERS and with bosky hair, gimlety eyes and snotty nostrils happen upon an interesting marionette, Pinocchia, sitting canted in tufts of grass in between slabs of stone with sporadic polar pools, on the outskirts of town. Air in its gelidity. Brother and sister watch with a mixture of bewilderment and fright when she lunges to her feet and, a whirling dervish, starts to strut aimlessly, through beeches, her treading erratic. Mutually they decide to tag (quietly) along, mechanically mimicking and even mocking her tipsy stride, the procession commencing negotiating through powdery rocks, the parade navigating those horrible ruins, marching helter-skelter. More mites, nippers numberless, join the wavering line, ebullient, experimental and silly, stomping pell-mell, zig-zagging as if alcohol-impaired. Adults recoil, arrested in alarm. Pets scatter like their lives depend on it. She is as though the Pied Piper of Hamlin, stumbling-bumbling as the Scarecrow character from 'The Wizard of Oz', deliberately taking the serpentine route. Gelatinous rain. Bitter winds come in rasps. Glacial environs. Rot, excrement and piss mephitis. Appalling destruction, a region enwombed in distress. She leads, as per instruction, the pre-teens to an abandoned warehouse where Off and his soldiers are waiting. The tadpoles are taken, kicking and screaming. Pinocchia whinnies unnaturally, throws a temper tantrum, and runs away, experiencing the sensation of being a ship sinking before having left the port. Her clodhopper shoes click like castanets on the slippery cement. Illumination's branching cyan veins in an anatomical megalopolis.

PINOCCHIA AVOIDS A BEDRAGGLED, ETHEREAL tomboy streethawker, plagues of obnoxious protesters, laborers on the jetty, and a gruesome pile of deliquescent, distended cadavers on muddy ground, at these birches, and eventually dashes through a fairytale forest with dripping foliage and sodden soil. Finally, she reaches an argentean lake under a micaceous firmament, ill-omen ominous. Her whole body is numb and tingly, as the sensation you get when your foot falls asleep. She's gnawed by despair. In murky aqua pura she sees her reflection and is shocked, for she looks less wooden and more human. She has aged too, maybe into adolescence. Her "flesh" to the touch has a distinctly hardened, leathern texture to it. She's despondent, beholding herself, because she has no history, family, friends, remembrances ... What is she left with? A life which hasn't lived. If she had a heart it'd sink. Complex cogitations orbit her noggin, collide like asteroids. Thrushes frolicsome. Hearing footfalls, she spins around. A couple of urchins, probably uncontrollable, possibly dangerous, approach sort of stealthily. One, Aurel, is angulose, and with an orange thatch; the other, Bamber, is plump, with chestnutty, strawish hair. They spring in a coordinated attack, most likely in order to rob and rape her. She dodges Bamber only gets punched in the chest by Aurel. Bamber mule-kicks her in the nates. She elbows (more akin to a nudge) Aurel in the ribs, turns as a top, removing herself from his grip, and flees, fast as she can, through saturated vegetation and into a barren field, splashing in icing puddles. Her stamina proves superior to that of her assaulters', who ultimately slow down kind of quickly, and collapse, winded. She weeps, jogging on the quaggy terrain. She reminds one of a person in some berserk rite stepping meticulously on red-hot coals; or, for that matter, someone inexpertly walking with stilts. A gravid gardener with a crimson headscarf gazes at a magnificent eagle swooping, framed against the silvery heavens. Fleet of furious battleships sail, and methodically, on the cinereal waters, steam pluming. Huddles of emaciated men and women tend to graves of loved ones in the cemetery. A rawboned wretch takes corn from a canary's cage, gums and swallows. He crouches to relieve his bowels and bladder. Frisky robins. Gamboling squirrels. Something metalline clamps viciously onto Pinocchia's ankle, vicing it. She is snagged in a weasel-trap. Exhausted, frustrated and agonized, she passes out in sapphire scintillation.

PINOCCHIA NIGHTMARES SHE WAKES in a slipshod shack in the middle of nowhere. An ursine jaeger had caught her in his nasty snare, intent on chopping her into chunks to use her as firewood, when the Blue Man, a crewcut (his barber is a butcher!) skeleton in striped tatters, rescues her, shoving the hunter, after a brief scuffle, off the cliff, a towering temple, and he plummets to his doom. She's in acute anguish, discerns the curious tattoo on the inside of his villous forearm. Luminosity like an optical illusion. Monochromatic overcast vault. Charcoal reservoir. Bevy of partridges. Satiny effulgence. Somber villagers, dedomiciled, toil up an ochreous hill in a straight line carrying precious belongings this frigid evening. Zephyrean melodies. Birds whistle, squabble. These granitoid female statues bent and broken, reminiscent of modest mourning virgins. A bell tolls forlornly. The Blue Man ladles beef stew into soup cups on the stove. He appears as death's corporeal caricature of a living male. Her mind automatically manipulates images through the prism of imagination, the way light through a projector burgeons into a movie on the screen. Her stomach glows, like she gulped a recently-blown glass-bowl. The festering sore of her existence continues to suppurate.

In this life she is a nutter restrained in a straitjacket. Oh, how she wants a mother and father to love her, nurture her, give her fervent hugs and honeyed kisses! The Blue Man snorts and shifts on an unstable stool, interrupting her reverie. These vagaries are, of course, necessary. She tests the floorboard of her brain with thoughts to gauge whether or not it'll hold. He grumbles, tells her the truth, his version of it, about her "Gestapo," precisely who and what he is - a malicious monster. She gazes at him, levelly, essaying to bolster her bearing. An abysm of quietude, for the nonce. Her heart smarts, as a fresh cut squirted with lemon juice. What a disaster. She feels deceived, like by the alchemy produced by a devious djinn to mislead her. She thinks of a mischievous Benedikt demeaning her. She trusted Gestapo, leaned on him for support, literally and figuratively. She felt with him as a minnow in the company of a shark in his oceanic universe. He's now an animal in the wilderness. She is nauseous, pats her diaphragm. It hurts, not unlike terra firma dug up by a merciless spade. Pearls of perspiration on her brow. She's consumed by ruthlessly devouring shame. Tears dampen and burn her chubby cheeks, her facial fibers moist, silken threads of refulgence woven through her lush lashes. Clutching her ligneous thighs. Relinquishing them in a trice. The Blue Man anticipates hissy fit. Lachrymose pour from her pores. Her feminized fingers, masculine mitts. Her physiognomy chirrs, contorted from the caterwauling. She issues animalian keening, rushing out into the dense thicket where the diminutive boys, Aurel and Bamber, arrive to intercept her.

ABUNDANT MOON. WEATHER'S METAMORPHOSES. Surf's soughs. An ordinary lighthouse beckons, beaconing winkingly in swirling fog, the demolished and dangerous megapolis in the background. Humdrum clay residences. A leveled hospital and hotel, the different levels of devastation superimposed on one another, making these overlapping layers of destruction. Farmers in their daily grind. Oleander bushes circumscribe an ossuary, its exterior stony, interior subterranean. A beige owl in a poplar blinks and hoots. Susurrant draughts. Aurel and Bamber lead Pinocchia through the snowy woods. Where is their destination? They gain on this plain, fresh-faced cadet, the rowdy riffraff pummeling him and taking the goodies he'd bought from a patisserie. Bruised clouds in a cerulean welkin. Dumb doves fly in ridiculous, pointless circles. The wide-eyed ruffians eagerly toss sweetmeats down their throats, get into a ludicrous, improvised game of tag, roughhousing on the crustal countryside. Aurel bragging his cousin is in jail reading and writing poetry after he was incarcerated for printing a subversive newspaper. Hiemal conditions. Algoid stars. The adolescents promise her paradise, which is a lot better than the complete chaos of the metropolis! She feels wilted, as a floweret after exhumation. Their voices are crackly, like they swallowed radios. Hers sounds as if her larynx is made of depauperated plant. Innumerous dead. Deplorable surrounds. The thugs thrust more delicacies into their gaping mouths. Hers is a pink slit. Sibilant drafts. She wishes she could get rid of the insomnia. She's fed up with being awake and alert all the time! She remembers knitting socks for

Gestapo, or Off, in the darkness when he was working the late shift, Lothar snoozing on the floor. She listened to Benedikt whimpering gurglingly, fervidly masturbating, the murmurous gargling dismaying. He stroked his cartilaginous cock, in its disgusting erectility. Whereupon he screeched as though a hawk, climaxing, the gross froth, a mythological foam (to give birth to an Aphrodite?) floating to the surface of the formalin. She had the irresistible urge to vomit. His cloven hooves, puckish puss ... The foetal enfant terrible ... She scanned Off's thoroughly weird cabinet of collected curiosities and extremely bizarre bric-a-brac, the knick-knacks accumulated over years of traveling, to best distract herself, alas futilely. He made bubbles, playfully, not unlike a baby in a bath, commented on her pudginess, filling her in on the fact he's her conscience, will tell her what's right and wrong, he's her scruples, to assist her in making decisions, helping her employ common sense. Cobalt vista. She has gotten older, absolutely, perhaps mid-teens. She saw the mirror image in translucent ice: poppy-fuchsia complexion, dirigible-breasts, malleable derma layer, sumptuously smooth, shapely and thickened limbs, fleshly hips, pliable-yet-solid tum and bum ... The transformation is, verily, startling. She has a pulse, a heartbeat, respirations, blood flowing ... Paunchy Pinocchia is glistering with life, and possesses the dignity of humanness. Her appearance frightens her. She is transmogrifying into something real, somebody she doesn't know. The blade hidden in her underwear is quite chilly against her skin. She had stolen the knife from the jaeger when he inadvertently dropped it in the middle of the fracas with the Blue Man. Abruptly, the lads attempt to sexually double-team her, Bamber slapping her prodigious posterior, Aurel trying to smooch her, to no avail. Adamantly she resists their advances, only they still grope her. Heavyset, she has weight and power on her side, fights them off. She is strong and they are weak. Defeated, they hasten away, discouraged, with fuming resignation, until Bamber backtracks, and pulls her ropy ponytail. She shrieks and swings at him. Aurel laughs like a lunatic. Bamber feigns indifference to her lack of enthusiasm. The three trudge, hike for many miles, traversing the icebound terrene. Thinnish spruces. She prays there aren't further overtures. Limp reeds. Venerable aspens. Coagulated cumuli. Sun pounds as blood behind an eye. She entertains hope they'll get bored of her and leave her alone. She is taken to a well-guarded, barbed-wire concentration camp and gets a glimpse of those anklebiters she rounded up. Her escorts've left her. Tremendous vacancy in her core. Her cardiac organ dies. Soldiers clomp, tanks clank.

OFF'S QUIRKY, PERSONALLY-SELECTED furniture is primarily made out of walnut and mahogany. These furnishings are strictly functional, spare and serviceable, devoid of style and substance. He isn't some interior decorator who has designed a tasteful showroom! His gift, genius, reader, is for science, and not hashing out logistics for the disposal of Jews! An anomalous divan in the dank quarters has dingy blankets that are bunched messily. Neglected garlic in an ashtray beside an antique lamp. Trellis climbing with vines. Redundant cherrywood chairs are stacked across the spacious lab. Pinocchia, arrayed in her long john ensemble, and discalced, is checked out by Benedikt, a gnat up her schnoz. She snaps he is vulgar and she hates him. He replies he swears he will violate her, vows to get into her orifices while she rests, announces she has "pomegranate tits," a "brambly bush," and a "colossal keister." It is a strain, maintaining her patience, keeping her restraint. He adopts a mean tone, manducating on figs, garbed in baggy pants and waistcoat, contemplates his wrist prior to kissing it like an icon, swathes himself in a scummy shawl as if shielding himself, pallid from the legacy of his rare, incurable malady, his gummy, grey, unsympathetic oculi set on her. He is corrupt, has a cormous cranium and gluey diaphoresis. He masticates on crackers, dispenses gibberish, diction larded with cliches, jargonised sentences convoluted and nonsensical constructions. He's a noose around her neck. She marks the smallfry, unmistakably, as a disgraceful lecher, a putrid pervert, an embryoid powder-keg of prurience, with an aggravating disposition. He puts on a top hat and frock coat for size. She has heard the rumor the thrill-seeking mini-monstrosity, with a penchant for the artful dodge and the self-assurance of a star athlete, had crept into the wan, tooth-rottingly-sweet-and-sickly, homuncular Hedwig's hyaline container, brimming with amniotic fluid, and strangled her, using his sticky funiculus, years ago. When he was done with her she looked not dissimilar to a plucked chicken with its heart ripped out, left on a sheaf of dog-eared paperbacks. Pinocchia shrugs and shudders. He's a shrimpy, Machiavellian sodomite, a freakish immoralist taken with the taboo. Her mind is distorted. The goblin gleans gratification from torturing her. He has no code of conduct, the hellion's chosen instrument, the needle, not unimportant, recognition of this restarted without any special effort on his part. The fiend is driven, destitute of constraint. Condensation smelling similar to baking apples. Daydreaming, she can dissolve like particles. She's a droplet squirted on a flower. Bile darts up her gullet as a bird taking off from its branch. Vague, fragmented sonnet with metaphors mixed. Creases manifest in an umbrageous pouch, spookily shifty, on the clapboard balcony. Blatantly she disregards Benedikt's belligerent courtroom antics, cross-examining her with fire-and-brimstone, choosing to pursue her meditations to find peace and quiet you'd get in snowfall. Flaxen fuzz on her nape not unlike a cat's fur standing on edge. Her tremors from nervous energy. Her serpentiform insides slide. Pings and pangs of her ivory incisors. Consternation thornyly pricks. Her trap is an effective seal, her stimulation having an amplified, reinforced resonance. Her brain and body fuse together to create a new essence, wiping out the dividing line. She is feeling as a golden retriever waiting for its owner to return; or a Greek slave anticipating her Roman master. Tired, she scrubs herself with soap in the tub and her doubts wash away with the dirt. She trots to reach her bathrobe. Arithmetical formulas in an arachnidan scrawl on the chalkboard.

Chemical symbols on scraps of cardboard. Weary, she is leisuresome, recumbent, the lice lingering on her nether regions bugging her. Her fattening face, vibrissa on upper lip, vibratile heart. Thinking the environment of war tyrannizes civilization. Benedikt commences his epileptic flailing on the olivaceous ottoman, puling like a piglet, very incorrigible and unutterably incomprehensible. The demon is more than adequate at goading, accomplished in using excellent, tried-and-true technique to torment her. He claims to be an "astute aphrodisiac." His customary paroxysms, unprompted, are grating. His horsy hinny. He's a jazz percussionist and aspiring arsonist. She yaps at him to go to Hell. He responds Off was kidnapped by rebels and is being held captive in a Tiger tank. She slips into the shower stall to properly change into clean attire. She's getting a vaginal yeast infection. She despises Benedikt. He gives her a sensation of seasickness, making her rock. She feels as a kitten fitting into a tight space, between a refrigerator and wall, whiskers serving as her senses. Off is someone who fills the vacuum within her. Without him she is a swan shot down into a quagmire and striving to swim out of it. Aromas of ambergris and musk. Fulgurant faltering through these roseate curtains covering latticed panes. Pinocchia observes pileous moths. Benedikt's maniacal whooping and she de-materializes in the luster subdued.

Pinocchia, with diarrhea, in the snowy central square is ambushed at a phantasmal conifer by Aurel and Bamber. A salvo of her flatulency. A glabrescent, wizened oldster. Violaceous pools of gasoline on the corrugated street. An elfin nymph picks at her molluskan nombril. An assemblage of carcasses. Fluctuant temperatures. A short, pasty witch expectorates invectives, laments her situation, and launches herself through this wrought-iron gate. Hail changes into drizzle. Uppity ladies gossip-mongering. Doleful prostitutes move not unlike respectable townsfolk at a funeral, henna'd by the brilliance. Soldiers charge with flamethrowers, helmets bobbling, boots thudding. It's relatively mild out. Military automobiles drive, wade in the shallows of shadows. Pedestrians spectate, warily trickle on muddy, cratered sidewalks. Noises splinter here and there. A pachydermous Pinocchia tells Aurel and Bamber what happened to Off. They confess they're the culprits responsible for the abduction. They will release him if she agrees to be sold to Direktor Ilse Low, proprietress of a done-up dive of a cabaret club. She'll have to work to earn money to pay the ransom. Mantilla of mizzle suspires. A racket subsides, punctuated by silence. Bustling, mucky avenues with a hurly-burly of humanity. A truck barrels, skids to a halt, and troops surge. It is a world gone topsy-turvy, an upside-down place where crimes are permitted, atrocities are rewarded, the profane is condoned, the sacred is tolerated, and the obscene is encouraged. Slight spate. Decaying cadavers. A marred bordello is a sanctuary for the lonely. A gang of juveniles beat a hasty tactical retreat from the police. Ammonial sprinkles. An electric light flickers on emerald grass of a dilapidated park. Anemic herd of hoi polloi mount a sludgy hill. Swirling clouds. Gravid sun.

OFF IGNITES A CIGAR WITH A MATCH at his untidy desk, cerebrating in the cellarly, tall-windowed, high-ceilinged room, that cavernous chamber belonging to an urban, middle-class, manorish structure, its width exceeding its height, with a rococo façade and schizoid decor: an imitation of unpretentiousness. In technology he has adapted to trends with his own innovative daring, with new methods of thought, intricate, flexible and courageous, affiliated more with primordial sorcery than unusual science, the crimps of ideations shown to him in a cerebral cloak. Cognitions in his gray matter - magical roots of a mandrake. Inspiration dawns on him as luminescence breaking through the thumb and finger of a man lounging in the shine and wanting to block the glare. He has lost actuality and found fantasy. He's a slave to the machine of his mind. In his chosen vocation he is like a skillful cyclist, pedaling frenetically, wheels jostling with competitive riders' in an evidently endless race. With an ape's agility he climbs a Jacob's ladder to rise above, get ahead. He will revolutionize, accomplish! He wishes to rule the kingdom of his occupation. No fair play on this field. Failure's a gliding presence, depression and doubt skulking in intervals of incitement. Gulping his brandy. Chark-cloudlets. His colleagues are charlatanic, cowards, posers, schemers and cockroaches, imitations of scientists. Among them he's a taunted bull

in the scientific arena, with them being the toreadors.
His associates are thorns in his side. To him, life is a
stinking cesspool and erudition is the sparkling stream.
He pounces on a solution to a problem as a lion on fresh
meat. Then he would treat it like an MD would a criti-
cally ill patient on his sickbed. He's a frequent visitor of
varietal pubs, stress of his circumstances the prime
mover of a nagging compulsion, the spineless (to him)
means of escaping his situation, which is an affliction
putting him at a disadvantage. A former chum (brusque
and ambitious, who tested the limits of omnipotence in
the laboratory) he attended university with in Stuttgart
once said lust is duty's demise. Off disagreed vehe-
mently. He remembers dear Gerda, his soulmate, a
kindred spirit, on the faculty of a reputable prep school
where she'd staked her claim on the curriculum, believing
the institution to be a training ground for hardships,
preparation for these possibilities, a toughening educa-
tional expedition where extreme exertion is expected to
increase collegial endurance in intellective pursuits. Oh,
yes, she was a beauteous bulldog, distinguished and
overbred, loving the limelight, the nightlife. Politeness
to her was a calcification of circumspection. He was
well-informed and duty-bound in service of the State,
his venerated country in an elevated era. He had a
commanding role, played his part, connected to the
network in a storm of change. Heeding her he was as a
saint hypnotised by a divine vision. Sometimes, however,
her carping, the verbal phrasings, and mannerisms,
could make him irritable. She was prone to jealousy. For
instance: she was for a duration lathered up into a frenzy,

suspicious of her husband's amazonian, Austrian secretary, who was also adorable and strutted like a stork, spreading her wings, systematically flirty with him, during those fractured times. Gerda ... his " Fräulein " ... She called him "Herr Doktor" ... He got resentful when her students came to see her when she was ailing, and he felt as Odysseus withstanding, like tissue paper molten lead, Penelope's courters in his domain, yet he kept his own counsel. The couple were separate, compatible chemical substances that absorbed one another; two coinciding in one. Their affection for each other was unchangingly infinite. His heart is a sensitive spot, thence light kindles. He was riding high. It was, with her, Heaven on Earth. He chews the cud, noodles around, compiles his ruminations in a catalog comprehensive. There they were, Off and Gerda, playing, excuse me, pulverizing, the poor piano, sundering the silence. They sat side-by-side on the bench, having forsaken standing on ground to take to flying in the sky, both bowed at that juncture, embroiled in a harmonious Chopin piece, the notes atonal flaming arrows setting the leaves of passion afire, the duo impelled towards the precipice of unreality, crustaceous hands scuttling crabwise on the b&w keys (reminding you of a shown savage's fangs) in the bangingly melodic tumult, after the cooking and cleaning were completed, naturally. She was a capable page-turner, her bombastic guffaws like they were detonated from a megaphone. She'd just lost her sister, Lore, to typhoid fever. Their excitement was a bubble at its popping point. They flew into a mellow, vital void. The convulsive, modern measure churned into a buttery softness, and into existence, his first foray into making life. There was considerable intellectual and imaginative investment. Clumps of gnarled, gaunt firs in the visculent tillage. He had an anuran aspect, why she aptly nicknamed him 'The Frog King,' written by the Brothers Grimm. It was his favorite bedtime story when he was but a whippersnapper. Their marriage was fantastic. They loved circling the connubial drain. They were comfortable financially, living on their respective salaries and the supplemental allowance she received from her father, a generous and gruff man of invincible integrity, a painter who ran his studio and a conductor of an orchestra and, lest we forget, a literary critic. So they had economical security. She had an awesome aura, maidenly and heroinely. She enjoyed serving on the board. Her personality was narcotizing, a drug he became addicted to, as she becalmed him. She could be frosted as a confection, sewing sarcasm into a sentence with imperceptible stitching. Sure, there were strains, stresses, power shifts, dips into tedium, and motiveless malignity in their relationship, only it was a lasting, outstanding partnership. He has memories of her being submissive, in her corsets and stilettos, fetishistic gear, wanting him to be dominant. And he obliged. She could be irrepressible and irresponsible, determined in her disobedience. Her nerve-shredding snickering sounded like insectean chittering with a hint of echo-haze. They dissected the composition in blinding brilliancy, peeling back the integument of the opus to best evaluate the muscle of the music. She was exhilarating as aged southern wine. She was a salve on the burn of him.

Reflections flicker over his mind akin to flame-shadows on a hearth. Her jade beret and velvet coat hang on the skeletal rack across the shabby room. Spears of light jab slantwise through the blinds. A pardi pawky banker known to him hacks at a gondola with an ax, yelling he is a "latch on society's spittoon." The celestial sphere glints as wet asphalt this pure noon, a creamy coruscation filtering through that shade. To vanish not unlike a mirage ... He sees his goals, achievable on account of his aptitude, abilities and application, in nearness, not farness, his peers as rivalrous prosecutors. Abstract homes. Fussing with a pair of clippers. Rivulets dribble off a torn canvas awning. An aristocratic, bonewhite bigwig Gruppenfuhrer lugs a cardtable down the dawn-blue hall irradiated by austerity, accompanied by an oafish amputee. A massive masseur Off'd pommeled months ago for some infraction or other skims by on a chuffing motorcycle, his lineaments paralyzed, looking as someone conscious and yearning for unconsciousness, who would accept fiction before fact, prefer a lie over the truth, seemingly demoralized. A bald-headed, jaundiced, beagle-faced, angulous Hauptsturmführer with muttonchop whiskers promenades like a royal person, an All-Highest Excellency, at a rate demanded by his rank. Off is familiar with him: the hyper-patriotic originator (known to be adeptly amiable and of ineffable cleverness) of the National Campaign, with its multiple layers of deftly-applied details, the final draft composed in an upholstered armchair in a writing-office next to Off's quarters. Off is not unmindful of its paramount importance. Dockworkers in an allocated area on the pier piping up as an opera chorus. Lothar nuzzles where his nether regions should be. Fucking flies like foreign agitators. He combs his oily bohemian's handlebar mustache and strand-intensive hair parted on the left. A daddy-longlegs crawls by a beaker. Drunkards dance in fulgor fading. A Panzer division marches. Proud Aryans "hurrah!" A middle-aged hunchback, lumpen and squinching, staggers like an orangutan. He has a developmental impairment, wears a bowler and it is askew, says he's a "Hitler acolyte," and disgorges language as loam, quoting from the Bible. Off squints, eyes encounter his. A walrusy guy provokes an effete streetcar-driver, tongue popping out like a stalk, and he thrashes as a fish that has blundered into a net. A columnar policeman, motivated by the quantitative procedures of protocol, spats with a shrimpy wino who is resisting arrest. A salamandrine Schutze at the entrance of a sprawling army barracks is a constellation in a militaristic orbit. Haphazard barrier. Heaps of rock, refuse. In a sequence of carousing, these carnival-esque females, begirding a blazing bonfire, an Adolf anthem record on the gramophone, their merriment superconvincing. A gnomish Oberscharführer with a rashy rictus inspects a trashcan and briefcase. Lothar licking himself. The newly nubile Pinocchia is a means to an end. He in the rambling, creaky manse imagines the curves of those calves, like wind-filled sails, and smooth as jellyfish. Hail door bolt-clicks. His scientific virtuosity has a vacuousness, this vortex of concepts lapping against his skull like waves a seawall, his focus altered by distractions, these occurrences compromising a condition. He feels as a shipwreck survivor on an island thousands of nautical miles from a coherent continent, experiencing a personal communion of the animate and inanimate. His deliberations fork and intertwine, and he is captivated - does order long for disorder? Does love crave hate? Does attraction need repulsion? His oral cavity is dry like a parched plain. Phenomena of an amorphous cumuli. The indescribable horizon in its harmony. He's restless as a gazelle by flickering levin. Moose antlers in the decorous foyer. Never-resolved firefight in phosphorescence waning. His inexhaustible emptiness. Blackbirds vigilant on partial rooftops. The enzymes of conjectures get things going to turn into an entity. Umpteen suppositions! Corridors large and small and with precious little content. Males, rejects from a theater troupe, loot a salon. Officers party in a U-boat stranded in evergreens and redwoods. Dreadful detail of death beyond ... Much damage ... Monstrous callousness ... Beery fumes ...

THE GALOOTRESS PINOCCHIA goes in the goopy rain, apprehension infiltrating her being as an alien organism, lion of her life mauling her, its teeth rending her throat, claws tearing her heart, jaws clamped on her existence, limbs bearing her away to loneliness. She has a baby bird's eyes, physog like a paranoid pumpkin, good-time girl's smirk and turnip shape, watching marvelous swallows adroitly flying, so free, to her perception forces of electricity in feathered form encircling the earth, conspicuous convulsing currents, her mind a map marked by many remembrances, her brain a book that has been closed for a period and is now open and she is flipping through the pages, perusing them, reading sentences of paragraphs, grasping their meanings to make mental pictures and modify them, flooding through sluices of receptivity, replenishing the reservoir, her withdrawal from people predetermined and in conformity with a deliberate militarily strategic retreat instinctively drawn up. She imagines the slugs of her digits writhing, her voice transforming into a mutant millipede and slinking off on an estimated two-hundred notes of legs. She recognises her personality traits as a patron does the food predictively cooked by a certain chef. Introspection is a steep, slippery slope. Ah! Realness indissolubly blends with unrealness. Teachers and students repair to a bomb shelter. She is battered but not unbowed, beaten only unbroken, anchored in choppy emotional waters, the present churned-up and foaming in the past of her vessel's wake. Vapor vouchsafes the definition of a valley. Biting breezes. It is an adjustment for her, not unlike a stroke victim adapting to learning how to speak again, the century of her entirety, inner and outer self, undergoing a rapid evolution. She's a demi-goddess dealing with diverse changes accordingly, the molecules of her musings material, flittering as motes in a lightbeam. Windblown folds of precipitational gossamer-drapery. It dies down and there is a split-second of prismatic gleaming. Limpid morning on the brink of an atrabilious afternoon. A frosted, humpbacked hillock, color of a bluebell, or an insect's wing, and radiant from those rays glistening like daggers. She strolls in layers of flannel, feeling as a lobster boiling alive. Gusts with sepulchral tones. Deliberately she subjects her thoughts to a state of solidification, in an intervention of cerebral independence, self-imposed and not insignificant, the impact immense, an intellective leap on her part, the cogitations as crystallized sifting salt; or they're sources in structures of sequences, connexions with an unaccountable intensity, making intermittent, indelible imprints on her grey matter, intuition imploring her, instinct informing her, synthesized in an unusual mass, and amoebanly flourishing, administering essential elements to the epochs of her essentia, an event that is a web weaving itself. The pendulum inevitably swings, is not null and void, making innumerable impressions. Dusk anesthetized by effulgence. Love, she thinks, amounts to lust. Her cardiac organ encased in hurt, and frozen, like some icy fountain, arteries refracted refulgence. Within the cocoon of Germany she metamorphoses. Off'd put his long legs on the rosewood table, monosyllabic, said he was fond of her, figuring the formula of her, an algebraic adorableness, arithmetized anatomy, she a factor, the sum of his situation, confusion a contribution to his conundrums, a multiplicity of problems, the dilemmas drifting as medusas on a sea's surface, floating like Mozartian leitmotifs. His innerworld stable, outerworld unstable. She was a minor and he admitted he wanted to devour her as a python would a rat. His images and ideas were separate substances mixed and stirred in his cerebellum, in his sombre mood summoning considerations of her. He influenced her interior and exterior universes. Face flushed, he had mentioned the fruit of her bosom, flower of her organ, the reflexion to obey the laws of his nature, and his environment evincing ennui. He perspired blood, language swollen with sorrow, and with more than a grain of truth, in the dead of night. Delicious caramel calm of coruscation pouring. He had joked about her "unalloyed abdomen," and "indestructible derrière," modulation altered, quivery, her torso in a tunic, head turbaned in a towel, so fattened and fair, the perfect model of rudimentary invention, her being exclusively Schumann-ballad-composed, corporeally with multi meanings, her body an allegory of others' anatomies, her compact entirety with its aggregation of analogies, his primate's knuckles brushing on her coarse-grained countenance, by diaphanous drapes of an unhygienic hostel with its aroma of Turkish tobacco, his affection with amplitude, the freezing rain lashing down, a frantic desire aroused in her, a wealth of possibilities in this treasury of a scenario, golden illumination insinuating itself, an illusion caused by an artificial soporific, emerging as flashes of energy and having the impression of an interregnum of an intimate, involved relation with her, approaching at all angles, her changes almost atmospheric, uncertainties fluids dissolving. She blushed, got into a bath-wrap, visage an unsolved puzzle. They were two phenomena, she the force, he the causation. Pinocchia, the ingenue, is cathedral (Byzantine Norman)- oblong, captive in chains of consequences, heart wrung by what she is seeing, sights revealed like linings of a reversed jacket, her reflections snapshots, showing the shrewd, cunning, blithering Benedikt, that pipsqueak deformity, the mechanism of her medulla oblongata geared with vagaries, these reveries a dawn breaking the gloam of her encephalon: the present is an amplifier of the past, death is life's deliverance. Her puberty is sprouting, no, exploding. Thoughts circling her mind - whirlpool round a rock. Nipping her doldrums in the bud. Brume effaces the frigid forest. Believing Off can change, as an atheist could become a Christian. What is change? A mould a particular individual places, or imposes, his personality into to make, passionately, a new, specific shape. The gamine, barrel-chested, leafs through a sheaf of recollections. Her brain is a religion, contemplations its prayers. Retrospections are subdivided by fractions of preference. Her imagined visions indivisible. Lorgnette in filthy slush. Off insisted her anatomic algebra had a plus, not minus, sign, her essence an earthly spectacle. Guns bark. Hail not unlike raining monocles. Pines charge the air with resin. Her menstrual aches. Puddles glow as tins of shoe polish. Nausea grips her stomach. Mausoleum of architectural distinction in artistic design with stucco sphinxes and aluminum harps and lyres. Her core feels radioactive. A polder croaks. Motors rattle. Sirens scream. Bombs thunk. She hurls herself into ruminations philosophical. Buildings departed. Cramps in her solar plexus. She is alone, like Robinson Crusoe. The travel wearying. Sector industrialised. Power station hums. Hers is a rocky road to discover a smooth path to ... A rangy, masculine towhead in a come-hither pose. A stillness, as before a storm. A sanatorium like a silo. Teeming troops. Impersonal, clammy sun. Showers as shattered glass, whereupon the precip spurts like out of a sliced jugular. Miasmal spiderweb. Oxygen breathes as a child. Scissory thunderbolts cut the clouds in a Chagall sky. Single-story hovel splotched with some scintillation. Lightning not unlike necklaces dangling on the feminine cervix of the firmament. Booms of grenades. Imploring bellows. Sharp shots. Reports of roars. A codger with a crowbar, between tombstones of cars, shoulder bandaged badly. Corpses in cruel, awkward postures dumped in gutters. Gypsies strip them clean and make off with their possessions. Pinocchia combats spasms of sickness, holding her Florentine hat, bowing humbly to a squadron of SS soldiers rushing on a spread stainless sheet of snow. This is a race of butchers, not surgeons, she thinks, abominates their "civilized mission." Cirri are skeins of cotton. Varnishing light. Wreckage of a sleigh. Lambency like from a Venetian master's masterpiece. She is sensitive and cynical. Athletically she ambulates. Biting her chapped upper lip she foxtrots to 'The Broken Doll.' Prelude of pistol-pops. Leaves drift akin to fascist and communist leaflets, 'Long Live Germany' written on them in large letters. She garbles to herself in a deathless, low-register vox, distingué as a Minerva shrine. A scimitar moon disappears and reappears as if a recalled construct from a dream of intellection. Levin scars the skin of empyrean. Fish, fruit and flowers on a bronze tray like a Flemish-school still-life. Clergy prostrated at an altar hewn of rime with pickaxes and chisels. Raps of drums, blare of trumpets. Tough rain licks as though a cat's rough tongue. She's hardened like a concrete monolithic statue. These zephyrean razors. Coffins in the dirty water as unmanned canoes. A Herculean fellow with suspicious, slanting oculuses. Brutal beatings. Random shootings. Gaggle of grouses. Mortar shells bursting. Bullets whistling. Burnings, burials, misdeeds and malice. She feels like an object, Off the craftsman who created her. He asserted, tickling the soles of her feet, a service which was, for her, pleasurable, both probing its quintessence, diving into its depths, that when he dies he will survive, for he put himself into her. He poked her armchair-back and elephant's legs, his lubricative dome rocking as a sailboat in the harbor. Geranium-cloudlets. Those convalescent warriors in arm-slings and leg-casts. Papery brine crumpled by combers. Leafage glissading as lizards. Nazis are a conglomeration of creatures at a hydrotherapeutic hut, surrounding a pianola. El Greco-ish carcasses on a Goyan countryside. Vehicular mooing. She has blown up not unlike a balloon, has become a rolling landmass, a mountainous meatball with a reptile's eyes, wiggling and wobbling, a continent without confines on its own eating binges. Ships skriek through the birch-silver aqua pura. Sirup-mire. Chromium-creek. Airplanes bombinate like elevators. This is as a sprint through Hades, the luminosity older than the Iliad. A stream, pine-red, sways like a curtain in gusts irregular. She's fat as silence. Hedges' swishing sonances in winds whip-hissing like bicycle tires on damp cement. Overcast welkin is a misty mirror. A dull pond's a palm with its mesh of wrinkles. Peasants in the daily toil of their drab lives. The sun expands and contracts as a pupil. Moppets go through the arctic thicket like mice through an abandoned abode. Fulgorous flecks. Jewish youngsters swing from drenched boughs. Foliage singed, trees scorched. Gainsborough-gorgeous landscape. Autumnal air. Snails with surrealistic shells deep-sunk in soil look like disembodied eyeballs. With the melting snow grassy knolls are green whitecaps in a littoral vineyard. Stars of David in an earthen space. In a Dali-distorted pasture in its icy splendour there's "Heil Hitler"-ing from a homely hoiden. Cadence of Pinocchia's steps. Her respirings sound as rifles rubbing on leather straps. Her belly seems to be a blimp which strives to soar into the woody heights. She's a massive Modiglianian model, hulkingly heavenly. Her sunflowery irises. She rests, sitting on a rotting log like a Tartar in his saddle. Natural witchcraft of the nocturnality. From her perspective the moon on the vista (with a pigment of a decaying iguana) is a tangerine on a sill. Dusk steals on her. Monk-habit-brown mounts. Her integument as luscious linen. Lice rampant in her marten-fur pubes. Skyline bleached by clouds. Icebound waterway squeaks. An oaken bookshelf. She has swelled like dough when the yeast does its thing. Her blinkers are blank as those of the blind. Blitzkrieg of levin. Defunct agricultural machinery. A blemished Sonderführer banters contentedly with this lean, fridgelight-fleshed Feldwebel, who looks at her not unlike a schoolmaster dissatisfied with a disappointing pupil. Stern warriors dure the wintriness, string up Jewish families. Sun's a widening saffron stain steeped in spotless cirri. Mongrels and their heads drooping as florets bending on neck-stems. Conch-cumulus. Her suspirations have the sonancy of a brushfire. Braille of scabs on her paws. Carrying her coat like a bride. Fans of ferns. She traipses through limpid drifts as fog through a bog. Armored detachments. Soldiers are hounds on the trail of a fox. Their silhouettes are shadows of death. Sleet sounds like glasses tinkling. The steppe with its detail as a Dürer engraving. Caterpillar furrows. The tanks' tracks make these brief fountains of dirt. She adapts to her conversions not unlike a Martian race does altering its nature in an incorporation with mankind. She drags herself as a hermit crab through a quagmire. A lanky laundress, concentrative, with swan-neck curves, crustaceous cast, and lips like a cricket's wings, who, in palpitations of precipitation, caresses of radiance and smacks of a soaker, is a statuette of some aquatic creature, objectivised by Pinocchia, an antidote to her ailments, a flame, hellfire blazing in her groin, stimulation lacerating her vascular organ, staring at the occultism of her shady, fictitious form on the ground smooth as glass, her fabricated figure projected on Pinocchia's optics like a slide from a magic lantern. That smile, shoulder, hip, knee ... The translucent river reflected as a serous, prone aurora borealis. The white stuff softens like sherbet in a cup. In the murkiness a frosty panorama is apparently opaque, as if seen through a waxy, floppy ear. Her jellylike corpus. Yelled orders. Motors grinding. Clanking contraptions. She has a craving for mussels and oysters! The horizon has these Watteau hues. Avian bombardments. She is sleepy like water. She feels as though she has a fever and delirium. Her deadrose bodyodor. She's a wintermoon. A fawn-faced, scurvy-scarred pubescent cloaked in a worm-chewed, wood-grey tablecloth says, "au revoix." Drencher like iron shavings. Grease-black mud. Her plucked eyebrows, unpainted nails. Inscrutable inscriptions on cedars and savins attributable to gunfighting. To her, the Fatherland had cast the first stone, tapped the vein of war. She is skittish as a bewitched kitty. Continuity of her crushing headache. Lunar halflight. Night metalliferously quiet. Milk-blue vault. Companies of quails. She bats her lashes, seared by sobs, considers herself a monstress. Department of sanitation details. She could be painted by Pascin! Her phizz clenched not unlike a fist. A muscular reindeer struts in a silent ritual. Her crease-cut hams. Careening as her shadow would if she were holding an oscillating lamp whilst walking. Breathing like a beast. Rustling verdure sounds as discalceated tootsies on stiff weeds. Sun in clouds is a lemon wrapped in gauze. A Mongolian personage the size and shape of a toenail and resembling a de Chirico character in wolfskin footwear sips punch on a porch with a wrathful glower. Intestinal intersections of channels. Cirrus-celia. Squalid cesspool. Timid touches of effulgence lip-pinkened. A maimed, spare Stabsgefreiter is a well-seasoned wood-carving in a melancholy madness, with a frail nape, bestial pies, and monkish mien snagged in a net of wrinkles, in glycerine refulgence. He has the gamy reek of wet elk ... Decomposing somatic sky bereft of secrecy. Blasts of shrapnel. More explosions. Her rosebud asshole itches, requires scratching. Tissue paper clouds. Resinously smelling mizzle. Shots bang like firecrackers. Mushy, gory grass. Her ironical moue. Chanting beck. Arches of aqueducts. Her limbs as the clubs of Hercules, rosy cheeks and strawberry mouth. She is a whitened and worn Andromeda, albeit an adipose one, held in the hug of a Prussian Perseus, and she acts out her acceptance; a decorative deception. She's goose-footed and pigeon-toed. Nippy oxygen. A brilliantined Off had molested her elbows, fondled her ankles like he would a mistress. Shimmer of radiant splendor, a sobering effect. Sonorous hail was light and hard as pearls. An odd fish, she was wrapped in a twilit curtain, like a perished soldier in the flag, ruminative, heart thumping as a thief's when stealing something, guts a mortal coil uncoiling, or cargo of a foundering ship, submitted to the hierarchy of thought, and taking liberties. This rhinoceros-horn moon. Her teeth chattered. Conoid coruscation played on the jamb of the doorway, made alien patterns on it. Their voices commingled like in a responsory. They paused in their animal romping, sparks flying as from a flaming catherine wheel. Her dammed-up emotions, apple-cheeks, caterpillar mustache. Hostilities were stirred up and all hell broke loose. Mob of resilient menials. Chills plucked her spine like fingers a string instrument. Her emotions wavered. Coffered ceiling, gilt-framed, rectangular mirror, severe chairs, sober table, gleaming linoleum in a classicized setting in harsh light. She is an integumented trellis of veins and nerves. She pictures him putting his sniffer in her fanny as a lion-tamer's head in a leonine maw. A cock crows and it resounds. She disappears and reappears in the hills like a swimmer in waves. For imported Camels and Lucky Strikes! Thunder cracking as drivers on balls on tees distant. Buoys bounce in the jet jetty as if juggled. Fly-dark heavens. Crippled refugees in rags on make-shift crutches leer at her and sputter as though water leaking out of a broken pipe. They are ravaged divinities expelled from a subterraneous grotto gallery. Plaster dust. Carbonized clouds. An uneasy skyline. She muses on an amatory adventure with Off, in a continuing ebb and flow, her bursiform gut, with its oceanic undula-tions, navel a dinghy, contracting not unlike a muscle when pricked by a needle. She's a red-and-purple flower whose petals, pinkish in bloom, are unfolded by his ape-fingers, his dormant desirousness revived, reactions in the recesses of their chemistry, his regret reawakening when restoring contact, he relating "open sesame," their affection blossoming as a cherry tree. He removes a line of his resistance like it is a geometric design, addition by subtraction, changing the points of the figure of his discipline, to suppress the sexuality, a web they'd woven together. He is an electrician. She's a conductor. Apart from him she is a lovelorn sufferer with symptoms of an affliction that's heart-disease. She's an amphibious thing stuck on land. The tenebrose tributaries of her daydreams disrupted by the illumination of realization. Cessation of skirmishing: tide receding from a beach. Crustal terrene. Actions of launched attacks. Time for her to go to work.

Direktor Ilse Low's Kabarett is an exotic, exceptional, pyramidal establishment with an avant-garde, Egyptian ambience called 'Überbretti,' where harsh realities are shoved aside for gallows humour, stylised satiric sketches, torch songs, transvestism, sarcasm, and cynicism, the comedy and theater prevailing, a public place for eclectic genders, social classes and races to meet on the dance floor. There is an intimacy and informal spirit to the performances, the crowds sitting at cozy, candle-lit tables consuming food and drink as the artists do their respective routines right in their midst. Hardships of existences are troubled waters in which these cabaretists fish. Pinocchia, in her late teens, deems it the center of moral degradation and, by the same token, an off-kilter, artificial, enclosed and thronging cosmos that welcomes her. Her first show, with her outfitted in a flamingo flapper and chorus shoes, open-toed and with cushioned suede insoles, and, subsequently, a burlesque sequin costume with flirtatious fringe, and, for the finale, a saloon seductress ensemble, was a smashing success. She was rough around the edges, her sensuous act needing more fine-tuning, only her talent is promising. She is cognizant Aurel and Bamber do not have Off, but she's having a ball here. Ilse can be described as a withered, sultry, cigarette-smoking shrew in a carrot-colored wig, garish makeup, and with a froggy croak to her inflection. She is a stern, sensual, unsettling presence, seated on the lime-green, slumping sofa, misproportioned feet on a lemon-yellow footstool, in the cramped and unkempt dressing-room where these drama-queens in unequal states of divestment shutter to and fro, eyeballing enormous Pinocchia, trying on a naughty cancan shimmyshaker dress, fumbling with the classic ankle-strap on those sandals. It is a full house downstairs, jam-packed, a whirl of activity, the joint a sellout, hopping and rocking to the music thunderous, the big band letting loose. She envisions a hideous Benedikt and cringes. He had said she was a "thickset babe with dimpled, blubbery haunches." Off said his life was a landscape he'd seen and forgotten, she was an underage virgin who is a living artwork, with traits of character, the medium changing, like a watercolor to a woodcut; nature's conjuring trick. His ramrod bearing. She was a stimulant, numbing his surface emotions and leaving the deeper ones alive. She was a wildchild and ladylike. Their bond a burden. He was a hunter and she was the quarry. Did she secretly want to be the prey, stuck by his spear? Would she shake him off as a though a duck shedding water from its back? She was sunshine and rainfall to him. The sleet oozed from the sky as if from the mouth of a drainpipe. He was spindle-shaped, looking like he was chiseled out of the surrounding silence, in Pierrot pajamas, a clown's costume. Sun in the cloud was a flash of recognition in the mind, or a round knee emerging from a pearly skirt. In the demolished burg she had the impression of being a bug, individuality illusory, that'd flown into an unfamiliar field, perception out of proportion. Lightning was strands of nerves, clouds blood vessels. She considered herself human and inhuman, the strata of her essence, with motion and meaning, with a slight split, the seeds of corporeality cultivated by science and nature working in conjunction. Her sensations rose and subsided as a fever. Was there a remedy for this "illness," medicine to prescribe? She felt like a weak woman constructed by a strong man. She leapt as a fish out of a stream, her passion fire in a grate, in the nerve center of a geometric cell. Her world was a rock face. Was she ascending or descending? Mountainous vault with slopes of cumuli. Waves of wind. Boundless energy in her being. Flickering of a lantern burning bright. She was a synapse in his brain, stimulus and response of affection in accord. He was the screw she loosened. Her throbbing heart was grabbed by the forceps of his essence and extracted. Would his penile stick float in her vaginal flood? Their relationship like attempting to drink the contents of a bottle of beer without the bottle. Bomber-planes of allies insectilely buzz overhead. Ilse in a cossie comments she's "cute and curvaceous," a "succulent sausage," gawking at her, and pinches her barn-butt and it pudding-jiggles when she yips and jumps. She's embarrassed, devalued, has the sensation she is sleeping with open eyes when they should be shut, that she is traveling through time as one groping for a door in the dark, blushes, shakes her head like a swimmer to get water out of her ear. Chiaroscuro as the crosses of Golgotha. Her employer's craggy, doughy, queerly cosmeticised frontage and warped-hourglass physique. A disturbed Pinocchia marches out ...

... AND, WANDERING, IN THE SNAPPY OXYGEN, she chances on Off, bumbling out of the Tiger tank and slipping in dingy snow, exasperated, brandishing his Luger from its sleek holster and shooting these shirtless, bound and blindfolded rebels, men and women, lined up and facing a dungy wall, in the skull, executing them, one after the other. He runs out of bullets and reloads, his guards boggled. He curses as a customer in a grocery store who cannot find his coins at the checkout counter. She is heartbroken, dejected, feeling like a cracked pistachio, a nonentity. Carnage and confusion. She strikes a bargain with the gigantean, bearded bartender, Hermann, his britches so tight they might imperil his paterfamilias prospects, she thinks, who has returned from extended military service because of a marginal injury to his pelvis, a Rabelaisian Gargantua who has a crush on her. He has made no bones about it. She makes the deal grudgingly. She must send the message loud and clear to the badboy streetkids, Aurel and Bamber, who've been harassing her since her inception, without cease. She has to take vengeance upon them. They shouldn't bully people! She asks him to name his price and he answers she could suck him off. She agrees to the terms and they shake on it. She insists intercourse (she has engrossed herself in books in her idle time) be ruled out. He nods as if spellbound, scrutinating her. She vagabond-roams. Resistance fighters are rounded up and assassinated in an annihilated library. A depilated, impudent humpback, palpably malnourished, with waxworks features and physical deformities noteworthy, porcupine-totters

on a baize lawn in the slums, in exaltation going over-
board in rambling on a "fund-raising committee in the
council chamber for national preservation," as though
he just left a session, trumpeting not unlike he's in a
regimental band. Climactic carmageddon. Artillery
assault within a twenty-kilometer radius. Pinocchia
feels like she's sugar ground in a mortar; or an item of
laundry, the moistness squeezed out of it. Her stomach
rumbles as an avalanche. Bugle-call of her farts.
Caliginous cloudlets like blackish cloths photographers
use, slinking in an aquamarine sky with streaks of scarlet
the hue of gums. Her (contrived) ambivalence drains as
blood from the head, her will running like a runnel.
Connubial commotion from a shack. She skunk-tod-
dles through the pit-aphotic brake, her lardaceous limbs
sheathed in corduroy. Inklings rise in her cranium as
nebula from Antarctic tundra. For a whisky and soda!
Ha-ha! Lurid light. Firmament flaming with fury. She
jogs and jolts like a cab over a bumpy road, intestines
tossed as a bundle of rags. Her consciousness and
subconsciousness insinuate out of her brain and bestow
on her encompassment undiluted imaginary visions,
impinging on the icy locale with erratic images of Death
in Nazi regalia in a Day of the Dead dance, some
prowling like foxes round a flock of grounded geese,
with reverent tones Hitleresque phraseologies smoldering from abysm-mouths, setting of the scene decked
out in a national colour scheme. Her respirations
sounding as a tapped muffled drum, cardiac organ as if
it's sinking in a deep well and rising to her head, frustrated beyond words, her back changing into aqua

pura. She is jellyfish-opalescent, swept by the current, paddling, astray. Is she a neurotic mired in perturbation? Her willpower as though it is a cat mangled by curs. Snake-smooth trees in a coruscational canopy. Sack-shaped, she follows the path of least resistance, believing herself to be nothing and wishing to be something. Parting puffy clouds uncomplicate the weightless welkin. Her comely character, rufescent cheeks, negroid lips. She has fallen into the rabbit hole. She wants to be an even greater thinker than Plato! Her coconut is chockablock with ideas imaginative, coming from the ends of the earth. One could turn her life story, with its Dostoyevskian drama and oceanic depth, into a fascinating film! She is a figure in a fountain, in the epicenter of a mental picture in a petrifactional state, and she is marinating in it, enveloped by the polar evening, drab garb flapping like a boat's sail. An express train knocks. A lustrous limousine strums. The flight of ideations at her outermost outstretched wingtips, her viscera knots loosening into loops, the cold at its worst. She sprays diarrhea in the shrubs as perfume, lineaments with this logical aspect, choppers pinched, mind moving like hurried breath clouding a pane. Her idealism prevalent, passion prevailing. Garrulous, militant hirelings, cadets bound together in the twilight as timber in a lumberyard. The sun getting closer is a tightening screw. A deadpanned, dumbfounded milquetoast paraplegic with a toothbrush-'stache dressed in a swallowtail jacket rotates in his throwaway wheelchair as a figurine in a cuckoo-clock, a marmoreal tyke keening. Her existence is like it's a chipmunk she's attempting to pierce with a pin. With maximum effort and minimal results, feeling as a subspecies of younglady, her clinical picture bleak, "afflicted" with an undiagnosable syndrome, her "condition" a pendulum swinging, she detours through destruction, an angel unwinged, a poem unwritten, looking different, attributed to the indescribable incandescence. She reduces the scope of her circumstances to a construct of a concept, constituted for her to evaluate, her aesthetic medulla oblongata an atom containing the chemical combinations of cogitations, coalescing into approximations of pathological, piecemeal manifestations with foundations exact and inexact, precise and imprecise, wise and unwise, her ethical energy spent in valuing virtue, devaluing vice, building up frameworks of meaningful systems within her, as a bird creating its nest with various twigs. She gorgeous, firmly fat, and lily-pale, polished like a china dish, fuzzy as a peach, a swimmer natating with the current. She's satiated, like from mother's milk. Musing on reason and unreason. Much cruelty and little compassion here in the Rhineland. Nanduti cirrus. A gale swears oaths of allegiance. Pinocchia ascribes her newfound clearness, credibly, to its influence. She gets stoked, flaring up, with her sexual arousal for Off, a revolutionary man and his superability, a flame consuming her entirety, her heart of stone deliquescing, on the edge of tears, a libidinous grandeur percolating within her, conceiving herself wearing a frilly blouse, unbuttoned, in a stratagem of salaciousness, a sliver of saggy midriff exposed, spread-eagled, in bondage, a lachrymous welling as from onion, powerless in front of the paragon of him: a girl parentally punished for misbehaving. He squishes her, steps on her, and doesn't tread lightly either. She's hog-tied, deep-throated, face-fucked, clutching her stiletto heels. Unendurable excitement. Insuppressible stimulation. She is precip which cannot fall, and overcomes it, the animalistic hysteria, not unlike a frozen lake starting to thaw, and the water begins to overflow, onto the melting ice-patches. Lacy vegetation. Growling in her gut echoes in an acoustic emptiness. Her virginity to her will be a cinder burned away by his fulminating cock. Her bulging body is a chandelier with veinal electrical wiring. A sexy song dispenses from the incredible instrument of her being, her snatch a canister containing a readymade potent potion, her sexuality a streamlet coming from the spring. They fuse, in her fantasy, coupling, evanescing, cooking in a white heat, converting into a dual-headed demi-god, rendered into ecstatic extinction, pies glazed in these lusty escapades, Off trim and virile, Pinocchia, ever-grinning, employing cheap tricks to spur him on, her pleasure, her impurity, disguised by the mask of purity. She's furbished in a Red Cross nurse's uniform, in an unformulated scenario, ample arms akimbo, glances askance at her doppelgänger in the ornate, quadratic mirror, a bonafide hulky, nappy Narcissus, it accentuating her surfaces and depths, her totality's suet somehow detaching itself from her person and attaching itself to his peepers, as a barnacle to a hull; or it is sewn there by an ephemeral seamstress. Chilling plateau. Batch of cracked spectacles and gross dentures.

Crackpotty, cadgy cadettes. Capsized ocean liner. Group of scribblers, an unconventional clique, pedantically prolix, with an emphasis on the sublimities of literature, potential of the panaceas of letters, like a club of mountaineers yammering on reaching the heights of lofty alps, on a sandy shore. In her "castle in the air" she doesn't want Off, her significant other, to extricate his penis from her pudendum. Garter-belt on her cadaveric, flabby flesh. Pondering empirical feeblemindedness, good and bad traits of the citizenry, pros and cons of warfare on a moral and economic scale, in her experimental cerebral station in peacetime, until screwball simpletons old as the hills disrupt her barnstorming. Tugging at the thread of thought and pulling in the fabric of understanding, thinking of his "departure" from his contemporaries; dubious impressions, the spooks, shadowy illusions. She sure can be surefooted and foolhardy! She feels as a drop in a cloud; a sleeper's evaporating dream; or that she is flying, the rubbery button on her broad breadbasket there to soften the landing. Creatural cumulus spraying an inky deluge. Reflections overlap like baggy clothes of lovers parked on a bench. Pit-a-patting precipitation. She limps, because of the boils, a tug-of-war within her between impulse and intuition, her pulse ticking as a metronome. She's an extant effigy. An avoirdupois aristocrat with a candid cast on a palatial bank at a Spanish-style palace exacerbates her uneasiness on the countryside digression. Static racket. Machine-gun rapid-fire. She turns a deaf ear to the din and blind eye to the sights. Troops like hounds of hell, hunterish, with their warlike mania, canine qualities, going two-steps-forward, one-step-back. Buoyancy of her gait. She is an orbiting star, falling fruit, an ample blockhead with convictions, remembering what Off, her praiseworthy creator, with authority and distinction, said to her whilst massaging her becorned "tootsie-wootsies," in the lagerish semilight, how they were one in the same. That's like saying God and the Devil are the same, the anus and the mouth are the same, on account they are holes. Rectal and oral openings ... exits and entrances ... She switches the subject ... Her coccyx smarts.

To get a swig of Bavarian beer! To her, she's regressing, not progressing, and shrinking, maybe, as if seen through a telescope from afar, locks blowing in snowless, wistful winds, tress looking as though a feather-duster. Unreality abolishes reality. The past for her pretends to be the present. She is a basketcase with the lid of life on her. Fern forest. Her whale-weighty presence in a tailored dress. Dreaminess in a rendezvous with wakefulness. Acid in her gullet. She hurdles chickenwire fencing. Rotten rooster and folding easel on a brown royal robe in hoary hedges. Sermonizing mistrals. Favorable temps. She whimpers not unlike an owl. Her existence has left her in the lurch, her life a seed not sprouting, it a pitchblack deepspace, her cranium convulsed with fabrications, such as Off, superimposed on the florid wallpaper in an expansive boudoir, stroking her stout neck, those chubby hips, kissing that sodden twat, her stocky, nude bigbody at his disposal, the rolls on her rear bobbing as bees on a flowerbed, his sandpapery chops seeking hers, blood rushing to her flaccid face. A panoramic view. Army encampment. She is in the mood for liqueur and sandwiches. Slag of bile in her volcanic venter. Her discouragement. Her foots stomping on sticks make this crackling sonancy, like flames under a cauldron. Accelerating her pace, as, perhaps, in a penetrating, preliminary space, revealing itself to be receptive, making an allowance for her anatomy, like in a Galileo Galilei metaphysical example to prove a point. She has the build of a curved vase. Vermian, vermeil lightning in the vasty sky. She's a positivist, not a negativist! Whiff of singed filament. She moves as a glandular secretion, waddles akin to a swan. Her certain automatism. Eminent personages make a to-do, trafficking balderdash, vocal fires burning out, their common ground a high-up aerodrome. The bunkum spreads not unlike an infection, with unanalyzable counterexamples on the cause of culture, philosophical knowledge, movie actors, and European nature, in an orgy of verbalizations. Pinocchia is a singular entity, she determines, useful, she deduces, in different ways, as dirt ... it can be used to grow vegetables or bury the deceased. She experiences these pin-pricking sensations in her kneecaps - a weaver's needles in a carpet - and she plods by a mortal morass of propagandizers, copious queens laying their eggs of agendas for the drones, buckled down, to productively dispense, the submissive specialists strung along, sedated by fundamental sentiment, unable, or unwilling,

to keep it short and simple, in the confines of the
Cause, their offspring playing cops and robbers and
cowboys and Indians, under unregulated conditions.
She tramples and breaks a pair of opera glasses. Her
B.O. stinks of poultry. Her flights of fancy flown at
high altitudes. She is a newborn transplanted to terra
firma. Pedestrians in double-file saunter down the slippery sidewalk in an established course, and deviate, like
billiard balls suddenly struck. She's making her future
up as she goes along, the past and present a foundation.
Her hearing organs hurt from all the noise, and thus
she feels as Ambrose out of Apuleius, ears eaten by
lemurs. Portraits of Goebbels, Goring and Himmler
defaced by excrement on a rimy landing. A gowned
(with a red armlet and swastika), Groszian golliwogg
with an absent-minded air, abbot-aspect, coarse shock,
and spidery facial lines, in a gothic pose, breathing
laborious, in transparent, humid illumination, washes
in a Drittes Reich marble basin, surrounded by au
natural children, skittering and flittering, arachnoid
angels around a piliferous hausfrau, natant like fish in an
aqueous den. To Pinocchia she is a bestial Diana circumscribed by lamb-headed nymphs. A reedy, merry twerp
with tumbleweed tresses. An intensification of deca-
dence, an acceptance of implications. She's at the mercy
of Passivism. Jauntily she curtseys, needing to urinate
and defecate. Briefcases and leatherbags. Personnel in
nonmilitary rollcall; civilian interactions on a parallel
plane, divided by horizontal and vertical lines and into
sections; cogs in the system one supposes; or planets in
orbit. They discuss Nationalism and Internationalism,

which regiments are getting results ... She takes inventory of their palaverous stock. She is overwhelmed, on the downward slide, bottom of the totem pole, keeping a monopoly on the saddened side of life. She's kill in lupine mandibles, can't get any relief from the lice. She is a brightened bulb. Sun's a flashlight. Merger of her soul and spirit in a fusion serene. In the kitchen of nature her adolescence is in the process of being dished up to be served. She's a chunk of peeled pear, a floret cut off at the stem, a day dying, or water, gathering at the lowest level. Is she following the right path in the wrong direction? Her heart is Jesus in the temple of her tubular trunk. She is a nice note hit in white noise, an eidolonic entity, her dreamy essence reproduced beyond an ever-changing vista of the visible. Her blooming bud-mouth. The orchid of her organ blossoming. Aqua pura of inspiration overflowing its banks in an outgushing of eagerness, her co-conscious deepdown, away from the top of her consciousness. Her presence beams like moonlight, mane a conflagration in the nipping gusts, being a plaster statue, cunt a carnation in an anatomical hothouse. Nucleus of meditations on her polyconvictions comprising a harmonious whole. Asshole mincemeat. She puts on a sportsjacket and flannel dress she had taken, gets a fresh breeze in her suety sails, rocks back and forth as a cradle, impervious to the world's boobytrap, camouflaged with branches and plants, her leaden feet creaking on the iced snow, sounding not unlike a rusty pump-handle, resisting the rubber band of a situation, though the elastic of determination is stabilizing her. She has an automated toy's persistence, an acrobat's precision of movement, that can't be reined in, held in check. She harrumphs, shambles, her mullings flitting as butterflies, the gelid, tangled wilderness, with its deathly quiet, the Mother of God Herself couldn't untangle. A residual rainbow. Glaciated terrain. Ammunition spent. Nightingale. Cloudburst. Sunshine. She grunts. Her armor-plate bum-cheeks, tom-tom knockers, and abdominal locomotive-boiler jig. Her bison's brawniness. She huffs and puffs. Her heart plays second fiddle to her head, encased in a formal Garden of Eden; a fly in the ointment. Melting pot of a cult of personality. Pinocchia is a Moreau-person, Michelangelo-sun-roundish, 'neath a cinereal sickle-moon in the periwinkle-and-hydrangea-pigmented skyline. She has reluctance about returning to HQ, with disruptive, depraved Benedikt, his inarguably unscrupulous tendencies, diligent debauchings, carnal crimes, unnumbered animosities, borne aloft on a crest of manipulation and into the millennium. He is frugal, tightfisted really, when it comes to honorable expenditure. She cannot deal with the jeering gremlin, his scrunched simious kisser. The little devil earns his bread and board, lab-lodgings, by dishwashing, with a pro's standard, spending his leftover wages, tidbit tips, on sweets 'n' cigs. He received an elementary education. Off, her idol, is out. Stained-glass bluish yonder. Her genitalial pincushion bristling with pubichair. Her torso has tension (infected with it, as a disease), sways torchlike, goosebumps blanketing her as moss a boulder. Declivitous hill. And she strives to compartmentalise her cravings for comestibles. Her ideatings are like

Christian beliefs. She's taken with diverse concepts, as a pet is with family members of a household, their bodily odors. Her cosmos is a semicircle, and she is the link joining its ends, her circumstances self-contained. She is a walker on a wire with no safety net, a woodworm boring through the plank of time. Her mammoth totality trembles like the earth's crust from a volcano eruptive. A hedgehoggy nun. The sunlit downpour's a vitreous globule veil, in its vastitude in an orange-grove quietened as a catatonics' ward. Her ponytail is a rope-ladder. The bridge of rationality is blown to smithereens by a bomb of irrationality. Her burly-simian silhouette swaggers. Aspic air, searingly cold, imposed on her. Soldiers debouching. Demented environs. She's stock increasing in value in time's (abnormally advanced) passing. She is grass sprouting thoroughly quickly. Her supernatural evolution is revolutionary. Her country is bowed like a broken laborer. Galumphing, she concludes she is a changing element, isolated in her development, in a phenomenal cultural compound, it exerting, with exactitude, an exemplary impact on her in the lost utopia, a collapsing Babel. She's reconciled with her reminiscences. "Love Letters" (Off's words for bullets) whizzing. More hallucinatory shit? Should she be declared sane or insane, locked up in a mental hospital? Her cardiac organ thunderclaps and she applies her observations to her surroundings, her scrumptious, tumid tummy taut as a mother's breast with milk, hypotheses coursing like runlets through a moorland. Afflated, her flatus has the sonancy of fired blanks. A corpulent corporal preps a latrine. She scampers over a ridge after having gotten a fleeting glimpse of him going ... A sere celestial sphere with cumuli could be mistaken for a misty glebe. Her vascular organ pounds. Her rosy, pouty lips are chapped. Her arms feeling as charred wood. A flea-infested paranoiac unfortunate out of some psychiatric institution gloms his rations. A crocodilian sentry castigates a jockey-diminutive weib, whose language has this ventriloquized effect. Trundling, her footsteps on the crusty snow make the sound of a gormandiser's grinding canines. Deliberating on the dummy and human conditions. Cerebral explorations on themes associated with centralism, individualism, collectivism, objectivity and subjectivity. She has an ice cream-type headache. Nietzschean-level theories of hers. She envisages the oil paintings of Gerda, hanging in the maimed antechamber, with its shapely proportions, and her manly, gorgeous, powdered presentation, mutely magnificent. Clusterings of nondescript commoners channeling. It is like, periodically, for her, occurrences "happen" to her, inundating her existence, these episodes setting themselves in motion, taking their own divergent directions, as an automobile skidding in muck one day, and skidding on slush the next! Flurries. She's a strapping, strolling ox, her stomachic summit swelling not unlike the sea in pulsating squalls. Her ears ring as telephones. Her conscience makes excessive demands on her psyche, her principles grasping for satisfaction. Her vortexical aimlessness. Her body culminates in a strangely splendid somatic symbol. She twiddles her thumbs, is inside and outside of herself, driven as if by magnetic pull and weird wanderlust, alert to the prospect she could arrive anywhere, gelatinous peepers glued to her monolithic legs, a freethinker prone to live peripherally in her own life. She was molehill, now she is mountain. Friendly farmhands. Her dueling dimples. Stumping, her entirety's feeling like an infected molar, an abscessed anatomy, and that she was beaten black and blue, only interiorly, not exteriorly, and she envisions a translucid, hyaloid sheet, frost on either side … Her wakeful status is a whisker away from a slumbersome status. Is this a transitional state on a grand scale? She wonders whether she is sleepwalking in a dreamscape. Smog. Does she belong in a madhouse? Her innards as though cement setting. A ragtag tabby pesters her and she shoos it away. It meows, scurries. Lothar gets stuck in a snowbank, repines, makes every effort to get out. She leaves him there. She has migrainoid dilemmas. She did her due diligence in investigating Off: he was a landowner, Bergsonian philosopher, stockbroker, pheasant-shooter, molecular physicist specialist, with a diplomatic background and an interest in Goethe, a rich, highborn businessman who was acceptably aloof and who cut an important figure, a habitué of golf links, houses of pleasure and racetracks who was raised in a Kafkaesque, ramshackle castle with a moat and fount out front. He was as unpredictable like a wild elephant, Gerda his legally-assigned keeper. Pinocchia's consumption of peanuts in liberal quantities. Her appetite is increasing. Is she famished! Oh, for roast pork! Sweat spews off her as sparks spraying from an anvil. Smaze over the florae and faunae. A sallow superintendent in wrist-and-ankle irons screeches his head off. Scintillant splinters in her retinas. Perspiration clings to her flesh as soil to shoes. She takes her existence seriously like a swimmer submerging would her lifejacket. She lumbers, picks out princely pickpockets, mosaics of mischievousness, with the utmost severity bound up in their joint enterprise. She has the sensation she is in fairyland, powerless to snap out of it, with her in a leading role, and she's receptive to the repetitious happenings. Germany has fallen as a house of cards and she is overinvolved in it, her criticisms of it chimerical. Her nation is the victim of an injustice, her country ransacked by the perpetrator of war, devastation the spawn of mankind. Moon's a spangled coin in pooling cloud. A Jewish toothpick and delectable lionet in nubility. Close-by clash. Pinocchia is a walking wound. Piled-up corpses. She lurches, a sizable cell, hardworking in the bodily planet. Here, guilt is synonymous with innocence. Her personal peace dissipates, her purpose embalmed in the amber of purposelessness. She's compelled to doff her duds, denude herself ... People, she thinks, cover themselves with clothing to conceal their nakedness, just as, to Voltaire, they use words to cover their thoughts. To be dishabille ... She slogs through willows. A porcine-pussed stringbean of a priest skitters. Newcomers and their tomfoolery on a makeshift football pitch of a battleground. They whistle and catcall. She is fetching!

TRANSITION OF TIME. Amniotic fluidic drizzle. Pinocchia feels like a slumberer in poorly-staged plays

(in successive superimposition) of a transient nightmare which branches as paths in different directions,
that she is a corroded effigy crumbling, and discon-
nects from sleep and connects to wake. She's a seraphic,
pallid perennial alighting upon turf, a gift wrapped in
rays, brought here from heaven, her exquisite, expectant
eyes a jeweler would strive to work with. Her wayward
excursion. A ripple in the loch circles like a hawk would
its prey. Rubbly ruins in nebula-dust. Fine, clement
weather. Pearlescent snowpack. Sketch of a soaring
steeple drawn by fog. Her cough is a clock striking
the hour. Visiting-cards of leafage with veinous scrawl
written in a charming plebeian style. Sea-bathing, her
armpits, quim and thighs clean-shaven, mustache gone
as well. She magnifies her musings with a mental microscope: the human race should be wiped out because it
is destroying the world! There could be the creation
of animated marionettes, equipped with the unisexual
fertilization capabilities of plants, intermarrying and
superadding to the puppet population, expanding with
extreme rapidity, with exciting chemistry and thrilling
variety, to produce a new and strange species, a potent
force, on this existing earth. She just has to grease the
skids. Inward debating. Swooping starlings. Is Off a
freak? She's Venus, he's Jove. She imagines the two of
them entwined as eyelashes, in a uterine cavern with
penial pillars, brains moving in time, bodies in space,
in their solar system calibrating the degrees of give and
take, the mysterious intimacy hard to identify, these
sensations difficult to describe, for she has never before
experienced them, a kind of concentric concupiscence

circling their scruples somehow, the pair sort of coin-ciding, not unlike a cornflower and buttercup in a vase, her sentiments searching out satisfactory responses, verbally and otherwise, from him. Cunnilinctus. She is ravishingly aflower, with subcutaneous veinal embroi-dery woven higgledy-piggledy through her pasty integument, her hippopotamic proportions having their distinctive characteristics, as an orchestra possesses its individual instruments. Analingus. Their psychological states are contradictions to their physical states, and yet there's a connexion ... to the fervor of infatuation in its initial phase, which is the itinerary of an illusion of ignorance, an oppression of common sense, a suppres-sion of actuality, the lovemaking a repeated trial run, the musical passages of a sweet sonata, melodies in minor and major keys, with elements of emotion. Her eyes are efflorescences, physog reddened as a turkey-cock. He seeks and finds her feet, seizes her hands. Violet-blue vault. Her lesions and sores. In his gloomy lair with its Mexican and Peruvian folk art, he, with his blade-like cheekbones, is tough and tender. Her affection for him, her attraction to him bursting like an impaired artery, her heart, apart from him, experiencing a phantom pain, as an amputee has in her missing appendage. Her ardor is a landmark in her life, fogged over and lost. Feelings renew themselves, as human cells. Parasitic prurience, cutthroat carnality, in the spacious sitting-room. His lurking, leering. Manipulated by him, controlled by him, she responds to his amative advances, obeys his commands, succumbs to his urges, performing oral sex on him (regretting the event afterwards) as he tells her of his origins, being a fisher-boy in a remote village. He wouldn't give up playing games with her and she couldn't say goodbye to him. Soon, she slumbers in his arms like a cherub in a cloudlet - a gentle transition, a contrasting chord plucked. Tenuous light. In an application of absorption her appreciation for him is a fading star. She visualizes their clandestine looks at each other when they got company, a rare affair. For instance, shortly after she was born his superiors (constituting obstacles for her; they were masters, Off their servant), full of subterfuges and surprises, examined her, led by none other than the macabre Mengele, while he explained the process, relating information, in an interval of fired impotence, that his concept of making her personality was comparable to a novelist who borrows from reality to fabricate an irreality, inventing an imaginary character. She was sweaty, boiling as water during an epidemic, her visible and audible universes in disarray, splayed in a johnny on the dinner-table in a drawing-room, treated like a tart taken from poverty and squalor, glabrate cunny and unshorn arsehole stinging, among all the gismos, she, a sensitive soul with proud perseverance, heeding the dead and ignoring the living. Pinocchia, the magnific moose on the loose, pumps the brakes of cerebrating. She feels as an ostrich that had buried its head in the sand for too long; that she's submersed, living in an aqueous kingdom of the Nereids; or she is crushed by a compressor. Erosion of empyrean. Extraordinary environment of the esplanade, mirk an extraneous merit, a vixenish versifier and thickskulled lout out there ringing bells. Suburban structures on streets furrowed. Rural-looking homes. Glazed, cutting gales. Lashing snow-band ceases, as if it snapped. She trots, collects her cogitations as though a hen herding its chicks, has the impression she's in pursuit of imaginary episodes, that she's aiding and abetting Off. Stone cottage. Shepherd's cabin. A monument's disposition has changed into differing versions, its appearance reformed by destruction, Pinocchia judging its decimation by distance, however, she alters this opinion the closer she gets, her vision fomented by viewpoint, evidence corroborated as she approaches. She is feeling like a tigress which will never be tamed. Her transformation into a teenager, her persistent, perpetual, preternatural growth corporealizes her essence, her diaphoresis a poisonous juice, she a venomous flower, a delicacy subsisting in her massiveness. A merciful moon. Her Deutschland is a heart gripped by man and war, and pumps death, dissent, famine, sorrow, sickness, and havoc. To her, caring is an artificial aspect of "action," the trait of contaminated character. Steambelching industrial centipede of a locomotive. Airmen in and out of an aerodrome are wasps coming and going from a hive. The Goliathan barkeep Hermann's hardened rod had fumbled in the depths of her throat as if he were fishing for something and failed to find it. She choked. She was instructed. She knelt on the parquet flooring, reluctantly, addled by anxiety, a beguiling enchantress to him, retched and wept in the uncleanly closet, complying with his orders to finger his feculent rectus as she simultaneously knobbed his unit, her cellulitic buttocks spread apart. Oral and anal antics. Her jumbo backside wagged. She felt like a loathly whore, gagged, chastised him. She puked copiously into the toilet. She pictured Benedikt, the incubus, and winced. Pressure breeds errors. A commotion has the elasticity of muscles. She goes on the gallop, impelled by idiosyncratic thoughts. The condemned suffer with the conditions of circumstances.

PINOCCHIA IS AS THOUGH ADAM without a God, the millennia shining on her, humanity without bondage, her brain having parted company with her body, breath faint, nerves converging like rivers in an atlas, has the blinkers of an edacious minor, and lizard-limbs, infinity simmering, coming to a boil. Iced asphalt. Believing she belongs in a psychiatric clinic, she should be smack-dab in the middle of it. The effulgence twinkles as a steamer signaling. Her idealism's a sigh contacting the possible. Unusual passers-by goggle at her. She is armed to the teeth with potential. Nippers embark on playing skittles and snooker. Her steak-sized shakers and toots. Soaker's like tiles dropping from roofs in a tornado. Fiction is fact. Unreality gets its wings clipped by reality. A fantasist, she aberrates. Fat tissue of cumuli plump up the firmament, graying its blue. Staring at the ruination of the city as if she's looking at it in the fragmented pieces of a splintered mirror. She feels like water overflowing a fountain, she is going in opposite directions at once. Grinning, bobbing cadavers in a ravine dark as evening. Her desire to be with Off smolders under the ashes. The fire in her groin flames up. He held the library ladder in idleness luxuriant, dissecting Rilke's poetry and Van Gogh's painting, and the hermaphroditism of the feminine and masculine soul and spirit, illumination invading a pane like a breach, penetrating as a lover. She wades into the shallows of her nature, confidence in her morality underfoot, only is careful not to drown in the abyss of these conditions. Her eyes glimmer like medals. Sun bedding on cirri. Her stomach murmurs as though a brook. Her oral cavity tastes of burned charcoal. The space she traipses into takes its shape and enters her like she enters it, her arrival a departure. She drifts as a feather floating on a breeze. Light stretches like it's on the rack. A cloud is a coconut with hair on its shell. Her imagination is a vacation from the everyday. Rationality is wine squeezed out of the grape of irrationality. Ideas and images change in her head as breath from inhaling and exhaling marathon runners in marrow-chilling air. Dusk eased by brume with an overlay of rain. Cirri are bacteria splitting the organic substance of the moon, dividing it practically evenly. She has put herself in a box and Germany sits on the lid. Searchbeams like they're sponsored by some sinister sect. Diesel engine of her duff. Her Rhineland is the heartache of Europe, a sheep in wolf's clothing. Her toad's gaze, face a piggybank, yap its slot, jellybeans as coins rattling around, mind marinating in an uncontaminated, concentrated liquid. A racehorse enclosure. Visions multiplied in the hall of mirrors of her "upper story." Thatched houses. She's a pawn on a Germanic chessboard, a marionette whose strings were snipped. Unpaved, rimed roads. She is a tack driven into the cork of her country. Letting one loose. Sky has an opaque sheen, like it's seen through unfocused binoculars. Her encephalon is glass showing her delusions. A rope's round her neck and her nation's pulling it. Germany's ethical fabric is unraveling. Give it an inch and it'll take a mile! She is a bird and her Deutschland's the feline. Her cranium is a coral island in a boundless brine with lambency pouring through verdant brainwork. Reason slips through the mesh of unreason. Tilling the sward of her cerebellum with tools of cerebration. Saliferous snow. Saline showers. Truth has taken refuge at the port of falsity. The tissue of passion, practical and purposeful, tears, the blaze in her belly doused. In a dream state on a pictorial plane without boundaries. Has good flown the coop of evil? Unspeakable distress, fear, turmoil, starvation, shame. Her tendons snap as tautened violin strings. Sun's an oculus rolled up so the white part is displayed. Surface layer of consciousness covers the current of co-consciousness. Her instinct is more physical than psychological, not unlike a geriatric hiker's arthritis predicting a turn in the weather. She passes gas. Her punchball potbelly is a spare tire inflating and deflating itself. Boughs' claws extend. She feels as an infected incisor, pain experienced when pressed. Her newfound freedom has a freshness - a maestra discovering her promise. Here there's crime with no punishment. Apathy is a solid way to soften the blows of what is happening. It's humiliating to be a human being. Gloppy sprinkles move like food in the esophagus. She is lost as a bat in luminosity; or like a domesticated dog out in the wild. Straws of thoughts woven into the nest of her belfry. Germany digests her as a predator its prey. Acidic mizzle. Her grey matter is a lighthouse beacon shedding its luminescent shafts on one notion after another. Vision of vapour: it is like the membrane of a flayed heart; a misrepresentation of a mirage. Kinship of sea and sky. Repellent moldy stink. A put-putting plane as a spiraling injured falcon. Her womb is a wound. Her entrails like tourniquets untied. Synthesized sights, sounds. Stench revolting. Excess of smoke. A Labrador-ish commoner with a trapper's topper avers he's a "mouse in a trap," and that "Hitler is a paradoxical Prometheus," he's been "uprooted from natural soil," nares equine-ish, ague asserting itself, aiming his eyes at her as a jaeger does at game, his admission he yearns to rent her behind's ramparts rather offensive and she closes her ears. He smiles, like he won a hard-earned victory. He's shadowy and sneaky, as though a cat burglar's accomplice about to make a getaway with the loot. Finally he shuts up. Her finely textured, frilly, scanty panties ride experimentally up the encrusted rift of her dense prat like an individual who is intent on committing suicide and is tentatively trying until at last succeeding. Regiment, in serried groupings, reserved mounted police, titubate. Sericate skyline. Spearheads of hail. Scaly trees. Sobs from sufferers. Pinocchia's sluggish bloodstream. Sturm and drang of a deluge. Warfare's a code she cannot crack. Furioso of gusts. The sun goes quite pale in the face. Thunder and lightning signalise a weather system ... foretaste of a storm to rage? Her illusions waft as wraiths, daydream on their own, independent of their maker, wayward like in a fantastical flood. Subhuman-sounding hollering from opposing forces. She's very squeamish in seeing strewn swollen remains. Rationality lays its heart on the street for irrationality to run over. Things are coming to a head. Grabbing her paunch as the scruff of a kitten's neck. She is morphing into a girthy grownup, personally winning the waiting game, but is on the cusp, her nation doing itself in, melting like a candle, a country that is a captive clutched by the captor of itself. She is a star, shining in infinitude. Elms are enormous avians with wings fanned. The Rhineland has made a woman out of her. Reliable reverberating refulgence. Symphonic warmup of winds and strings from a military camp. Adulthood is a sequel to her childhood. Her wardrobe falls as a bunch of annuals loosened. She is nearly in the buff, except for a camisole. She blinks like a fish, has gooseflesh. Wordless language of the irradiation. Death, to her, is a demon hiding behind life. She deliquesces as an icicle on a heater. Snowflakes like soap bubbles. She causes a stir in the wintry oxygen. Those cloudlets are facets of crystal in the amorphous azure. Edifices in enforced unification and with an aura of pomposity. Her realizations are attracted to her mind as moths to a candle-flame. Sun's a blush rising to the cheeks of clouds. Her energy eclipsed by enervation. She's flushed, tiring. The metropolis and the devastation the fighting has bequeathed to it. She is a somatic sundial, an annular segment glistening, blenched in durable glitter which lavishes itself upon a glaucous canal too. Her hadrosaurian heft.

Haft-precip. A silver stream is a startled solvent genie. Downtown inundated by watery light, turning it into Venice. A hale convent-cutey's allegorical anatomy. She utilizes a swing-bridge, systematically surveying it as some analogous object. Tagalongs of trash. Unreason suffocates reason. The masses dash into their burrow-dwellings like rabbits. Avenues are a series of detours, making a maze. Attack met by resistance. Cirri created as if dust raised from ranks of marchers; or it's froth foaming out of the maw of the vault. Her bellrope of ponytail. Doberman in fine fettle laps against her like surf does rock. Failing furies. Bale of fabric turned out of a tavern, with malfunctioning management, changing into this antiquated pattern of Toms, Dicks, and Harrys. Heaven is as though it is a volcanic crater emitting rumbles like a warning for an eruption, and a lava-soaker commences. Her solar plexus feels as a mountain dam. Her entirety tightened. Forestal fecundation, penumbrally sharpened. Flittering burning embers are not unlike shots fired in the dark, in slow-motion. Compact, commonplace homesteads are as silentious announcements. Impending moon in the cover of cumulus. Shadows stumble like phantoms searching for human hosts to inhabit. Her unidimensional cognitions. The seashore foreshortened by vantage-point. Freezing precipitation thrown down as bait to bite. She tugs at her strands like mooring rope; or the locks are pulled as in a theater's loft. Fuzz on her nuque like a plant's petals when touched. The Zephyrs whistle as through teeth. She's got the sensation she's incomplete, like a block of marble anticipating being sculpted into a statue by a virtuosic master. Fissures on her brow as echoes of Cupid's bows. The recurring pour like a refrain. Overstimulated dickens horseplaying. Her footsteps in the whitestuff with the sonance of chompers crunching, fulgurant flecks in her lamps, ensconced in their sockets, as odd, hairy bugs burrowing in these orbit-holes. Eye of the sun with cataract-cloud. Jewish police, Star-of-David stamped, stand like olive trees at Jericho, convivially converse with student gravediggers, in measureless worriment, seraphim of the scriptures. The yellow of her ringlets remindful of the pigment of the stain a corpse leaves on something. Scraggy packs of mutts scour for scraps. She is spontaneous and swift, put in time's hasty passage. Pushing on. Families in apartments, conditions deplorable, as jailbirds in prison cells, waiting for liberation. Burps, moans, sneezes, groans. She is encumbered by an internal struggle - Jacob with the Angel. Her love, divergent from the norm, runs over Off like a river a boulder, her state of being, with an uncommon condition, rising and falling as the tide, impressions of events parts put into a sequence, fantasies melting like Icarus's wings with the altitude. She has taken shelter under his protective roof. Dilution of humanity: draining of the swamp. Cultural chimera. Public - pooches fetching ideals! She feels as a germ in an operation area, Off the surgeon who forgot to wash his hands. Purling feeder. Woodland mutterings. Her mumbling. The spritzer has the sonancy of an alchemist's fire crackling in the precipitation. A buxom dairy maid, with a Juno-esque plaster head, a bull in the herd, voids in the spate, her impulse to vent obscenities ... A puny, schmutzig old fella and lank lady chop a raw potato on a music box. Dingy kinder, in holes, hungered and freezing, barefooted and toothless, hauling a deer spitted on a pole and enfolded in a Nazi flag. Wunderbar horizon, Turkischblut-tinctured. Could she go for venison, slathered in gravy, and champagne! A mungy mademoiselle says "Prosit" on concrete in its gelidness. The Fatherland's the equivalent of a man on a mission. She has an oscillating recognizance of Benedikt's cellophane skin and its shellac of sweat, humping, hornily, Off's Dutch lamp and Saxon china, looking like it was conceived by Dix. An oxidized tractor. Handclaps of thunder and nictitating levin. Rampant barbarism. Jews are killed wholesale, murdered in a slummy suburb, dreary and expressionistic, by SS guards. A Schumann record spins, a penile microphone inserted into the vaginal gramophone. A rouged, perspirant, appearingly perishing-wild-boarish officer's vile guffaw and eloquent glance from the brambles. He has ivory tusks and a pig's bristles. She's far from the madding crowd. Unhappy houses coal dust-blanketed. Her exploration of treacherous territories a jolting junket. An umber umbrella. Bomb-riddled region. Skeletonised historic buildings powdered. Platoon patrols scud in hobnailed boots and carry tommy-guns in stage footlights of moonbeams glistering as steel. She is an imposing Herculean honey, a lass loaded with a tonnage of weight, garbed in a form-fitting suit of Berlin cut, and a shabby fur she had purloined, going in a ghostish grace. Springy serpentine curls. Caftan and cap, formerly fashionable. Her prizefighter's nose. Her mind's eye is dilated.

Recruits in mobilization make these maneuvers around rocks of demolition. Apparently dull boulevard. A babyfaced butterball, blindfolded, shoots at a flying kite, his peers cracking up. Pinocchia stares at it like a hellbent hypnotist, seems about to pass out. She feels as a typhlotic, misdirected girl, silent like a deaf-mute in bravura Bachian arias of breezes. The cellulite on her legs visually comparable to a white wall riddled with bullets from a firing squad. She gets warmed by wine. Sentries watch gates to a morbid ghetto containing its ragged, feverine denizens, as if at Sodom. She's fair, faint, doll-pies clear, and chilled, advancing as though an impassive Angel of Jehovah. Majestic sycamores. The dead lay in carts in sludge, not unlike wooden works, livid and in rigor mortis, rictuses devoured by rats. Sky like soiled paper. An icy inlet's gulls wail as complaining tots. Her plaited mane like a knitted tie. She grazes the faun's beard of her pubic plat with her filed fingernails, is gnawed by gusts. Feather-stuffing pluming out if a torn mattress, ripped down the middle, as water from a whale's spout; or like swimmers after a dive rising to the top from the bottom of a lake. Drawers from a dresser. Crockery on a cot. Tumor of the moon. Range enlivened by brilliance. Dirge of tugs steaming as teakettles. Weather's dictator-volatile. An effeminate florist appareled in overalls, skull shaped like an earthenware pot, reeking of Brie cheese and kerosene, eyelids batting, glimming the bosomy Pinocchia, her whopping hindquarters. Artillery trucks floor it, coasting as shadows of cirri mirrored on a pond. Parasol with a flounce. Soviet bombers bumble, hammer the unrecognizable megapolis. Air tumescent with wind. The incomparable aircraft. Signs of slaughter in limitless farmland. She passes similar to a comet under Jews, young and old, stripped and hanging from snowy branches. Fulgor touches her not dissimilar to an insect's wing. A dachshund and fox terrier hie. Whims of the phosphorescence. Lyrical leaves frisking on Siberian sod. Wilds defiled by war. Screen of bushes. Jeremiads of jays. The sun is a tonsure. She's a Proustian goddess, fulguratingly enflamed, sheering like some marine monster. Her anguine guts. Fuliginous cumuli. She is Manet-august. Her voice hoarse. Elegies of robins. She sings a song in a husky cadence. Illumination ingresses, furtive intellections in formless classicality, waver as the long legs of chorus gals. Ripples in a rill like circles beneath the eyes; or else wrinkles on temples. Pellucid rays, Renoir-esque, on the carrion of a mare, full-hipped, in an orchid, on brochures and vestments, wide-open eyes clotted with blood and mud. Her celia as ochroid lashes of a sunflower oculus. Units march in columns like army ants on an earthen floor. Her gasps have the sonance of bare feet shuffling through wheat, and the sound ... looks at her. One admittedly cannot explain it, but it does. Is it because she is drugged with weariness? Tan, aguilliform glint. Moon's a large lung filled with radiant fluid, expanding and contracting, with a network of bronchial tubes of cloud and veins of levin. Redolence of putrefying matter. Spades, rakes and hoes. In a marshy stretch ducks quack, flap hither and yon. Smell of gasoline, oil, burned flesh, leather and rubber. A disemboweled armoured vehicle.

Her metalloid tootsies pound on the cast-iron plate of terrain. The atmosphere is cool and hardened as the contents sitting in a pot on an unlit stove. Fluting notes of her farts, warm and wistful. Brigade in formation congregated at a munitions manufacturer like for a prayer meeting at a house of worship. In this environment she feels as if she has vertigo, and with Off she is able to get low. With him she is a creature finding a spot to change into a pupa; a garish glove on a noble hand, fitting over his sinewy fingers like eagle's talons. Off with her and Benedikt is a high priest with his (abnormal) acolytes. She's a bride serenaded by Off. Is she made of flesh, bone and blood, or is she an abstraction? Her vivid pigment radiates as though the colours of flowers following rainfall. There's a rip in the veil of order and the void of disorder peers out. Espaliered oaks. Her blowtorch breathing. She is Zarathustra's mountain. The day wanes like the emanation of a gas lamp falls, shadows a surging mass. Clouds drift as laundry coasting on a watercourse, the terra firma having something visually in common with an overcast celestial sphere. Disquiet fills her body, shaped like a sack of gravel (such a superficial transformation; she was wrapped in a cocoon and broke through!) as helium a balloon. Her development cannot be arrested. A gaunt and gouty (he had complained before) wretch with meditative lines in his forehead hangs like a leaf from a tree in a compression of nothingness. Cumuli are monstrous serpents uncurling and rearing their heads in the nest of sky. She feels as a creation of the wild, or that she came from some other planet to this plane. Could she be removed from the universe like a stain from a dress? Shivers trail up her spine as tingles on a musician's vertebrae as she plays with incredible inspiration, her locks vibrating like the strings of a cello stroked by a bow. A filly's cadaver positioned as the German Cross in a sepia snowbank. Torrent has the essence of staples and petrol. Carcasses of machinery. Rapacious crows peck at rancid rodents on the roadside. She's off the beaten track. A cartridge belt and rusty rifle fixed with a triangulose bayonet. Husk of a tank. Drizzle sizzles like a hot iron put in liquid. Plain as porous integument viewed through a microscope. Pulsing arteries of sprinkles. The horizon's a hand coated with cloudlet-calluses. The lamenting night sets in with uncertainty. Rodin-ish adumbration. Icebound bay beginning to thaw. Tang of dampened sawdust. The moon is a blob of paste on the blotting paper of the empyrean. Plantage pointy not unlike Persian slippers. Air sloughs the algor. A hawk, rubified by the twilight, is an angel of doom. A plethora of these paratroopers' heads stick out of the ice (as a hockey rink) looking as if they were beheaded, are lifeless, imprisoned thusly. Her Rubensian figure skates around them. Shrieky birdy entreaties. Is this the end of the road? Is she living on borrowed time?

PINOCCHIA ISN'T A FASHION PLATE, she is more a fashion platter. Her lascivious act on stage is titillating, sexy to all and sundry, although in her opinion it's a most lazy and obscene performance, by her lofty standards. Awestruck audience. The big band's instrumentalized rendition of 'Lil' Marlene' grooving and slamming. A woundup clockwork and overripe, looking as though she's on the verge of her seams splitting, she, gluttonous, preferring pastry and sherbet (tonight stuffed to the gills with the choicest cakes and pies), goes with gusto, her raunchy gyrating electrifying, the hemisphere of her hind bouncing, robustious bust quaking, glorious pot jouncing, mast-limbs balletically expressive. She is an immortal temptress, an eternal entity, the elephantine oafess giving elegant entertainment to the lush louts. And she's aggressively athletic, her sturdy poise impressive, spontaneous 'choreographic' creativity free of inhibition, lashing out for the boorish clientage like lightning and thunder during a storm of improvisation. She's a chanteuse in risqué raiment with accompanying swingin' tunes, surviving on a pittance for pay in the kitschy dump, relying on primitive patrons for tips. She has an apt businesslike approach to her profession, ambition tackled with reckless abandon, a humongous freak of nature who is a driving force in the honky-tonk club. Mainly she relishes being a celebrated cabaret singer/dancer and attracts her fair share of admirers, the majority of them lower primate gallants. She tangos as if she is apoplectic, an unladylike prima donna. Then she dons an indigoid wiglet, a snuff-hued falcon perched on her wrist, clinging to the protective glove, and polka-prances. Ilse incites the crowd. A petite, carroty danseuse/waitress with a trout-mug encourages her. A grizzled gargoyle with black-olive eyes compliments Pinocchia with conviction from the front row, appreciating her griseous gristle-omphalos like a jeweler a priceless gem, craving her, yenning to dispatch her. She's encased in a scandalous getup, arousing his appetence. A mole on his creased cheek as a sooty, unmollescent snowflake. She has the sensation of being a fowlish fatso ogled by a lowly worm. Her nails, finger and toe, are not unlike dragonfly wings, hair wound into a beehive, surplus of jelly-belly waggling, plethoric postern wiggling, petaliferous digits wriggling, molluskan navel exposed in the ardent rhumba. She is virginal, impenetrable, immature, confident, and of curious quality, accustomed to the avaricious attention lately. She sambas, jitters, shimmies. Smoke, cigarette and cigar, in the joint with its libidinous patronage, as though incense in a vestry. Pinocchia is a heretofore unspoiled, unsurmounted, mondo mesa offering the crazy clients a tremendous view. She won't be unobtrusive. Her log-legs bristle with silverfish-feelers. Folding her scrubby arms. Her zillion pores discharge perspiration like her body is a washcloth wringing out water. She's a sexual sponge sopping up covetous stares, bringing the faithful flock into accord with her unassailable anatomy, beautiful and brawny. Grecian knot of her nombril. Guys' gazes like electric contacts flowing in circuitous optics. Gorilline Hermann soughs, fondles her fanny in the deserted hall, says he wants to finger her lubed cunt, crapulent asshole, and she elbows him in the sternum. He chortles. The delinquents Aurel and Bamber can be found in the coppice, he says, gropes her, mentions improper intimacy. She rebuffs him. Rejected, he fesses he's infatuated with her, he's inadequate.

THE RAGAMUFFINS, AUREL AND BAMBER, are hanging by their snapped, bruised necks from boughs in the frosty forest. Pinocchia is horrified, and mouths their names. A terrible scene for her to see. Her heart thumps. Acid burns in her stomach. She's carried in the tide of events and can't reach the banks for safety, resigns herself to hoping she gets to the dam of resolution. Sulfuric odor. Blustery daytime. She is crestfallen. She discovers her arms've turned wooden. Her genitals as well. At her homebase, the laboratory, that gloamy cavern with its superabundance of junk, in a ministry-ish villa, the neurotic Off looks at as intensely as a mountain climber does an Everestic peak, with the essence of an intimate, inspired and indulgent ritual of covert, enigmatic experimentation, especially the concoctions and cocktails of his creation, where no one may venture without relenting, surely succumbing to its characteristic chemic redolence, a moribund, marooned environment which endures nearly magically medieval practices, occasionally, under the pretense of Third Reich productivity, for the purposes of enhancing German nationalism, she snivels, pouring fuel on her torso and limbs, insufferable, infantile Benedikt, kept in a diaper, running riot, playing tennis by himself, wielding the racket like a barbarian his battle-ax, whacking the ball against the paneling, a prototype produced with a tenor of craftsmanship, and, before long, partaking of his stash of hashish on the carmine couch. Divulging he has an "anal authority," he's a "rectal ruler." He entitles himself with the fanfare befitting of a sovereign, as her invaluable personal advisor, and she, taken aback, recoils, won't give a precious inch, nauseated from crown to sole. She needs him like a handless gent requires mittens! His sap-skin. He recovers his naturalness, previously nullified, pressing the advantage, not letting go of his catch, these proceedings only he can influence, engrossed in the intrigue of a potboiler, his machinations miracles. She's feeling as a branch about to break, an alien abroad, and grouses. He cackles, fixing stonily on her, takes a breather from the low-toned conversation, giving the discussion virtually a new dimension. She sniffles, becomes immune to the impression, savors the refreshments of lemonade and cookies. The caddish creep attempts, asininely, to play a kazoo in the formaldehyde after he'd finished filing reports, egging her on, a flea in her ear, and she lights a match. "Torch yourself!" He implores, sniggles, changes into a sorry sari. Ha-haing and ho-hoing. The flame is blown out when the metal door opens with a cheep. It closes with a bang. Off stands stoically. He was out on duty, training a battalion, avid as apostles. He had held her head as Hamlet the skull of Yorick, in an alle by a disabled brücke, she a puppet in PJs. They'd packed up shop on the snowy strasse by a busy platz and S-bahn. He told her he preferred to return to being a civil engineer than leading drills. She had seen him, her "Gestapo," in his immaculately pressed, raven-pitch uniform and impeccably polished, black boots, at a chronicled kirche, in closeness to a humming and popping markt in the mitte, near the damm and willow see, haranguing greenhorns, shuffling them not unlike documents, with the harshest hostility. They were trodden on and torn at ... He pauses, briefly, panting, and unzips his fly. Time courses as waste in a sewer. Leven flashes of her ideations, incandescence of her imaginings, her pallor with tones neutral. She experiences a sensation of living her life sandwiched between identic mirrors. White wigs of clouds. Benedikt, the golem, is giddy in childish expectation, his dermalayer like flypaper. The sticky pellets of his peepers reflect duplicate images of her. Condensation reeks of pencil-chips. Her cardiac organ plunges congruous to a meteorite. Teasingly she strips for Off, straddles the satinwood chair. He salivates, strokes himself, caresses her chin. Her mouth gapes to fellate him, thumb prepares to violate him. He is willing. Her brain and body have separated themselves. Benedikt tee-hees, bunny-hugs a mechanical duck. On the sly she withdraws the hunter's dagger from its shiny sheathe, massages his tautened scrotum, questing prick, using her free ham, and castrates him. She watches him dispassionately as he cants congruent to a schoolgirl essaying to convince the headmistress how much she has to micturate, grabbing his blood-soaked crotch and howling like a hound, sinking to the floor. Benedikt bleats as a lamb. His glee gone. She glares at him, going berserk, attired in his stupid oriental regalia. Off lay there, whining, bleeding to death. "Murderess!" Benedikt cries. "Savagess!" His pill-pies. Her tum clenches akin to a fist, vascular organ beats. She stares blankly at Off's crumpled form in a hematic puddle. A gaseous eructation. She'd sliced off his member with surgical accuracy and authority and thrown it aside like a rotten prawn. She yanks Benedikt, squealing and spitting, out of his jar, spilling a little fluid, and presses him, floundering, into Off's groyne, to drown him in the sanguine. She wheezes. He mewls. She expectorates. His flesh as lacquerwork. It's an over-the-top, real-life Grand Guignol. Unreason is in competition with reason; a lucent, recondite dualism she delves into, the thoughts ultimately diverging from one another. She notices she has pussy-pleats. Her supply of blubber - the rolls of flab droop like pennants in a calm. Off whispered to her, tucking her into bed one jet night, that he refused to sacrifice himself for the Empire, instead he would save himself for it. He didn't keep his nose clean, he kept it snotty, to be on the razor's edge. He declared Hitler would be victorious. He would triumph! He swore his allegiance to the Führer, finger-fucking her. The ramifications of reporting her nonhuman issues to him ... how would he have reacted? She had her reservations. Could she have drawn the admission out of herself, as a witchdoctor using a branchlet to draw the infection out of the inflicted? She's a wilted rose, and egg-fragile. Spirals of birds. Mobility takes control of her and she gallops like a gelding, emancipated from the stable, liberated from harness and saddle, hooves thwacking on the iced lane. Her abdominal apparatus is operating up to par. She is ripe fruit falling, and has, momentarily, regained her composure. Cirri heading towards the sun:

a visionary's conception of visualized stimuli reaching the grey matter of a cosmic body. A totaled city. Hers.

PINOCCHIA IS MADE OF FULL FLESH AND BONE once more, and loves it, until she realizes her trunk, arms and legs are weakening, her features fading. She was transfixed by Off as a cobra by a fakir. Her dazzle's delayed by the strengthening day. Is her condition curable? Is her prognosis dire, like she has leukemia? She's bloated and aged. Her spirit has vanished and her soul is waning. Is she attacked by advanced cancer? Her devotion to the Deutschland cannot be questioned, or answered. The megalopolis mosaic is eerily muted. She contemplates the lambency-gilded, freezing-cold aqua pura, considers it as if Christ himself is bathing in it and she is St. John, her horn encrusted, as though a chimney, bell-clam dry and cracked, tongue a tulip, wearing this toque-robe, a carpaccio cloak, like a dress. Wiping Off's blood from her shaker as a barber shaving-cream from the razor. A fresco-firmament painted with cherubic cumuli, in celestial confraternity, fervid flight, the tiny beings defying the laws of gravity, such a heavenly, winged, morphological species soaring. In a vaporous piazza she feels like a tourist in the 'Arabian Nights.' Her heart is a beaming sun over a stomachic chasm, the machinery of her middle working well. She is at this minute a whale-ish woman, with "extra padding" on her frame, becoming mannish, in spite of her gymnastic routine to maintain fitness, her tuchas terraced with its flight of beefy stairs and with a filigree of cellulite, her bottom a moonscape, its crusty crevice a poacher's trail leading to … The heels of her feet are coarsened with carapaces of calluses. She is as a sponge that has soaked up the spilled liquescent medium of knowledge, and has maturity gained from experience, but is losing her balance, deviating from the direction of orientation. She's no longer the chick right out of the egg. Her emotional inertia pronounced. Her sore bum, scabby umbilicus. Her midriff hums like a hornet's nest with hunger. Her bowels as pilaf with too much pepper. Her mind in febrility. Beryl welkin. Banshee-wailing air-raid siren-warning. Letting out gas like helium from a balloon. Without Off she is a regular room with ordinary acoustics. With him, she is one with extraordinary resonance. She is a sexualist. He was an eroticist. With him she was a force made mysterious, a silence shattered. She wasn't immune from his influence, nor did she want to be. He was the sun shining on her from all sides, and she didn't need to seek relief in the shade. Her consciousness above and subconsciousness below the mill-wheel of her brain, the watery cogitations (on the physiology and psychology of her relationship with him) with a consistent inflow and outflow on both levels. She'd withstood her menstrual cramps, had the token pretense of being covered, lovesome, meaty lump of physique contained in flimsy negligee, language bland as dispensing a weather report, seated on the shoe-bench, enduring the risings and ebbings of stomachaches. He was beguiled by her bewitching beauty, his mind struck dumb by it. The "birthmark" on her bulging tummy like a coffee bean. Barleycorns on her big foots. Pancake powder on her chubby cheeks made them puffs of clouds. Her pulse throbbed. She recalled a shot-putter, he a pole-vaulter. Salmon luminosity. Thinking of the satanic, proud Off, and the thinning strands pasted with pomade on his pallid scalp, seraphic smirk, elongated earlobes. She can hear his strangled modulation. He was dapper, with dignity, and she was a mere marionette, joyous on his knobbly knee, in her undies and brassiere, preening herself, in jubilation, alongside the detritus of a depository, in a dank, dungy sub-basement. She was loyal as a silhouette. He combed his unctuous hair, felt her portly totality, stated his supervisors had disdain for him, deemed him a radical boozer who wasted his potential on pipe dreams, these peers regarding him as a chip off the ole block, an eccentric black sheep punching bag they hit on a regular basis. He swilled grog from a thermos flask. She had suggested an upkeep of his mustache and he, without hesitation, began trimming it. "Son of a bitch!" He'd nicked himself, and with a theatrical flourish. His countenance was scrunched, smoking a corncob pipe. She inhaled and exhaled the fumes dramatically, coughed, lungs burning. She snatched at flies, showing her curlycue belly button. He eyeballed it and the irreproachable glutted sun of her gluteus maximus. She was glad! With the smeared shaving cream he was circus clown-semblanced. They were hydrogen and oxygen. She encountered puberty and chocolate, fungus-pale and chipper, battered mosquitoes, utilizing her hand as a swatter, towel worn like a Muslim's headdress, after a bubbly, lukewarm bath, her Byzantine brainstorms lush. He was giving her a relaxing foot-rub when he had to hurry off to a meeting, the conference he insisted he was obliged to participate in. And she was tempted to dash after him ... alas ... Zooms of enemy airplanes emanate from the contusioned sky. Prayer-beads of rain-drops. Time lumbers as a cavalry camel. Infrastructure's instability. Luminescence inundates a railway tunnel's entrance, exit. A trolley stalls. Vitric millpond. Illusional, immense vista. Ravens' yawps. She espies the Blue Man's lifeless body lying not unlike driftwood on the shore. She promptly digs a grave and properly buries him, feeling shellshocked, gut a gassy chamber, believes herself to be the saddest living doll in history. This cathedran crematory, a "death factory," conflagrant. Ash as confetti. Cirri with a canine fidelity to the navy skyline. Illumination interlacing. These muddied streets converging. The town's mediocre, meditative, in mend-er-mist, out of a tale, like a darkened, dampish dream she is revisiting. She experiences the sensation she's exiled from her own existence, her blood pressure rising as a dirge, in the numbing chill. Ostentation of light. Labored brilliancy of the moon. Dovetailing seagulls. Here is resplendent Germany, where she has pitched her tent. Traffic radiates inward and outward. A dainty, tranquil chateau with a shorn lawn and clipped garden. Idealists' demonstrations: are they a blasphemous, inju-rious insult to the Godly Fatherland? Fog and fulgor make the browned municipality blurry, it resembling a double-exposed photograph. A pixie-ish victim is put on a stretcher and lifted into an ambulance. The

Regime represents the nadir of moral failure, according to Pinocchia. Obstinate pigeonry impale breadcrusts with their beaks. Petrified and primal line at a cistern. Dungheap malodor. Tuneful birdsong. A train loaded with a freight of affrighted families crammed in those cars departs the steamy station. Plodding, she feels as if she is a mule dragging a wagon through a mire. She looks at the sun-showers as though they're poison-darts. She's asphyxiating uselessly in the atmospheric changes in her life. She is a parasite nestled in the decaying flesh of her country when she is trying to get back into the saddle, the eventlets interfering ... Invigorating, rapturous radiance. A young lot on the prowl. Aegean-blue heaven. Picture-book prospect. In an apathetic climate there's a deficit of decency. Rationality shrinks from irrationality. Reality's diminished by unreality. Good is evil reborn. Saneness is the fish snapping at the bait on the line of insaneness. Humanity in her nation is affronted by a lack of it. She settles in her own skin. Cumuli compete for supremacy in the splendent azure. She is frustrated, disheartened, outraged. Her hands are tied. Where does one draw the line? She is Atlas holding up the Globe.

As AT THE start, HER BIRTH, the writing is on the wall. She just has to open her eyes to read it. They are shut. Her psychological and physical lethargy. There's no why here, she concludes, only when. The megapolis is a viper's nest. The window-washer dissipates. Her vermiculate viscera squiggly. In the foundry of mortality her personality is cast and poured into the mould of her identity. Bombing bedlam. She has run the gamut of experience, confronting intimidatory setbacks, the consistent challenges of obstacles surmounted, and she is able to handle the blows. Her geist is mighty. Some dustmotes dance in a lightshaft. Constant sounds of a donnybrook. Urbanites leak out of the flared nostrils of the metro not unlike a nosebleed. Pinocchia is huge. The continual fray has taken its toll. She's in a somnambulistic state. Her acceptance of war is intact and entire. The camps and prisons are all over the hills and far away. Wafts incessant. Many explosions. Gangly, twisted shrubbery as mutated antennae. She is at the mercy of flu symptoms. Her congested respirings have the sonance of cicada chirrups. Schlepping on a gravelly road. Where is her destination? The possibilities are locked in mortal combat in her cranium. Her former isolation is confirmed by her current freedom. Emancipation came at a cost. She knows her fate will be a shock to her system. She is effluvium, shifting shapes, and muses on Germany's greatness, its potential for power. She reckons she's a mutant out of a second-rate science-fiction novel. To be wasp-waisted and statuesque and living in a place of privilege! She can't miss supper! She'd give anything for a dinner of bread, cheese and schnapps. Her lamps are moistened chestnuts this frigid morn. Pinebark claiming a chicory aroma in the murk. How can she be homesick when she is already home? She feels a solicitous sensitivity, riding along, like Europa on the Bull, her blood-vessels teeny-weeny ice-chips melting in a bodily thaw. She's a space hitherto unfilled, basin emptied, toy left by a babe, deliquescing snowflake, mouse batted by the cat of destiny, dishwater going into the sewer ... She remembers Aurel and Bamber ... Decadent Europe, inescapable. Smoke rises from two holes in the green ground where bodies burn as cigsmoke from upturned nares. The rancid fetor is inconceivable. She is a whole morphing into a super-whole. Blasting flatulency. She's on the hamster-wheel through the rubbly remnants of the city - Virgil in a germanic Inferno. Built bricklayers like out of a secret society. Slim sylph with a humble comportment. Pinocchia ties a kerchief on her head, waiting on the platform of a diving-tower, seeing the expanse of a pota-to-field where a boyish gnome carrying a strapped snare-drum and sticks crawls into the skirts of a blocky old granny sitting on a rock (or stool?) by a declining fire. Pinocchia stands as a shadow; or like an actress readied for her cue on the side of a stage. Her will blazes through her being. Nature's brisk breath brushes on her bovinic neck. Her life has been fraught with adventure. Her existence is an egg, and the yolk of her youth will become the bird of her adulthood, and it is ozone-fresh, she inexpressibly embedded in it, the binding of the past ungluing in the present, her mostly-cooled core warming up. Humility's a stimulant. Her ruminations are jumbled in contextual combinations. Nerve-strands of rays from the central nodal point of the sun. In the meat house of slumber she cures the bacon of wake. She renounces her responsibilities, the sword of assurance running her through, her reality an extension of her irreality. Orthogonal asylum situated at a forget-me-not-blue ravine. A spry slattern. A fuddy-duddy in garments garish blusters. The frozen territory rolls beneath her. She has difficulties with her digestive tract. Her breadbasket is heated as a country stove, innards a ball of string undone. Her blond mane's lamb's wool and she fiddles with a stray curl, befogged by indefiniteness. Her petticoats sway on her demilune calves and adipose butt as she sashays, consuming time, recalling Benedikt, in his dirndl, drinking dregs, his absurd tittle-tattling, slanderous shit, sweeping like a hurricane, acting as a proprietor of a place of ill-fame, where she felt compromised in his company, the surrounds, not complicit in cultivating their incompatibility. Stalking onward, opaque blinders misting. Her booming flatus. She's got a splinter in her side. She was lean, is now large. A rainbow revealed in a brackish pool is a peacock's tail unfurling. Hardening coating of snow. She travels like a carpenter's apprentice, ego a squashed grasshopper. She traverses the terrene as an anarchistic angel. An icy knoll relates to a collapsed soufflé prepared by an inept chef. Flatulent detonations. Her sharp edges have been smoothed over. An elk, mid-size, gallivants. Its antlers brush the undergrowth, called to its routine. Her heart is a giddy teen, careening around, unscheduled, in a turret, enjoying her liberty, with explicable exuberance; or it is, in her chest, a torch in a cave. Her fingers are warm, unexplainably, like a barber's curling irons. She is still in a mucky muddle (hot chocolate chilled), as if she's positioned atop a pillar; or posed as though the

Virgin Mary on the Serpent's cardboard-flat head, feeling like she is ripped to shreds and left, as scraps of a document. She's torn apart, spoils for a bowl of bonbons. A slender naiad. A play program, stamp album, varnished riding boots, and pots and pans on a wickerwork chair. Fresh white stuff enriches the environment. Combative conundrum. The struggle like a classical tragedy on the stage. A world deteriorating. She has a sensation she is a substance in a corrupted form, exposed to other elements; or she is a chord plucked from a guitar's strings. Her tendency to tubularity. Store of Viennese architecture. An ally, for her, is necessary. Should she join a counter-organization? The threads of her life don't mesh. She ponders this: put people on their knees and they'll kneel; place them on all-fours and they will crawl. She achieves mental catharsis with these ideas, gives herself a talking-to, language sliding out reptilianly and glistering as objects in coruscation. The womanly/manly curvature of her shape finds refuge in the prolongation of emergent obscuration. She juts like a ledge in a brumal blear. Her ashen lashes. Unexpected outbreak of chiaroscuro unencumbered by foliage. Showers jingle as spurs. Her careworn cast. Winds stinging slap her in the face. Boys and girls, bonded by hardships, toss a handbag, flit more or less like embers in the piercingly arctic air. Their parents, a sect of sorts, descant/dissect socialism, capitalism, and other miscellaneous subjects, the sparks of opinions igniting a firestorm of debate. Scrolling sprinkles. Their sentences disappear as moppets in a tarn. There's a ringing in her ears from the blasting - a castrati choir. Memories surface like boulders when floodwater recedes. The incident where Off and Benedikt died: she let things take their course, the situation developed from its surroundings, as a creature in its natural environment, an individual in his/her native village. It happened in a mode of spontaneous, necessitous action, her conduct, to her, passing muster. She wishes she were far from the event like a distant nebula. Death is life's spectrum. Vice's virtue's counterpart. Evil is good's interruption. By Off dying he let go of her strings. Sorrow is leached from her system. She leaps as a spark. With their not insignificant energies her refracted reflections present a complicated, and incomplete, insight, with incoherent, complex combinations of concepts, plenteous interpretations without conclusions. She's thick-lipped and reddened like the sun setting, eating a plate of produce and prunes, has on her cardigan, peasoup-blurred. Her expressive lineaments appropriate arrogant furrows which line the facial lard. The Rhineland's as a scab that won't heal for it's consistently picked at. Boldly exposed, she feels like a ripe peach rising up from a branch and not falling to the ground; or as a cracked and peeled nut. Trees look not unlike slumberers waving off flies on the winding bicycle path, the snowy shrubs frothing. She sports a ferocious smile, has goose pimples, hits her stride as an overexcited youth, acid jetting in her gullet like juice spurting from a peeled tangerine, pigskin gloves doing the trick, sin drawn out of her as a thorn parentally sucked out of a thumb, the salve of salvation soothing it. Her clothes have the primary colors of a modern painting. The city behind her, in a hermetic vicinity permeated by night, is a concession to commotion. Her entirety's a dowsing rod pointing to a hidden spring of manumission in a moonless gloaming, teeth, bared, white like an institutional uniform, thinking the capital's outer life is ending, culture's inner life is beginning. Off had lavished sensual adoration and admiration on her. He chewed the cud, ornithically pecked, had his hand in the pie. To forget her problems! She endeavors, in vain. Chain of episodes linked by fate. A trio of tanks burning as tremendous candles. Deutschland is a black hole pulling her, the light, in. Horrific screams are this Shostakovich symphony. She's in a state between trance and sleep, in self-imposed banishment from her existence, her morbidly obese, beautiful body in fullest flower, a firestorm of energy freezing her person. Her nation is a heart with a knife through it, swallowing its pride, a kingdom slipping into oblivion, failing to rise to excellence, and plummeting over the proverbial cliff. Arterial ultraviolet lightlances in her somatic spectrum, demands made on her muscles, her anatomy an anaconda with a rodent in its belly, speculations boiling in her brain like a purling beck in a mountain range. There's a sensuous symbolism in the phenomena of her pillowy bosoms, the combustion motor of her tushy. She has the spryness of a mime. A hearse burning. Her life is a long, drawn-out process, her destiny not sure of itself. Her instincts have a compass influence. Putrid stench. Frenetic synaptic thunder and lightning rumbling and crackling in the skull of sky. Leafage rustling as culottes. Cuspate crag. Clear cataract of reminiscences gush into her cranium.

Madness is musical. Denial's unmusical. Fact and fiction are in hand-to-hand combat. Pressing pressure in her bladder. Forward - march! A gulch had filled with rain, velvet-sloe, like a breast with milk. Her groinal pinging, panging. She is pulled toward something, as a bear toward a honey jar, her shadow moving not unlike a murderer, hair a fan opening and closing, nipples shaking as pebbles when a train passes. She shudders. She requires her rear to be booted to continue, swathed in scintillation, purified by it, soul-pokes, spirit-prods, malleable integument luscious as a Turkish carpet, motility meticulous, the tingling in her stomach like a head has after a nosebleed. Perennials flicker as candle-flames. Germany has methodically come to grief. It is a long-lost living thing with no understanding of itself, a critter chasing its own tail, this proving to be prob-lematic, like attempting to hammer a nail into a swimming pollywog! Her barging canter. The sympathy she has for her country ... She perceives breeds of quick-witted modernists and revolutionists across the border, and a frazzled fella with a frizzy horn of hair using pleading sign language to uncomprehending, rugged soldiers.

PINOCCHIA PICTURES OFF: they were a couple of unstable explosive powders, the two juxtaposed on the same plane, cheek-by-jowl, unsophisticated carvings on a chapel's altar. Onto love they grafted lust. They were a Wagner duet; a liaisonal 'Lohengrin.' She was a part of

Gomorrah, he of Sodom. Their carnal pleasures could be divergent, or their desire could be dual. Tramway tickets flutter. She cruises as a yacht. She's the embodiment of an empire, restructuring itself, rebuilding to attain its goals, recreating herself with ability. Oblivion is a custom she adopts. Her solar plexus is volcanically molten. War - a disastrous manmade folly. Abrasioned cloudlets produce condensation. Her emotions not unlike shares and stocks rising and falling, trends depending on the market. A dolled damsel adorns a wide avenue, crepey throat enriched with brilliants, her neck amply supplied with studs, a winsome lift-boy, fair-complected, fine as Dresden china, paying her mind, she profiting from his perversity. Snowy bushes are powdered toupees. Misfits cram tuna like esurient cannibals, expressions as animals sensing danger, spoken sentences exploding similar to shell-bursts, imitating intelligence, striplings glaring bludgeoningly, in an increasing and decreasing system-atic function, a humanly frequency, argot circulating hazily, at random, not dissimilar to gasses. Cock-a-doodle-doing. Woofs of mongrels. Chicken-clucks. She squeezes out visions like feces, flowing as a conflu-ence of currents of an electric therapy machine. She has got a barrelish build, drudges like an automaton, swelling as a channel in a tropical storm. She is a mitten turned inside-out, a slug squirming in sand, knockers' nips redhot tips of fiery arrows, toes cigarette-stubs. Wanting to spike herself on a lightning-rod. She faces her fantasies (Off at her navel like an eavesdropper at a keyhole) like she's in a conflagration with its sincere, paralyzing heat. She's husky, singlehearted, separated from herself, in momentary immotility, in repose, and suddenly propels herself as if she were shot out of a cannon, blood brought to her brain, a supercharged entity, heavenly and hellish, feminine and masculine, a standard-bearer with resolve and conviction, pallor tobacco-tinged, a non-celebrated, automatous semi-civilian, delivered from a hoodoo uterine conjuring in intergalactic space, that is, society. Her suspirations sound like a beaten kettledrum, intestines feeling as though they're slag of smoldering flame. A frilled bib. Bouillon puddles. Water, to her ... you can drink in it to live or drown in it to die ... A creamed casino. Structures insecure as paper-boats put in a pond. She remembers Benedikt, in his horn-rimmed bifocals and wobbly pannier, neat like a maid's bed, a cartoonish tot, an individual affiliated with immortality, shivering as if he had the DTs, and his all-surpassing aptitude for aggravation, the holy terror hooked on quinine, marijuana, morphine and opium, and addicted to alcohol. Fractured flowerpots on flaking windowsills. Grungy panes. Her mane was tousled. She tried to tune him out. No mean feat. An immoralist, impudent, he got into an open-necked nightshirt and loincloth, employing his umbilical cord lasso-like, yee-hawing as though he were a cowboy. She plunked on the settee. He made her skin crawl. In his presence she felt like she was on an ocean voyage, seasick, wave-walloped, her stomach sinking as the sun. A garrison paraded. The moon was a stamp on the dough of the empyrean. Humanitarianismic efforts. His dreary gaze. Steam-bath fog. Warring ferment, ambitious, took the form of accomplishment of power achievement. Patting her mussed mop. Springs of considerations bubble up in her noggin. She is ambulant, a bouncing ball, amoeban mind expanding itself automatically. Brats being scolded by a fleshy, surly SS-Brigadeführer playing with a yo-yo on a promenade - cherubs flying around the Father-God. He announces Hitler wants to recreate the world in His image. Grace notes of rain. Sabers of illumination. Eros-wings of her fat flapping. She is crocus-whitish, flitting as an insect in a fairy-land. She's heavyset and handsome, limbs drawn bows, light-footedly nomadic, exuding resilience and inge-nuity, in wandering. Her ringlets like smoke curling. Her heart pumps as a housebreaker's, or a caged slave's, moral fiber fraying, seductive smile like a model's in Renaissance art, chompers chaste-lily-inside-yellow, catapulting herself on in a universe turning on the axis of transmogrification. She is a solar mass, inner being a concealed jewel, pair of lips parting as lepidopteran wings when it leaves an aromatic annual, dancing to nature's tune, the safety net of contemplations stretched over her encephalon. An eagle soars. Thoughts are wavelets rippling out into ever-widening perimeters. She imbibes the experiences her life has poured for her, ingests the circumstances her existence (with her feeling extraneous, ephemeral in it) has provided for her. Her arms and legs are straight as sunshafts. Grille of leafless boughs. Congregation of loungers. Winter's dusk. She prays the choo choo of lousy occurrences derails and fate lays down tracks in the positive, not the negative, direction, although she's afraid progress will

be a slimy molluscoid trail. Her cardiac organ's drum-
beats. Her passive resistance to revived winds. Her locks
straggle over her eyes. She shambles on, prepared and
provisioned, a welter of her cerebrations elements of
an equation, endeavors to find her purpose; a messi-
anic marionette who redeems mankind, the human
race, restoring it to its proper place, its perspective and
prosperity. Her heft's a handicap; she is a bell-shaped
giantess, a comical sight, causing an earthquake with
every step taken, fixing herself like a bird grooming
its feathers. She's a nova across the countryside trans-
figured. The mayhem circumscribing her becoming
mundane. Gordian knot of cogitations in her noodle. A
sonata from somewhere. She has the sensation she is a
bacterium in a national solution. A tavern transformed
into an ad hoc hospital. Sleet's seeds cast by a farmer
with a Vandyke-cirrus beard in the pasturage of welkin.
Pinocchia is cow-eyed, vellum-toned, potato-formed,
has a speech-impediment and worried forehead, near
albino and adult, aging rapidly, enclosed by her environment with its dynamic forces represented by nature.
She is turned out in a vicar's cassock, prances as a prairie
cock, enunciates (vocal chords like they were dusted
with baking soda) "Viribus unitis," teeth eroded, drags
on a Virginia cigar, and waves nonchalantly (looking
like she is giving a Nazi salute) at an oncoming convoy
of Gestapo in their luxury vehicles. How the mighty
have fallen! They blatantly ignore her. She wishes she'd
taken Lothar apart, to discover what makes him tick.

EMBERS IN ELUSION GLINT AS MINIMAL MIDGES in marigold light. Manifesting meteorology. Breezes flick through pages of leaves inquisitorially on frozen branches. Colonnade crenellated with tire tracks. Pinocchia's bull elephant haunches wiggle not unlike custard. The zaftig sweetling has a splitting headache. Her poppy-bobbies still burgeoning. Off had a corporeal correspondence with Caesar following a fistfight. Her leonine languor. An illustrated magazine. In a chintzily rehabilitated dormitory settlement with its chronic vermin infestation he'd presented her with costly gifts. She received bourbon. Her mouth was tubed. She was assailed by appetite, took off her dress, wore pantyhose and clogs, glossy tresses with high-voltage effervescence. Her full name was given to her: Pinocchia Doll. She was Michelangelanly marvelous, plopped in a rustic birchwood chair, armed with carnal knowledge, bodily scale stupendous, glugging cognac, gorging candies, savoring the panoply of treats in the room apparently countrified. His cock was a springing snake. He stared at her with deliberate appraisal, assimilated everything anatomic, his dick a watchtower. She got up with a pneumatic snicker and put on these chamois gloves. She was ostensibly male and female in the viscid brilliancy. He sat on this quilted couch, penis a flogging-post (unopposed by the unbuttoned pants) while she bent over the chamber pot, a pretty porker scoffing buttered biscuits, and dream-deranged. Swathes of maples. Azure was a cerulean smear. She was wicked, emboldened, that enchanting ensemble applied with energetic enterprise. Her inflection was canorous, bent to blow him. He chugged brandy out of a decanter. Her rhinoceri-rump breasts. Her spluttering farts. Assonant gusts. Motorbike with sidecar parked at a doorless fridge. She was taken down a peg. He thumbed her vagina and derrière, called her his "petkins." She was knocked off her high horse. By-the-book, dyed-in-the-wool Sonders and stewards keep their eagle-eyes on evacuees detraining, engine sounding exhausted. Her didgeridoo-sonanced respirations. To get stringent ale, poached duck, cold cuts, and meat pie! A parous bar-maiden, jugs juddering in bisque arc lights. A fractious Valkyrie with a crewcut smokes cigarillos, built as a bulging rucksack, inundates like liquid. Prostheses, hairbrushes, and handkerchiefs. Gummy spate. A special squad satirically wassails on a crossing lorry and in a disused crematory, swept and hosed. Thuggish thicket in a transitional interlude of zephyrean strains. Cattle-compartments smell of rot. She loomed, was paper-white and docker-proportioned, knickers in a twist, as he, bemedaled, perused five memoranda, ablazed in annoyance, lady's lips pursed, and chaired himself. She was fussy, salami-digits playing air-organ on her taffeta'd lap, fooled with an expensive necklace noosed on her bullfrog's throat. The parlor shook as if there was an earthquake, only it was the repercussive force of the bombing, in its periodicy. Her buttocks were shock-absorbers. She wanted to be a silver lining in the stormy sky of his life. Her palms had tacky perspiration. His lamps toured the topography of her torso, felt the gravitational pull, the purity of its power, and the torpedoes of her calves, wan as angora rabbits, ceased slurping his soup with a sagacious attitude, sweating like his pores were invisible taps leaking, in wriggling coruscation from the quaint candelabra. She, low-slung, over-stuffed, tubbily large, leaned, loyal as a hausfrau, his hands on the tenpins of her legs, concrete feet. A blast and she ducked. He hardly flinched. He spanked her purple. She was a force of nature, not to be reckoned with. Fanny smacked, she told him about her nightmare in which she was in her birthday suit, save for a greatcoat, digging a ditch lit by a lantern when corpses of Jews, hominal scaffolding, rolled like a landslide, and she fell as a scarecrow, aiming to grab her copy of Buddenbrooks, but was crushed. He was a trifle baffled and bemused. Concerning the regime, he claimed the clowns were running the circus. She was the size of a grizzly, munched on a stick of licorice not unlike a tortoise would on a leaf of lettuce. Her tuchis was toneless. Odor of carrion and methanol. In a mephitic meadow, at a flatbed by a picnic table, an epicene, namby-pamby draftee hobnobbed with an anarchical, wandlike lad who'd clipped a clothespin on his bill. Off skewered Pinocchia. The gigantesque Goldilocks seal-barked. After the dirty deed he read memos on a sofa. She waddled, devoured a currant bun, ensilvered by the splendor, back undulating as the tide, arms moving like snipping shears. Stars were fireflies. He had given her swanky earrings and a wristwatch, even a wedding-band. Did the items belong to dead Jews? Was she devaluing herself into moral desti-tution by taking them? What was next, gold molars? He carried a concentrationary stench with him. In a funk she had hemmed and hawed on accepting the (filched?)

presents. At a salvageable, soaked farmstead, icy pellets on atrophied branches were, to her, fillings extracted from oral cavities. Her gaze went ceilingward, withstanding a discomfiting procedure, when she got a few cocktails and several toffees into her, goodies he'd snatched at a party. She was dead-pale, reamed on a desk. She was a willing debauchee in these depravities. She consulted her buck-nude, rotund reflection in the sullied window. Corkscrewing her, his concentration was constrained, as some schoolboy applying himself to doing his home-work; or he was an Egyptian slave, whipped into constructing a pyramid. Squishing, squelching, squirting … He told her of his role in arresting lesbian lovers, Aryan Lilly, "Aimee," and Jewish princess Felice, "Jaguar." There were flames and fumes to contend with. The Gestapo raided the trendy flat where there was a wanton writhing happening on Arabic carpeting. The women were taken into custody, stark-naked, humiliated and hysterical. This information made an impression on her. She was fitting her foots into galoshes. He drove her again, riding her hard in a sodden attic which was like a bunk-room from a guardhouse, over an out-of-business bakery. She slugged vodka right out of the bottle. Perspiry beadlets on her spongy skin. She was as a clay sculpture in a municipal fount. The mamba of his member had slunk into her linty sphincter. He summoned her and she solicited him. A batch of polit-ical criminals were corralled like cattle below. Pinocchia possessed the mass of Jupiter. Off sipped synthetic coffee. Rations were being reduced. They chugged along. He bulldozed her. Their sex looked sped up, as thespians in a silent picture. Brutalized, she bawled. On a duney sandpit a wheelbarrow was upended, a freckly man, shock like sable seaweed, pennanted in the unabated drafts, sat on it, crossed his well-fleshed legs, wearing a mirthless moue, uncovered arms sleeved in tattoos. Punishment-cells with high-tension fencing turned into manifold mortuaries. She sucked down the sanguinary burgundy and seafood appetizers. She, a humanoid combine harvester, freed sweets from a bag. A tennis court was a dumping ground for cadavers. She lighted a cheroot. A uriniferous tang to the oxygen. His oleaginous hairstrands created an ovality of a frame for his dandriffy pate. She ate a Hershey bar. Its wrapper was crinkly. They were having a tete-a-tete in a hedgerowed, recherché chalet near a playground with its sand and scrub and circumambient air. He was changing the dressing, with its drainage, on her infected instep. She had a systematic subsense he was aroused, with the unstockinged nub and its plentiful pus, its stink of putrefaction. His penitentiary pout. A shaggy pony malingered, leapfrogged a ghoulish carcass, jaywalked into the cartage, and wound up in a conservatory, in its sad state. He spoke of the New Order, weaponized poison gas, and all being fair in love and war. She never lost her composure. It was easier being a puppet, made of wood! He tendered relieving words. His fag end was a lighting bug. Rancid waftage. Her loud raspberry lipstick was a smudgy silentious skriek after their coital crusade. Smoke befouled her breath. Corpses, wraithy, of indistinguishable gender were affixed to the asphalt, the thoroughfare implausibly overburdened with them.

She was the spearhead in their bestial joust. For him, she alleviated, partially, the degeneracy. Revenant cain-raisers gallivanted. An 8-cylinder motor coach beeped at them and they hollered "Heil Hitler!" In the piddling bathroom pullulating with warmth, her blood geysered as an oil strike, tarrying before the looking glass. Her inguinal burbling. The environs enveloped in solemnity. A cloudlet is a flower in the buttonhole of moon over a landscape lapsing into quiescence. She gives it a searching look. Civilians in showy habiliments (fezzes and sheepskins) raise a rumpus, intonations quavery, grouse-shooting. She fixes her protuberant peepers on them. Yiddish singsong. Melodious birds restless like bees. Her country has enough rope to hang itself with! There's an unbridgeable gap between reason and unreason. Irrationality is a spur to rationality. Reality's bogged down by unreality. Order is a diver who went deep into disorder and's straining for the surface. Shimmer of skyline with billowing swells of cumuli above a grand, polar region, laurels and lindens committed to it, the day approaching its apex. With her rolls of flab she, wide-nosed, broad-chested, and velvet-haired, bereft of vanity, was an earthward fogbank. Her golden locks glowing as burning candles, flatulency sounding like the drawn-out mating-cry of an ass, her bulk slackening, losing its definition, her shapeliness decomposing. She's vaguely linked to a bungled, obscure existence. She sways as a hammock slung 'tween two trees. The night has brightness, defi-nite, indefinable. A stream not unlike fermenting wine in the shoreless scintillation. She experiences a solar eclipse of the soul. She'd yanked up her pj's top, at the towel-rack, and surveyed herself. She was powerful, glistened, sweaty from fucking. He recleared his throat. She was his pet project, he said, drilling her. She was Sherman-sized. Her rueful grimace. He steamrolled her. Whereupon they swigged armagnac. She humped him in a trice. There was distance, difficulties. The murk as heat coming from a radiator. A Waffen brigade, bearish bruisers, goose-stepped, sang songs of the Deutschland, were fitted to their silhouettes. He had played her like a flute, pulled the wool over her eyes, lied as a rug. His monkeyshines were mesmerizing. An ardent toss and her parts felt like they were left in the crema when she orgasmed. She was supplied with a sedative beforehand. He slapped her and she staggered. He boasted about offing old people and kids, settling on a divan, champing on a green salad doused in Italian dressing and commenced cutting a wedge of muenster. More than just the Jews' rights were stripped. Offering her a pickled beet. She took it, from the davenport. His Luger was unholstered on the hearth in an idyllic hunting lodge an associate lent him, with its sylvan surrounds. She was wearing an embroidered tunic, shorts (always tugging at the cord) and jodhpurs, scampering, had the surety of her "prettifulness," as he playfully chased her, a ponderous, predative pervert. He was a "handsome Hansel" and she was a "gorgeous Gretel." A spindly schnook pitchforked a hayrick. Her keester shivered as shaken creme brûlée, fulgurant flamelets undulated in her irises. Her snout stung where he struck her, numb, like it was shot up with Novocain.

Her posterior was feeling as a prosthetic. Was he a cog in the Nazi machine? A mastermind controlling it? Soldiers stomped, machine-guns strapped over their shoulders, wore gas masks, seemingly insectan. Pinocchia and Off oinked in an ovaline ossuary on the outer perimeter, bones gone, on a pile of discarded drapes, wreathes and banners, in addition to a heap of wank mags, on the mackerel-hued brick, their sexing on the sportive side. She had the sensation of being inorganic, lifeless, manmade. His face crunched up when he came. She didn't climax. He went limp. They shared the quiet. He commented on Rommel, the victories and defeats, Stalingrad, and the singular Kaffeehaus where he met Gerda, a Marxist mademoiselle, activistic tub-thumper, when he was a penpusher at the secret police HQ. Gale-driven, cross-hatched spritzing. It was colder than a witch's tit. Cordite reek. Hail like damn ball bearings. A downed kite was a broken buzzard in snowy hedges. Stipples of rain. She held his cuboid coconut in her forepaws when it yawed. He was a prehistoric carnivore with her. They were in a fragrant flatlet (scented with incense and cigarettes) in a redbrick playhouse, when he bloviated on the Third Reich while she accoutered herself in a kimono, libidinally levitational. He smashed her as France, demolished her like Poland, decimated her as England. She attended to her pewtery muff. He looked on with the voids of his pies, coal-blackish. Whale-firestacks spat spouts of fire, sprouting out of those funnels towering. She roved like a spotlight on stage, and he got a gander at her anal borehole, a fecal plum-pit, when she bowed for the carafe of gin, cloddish cheeks drawn asunder as theatrical curtains. She was flopsy, in a swoon, flatfooted, in a cumbrous clump, admitting she was feeling like a decapitated and dismembered dummy, and that, without him, in his "wizard's workshop," she was becoming less human, more puppety. She was cornflower-fresh, coy, putting on a camisole, with an aroma of armpit, in a semblance of concerted ladylike correctitude. Emanation in its fluidity. A teddy bear, in its minatory inanimation, lingered in the cobwebbed corner with these valuables Off'd lifted. A seedy cellar of a boarding house and Pinocchia, the smocked, mondo maumet, got vertigo of elation. Her mucho midsection was apparently iced in sugar-coating. A megaphone was strangulated by a stethoscope. A round of intercourse. There were coos, trills, ululations, suspirations and warbles in the copulatory engagement. Her hotbreath, babyfat, windbreaking. Cube of provolone. Her tootsies the size of bullhorns. Autobahn to fornication was a cinch. Bookkeeping paperwork. High-spirited, gung-ho slewing in the slush of lovemaking, with whiplashes and bodyblows, snot and saliva. Her garters. His needle in her haystack. With her fabrication, he wasn't intending on reinventing the wheel, mind you, merely revamping the traction. For her, the sodomy, with vim and vigor, was an immolation on the pyre of the profane. In a carnal cataract he choired his pleasure. The pour as projectile vomitus. They swiveled in intimacy, in a resurgence of vivacity, in the swishing sheets. SS, with verve, came and went. The infatuates were pieces of a puzzle fitting into place. Her backside throbbed like the sun pulsing. Sonders, displaying solidarity, skillfully sang the national anthem in a fool's (frigid) paradise. They broke loose in a euphonious storm. She was sprawled, a marionette with her strings snipped, athwart the puffy bedding. His drunken diction deteriorated. Her wurst-wrist, hillock hind. Cadavers of integumented wishbones at gassing vans. She slurped weak vegetable soup, was a white stripe down the middle of a black blanket - a skunky sight he reckoned. For her, being "born" a puppet was not a badge of honor, it was a mark of shame. She sat, nates aching, readied for a quickie. And she gloated over her gifts, punchy, as a preteen over presents at Christmastime. His tried and tested ploys worked well with her. Riverful of phosphorescence. She was a massive minx. Busy pipes. Rivulets of diaphoresis. Laxatives. Yogurt. Lanes and yards. Her stout shoes. Log fire. He was a ship guided by the star of her. Folds of frost. Preludial passion. He was a train in her tunnel. At this mountain retreat there were photographs of a Jewish family, taken with shades of painterly artistry, on the mantelpiece. Her pelvic pain. He'd jabbed lancingly. They were remorselessly soused. She felt sicced-on. His stabbing penis with its potencies was a mobilized weapon. Her rectal cranberry was not spared. It buzzed with stinging discomfort. By the washbasin he blabbed on Speer, good and bad, right and wrong. The lodge was called an "eagle's nest" by him. To her it was a lion's den. She plopped on a footstool. The nippy whisks wha wha wha'd. His blah blah blahs. She was, with each passing day, turning lovely, rumpy, buxomy, comical in cosmetics. She could be deliberately demure, a commendable calculation, giving her, in military terms, a distinct advantage. Fleshly pendulosities of her labial lips. She was tolerably tubulose. Flaps of fleisch established for viewing. She filed her crescentoid fingernails, a downhearted killjoy, remarking on the death-factories. Gunshots. Shouts. Shelling. He gave her an interrogative glower. She was rocky, as something constructed with subpar materials and shoddy workmanship, in her highest heels, busche beauteous, arsche amazing. He was alive and she was dead. Jews were bacteria to him, were meek and not inheriting the earth. Not in his lifetime. Not on his watch. He was an integral part of the master race. Her Brobdingnagian being not unlike a blacksmith's workslab. Their coupling was tearing, slithery and slippery. She was a strafed city when he was done with her. She felt as a Jew assisting the enemy. Torrent was a spray of spittle. She was a prettified Pantagruel. She was the Earth obedient to the laws of physics, turning on her axis, looping around the sun of him. She was a gas chamber, made to appear like a shower room, with a nozzle-nose and vaginal drain. This was a wolf's lair. Nuisance raids tapered as rain. Her dinosauric/thunderclap footsteps. Her rugby ball behind and belly. She had an Aztecean appetite. He was a mamzer, with a mandrill's mien. She was an Aryan tower of power. Her bodily borders were penetrated. Gangrenous mephitis of her cunt. She was euphoric with nationalist hellfire. Dignitary motorcade. She was a report, open-and-shut. Their friendship was pregnant with potential. A quarter-centimeter of crud on glass tinted. He taught her, in a thong and purring, a lesson

on how to casually frisk someone, and she made a song
and dance of it.

OFF HAD ENTERED PINOCCHIA in increasingly popular
underground wrestling/cock-fighting contests, held,
mainly, in a Budapestal edifice. It was hand-to-hand
combat, rock 'em sock 'em conflict in a roped ring with
a referee. She was Anna Konda, exhibited in a snakeskin
leotard and jackboots, going through the competition
like a dozer through a mound of cadavers, a wreck-
ingball through tinfoil, crushing her opponents. Her
strength was tremendous, her cardio terrible, which
meant she had to finish them fast. She was Churchill-
chunky-and-rubicund. Einstein-hair clouds in the sky
the color of watery ink. Her belugan beine with its cafe
blancmange pigment, fatjerking as flames of a bonfire,
taking a poo-poo and pee-pee in a kiddie potty. There
were fraudulent Klees and Kandinskys occupying a
corner, exclusively established in it. She was tanked-vol-
uble, shining not unlike ice, laughably trashed, with her
Lowenbrau. His hand went for her heinie, thumb sent
on a fool's errand, and withdrew it in a fuddlement.
Their coition was pulled from a penny dreadful, or some
sword and sorcery novelette. She baa'd as a sheep headed
for the slaughterhouse. Mellow lilt of winds uttered in
her hearing, at the acme of activity. Bookshop's window
with political posters at a streetcar stop. The grime-gray
heavens took on the stasis of storm. Their twenty-four
hour bender in a space above the florist's. Populous

distance. Clueless holiday crowd. He was replicated in her eyes. Nuts of his teeth. Her derma like tracing paper. Clans of rooks waltzed round a bandstand. Gain of portentous gonging. Her mountaineer's cap and knapsack. His heated hatred cooled off. They did this and that, his way and her way. She was decent. He was denazified. Quiet whoosh of his rocket as she stripped and bathed and re-clothed herself. An electric eureka. They partook of peppermint schnapps. She, a reverse-(gynecoid) Ganesha, with an elephant's body and human head, evaded an argument on Eichmann. She clung to him like an odor to fabric, felt as sinful Saul turning into Paul, a state to which she was subordinate, her anatomy acting in accord with nature. Snowy streets were filled with modern transportation. She was a corpulent carnation nodding on its stem. In her nightshirt she was a big fish flapping under the surface of a stream. Grecian coils of her curls, none-too-wise forehead, derma layer like blotting paper, bronze pubical hair as a lion's beard, body protesting her brain's orders, real life eluding her like it's an eel she's grasping with bare hands, eyes popped as a snail's. For her existence to be an exam and she is the prize pupil! With him she was an executioner with a victim. She was a tigress and he was fresh meat. Her heart was a falling star, sounded like a brass band, her being feeling as a child's that was beaten, every inch battered, stomach a sepulcher of shriveled sorrow, secretions of thoughts cascading. She's a rose pulled from a magician's hat, forsaken decoration, lapdog evicted from its home, plaything neglected by a boy, her essence a circle, a circumference with no center. She passes like a cloud, clears her mind not unlike a hunter disemboweling an animal. Her country is a shady spot and she is sunshine filling it. Caricatures of her cogitations, illustrations of her illuminations. Vendetta of weather. Her nation's a field mowed down to provide fodder for the future of Europe. Plato's myth bought into - God (Off) had halved her into a male and female entity. She's a hale and hearty puppetoid Pygmalion. She is tight as a sailboat's rigging. Germany is bleeding to death, the protective bandages of reason, order and rationality removed by mankind. She'll wash its wounds clean! She feels like day without a night; or a chasm which should be covered up. Her goatish caperings, with manifest overagility, in leaps and bounds, diametrically opposite a rectangular garden in honeyed light, a heroine heading toward her destiny, her locks bouncing as hailstones. Off had crept on her like a many-legged insect mounting a leaf. They were two people in one. She has a round physical mass: a turkey with the substance of stuffing. Curvature of her hips. Her expressions as the play of sea and sky in dawnlight. Innocence, to her, is proof against guilt. A hamlet is an object, and her ruminations come to a stop, not unlike in a blind alley. Horizon vivid as a hallucination. A melting icicle is a substance pouring out of a stalactiferous test tube.

Pinocchia, feeling as an AWOL reservist, teeth stumps, dermis eggshell-white, scratches an itch on her triple-chin, has a Russian-doll look. She has a desert-flower earthiness. The unity of her soul and spirit are observed with clarity, countenance suggesting a tragic mask. Ashen eventide in the alpine mead accepts the nourishing and consuming chiaroscuro. The tide of recollection flows and ebbs, leaving behind the flotsam and jetsam of realization behind. She sticks out like a sore thumb. In a gears-grinding voice she says, "Genocide is a Genesis," and sarcastically wave-salutes the German soldiers slogging through a marsh. Her gesture is wooden.

FINIS OPERIS.

Hair-Raiser

EMBOLIZED EMPYREAN, MADE MÖBIUSOID by the overcast obscurant. In fulgurous intervals buildings are apparently insectile. Propinquous, squished edifices with clotheslines hanging between them, their fenced, drab, litter-and-toy-strewn yards, all mashed together. Sociopathic commuters slalom to avoid the moon-crater potholes. Ozone's grungy. The harbor is cruddy. Indifferent infrastructure. Streets, stark and narrow, are clotted with cars commandeered by primarily crazy folks unkeen on packing patience. Reeky landfill, a barbed-wired, fly-shrouded smirch of territory, day-and-nightingly befogged in a menacing magenta in the old U.S.A.. Coastline is undulating in smog. So but also Raphael, volleyballer-tall, cream-complexioned, a boyishly beautiful gamine with a brown Moe Howardly/lesbianic bowl-cut, sloe Sleestak-eyes, buttony nose, maraschino mouth, and Italianate integument, a serious puppet-film fan, now dressed in a teal hoodie, itsy-bitsy bikini undies, and rubber swampers, in her janitor's closet of a multi-odored bedroom, sprawls on the mattress, her long limbs crisscrossing like searchlights in a vintage b&w prison drama as she stretches, tight from tension, cortex jazzed, system sucrotically wired from binge-snacking (she could never resist the sugary siren's song of baklava; it is real impressive she remains so darn skinny!), tuckered and ticked off from rounds of bouts with her batsoid, blandly pretty mother, Virginie, a sequin-peepered, sunscreen-slathered, pear-shaped stunner with a permanent haunted-hunted-deer expression on her cute visage, skin soft and smooth as a baby's butt, and 1980s-era Aquanet-teased perm, who wore a woven poncho, brief miniskirt and Helenic sandals. She's SlimJim-thin with slightly thicker thighs and bum. They live in an apartment comparable, visually at least, to a shrink's waiting area, only if it were chaotically cluttered, the cleaning crew having given up the ghost dammit because they couldn't keep up, above the hair salon she owns below. The series of arguments were started and not finished and Lord knows when there'll be a rematch. Raphael flexes fluidly and freely and well, needs a sauna-steamy bath. She's hopped to the gills; good indeed for her emotional state. All's currently calm. The hallway is hospital-lobbyish, with plain chairs, plastic plants, framed Ansel Adams-esque pictures, and polished tiling. The epic spat was over a raffle ticket. The fight was verbally balletic and ballsy, the two going head-to-head, toe-to-toe, the combatants compellingly spontaneous, vocally rumbling with strategic cornerings and confrontations, verbally squaring off in the ornate parlor with its varicolored wallpaper out of some commercial studio. Gnats bobbed on the befouled air. Both were tanked on nerve-shattering amounts of coffee that eventually impelled them to the john which ultimately proved to be the end of the skirmish. Toser, Virginie's occasional live-in lover, cutting a weird, bouffant-toupee'd, Mephisophelean figure, an asthmatic, angulose, LipoVac'd, suave (charm murderously fatal that could sell you property in exotic locales), silk-suited, spray-tanned, lousy lounge-lizardly singer and part-time dietician and workout guru who looks not unlike a Botoxed Fire Marshall Bill from 'In Living Color' if he got plastic surgery to resemble an iguanid Andy Warhol, and with a breech that appears as though it's a football punctured by a sharp object. Checking her out on a fairly regular basis he was like something simious taking a gadget apart and putting it back together again ... Ocularly. Raphael actually saw his act one evening and he was swinging the micro- phone cord and marching in place as Roger Daltrey at Woodstock, possessing Motown moves with Vegas vigor, doo-wopping and crooning Tony Bennettoidally, during a ballad making a pistol out of his hand while belting, spinning it as a Western-gunslinger by flicking his Popsicle-stick wrist, the other, free hand spidering a non-hip, tonnage of jewelry gladiatorial, cracking wise and waxing lyrical in-between lame tunes, mono- logue getting mushier and vapider by the minute, the sparse, besotted audience either nodding in approval or nodding off altogether, one unsteady, dwarven, glossy and glabrous elderly man in a special lifeguardish chair amongst the "crowd" sneezing and wiping his bulbiform, varicose schnoz with a white hankie, waving it as a sort of surrender flag. Virginie was screeching and clapping as a typical teenybopper and Raphael was extremely embarrassed, like she ripped a raspberry at a formal function. Anyway, Toser, with a creepy Lincoln-statue smile, watched daughter and mom tussle, spectating dumbly, pies going back and forth like he was courtside at Wimbledon. He's quite a maroon with raisinesque blinkers and the cajones to believe he can competently perform for people. He'd floated as a reptilian radon into Virginie's plateau'd life. He butters his bread on both sides. The quarrels had different scenaria. Sprinkles' spatters on the mag-shiny panes with velvet stage-curtains. Full-facial sight of herself in them. She sighs. Soul-sapping humidity. Post-storm thunder mutters. Lightning gouges the flesh of firmament. Mosquitos' whines. Strange chemical (combinations and compounds unknown) horizon oranger than it ought properly to be. Thoughts run through her mental projector. Her head's gonna roll if she doesn't do her math homework, due tomorrow. It's her senior year at school and it sucks for she is failing badly. She is up shit's creek w/o paddle. Her spirit sags. She requires a Higher-Powerish intervention. Her B.O. has a yeasty stink. Avian adipose on the bony welkin. Hissy fart out of her V'd fanny toot sweet this very. City's a mess. Heaven drools. Winds are mean. Soaker sways. Birches groan. Risen moon is a curvy horn. Claws of planes scratch for a duration. Her dull-gray custodial quarters. She feels as if her coconut is a kind of drum-receptacle leaking poisonous fumes, these industrial solvents in a waste dump. Several Winnebaga parked out front at the metered curb as though by student drivers. A range of runners attired in neon spandex tops and shorts stampede down the breakdown lane not unlike Texas cattle out of control. Elmer's-sticky oxygen. Toxicly-affected atmosphere. She ingests a chocolate cannoli and imbibes kiwi juice, popping oculi making her look throttled, lost in a funk. Her mom's shop's sign puts a spin, literally, on the trusty traditional barber-pole thingie, having this insane tornado, twisty as heck, her name coupled with clippers-and-comb ensemble slithering serpentoid out of its vortex, designed like a radically cool orientoid dragon-and-sword-type deal you'd customarily see on a neat banner of an MMA gym. Gusts squall at the tops of their lungs. Miserable mugginess. Church's steeple is a brick-and-glass witch's hat.

Rush hour rash on the bum-crack of highway, a four-laner. Cars fluorescent-lit and unstriking career and kerwham as in 'Speed Racer,' engines sounding tinny, headlights staring steadily, almost studious, tires ministering the cement with pressurized hisses. Sun yo-yos in slo-mo. Jackable rides on the median strip. Billboard unfestooned. Zephyrean purring. Amberous, domic sky with encroaching sailor-hat whitish clouds slumps, seems stunned somehow. Satin cataract of coruscation. Tangled ossified trees. When Raphael, in a melancholic torpor, with cellular lassitude, mentally numb, given a shot of psychological novocaine, her core system disquieted, voices she thinks Virginie must suffer from perpetual PMS, a Lilliputian lad, Hud, countenance suggesting a can that was crumpled and straightened out again, clad in this skateboarding gear, along with Spielbergian chums Feamster, a chubby, whiffled kid, and twins Kite, jockish, male, and Korona, female, nerdy with honker and hornrims, appealing and not, each wearing similar stuff, manifest on the windowsill. WTF?! She has a reversal-of-misfortune vibe. Raphael, slack-jawed, calls herself a dipsoid, insists she's frigging freaking. No doubt. The elfin adolescents commence a ragtime chicken-dance and Raphael giggles. Did someone sadistic spike her goodies? Kite, cackling, gives Korona a wedgie. She insists he's a lame-brain and he ta-das, claims she is a dudette who should unwind in his backyard. Feamster, barrel-chested, picks a nasty snot and eats it. Raphael admits her temper erupts like a geyser, she's sick about the donnybrook with Virginie, who is undergoing a Kafkaesque psychological Metamorphosis, her own, Raphael's, independent streak, is wider than Lakers great Kareem's wing-span. Discipline? Does a Frequent Flyer appreciate cross-country trips? Hud, with his thoroughly carnival-barker personality, convinces Raphael (the main selling point is the enticing idea of escapism, her craving an anesthetic as a chemic compulsion; the demonic cock-crowing SOP for shrinkage) to pinch her navel twice with her forefinger and thumb and cock-a-doodle-doo thrice and suddenly she trembles and shrinks in a smeary blur.

She is their size! Jesus Christ! She huddles with her new pals and hugs them. Hud tells her she'll enjoy 24/7s of near-death experiences. Holding hands the buds cliff-jump off the ledge into a strolling septuagenarian woman's silver mane. It is a lot like a helicopter drop exercise and falling straight into a severe, fertilely lush, unmacheteable forest.

RAPHAEL IS OBVIOUSLY OVERWHELMED by what she witnesses in the new world: these blubbering baboons in bubbles; lardaceous lady vivisectioning a sinewy guy, his internal organs transmogrifying into melting Dali-esque snails; plaid dolphins swimming in a gelatinous ocean; fetal creatures umbilically bungee-cord-diving off towering cliffs into a semen-spitting fountain; osteoporotically bent, garish flowers; cubed fruit; insectean cherry blossoms; porcelain marionettes in kinky positions on fractured furniture in sparkling snow; baby carriages made of kelly jelly changing into enormous armadillos in a nice golden glow; colossal clocks; shish kebab of human translucent torsos, their tatts tangoing; larval lice bouncing as jumping-beans on seborrheic scurf-soil; Ferris wheel of gigantean computers and typewriters ... Navy-blue vista is a verb, green earth is the noun. Impressionist pines. Pudgy pigeons. Bees buzz like an intercom. Martian region, a Red Planetoid range with normalized idyllic country in the middle. Dye-monsoon. Emerald ducks circularly glide on the surface of a pea soup pond in ponderous winelight.

Matisse-motif'd ocean. Rhombusoid sun. Orange Crush runnel and its hellaciously micromassive volumes of radioactive waste. Conceptual decelerated relativity of time in flux. Anthropomorphic Gummi Bears natate in a suety swimming-hole in a Dustbowlish country. Pubescent picnickers, in gay-hued bathing-suits, mill. Warbly luau music plays. Beach-party on kitty-litter sand. A tawny tyke in a burgundy tankini fiddles with her flaxen curlies and takes a whiz in an unpruned hirsute hedge. Garish, cylindrical dachshund-blimps gaily float and woof, stubby legs dog-paddling uselessly. No-shit slingshotty, swooned caterpillars. Abruptly, Hud pokes Raphael in the eye and Feamster boots her in the behind and Kite bonks her on the cranium, not thrilling her one bit. She does her darnedest to fend the rascally ruffians off. Her growl is guttural, doing a spin-o'-rama and elbowing Hud in the gut, slapping Feamster's jowls, and hitting Kite in the shin. Attack met by resistance. It looks as some slapstick routine. Already she is homicidally tired of the twits and their maddening, unentertaining stunts. If the outrageous behavior continues would there be psychic damage in the longish term? Whereupon she realizes she is primitively naked, is instantly mortified, feeling absolutely ridiculous, but relaxes a tad in discovering the others are too. She was just so blown away by the surroundings she didn't notice initially. She's insecure being without a stitch, in desperate emotional straits, has the sensation of being a shaved and caged hamster in a laboratory observed by youthful, eccentric and denuded scientists. Then she imagines she's at a nudist camp. Shreds of utterances drift like dandelions. Intonations rustling as autumnal leaves. Smoke exhumes from the desert. Stars burn and bird-flap. Emberous tobacco particles. Environment sniffs with congestion. Hud without warning gooses Raphael and she knees him in the nuts. Feamster kicks her in the keester. Hud is pigpiled upon. She could go for higherbrow company. She shuts her grey matter off like it's a control switch. They're coal-miner-filthy, are not the brightest bulbs in the juvenescent box. Expressionless, Korona's incisor-fangs protrude as tiny tusks from her slot-choppers. Her smarts aren't speedy and she has an armpitty aroma and she's witheringly slight. Hud, ogling Raphael with ear-smoldering fixation, announces they're agendaless, declares in addition they're ulterior motiveless. Kite focuses on her washboard-stomach. Feamster pays attention to her curvaceous hips, majestic gazangas, hinyackas like you read about. Korona gazes at her humongous tootsies andflaunted yabos. Breezes sound as struck matches. Gritty drizzle. Chiaroscuro pallid-cheese-achromatic. Aftershave-aquamarine lagoon malperspectived by seeping mist. A bough squeaks not unlike a porchswing. Rain kersplats. Fast sunrises/sets as over the Pacific. Titanic tarot-cards domino-topple. Dew gives everything a confected aspect. Mini-mohawk of turd on a slate. Thunder goes whammo. Rice Krispie sound of sprinkles. Parabnormal penumbra. Cloud in the vitreous vista is breath expanding on a window. A metallic starling flies in the exact motion of someone rotating a kink out of a shoulder. Discourse without subtleness. Korona's ceaseless coughing. The sun is reminiscent of a dead fish's eye in crushed ice of cloud. Raphael's axilla aroma suggests digested vegetables and barnyard livestock in blistering dogdays. Her copious earwax gives the impression she has bister foam earplugs in and she breathes like she has an astronaut's helmet on. Hud thinks she's monstrously towering, looks as an ecologically mutated fowl, and is petrifyingly alluring. Cinnamon pollen. Oxygen has a Listerine savor. Gales whirring like processors' gears and making tumbleweeds corkscrew. On a wedge of grassy slope a mob of howler-monkeys swaggering and shrieking. Seagulls fly, appear as hoary ad-cards fluttering out of a magazine. This completely outlandish universe must be seen to be believed.

THE GALUMPHERS AND BLARNEYERS lung-bustingly clump like Claymation characters up a dandriffy knoll and through a squishy swamp with panther-black bleachers elongating as shadows and dotted with lozenges of brilliancy. Skirling gales shush with an apnean gargle. Nonstop yammering and yukking. Spate's piano-strings vibrating. Raphael, inverted-broom-semblanced, infamously fatiguable, cardio-wise, sluggardly hoofs, heart sounding undampered, sluggishly trudges with rhythmical economy, is sore from the hiking and's sugar-crashing. She feels like a cog widgeted into a wheel, plods wearily, frog-soft bawagos mamboing. On the air's amperage she drifts on electric currents, circuitry crackly. She is paid attention to, an emphasis on her physicality. Hud's shock's mush-roomed. He fervently opines her sexuality is unconsummated. Kite's theory is she's a nascent dyke. To Feamster, dabbing his anvil-like head using a bandana, her mouth is a tomato, her ass is artillery, her bosoms are baby kangaroos in a pouch. Her featured comeliness in conjunction with her gloriously lithe build is congruous. Korona plays a Mattel Electronics hand-held game that tweets, blurps, chirrups, bleeps and blips invariantly. Her knees are cross-hatched with Band-Aids. Alien wasteland in the center of a fantastic field is forbidding. Blunt snoot of sun on the yawning claret vista. So far it has been an outstanding experi-ence, incredibly, impossibly visional, although her tour guides are insensitive irritants. They love tugging on her mental pubes. She doesn't have the opportunity to brace herself for the direct swung sucker-punch to her solar plexus courtesy of Hud, his li'l prick perversely telescoping, the resultant fist-to-flesh noise making a queasy whacked-melony sound. Her adrenal jolt a rev-upper. She rests, recovers, unresponding, self-ori-ented, tightly wound, and resumes, tunes them out as radios, the brats, huffing and puffing, on her tail terrier-ishly. There's a visible voltage of suspense. She would be straightforwarder only doesn't want to be upsetting. Others would have nullo problemo being a callous cooze but not her. Various snarky conversations rise and fall, echoes recessive. Her respirations fill her aural atmosphere. Hauling herself shimmyingly in a Hawaiianized gait she could be hula-ing. She has an ashtray taste. Ointment-oxygen. Pearlescent sky with baggy cirri. Lily pads in a murky moat like paper place-mats. Crazed temp-swings. Ruby rocks. Midgets, five a-breast, schmooze in a tea-party of a demonstrating line, sipping and pumping their fists simultaneously in a large lavender valley. Mammary-mountains. Peroxidic maelstrom. Piliferous spinney. A gang raimented in Harleywear play pool (reminding one of refugees from a GWAR concert on a rejected 'Logan's Run' set) in a lovely orchard, Hawgs astonishingly upright w/o kickstands. A mantis bartender with jailhouse ink chomping on a toothpick grins and stoops and polishes his idling chopper, and it blats when he revs the throttle. He ends up popping wheelies. Public urinals of gravestones in a surreal cemetery with an amazing beer-foamy brook in proximity. Nacreous nebulosity of monoxides over the jut of a promontory. Stars are suppurating sores on the sarcous skyline. Their residence exteriorly is reminiscent of a barracks, a big, blasé, commodious cake, Nestles Quik-colored and in an absurd state of crummy repair, accompanied by a few picnic benches, situated on a dandruff hill on scalpiferous terrain and circumscribed by filamental ferns and forsythia. Armored-vehicle dump-sters in which hardcore straycats rummage, meows trebling and bassing off the metalliferous sides. Verminal twitters also. Darkness advances as a typhlotic tarantula. Parentheses of sleet slow-dripping like from a faulty faucet. Speech sounds as pig-Latin baby-talk on acid, balloon and burst. Stainless-steel fence ungleaming and in an iffy state of upkeep. Wheelchair ramp with bumper-stickers on it. Raphael's partial profile. Penny tang in her mouth. Animalic din of fighting and fucking. There are paved passages like Projects' driveways. The main reason they're illusorily foreshortened to her is perspectival. They diminish, recede in the brume. Loud dragsters billow like sails and go limp as flags. Lindens shed pollen like wigs do powder. She puts on a painfully pale smock and zip-upable Reeboks, and instantaneously takes 'em off 'cause they are too restrictive. Her gullet feels as a grill with coal in it. Perfumy mistrals kettle-whistle. Pyramid of vans. Sodiumal security-lights. Cinereal beards of hornets' nests from the peeling gutter. A stalactiform one in the vicinity. Interiorly it suggests a homeless shelter and has the stench of urine and feces, with numerous oily, sarcophagal cots with greasy army blankets and stacked, stained pillows and there's noticeable insectean activity. Waffled metalloid stairs. Ominous furnishings not unlike medieval torture-contraptions. Carpetless steps. Den so jam-packed with junk it's unvacuumable. Dancerly tap-shoe-clicks of the drencher. Cockeyed windows with mandibular shutters. Burn-pinkening dawn. Bioluminescent bugs. There was an opaline dusk. Suspiring showers. Coffinous ottoman hide-tan. The sty's environs having vaudevillian-dormer-social-intercourse. Keggers on cabana-chairs, the stains as if oil-changes went wrong on them. Plasticine cygnet on the mantel and a cyke, this pictorial representation of Custer's Last Stand. Cognomened footlockers aligned lengthwise in the hellish hall. Cloudlets assume abstract shapes in the gunmetal-grey horizon. Liberated, abroad felines forage in the squalid rubbish buckets. Unlit loading dock. Raphael surveys the ghastly dump dead-eyed, wordless, whey-face scrunched, assessing, in detail, spectral, sickened, staring. They clear out and she cleans up. She should've slipped on a white suit and oxygen mask! She puts a quarter in a vending machine and it projectile-vomits a Zagnut bar. Revealed, in the raw, she sweeps, dusts, vacs, sprays, scrubs, and spends a significant block hosing excrement and semen off the massive Lucite walls. It's a menial yet honest job. And she applies herself, toting the barge, lifting that bale, hurtling to and fro, pendular like a metronome, breathing with the sonance of bubblegum-cards in wheels of a ridden bicycle. Her sprocketed, simian, gangling motions as she, with a shard-squint, hoovers morphic mold, practically polymerized, in afterimages of illumination, whaling the abode as Moby Dick. She gets her domestic affairs in order, negotiates a mausoleum-diametered study, approaches the chores as though encountering a cosmic mystery, gives a valiant go, pulls a steamroll-and-run-driver on the dwelling. A virtual disinfecting bombardment. You got her pipe-cleaner limbs haphazardly bending, garbage-bag-twist-tie-flexible, upper-thigh cottage cheese of cellulite. She has slinky strides and gives furtive glances. With her bravely bending, crawling and slinking, boldly in the buff, thus wholly exposed, tush-conscious (a booger-shaped mole due east of her fuzzy anus), she gives the boys boners and causes their jaws to hit the floor. Their johnsons are periscopically up; or they're missiles launched from scrotal silos incrementally. Their excitement engaged to the max. Customarily they call their erections "penis promotions." Her beauteous bottom. To her they are at a larval maturity point. Feamster conveys her howitzers are aimed like missiles. She has a willowy frame, reedy inflection, countable blemishes, muscular calves as bratwursts, and breasts like bulbaceous, conical paper cups. Youthful glands go bananas, the awesome display cholesterol-raisingly intense. Aches of her abdomen and groinpull hamper her. She articulates her uncomfort. Korona tsks her tongue and sulks demonstratively. The girl is flabby and penguin-toed and needly and pathologically reserved and receives the lion's share of shit from her cronies, not a tried-and-tested team-player, on the fringe, the openest of them. Her plaintiff oratory sounds as bus-brakes. Fragrance of laundromat exhaust. Feamster with minuscular retinal flash-cards blurts this chick Raphael is a babe. He'd bet a bank-account-depleting tensky she's a pro model. He proffers it with pluck, in spite of his financial insecurity. Kite adds she's what the doctor ordered. Hearts furnace-whoom. Sun is a disk. The crew throwing darts, playing foosball, doing this and that. Teeming, striated, cauldron-blackish, infernous interstate has hydrant-sized, Gaugin-colored seahorses pinballing back and forth on a westward sojourn, ejaculatorily shooting and careening like calligraphy. Raphael would wager altitudinously high-domination currency there will be an accident eventually. Her tuchas is toast. It adopts different forms and guises in her motility. She is kneeling penitent on the nasal-green grass, hooking up the kinked garden hose, hunching over, getting on all-fours, splayed, open for observation. Her movements are communication codes. Her peach-lanate prat (pruny in this advanced-yoga position) to Hud lay a click north of perfection. For him her anatomy is an audit and he's dedicatedly doing his job by analyzing it. Her spread duff is impregnately protected and to him spinning on its axis. The Four Horsemen to him are boobs and buns. He looks as a rabbit about to be roadkilled, his penile worm springing like a joke-store's cloth-snake from a nut-can. He tosses a beanbag. Kite and Korona play keep-away with a pack of Wintergreen Mentos from Feamster, who is jitterbugging, contorting acrobatically, relative fluidity belying his bulk. Unemboweled phone on the fluffy loam. Eventide's licoricey-ebon-and-sticky. Night'd strip-mined the day. Minutely climate change. Scent of sawdust. Millpond hollandaise-colored with an eggy-filmy plasm. Lionhide banks. Stand-up comedy of freaky jugglers in cadet-bluish leotards and floppy jester-footwear on parkish benches verdigrised at a dirtyglass duckpond with concentric circles created by a multitude of dragonflies. Elephant skin meadow. Willows, nubbly and deciduous, weep leaves. An arc of decamping, cartwheeling, cooing pigeons, a collection with cohesion, the flock Frisbee-gliding, making loopy ellipses. Bluff dun and crunchy as Shredded Wheat cereal. The crescentiform, earth-tone moon gets lopped by cumuli and regenerates itself like a lizard's tail when they're gone. Hud essays to tear a phone book in a screen of spate, to no aveil. His black eyes make him a Zorro mask. Dead-bird-milky-blue hillock has origami-animals on it creating noises as voices from the grave. Feamster, not the swiftest ship in the knowledgeable fleet, soft as a fucking grape, is seated on a stool sucking on a penknife, pinwheel-eyed, his vegetabilization from the LSD, on his giant highatus espying boulders of

Brussels sprouts whimpering like 'Precious Pup' in Fisher-Price beds with ultraviolet lamps on a Nile-green knoll in dandruff-flurries, an unblinking stump stinking of bologna-left-in-summer-heat descrying the moon, a roaring skull in respiritic beams out of popular entertainment. What a rush! His is a diagonal room, a legal-pad yellow sandwich-sarcophagus, filled with horizontality. His Sidon mirror shows a homodontic smirk and phocomelic limbs. He's a boat in a fog, eyeballs gritty as if sand was thrown in them, with a hemorrhagic stroke-victim's vegetated expression. His breathing subaudible. Bipedal mongrels, narcoleptic, REM-slumber on a public sidewalk at a Cumberland Farmsish convenience-store called 'Water Lou Gehrig's,' some speaking Chaucerian English. An epicene chap with lobstery eye-stalks and Lands' Endified with conspicuous temporal-lobe conundra moves like he's got ball-and-socket joints. Droog-esque bloke in an electric wheelchair. Graphite landscape in the rain is grainy-porous-photograph-semblanced. There's deficit in Kite's attention. He has on his shoplifted sombrero. Pulse-lines of lightning. Hud ogles Raphael, has a woodie, realizing him sponge-bathing her, as he forensically figures out a '90s computer post-modem. He has a deep-focus fever-dream, her middle rippling like petroleum-fumes. To him she's a take-overer, usurper, pad-plunderer. She is splits-stretching and pantyless on a balance-beam in the Gold'sine gym. She's always at attention's center, a nervous system-overheater, an eye of the pyrotechnical-glandulose storm, a monkey-wrench in the ointment of the three-dimensionality of their planet. His shillelagh uprising. Her tiggobitties the whiteness and shape of peeled boiled eggs. She'd stripped as though ripping the skin off a sausage. His hormonal machinery's horsepower ... Her lithesome gorgeousness is fatalistical. Nipples like artillery shells, pooter-cheeksies high-watt bulbs. His mentation cranked. She moves as a cracked whip. His synaptic twitchery. Her vampire-whitish chest sea-heaves. The only turnoff about her is the biodegradive b.o.. Superimposing a potted plant she is a multi-armed Hindu goddess. The intercom's buzzer is belling. On the HD Hitachi Ward is preaching to Beaver and Wally. Rainbow spots are many-hued M&M's. Prematurely potbellied (an abdominous accordion) and malarially sweating, Korona is violinishly curvy, unmuscled, nontoned, the most passivest of papooses (in the yore-days a fury), has the oblate head of a reptile, mondo matako, and rump-roast-sized feet, in a tie-dye t-shirt and bandanna, adjusts her owl-glasses and leans a little, like she got suckered in the groin, a brooha in her bottom, the bum feeling as a bulbful of excrement, acid in her gullet going up like vapor a chimney, discomfort sharpening her senses, expanding her perception. She inhales from her Marlboro and exhales two steer-horns of smoke from her porcine nostrils. Dandriffy snow. Her face feels tautened, as if she's sitting too close to a fire in its place. She hates her ketchup-bottlish body, bloated belly bowing out like in mounting gaseous pressure. Her deerskin suntan. Exit-sign red of her heels, she schlepping with her into-the-hurricane gait. To her, Raphael's glutes are two smooth scoops of strawberry ice cream. Prior to her, Raphael, coming here, Korona withstood bad-trip elements, was getting cabin-feverish, becoming agoraphobic, the others' comments, knife-twists, confirmed this. The dipshits put her through the mincer. Her lucid and vivid visions had cumulative and crushing qualities. It is pouring like hell. Kite, mirthlessly, mucoidally chuckling, Heimlichs Feamster, who is bovinically lowing and whose hair is CCM-helmety. Korona flamboyantly makes angels in the mulch. Her double-chin reconfigures itself. There's a used-prophylactic-scar on her sternum. Her gasps as though in a courtroom when a controversial verdict is read aloud.

Hours truly witching. Adrenal warmth. Air smelling coppery. Demufflered jeeps. A tomahawk-shaped octogenarian, weather-bleached, with a demonized dial, lemon-yellow and lime-green like the guts of a squashed bug, chops opening and closing as a drawbridge raises and lowers, with tortoise-shell rims, disintegrating dentures, and municipal sewage mephitis, scuttles centipedishly, quick not unlike a silverfish. Indigotic empyreal eye has a (solar) system of star-exploded arteries in it. Cirri are spongy splotches of fungal decay. Here's on the level of being locked in the loony bin where the inmates ironly govern the asylum. The silver lining is, for Raphael, that she is separated from the familiar world of woe she came from, so there is a smidgen of consolation to be gotten. Here is the forever-dangling carrot, a dimension that has connotation, not denotation, an outline of a concept, a far cry from the dead-end mean streets she was accustomed to. There are paths to take and no destination. There's no emotional encagement. She fits in, abstractionally anyway, is firmly included in the young kabuki theater. She's unalone, doesn't have to succumb to peer-pressure, can exist on an elementary level. She is on the straight and narrow, has cleaned up her act. She has learned lessons. She wonders if going back would be the kiss of death. Her head hurts, a migrainoid ratchet cranking two turns. Her heartrate speedens. She isn't elated. She refuses to bitch. This place could be pleasanter. There are jockeyings for position, normal B.S. and power plays. No one touches base. They steal it, or fling it, as a baseball manager throwing a temper tantrum to protest an ump's call. There are life-and-death dramas, a crisis of conflict at every turn, the verbiage unshutoffable. Their elaborate machinations are tedious. She keeps eyes peeled and ears cocked. Innerly she swears there'll be responses to their nonsense, cathartic nonviolent payback. She's intuitive lately in gauging the barometer of beefs, monitoring the squabbles with an instinctual Geiger counter, and she can capably omnissently predict potential problems with an uncanny sixth sense. And seeing smoke-detector blinks and jugular veins pulsing are clues as well. She grazes ruminantly on a marshmallowy treat, carried in uncomfortable-looking corduroys, thicket of acupuncture needles throbbing in her sunbaked back. She has welts on her eggplant-knockers from an asinine snafu with a Ford Mustang GT's motor. She ski-jumper leans to fuss with the jalousie in protective plastic wrap. Daytona of cockroaches on the checkered tiling. Sun and moon swiftly swop places and bell-swing. Fuchsia river is a lined gigantean palm. Crystal frost of cloud. Holmeses in hoodies like hawks, wiredness barbed, are a Greek chorus of citified argot, conversing in an oppidan, primatal language as shock-waves, no-attention paying, bicker in razzles and dazzles of rays. Obscenities are exchanged. Rinse, repeat. On a whim she shucks, soused, dolled up, runny mascara lending her a messy Lone Ranger mask, tottering perilously in platforms, peeled-potato white, the kiddos playing backgammon, pies aprowl, mugs predatory, velociously jabbering and sipping Polar seltzer. Her slurred vocalizing sounds like klaxoning, slack-fish-on-a-hook-mouthed, in a full-body sweat, goosebumped, lips sealed, she with a Nietzschean ambience of activized individualism, vacant-cow-eyed and greasy-feverish, dancing uninhibitedly stiffly, in a kooky crane stance, listening to The Carpenters. Her pageboy haircut a crown of tufts, derma layer the pigment of overripe pumpkin. She bends stiffly, as if she's got a back-brace on. Levin sounds like a mike's feedback, looks as though it is a zig-zag trace of the Rockies. Her doll's-hair bush. Her nose is a conjunction between clauses of ears, signifying cuteness. She's a diamond in a rough household, trots like a fox-hunting hound, dimples of mirth on the backs of her thighs, crinkling them, striding Indianishly, has an ungodly floral odor, a sick sweetness, ironizing the irony her mom's a hair-dresser and here she is in a hair-world. Wow! Her thought-soap-bubbles, text within waving as aviators' scarves, like ones from a toddler's bath, float and burst, the "pops" as heater-hisses. Feamster sweeps in flourishyly, square head turbanned by towel, penguin-built, pecker a semi, ham steady on his joystick, pumping his penial primer, fleshly chest rising and falling at the rate the sun goes up and down, tries in vain to pinch her, and she warns him to "watch it, bucko." His big toe's nail the colour of turtleshell. He uses a swatter to stun a fattish fly on the fiberboard cellar-stairs, and removes its wing. He has facial tics. The maimed insect scuttles in crazed circles til Korona, martyrishly magnific, puts it out of its misery by smacking it with a mildewy, folded newspaper. She says unbidden remembrances are ladles sampling her sorrow. Ceiling-fan circulates rapidly like a clock's arms in a filmic time-travel interval. The kids' cots with crib-railings tightly made. She can't bond with them, confide in them. Her brain with cogitations is a light-fixture full of dried bugs. Bar-graph of lightning. Bayou-blue Mount Doom eminence. The sky breathes and the sun beats as a humongous heart. Leaves a parched brunet. Garden, indifferently upkept, spiny and brown-green. Mugginess sickeninger than ever. Photos on the fridge like they are pics of missing children you'd find on milk cartons. A 'backer-brawny Pakistani happycamper in yuppiewear sells Bufferinish narcs to 'Yellow Submarine' buffoonish Blue Meanies (drawn by Frida Kahlo) already narculated, their voices with the sonancy of squeaky bedsprings. They scribble on amethyst vellum, their writing drawing, ebubbliently drifting in the lotus position. A burro with Pillsbury Doughboy-limbs prances. It has floppy-ears and buck-teeth. Raphael appears thin and thick at the same time, her posture immaculate. Putting on a brassier at this point would be tittymount to strapping herself into a straitjacket she is so used to being nudistic now. Her footsies with a putrid-fruit stench, melon on a hemorrhoid-pillow, in starkers, bod inhumanly improbable. Her virgin white face so bright it is like all the sun's shine has gone into it. She longs for home and hearth. Existing in this nuclear rat-hole is a shell-game. Cerebral hemorrhage of the sun. She is exquisitely charming, poised as a secretarial pen mid-draft, railish, rooty, ribby, acnean scarred hollows in her haunches. She whumps into the pine-paneled wall of the atriumine commons. Feeling like a shark swerving through a reef. Kite affirms she's the sexiest skyscraper, in top shape. Hud and Feamster nod in avid agreement. Korona meanwhile remains neutral and munches on Ritz crackers. Moisture encases her. When it comes to pulchritude she knows she's not even in Raphael's zip code. She has the incognitoizing aura of invisibility, Korona does. Air like mopwater. Oceanic sounds of the ceiling's fan. Steerhorn of moon. Celestial sphere chocked with cloudlets. Diarrheatic spatter of rain. Zaftig gerbils in glycerinine-clear liquid-crystal displays. Welkin's way clearer. Extracurriculars of half-nelsons given between Hud and Kite. Korona undeformed by her makeuplessness has bystander status, with an impersonal carved-pumpkingrin, unexceptional specs repaired with electrician's tape. She says"owie" when Hud sucker-socks Kite in the groin, and makes a mustache out of her indexer to stymie a sneeze, voice breathy. She smears Clearasil on her chin. Slug-mark on her right shoulder-blade. They look as if they are Ludditic Touretters doing calisthenic exercises, forced together by something nucleic. She tells 'em, deadly-serious, stony-faced, they're not cerebral colossi. 3-D brine. Laser-jet echinoderms sprout spikes. Mythic elms look to've grown the ground instead of the other way around. Aluminumoid ambulance with hackysacks left on its hood. Hud Breakdances. Kite and Korona as though they're Native-Americans on the warpath. Slutty, haggish, bladish-bodied hoydens, intense-faced, wolf dates outa cartons and tear-ass up an illusory, integument-pigmented incline which matte-dissolves. You'd be hard-pressed to not consider them hookers, gaunted to within their lives, in whorish regalia. Sky isolates itself from clouds. Sepia-fleshed asses, unshaven and with exposure-scuz and socks for gloves and in a mass stupor look discarded, deposited with shopping-carts filled with garbage bags of their worldly belongings and recyclable bottles and cans, remindful of the Grinch's Santa-sacks with the Who's purloined presents. Wind's keen and wheezy and autumnish. Stars like Xmas bulbs. In the mercuric effulgence the butchest lesbian Raphael has ever seen is crew-cutted, cavern-cheeked, tufted-nared, and breastless, a conspicuous caloric consumer, a blubberer fitness-deprived, her sour burny malodor with a decomposition-element of reek, fly-fishing with an interracial entourage (making a ratty-squeaky stink), futzing with her rod's line and with a rictal smile (showcasing quandariacal teeth) yanking chains. Dressed in nothing save a raglan sweater she is stooped, dispenses rectal complaints, doughy arms akimbo, ventures an Asian acquaintance wearing sneaks pooped her pants, goes "eeeyyyuuu," abutting a bronze boulder, her anatomic angle allowing this harlequin refulgence to adjust itself, holding her lax gut as a gunshot hambone starlet in a Western movie, illed by a dollop of dogmess, her russety cat's-eye rosebud, a brownstar to Raphael, pungent like a Magic Marker, laid bare, its arse, couple of pitbulls in a pillowcase, constellated with pimples, goes death-silent. Carnivorous flora and fauna's a grand-scale, knuckle-biting-inducing, public-health problem make no mistake, can intimidate the bejeesus out of you. The violetish plains-gas is up there too. Lacteal lightshaft with immense dimensions diffracts in the portière, and the spear decocts, regentrifies itself. Fannish verdure. Cesarean slice of a trail towed by a puny private plane on the stomachic skyline. Sand sound of spate with drainage mephitis and diagonal quality to it. Countryside looks miniaturized, as if it's a landscape diorama in a glass paperweight. A wino, the poor wretched creature, canines birch-brownish and dime-grayish, chomps bona fried chicken, makes a production out of it, the walking dead, with corroded falsies and undeliberate nonchalant stealth, part of the wayward mad, gropes for purchase, perambulating, jay-stumbles, bolt-upright, through a busy intersection, crashes pratfallishly can-over-teakettle into crates of bluely berries, the racket ricocheting. Swounding swotters. Limbo-and-turkey-shoot contest going on. Dinner-mint bluish lagune. Scotch-plaid rainbow. Whap of wings. Shark-belly grey-white embankment. A cherubical Chinkette sybaritically entranced floats chromatic colostomy bag-balloons, wears waders and plays a kazoo, traverses pocket-pitch, cruciform beaten tracks, and dangles from a fire-escape's pull-ladder hanging as though a necktie. An attractiver minority, spic mayhaps, smelling carbonated, with cheeks sunken, makes her hand into a pistol and aims it at the Chinagal's helical nombril and, not devroid of central nobility, expectorates lalations of hip, burghal lingua franca, lambasting junior hooligans (in roiling steam) trying to torment them. Kite hunts Korona, shoots a suction-cup-tipped arrow from a toy bow, barely missing her dental-white rump. Raphael experiences tingles from scalp to sole. She osmosizes gawks, can create climacteric changes in you. Hyperfertilized acreage. Graying heavens corrupted by an orbiting copter; a manmade defile. Wind sounds like crowd cheer. Feamster's tabletop-flat head's buzzcut looks as if it was done with hedge-clippers. His hyperemic organ. He's woody-whiffing. Korona's vari-cotic, demilunic calves in the gingerbread-light. She is kyphotically hunched. Comet of jismic scum on the sink. Faulknerian roadlet of doom. Volva parallel parked along it for a Special-Olympics-ish shindig/competition at a parish church venue. Branches windmill. Vietnamese transvestals have free rain in the fibroid pouring. Mounted fiberboard shelving holds old-fashioned videos (all alpha-betized) contained in parenthetical Oscar-ish statuette figurines. Oculus of a Magnavox console. Candy-colored cloudlets as though cresting combers, breakers shattering ever-slowly. Hud and Feamster catapult one another on the seesaw. Kite pulls Korona from the hoop of a float not unlike a cork from a bottle.

IN THE UNKIND KITCHEN with its general crud, Raphael, still feeling exhibitionistic, in the altogether, Schiele-rangy, refugee-famished, P.O.W.-scrawny, in puzzling chef's hat, cardinal Nehru slippers and aberrant apron, on an eye-rattling, tremendous abundance of caffeine, blushed and beaded, preparing a yummy, unforeignish and unremarkable meal of corporate food, basically spaghetti and hot dogs, warns the juvies she's an essentially inexperienced cook, a rank amateur, so shut it, do not hazard a crack about the course, or anything remotely connected to culinary commentary. She wraithily wanders, globose bodacious tatas jigging and rendered littler in the full spectrum of brilliance and cubist shadow, posture indecisive, figure-eighting around a shipment with impressive footwork and sallying for the refrigerated cabinet of a milk dispenser. They aren't exactly lining up in droves and trampling each another, though they are lampooning her efforts, lying on the dungy divan and vinyl couch, biting their knuckles in mock-horror. They're a quadra-celled organism. She is determined to concoct deliverable dishes, using survivalist pots she heard were bought on sale at a supply outlet. She's a babe-in-the-woods, tossing a salad at the teak table, thence hurling herself to the feverish stove, opening and shutting the oven without confidence. Precip as goo. Day drains into the sump of night. Crows congested on telephone wires heckle, their flight pirouettic. The moon is speciously seen through a viewfinder's lens's fish-eye. Army cots have the faint imprints of bodies. Korona, uncomposed, in shower-thongs (footsteps making a rubbery-squeaky echo like someone using crutches) and hair-curlers, stiff-arms Kite in the thorax in the upscaler lounge near the lockers with a fridgelet and seamen-ish trunks. His teeth-grinding with the sonance of a Bolex. Feamster rheumy-eyed carries his plate of pancakes as an emblem of authority. Hud holds a dated, clunky cell, staplery, under his lower jaw violin-fashion as he beats batter for the nightly flapjacks. The phone looks crocodilian. The Coca-Cola-colored cumulus of his frozen-sea-crest coif is perceptibly underwater and reflected in the pane with its bullet-headed rain-drops, treads like he's brittle-boned (oldster footage) and plops into the reception-area's flame-retardant swivel-chair in front of the tube for the much-anticipated Hanna-Barberathon. Korona accuses Kite of having a pussy and he retorts she has balls. They giggle, inbent, glandular, grappling, with their own burbly dialect. He takes guff from her. He prepares himself for the painage, as a concession letting her win for a settlement. They tussle, sprawl, Kite staring down the barrel of her loamy clay behind redolent of underarm, overused blow-dryer, and the dentalishly sweet, poised perversely. Her shade-producing udder like a slashed tire. His rod as a cattle-prod. He escapes and regroups. Another brief flurry of a ruckus, brachiatishly leaping. She tugs on his cowlick and he yips and shoves her sorta circumspectly. She karate-chops his scalp-pinkened forearm. He sucks on a pencil like it's a lollipop. He makes this comment her buttocks resemble lumpen loaves of wheaty bread. She picks her cranberry (fecally-rimmed as lipstick on a mug) and he exaggerates retching. Doves kinda brood by puddled petrol-rainbows. Shale-sleet. Vault swollen with clouds. Earth tumid with water. Rococo, ectoplasmically-stained patio-furniture. Korona plays Kite like a finely-tuned instrument in the kamikaze-style scuffle. They writhe and weave through each other. At the coat rack and radiator Raphael partakes of the marvelous pharmacy punch. She has to pee as a racehorse. Her suntan the pigment of Kahlua and milk. To Hud she's a world-class hottie who could be the covergirl of a beauty brochure. She can break his virginal chain anytime! Before 'Touche Turtle and Dum Dum' he is in a transfixed state. Korona curses she has dingleberries on her asshole, picks the poppy-seeds from her bagel. They're numerous cards short of a full deck, skewed versions of those spacey, flaky. Their mops make a pall. In the Aruban anteroom Feamster pricks his pinkie with a diaper-pin. His hands the size of catcher's mitts, built like a noxious-waste drum. Buddhic teddy bear splay-limbed on his lap. His inflamed ears aprick he listens to a Mermanoid show-tune on the boombox. Hail's quotes for sentences of sylvan scenery. The precip is oxymoronic against the moon's beam. Afterwards, alone, exhausted, having bathed in the recently-scoured Volkswagen-sized tub, Raphael sits in an institutional chair, mud-masked, cuke-blindered, cotton-balls crammed 'tween her toes, the nails painted a jaunty jade, dishabille except for stegosaurus-slippers, a raunchy terry robe on her lap, engorges tamales and burritos and swigs tequila (pleasurable palate-wrecker) and decides to get utterly more toasted ... And winds up sleeping, okay, passing out, vulnerable, front-down on a hammock and dangling over a multi-planked blond platform, taut backside, the color of squash, splayed, the ingenue spreading as broth's steam on a window's glass, lengthy, shapely-wiener legs hanging on either side, limbs extended to all compass points, totally snoring up a storm, zucchini-titties compressed, adorable pixie-mop sticking up like she stuck a wet finger in an electrical socket, when Korona, rubber-gloved, lab-coated, bird-of-prey puss, pizza-complected (heavy on the tomatoes), wincing, Redhot-candy lamps squinching, Krazy-Glues her, Raphael's, hind-cheeks together. Hud and Feamster mural her with temporary tattoos and fit an athletic supporter on her coconut. Feamster, perspiring as if he's suffering a stroke, stumpy, ivory incisors shown, Morse-Code-blinks, aspect rictusized, flatus having the sonancy of a whoopee-cushion plunked on, wobbling like he's stricken with Tourette's syndrome, facet downcasted, admits his brain feels vegetabilized, confesses his mind isn't in possession of his body, aspen-shivering, as though he's having an epileptic seizure, blacking out reality, looming lunarly, applying the tatts tenderly to Raphael's olive, elongated-emery-board-back and aerobical-ly-toned tuchis (a past-believing posterior, one that's speciously been hitherto fed nothing save for organic, low-fat dairy products), beseeching a God-ish entity Upstairs who doesn't give one fuckola he's got his hams hyper-bongo-drumming an au naturel, zonked gal. Hollow-loggish percussion. He has zero hope this divine-intervention assistance will happen. To him it is a bonerfied minor miracle they are managing to pull this off. He has a crabshell-cranium and the beginnings of wattles. Kite makes a comment her, Raphael's, body-odor's comparable to an overused dish-rag, tickles the carmined soles of her feet with their heater-stink and Raphael comes to with a start, mouth cottony, skulking for the hopper, horsy-whinnying in anguish, flatulence spluttering, sounding like tomatoes smashed with a mallet, clenching her heinie, still loaded, screaming at a high-range pitch, as an air-raid siren, which could probably rattle your fillings, looking like she's cantering on live coals, in a quirky panoply of movements, bo's'n-staggery, she a vapor trail, nates sucked in as facial cheeks, filly-galloping, clutching her Pillsbury-pale booty (in the alabastrine illumination), neighing, gripping her rear region, rushing in a bad medical fashion, cabbaging her buttocks, lurching, cream cheese-fundament jiggling, in a frantic, undigni-fied shuffle, getting pelted by tennis balls shot from the cannonesque Lobster Elite Liberty Machine (not cali-brated for misprision) operated by the guttersnipe specimens, an eventful fact not helping one jot, ramming into the gender-unspecific lavatory, and she explodes on the horseshoe-shaped toilet, wailing in agony. Her oculi are so crossed she could be an ice-hockey center seeing her right-and-left wingers at the same time, apprising the thankfully wash-offable Maori-ornamental deco-rating her derma that feels sadistically Indian rub-burned. Her rectal berry stings like a sonofabitch. These imps, laughing manically, are mischievous thorns in her Achilles' tendon. They are vigorously pestiferous, should fry in an eternal pan! They've got more virtuoso slice 'n' dice tricks than Ginsu-knives. Her final straw/ camel's back moment. The a.m.s/p.m.s of tomfoolery's wearisome. She's been the recipient of their boom-lowering in the free-for-alls. For instance, when the rapacious, ravenous ragamuffins gang-tackled her, a wave breaking on her, she offered little resistance. She timbered akin to a felled tree. She has had enough of the idiotic, culty coterie. They are hangnails she must clip, bothersome to the maximus. Her risen hackles. She has the Intellective and spiritual energies of a sunning reptile. Defecating as a lunatic she misses her Jill-of-all-trades mom, who pays the bills and she herself bitches constantly, and her blighted, bombed-out town. She cannot deprogram her problems by remote. Her parents've split. She pulls the indigoid, nonunique comforter on her chipped shoulders like a cape, remembers her natural father, a security guard at a local bank, giving Virginie a continuous walloping, so fucked-uppedly scheduled were the thumpings he may well have written them as appointments on a calendar, beating her as flames, beady-eyes piggied, timing the blows, measuring the shots. It was a legendarily difficult marriage, dysfunctional to the hilt. Thoughts of him sink in the aqua pura of memory, only every so often the remembrances bubble. They burp up and dribble down. The Heineken-devoted dad, with his DUI issues, went on his weekly visit to chat with his crotchety probation officer, when Virginie's brother whipped the U-Haul into the driveway, filling it with their belongings, and they bailed pronto. She mulls over her kidney-shaped omphalos tucked in her chamois cloth-softened tummy. Whisks aggrieve the brittle vegetation. Flaming phosphenes of glowflies behind lids of light. Phone booth

Porta Potty. Hairy esparto. She deems herself unbright, the backlight of life illuminating this. Her existence is a dead horse she's fed up of whipping. Feeling not unlike she's existing in an air-traffic control tower - too much occurs too quickly; a gerbil on the wheel; and as a mouse in a maze suspecting there's no bona fide cheese waiting, but she doesn't wanna jinx anything, like a pitcher in late innings throwing a no-hitter who doesn't wish to risk losing what he's gained by mixing pitch selection unnecessarily. She's languishing on the shitter. Korona, schoolgirl-straight, plausibly Satanically possessed, a gap-toothed, unfledged witch, insousistently raps on the pressurized, revolving, reinforced, fine-grain-wood door of the recesstacle restroom considering she's got to go. Raphael blocks her out, tries on a Navajo necklace, Caldor-brand blouse, worsted paratrooper pants (that should be laundered), and sporty slides. Her Bowie-blade figure's musculature is outlined. She swills mescal and blazes a doobster (nipple-erectingly powerful; no small potatoes) and does t'ai-chi. Every diem could she indulge. She is discomposed, attributable to her being clinically claustrophobic. She has delirium-tremens-type head-trips, drinking herself blind as a full-blown spiritous one, getting irretrievably sloshed, her cogitations turboed. These cynical metro canines bark, saddled with unre-solved animalian issues. Crucifi of swooping starlings parallactically wing from the polluted estuarial bay. Palms' fronds Nazi-salute. Empyrean's postnasal drip. This hydrocephalic, tubby, bumpkinish poofta's high-wattage grimace is drawers-foulingly frightening, ascending on an incarnadine cliff's Filene'sish escalator. Mass migrations of skittery prehistoric beasts, locustlike, descending on the vastity of expanse purportaged to be unnavigable terrene. Wooly smokiness on a plateau. Surf sounds as struck muffled cymbals. Griggy grimalkin. Wheat-pallored feti with negroid Afros, Werther's butterscotch peepers, and rosy spincteric moufs are reggaen pot-heads. Oxygen has the consistency of quicksand. Korona's throaty threnody.

RAPHAEL SMEARS MOISTURIZING LOTION on her frighteningly divested self, gets roasted way into the wee hrs, her spoken language a narcotized garble, threads of uncertainty strung through her entirety. She'd stripped off her tunic and trousers, folded them, and set them on the lacquered dresser. Her ill-pallid toots treed with purply, pulsing veinlets. Yowza! The caramel/mocha/yeasty/date/hoppy stout, diabetes in a bottle, is decadent and dynamic, a goshdang doozy ... She contemplates commencing a hardcover copy of 'The Death of Ivan Ilych.' Libation with literature! She creates a digital spire, sees Doppler Effects. Her passed gas in the manner of automatic weapon. She rises from the converticouch, one haunch more broiled than the other, like a forever-reaching heliotrope, strikes you as bodyly stemmy with a flowery head. Her presence, a lance of light incarnate, penetrates the domicile. Her absence in all probability would render it vacuous. Pressure metastasizes in her drum-tight core. She inserts herself into the commode, her evacuation a deja vu of yesterday's dump. Her features make this bulldoggy expression. A Sterno stench. Phosphorescence, inclining and declining, is infectious, and all's amputated because of it. Life-size Lionel trains snail-crawl on tracks oiled, snapped together, and put down by NFL-hugeous hands in brassy, stuttered, elliptical emanation. She wipes her private organs. Hud and Kite play priceless, wicked vintage video-arcade games under a torn tarp. Korona, pencil-straight, gnawing her cuticles, paces congruent to a sentry. Feamster's gesticulations orchestral, all of them making savage-noises, warrior-active, respirations, sucking wind, sounding as sawing logs, seemingly atom-smashingly colliding. Kite gropes Korona with a gag palm-shocker and she yelps and skips. Their puerile pranks, driven home, are, to Raphael, unamusing. They are hardly the neatnikest kiddos, and unquestionably developmentally arrested. Natives are restless. Noise is deafening, even with the acoustic damping-tile on the goddamned walls. She has the sensation she is living on a dunk-tank. Their goodwill halfcrazed. Kite on the futon calls Korona a tubate retard. To Raphael she's got Asperger's, or a form of autism, or has Obsessive Compulsive Disorder, and's shiny-chinned and wet-lipped. She's got a thunderously tuberculoid laugh and rancid-chicory trace, slathered with a goaltender-mask of zit-cream. She is nonironic, unstudyable, essence unabsorbable. Vapor condenses to drizzle. An avian pinwheel. The twits, pesky virtuosi, have an uproarious cookout. Blearily Raphael regards her hyphenated umbilicus, usually a sloppy knot. She's gonzo on tranqs. She hearkens Philip Glass. Through the concave, plasticized, unopenable window dithering in the no-nonsense downpour the twerps' esoteric food to her is a futuristic cityscape. Her blinks like she is sending out signals into the ether. Rainfall snicks as bullets put into a chamber. A narcose Raphael is braless and flannel-shirted (powder-blue and unbuttoned), beryl boxsies puddled at her foots, goggle-eyed, shuddering as a clubbed seal, from strain, a cheap belt not unlike a Jesuitical collar (a costume part inadvertently left on) woppsed round her waist, planch-midsection and exquisite derrière with cross-hatches of scrapes, sphincter on the verge of failing, wiry being in the palsied lambency, fixing the rickety ol' Gravity camper-chair with flaccid, overplump cushions next to the tilted card-table prior to nautically sliding into it. Exoskeletonized in the gloam, frame frail in swimming columns of the full moon's luminosity, she is surprised they haven't insurged and terrorized her. Unease has taken root in her entirety and grown as a mold, like her insides are spoiled food. She rocks side-to-side, as a ship on choppy waters. Her period is a cunt times ten. Her perspiry coins glistening. She muses, her fungal tang moderate. In the blinding clarity of hindsight she should've never left home. Dihedral triangle of her muff. She doffs her Keds and dons her socks. Her stork-shaped silhouette angular. She's sitting Indian-style, has on a fisherman's cap with bent, proboscoid bill, the queer sick-sweet burnt-urn fetor of her tootsie-wootsies insinuating itself into the coagulated atmosphere. Kite's asinine akido, lantern jaw, macho posturing/performing. Feamster's butcher-block skull and Promethean paunch.

A tugboat flies on the water like an aeroplane in the sky. Advertisement dirigibles struggle for primacy on-high, mediation of geese Canadian. The welkin lightens to a distinct nonhue. Sparks of fireflies. Unsettlingly unstable, plush chairs on a patternless shag carpet in the milky corridor. On the geometry of her body is a Tautochrone, or Isochrone (from Greek prefixes tauto, meaning same, or iso, equal, and chrono, time) Problem: diaphoresis drops diligently slide down the cycloid curve of her angled midriff. Humidity has gotten significantly terribler. She feels morose, melancholic, clinically depressed, copes with denial and distress. Stolid, variegated, sloppy spokes of headbeams illumine her, rotating, as from a rotary, which is odd for there aren't any automobiles. Skeeters wang off the windowpanes. She's left to her own introspective devices. Natal gurgle of pipes. Cobalt lava-lamp. Fresh coat of varnish patinas the Portuguese mahogany flooring. Docked-fish-gulping waftage. Landscape's a gigantean disembodied smirk. The moon is an oblong beef patty. Jagged lividity of lightning. Dark's black like an innercity alleyway. Shutters hinge-scritch. She revels in her spatial privacy. Ferociously expensive valance curtains of a trillionaire (yeah, an embellishment) with floral themes. Hud pretends to perform emergency CPR on Feamster, whose play-acting is incompetent. Their rampant rambunctiousness could bring anyone down. They imitate zombies. She has racked up an accumulation of abrasions from the gamboling. Drafty pantry. Follicle-shrubbery. Sprinkles' tinkles have a customer-bell sonance. Abed, tress unarranged, face slumberously tumescent, she observes them.

They grunt and bash into one other as bumper-cars, actions baroque. Their rebel-yelling. Asterisks of mizzle. Foil-stream. Startling view. Thundering sky with metal-line glints of leven permutations. Her belly feeling denser. She is replete with jitters, comes across as frazzled, as after a freakas. The lane is a prolix polyurethane lung with poltergeistish sycamores materializing like you have a fever, bulging, blurring and settling. A plain stoop you'd normally find in a low-rent district. Tumbler with grainy material residue. Generic venetian blinds lowered. Plumes of aluminumal clouds. Static siss of a Kaopectate-coloured lake. Gloomy heaven. Fake-wood floor bearing trash. Asbestosy air. The entertainment console congruent to a fighter-plane's instrument panel. Shake 'n Bake, Kellogg's and Betty Crocker boxes on an enamelish desk. Hud is a veteran of relaxation in a stuffed-animaled director's chair, spikes his Swiss Miss cocoa with a Bartles & Jaymes wine cooler. His silence a tensed malevolence. Raphael to him's a person-silencer, head-spinner, corporeally fabulous. In the undistinctive foyer, beside the 'You Are Not Here' directory posted in smoked glass, with humdrum, Norwegian-blond doors, Rubikulous ashcans and chestnut carpet, a vent sibilant, its gargles inguinal, surroundings the optical equivalent of treacly, monotonous shopping-mall music, Raphael, for a genuflectory Kite and Korona, makes her middy morbidly round like she's pregnant, parturiently waddles, and they are hysterical, establish quite a hubbub. She confides in Korona in describing the heebie-jeebie-prompting dream where she was a sedated patient in a hectic hospital, her room the size of a confessional booth, and an avoirdupois, Armenoid nurse with wasp-nest tress, burgeoning chins, perspiry mustache, anthropoid forehead, and solo elongated eyebrow, her aspect specific and unpleasant, planate snout twitching as Samantha's in 'Bewitched,' held these suitcases over her, an inert and passive St. Bernard that'd seen better epochs rigid like a rocking-horse in the hallway. Its snorts sounded suffocated. Wood-carving Doctors' movements were quanta-quickish, whizzing as time's passage. There was this multilevelled confrontation which changed into garden-variety Muzak. What was especially eerie for her in the nightmare was she was audibilized when she articulated, only the medical staff were like thespian props, mute, peripheral presences, actor extras on a sitcom set, their Intonations chip-munkish, in an aural anomaly, Babel-babble, more seen than heard. What they said she didn't know from shinola. Inflections had the whiny sound of mosquitoes on meth. Emanation was an epiphanyish visitation. Speed bumps of lightning. Precipitation was finger-wiggly quotation marks. Fulgid figurants. A 'Ren and Stimpy' episode was on the archaic television ... Korona was in toto stumped. Saline-drip showering. Hud wants to be erotically enmeshed with her, feels guilt-ridden, very ashamed, at the terminus of his amorous tether. His romantic overtures would be really slick and solicitous. He'd dissuade her from dating. He's enthralled, her sensual movements as a slow-tease stripper. They are sham motions, sensuous, provocative, designed to titil-late. Her afflatus is crude code. She had deposited plenteously. Her backside feels raped, her esophagus strangled. Her customary Dutchboy is mobster-slicked-back. His gandering is an optic, unviolent violation. He samples gnarly-tasting distilled spirits. French curls of smoke overdeliberately blown from his Benson & Hedges cigarette, smoky sabertoothed-tiger tusks extruding from his flared nares. Her heels tough like an attaché case. Her deck-of-cards riffle of cachinnation and teakettle's wheeze. Her paddle-large feet with a balsamy, low tide, sour-medicinal sub-odor to them. His lust spreads as melted margarine through the mauve, ambient alcove pried out of a substance-dependent treatment facility. She is chestily stacked, and sans skivvies (in a G-string and sports-bra), ties a vermilion velveteen gift-ribbon around her photogenic, succulent-stalk neck and jars preserves with the twins. Her farting sounds heliated. Her mind shaken like a margarita, being as a maraca. She hasn't a clue as to how she acquired a spiffy shiner. Kite plays Russian Roulette with Korona using a squirt-gun at an administrative filing cabinet. A stagy-hammy embryoglio occurring and rikky-ticking into the background, Kite having fleen, jonesy for pie. The beef sounds not unlike shitfaced voice-boxes runover by a velocious 'Vette, aspirated breathing like they've got an ammonia thing. A crapload of baggage brought into the brouhaha. Feamster holds a plate of brownies as a crucifix at Kite who is like he is Sataninely possessed. Raphael, pencil-necked, tailly figure revenanty, does needlepoint and keeps her ant-eyes, lids rolled as windowshades, on the Spam. The grudge-match symphony turns into Muzak. Ruddled irradiation. Chinooks' parental hushing. The bulbs of hindquarters of this nubile nymph Raphael with highest watts. The disguisability of his desire is difficult. The escapist product fireplug-formed Feamster is spellbound by to Hud is an anamorphic novelty, an unresolvable narrative, a prime example of a commercialistic function of the consumer/capitalist mechanism. And his dentition apathy is disconcerting. Picturesque panorama. Hud dreams of mashing the meat of Raphael's mammaries into purée. His hormonal system's pressure is on the cusp of blowing. His cortex rattles like marbles. The garbage disposal gurgles. Hud on the lunatic-fringe causes her stomach to get anxious. She imagines him being a slobbering onanistic sex-addict. His libido seeps as lachrymucus. He snuffles, shifts, smooshes his ballsack. She'd glanced, blessedly saw the obliquest part of the prurient act. He brazenly touches himself again, a revved-up chain-saw. She devours a mammoth bran muffin and dispatches a flat tonic. He gives her cases of the skitters and willies. Combustional hellish-heather celestial sphere. Building-blockish shack. Groomed foliage. Poorly-postured, meditative, mint-white nutmegs and curries. Piney environment evacuates ethyl. Inutile, cubular lanterns. She glimpses him, aghasted, finishes a candied yam and leaves hastily in a noiseless galopade with a segmented quality. He hurriedly goes after her. Unexpectedly, in her cubbyhole, this motherfucking cumbrous Don Ho dung beetle pops up clad in a tuxedo and warbles 'Tiny Bubbles' and strumming a deliquescing ukulele. Shampoo-and-conditioner hurricane erupts. She's gonna hurl, gotta jet. Her scream is like a storm.

Raphael wakes, has pings and pangs, bruises and cuts defacing her body, tied to the bedposts, eyes crusty, Toser's repellent wig covering her swollen face. Virginie, newborn-bawling violently, in a dress as a surgical gown, is scissoring the pantyhose binds. Toser's bald and sobbing and moaning and writhing on the floor in the disastrous hotel room bleeding from the neck where Virginie stabbed him. Virginie wraps Raphael, wrackingly weeping and still extremely groggy from the substances he had given her along with the alcohol, in a spare sheet. Sitcoms 'Happy Daze' and, subsequently, 'Three's Crummier,' are on the cable-equipped television. Euclidean grid of the sky, deepwater-glaucous, with cirri-lines (looking like razor-bladed cocaine) and star-coordinates. Ssshhh of spritz. Virginie explains to her daughter she, Raphael, was spotted earlier by classmates who were hanging out in the CVS parking lot, licking numbers and cellphone-yakking, her head, Raphael's, rolling as a blind person's, or lolling like a Raggedy Ann doll's, drunk and/or drugged, assisted by this parlor-tanned, rawboned dude out of a station wagon, and they contacted Virginie promptly. How she found her. Raphael's resurrection smacks of last hurrah. She nibbles on her broken nails as a movie-goer on popcorn, fusses with the covers, busted-up, rapined and ravaged. The unswallowable story, a tale told in rapid-fire, in the hair-dimension, tastes fine to her. Virginie is bewildered. They are 20-plus miles from home. 7acknowledges his grotesque, gollywoggy, sausage-legs and gnarly, trollesque, furry foots with horrid, curly, yellow nails beneath runny nylons. Virginie, gorgeous game-hen's kisser placid, swiftly squats and smothers him with his stupid piece, swears it is done, it is over. Weakened significantly from the wound he doesn't struggle much. He dies fairly quickly, undramatically. Raphael in the meantime blinks as an airport tower's tip. She cannot deal. Ruminatively she regards him. In an empty expanse the vacuous quiet is self-enclosed. She stands here, strongly, and there, in an absent-minded self-embrace, blank, detached in neural calm, her essence radiating into an edgeless void, a quiet nothingness, in the rather limitless chill of her own space, just so.

FINIS OPERIS.

Penile Axillae

ANGELIC (with VICTORIA'S SECRET-styled wings), aurulent Arianne, tongue-twister there, was a burly, blond tweeny beauty who smelled strangely of wet dog, peat moss, damp basement, and tree bark, had a cute pug-nose, tawny tan, and teeth so bright you could read by them, a slightly sexier, downscaled allosaurus in size. Hey, I ain't no asshat. Pud perhaps. Tool maybe. Well, you're giving me the stink-eye, mad-dogging me, pal. I'm not crossing my wires here. Where to begin. I will start. So, it's hard as hell to explain ... It is just a big-time weird physical deformity. Even the doctors think it's fucking freaky. Totally strange. Well, uh, they don't word it so street-ishly, but ya get my drift. I'm an anatomical original, buddy, like that Elephant Man dude. I suppose shit got all screwy in my ma's womb from the fiendish drinking and drugging. Didn't help my development much. I'll tell you. I was born thirty-plus years ago with a fully-functional penis and accompanying testes protruding from my left armpit. Them's the bitching breaks, guy. Um, I'm a living special-effect, a human sound-bite, baby! From what I understand I'm the only person on medical record to have this condition. Can I smoke? Lame. And they gave my most peculiar malformation a term: Penile Axilla. As in penis armpit. Neat, right? Yep. You betcha. Applying deodorant is an epical cunt. You gotta go around the unit. Dick and testicles. Sucks balls. Goddamn. I'm forced to wear these loose-fitting shirts usually for the frigging fat. Unbelievable. I've got a buff bod. Gotta hide it. Once in a while the thing slips outta the harness and tickles my tit. Which causes problems sure. Following me, captain? Not erect the prick is quite a mollusk of a member. With a hardon it's a pulsing goshdarn python. David below and Goliath above. Swear to Jesus. I cannot piss out of it but I can indeed fuck with it. Sometimes I get a double boing. Christ, I'm sensitive, though, ashamed. About the situation. Pain in the gonads, comrade. I guess I am a circus act in waiting, however, with the somatic irregularity I suppose I get more can than Campbell's. True. More pussy than like tampons. No lie. Procise here doesn't fib one damn bit. I'm aware too I'm talking like I'm getting paid by the syllable. After a cup of coffee I turn into an R-rated shock-jock. Usually my self-esteem is sorta in the sewer, only when caffeinated, or drunk, which was damn really often before my incarceration in this fine facility, I could be kinda cocky. I got more breasts than a mammogram machine. Once, in a seedy bar, cocked out of my brain, there was a blue-moon time when I took the sluggy sucker out of its holster to let people gawk and groan and stuff. Hilarious, trust me, chum. I stroked the rigid shaft, as if it was a little pet. Several, erm, more than a few ladies ran for the exit like the joint was on fire. Thought it was wicked gross. Can't say I blamed them. I face facts - the dink is disgusting. Pulling a crazy stunt like that wasn't sharp of me. Can I plead guilty for false imprisonment? Haha! Singular reason I'm doing the interview. During my checkups I'd gauge the nurses' expressions when seated on those tissue-papered tables in clinical offices embarrassed to a near-death-experience level, seeing their professional faces evincing repulsion, countenances carrying a conspicuous toxic texture, if it means anything. Pardon my Earhartian flights of fancy ... I am realist, a miscreation. I'm self-pitying again. Spreading it on peanut butter-thick. I don't wanna bleed for ya. Spinning my wheels. What else I got's retrograde amnesia, sleep apnea ... I'm not chain-yanking ... Spastic dysphonia, microcheilia, taphephobia, chronic otalgia, tetism, ADHD, amusia, and lest I forget prosopagnosia ... Recently I've had rectal probing done by my not-nice-one-bit cell-mate who is conceivably and commonly referred to as Black Brutus, and this hasn't helped one iota in my anal no-violation healing process. And my undies are loose. I admit when I glance at my reflection in the mirror I recognize I'm not an ugly sonofabitzkie at all. Far from it. As long as the gastropodal prick is strapped in snug I'm fine. I might get more snatch than a gynecologist, more twat than Tucks, more racks than porn mags. This deal bites. I'm hosed. Self-sympathizing garbage. Lordy! I abundantly apologize. Compelled I am to confess Johnny-on-the-spot I have used the penial sausage to my advantage. Surprise. Shock-horror. Why I'm in the slammer speaking to a shrink. Oops. Psychiatrist. Sorry. Prosecution had a rough road to travel in the court to try and nail yours truly at trial, attempting to convince the jury without a reasonable doubt I used my thingie as a weapon of rape. Long haul. Last week I was told by my staggeringly expensive, smokinghot, tightassed, allangles,bombshelllawyerwith'CloseEncounters'-alien-long limbs, hands and feet, my case will make law textbooks. My name in print! Yahoo! At any rate, the judicial system reamed me. Get to it? No problem. Arianne was a brawny, free-spirited, hippy hippie-chick with howitzers if there ever was one, a once-in-while naturist, a modern-day flower-child. One lukewarm, awesomely autumnal evening I'd met her in the dairy department at a garden-variety grocery store and I invited her over and we pounded down beers like no frickin' tomorrow at my pit-place. I thought she was a honey from heaven and in the same ballpark as supermodels. On par with 'em. A heavier version. She informed me she had hidden tats, nipple-rings, genitalial-studs and other miscellaneous body-piercing paraphernalia. Didn't matter much. She dispensed info she was ripped at her cavalier soon-to-be-ex-boyfriend because she lost across-the-board an argument concerning ABV of a certain beverage and requested a rematch on account of she deserved a shot at the title and was rejected outright and as a result she said to him he should mosey on and leave like a minute ago 'cause he wasn't motivated for a nother bout of verbal fisticuffs and she wanted to get laid by someone else's schlong and in addition mentioned her mood swings as a possible catalyst for the inevitable breakup and also their relationship was not rich and rewarding in any way and I was a willing participant to help her out in this David Copperfield-tricky matter, conveyed by my sycophantic spiel. Nutcakes. She was supposedly a switch-hitter. Who cared? We were both Stalingrad-bombed, smelt of breweries. I wanted to pitch to her, at the plate. We were close-only-not-touching on the zillion-spring sofa. My seedy eyes bugged out of their sockets like a night-sky-scoper's in Roswell, NM., rubbernecking the birdcage of her ribs and my dual dongs spring-boarded on the upswing of erectility and I was marathon-runnerly respiring and my conscience thank goodness was unaccounted for and I was praying for a miracle of hormonal hijinks to happen pronto. I weighed my options. Risk vs. reward in a WWE-ish wrestling match of uncertainty. I hoped my number was picked. Pluses were pitted against minuses in a cage match. Everything was happening fast and slow simultaneously, like when your car is gonna crash into an oncoming 18-wheeler truck which is unfortunately in the wrong lane. Yours. There I was, busting a move on this big babe with an IQ of a notch under 55 at happy hour, perspiration spurting from my every pore as geysers, and I was gone, man. Poof. Honest injun, I scored as frequently as Dennis Rodman. On the court. To suggest I bothered women is comparable to calling a killer whale in your tub when you wanna bathe a minor irritant. I was cooler than Green Bay's Lambeau Field's frozen tundra in January. I wanted to bend her over, break her will, make her mine, bust her like a branch. I was careful, used a psychological prophylactic, didn't want to impregnate her mind with my lecherous ideas. I wasn't going to torpedo my efforts. Bee-buzzed, I was on an oral roll. She could be witheringly sarcastic and glacially cold and corrosively snide and catatonically distant. I felt as a lump of chewing gum, stuck under a desk, out of the way, where I wouldn't wind up on the sole of her sneaker. I was the Invisible Man. She was Stepford Wife-frigid. I scooped more chicks than Austin Powers. Missed more bunnies than a blind hunter. I strived to resist that siren's song, held onto my boat for dear life. Yet I wanted this snookie to nibble on my line. She abruptly announced she wanted to eat out. I regarded such unexceptional establishments like Taco Bell as a prime place for fine dining. My passion for her was ... Progressive. She filled me in on her 'Eight Is Enough'-cultish twinkle-toothed family. This irrelevant info would def end up in my memory safe-deposit box. We were involved in a Picasso-abstract, nip 'n' tuck convo, atmosphere like high-voltage. I was intoxicatedly smart-alecky, a hipper-than-thou, sharp-tongued, irony-oozing dirtbag. My dynamic duo: throbbing dowsing rods and I was literally navel-gazing and cruising for a bruising. We were cat-and-mousing it. She was buying what I was selling. My jokes occasionally fell wafer-flat. I shot for her moon. She suddenly inebriatedly interjected she was feeling abandoned and alone on a deserted island in life and copiously crying, whereupon I took the necessary nautical navigational action to reach and outright rescue her, butterflying and backstroking ... Ever have intercourse and get blown at the same time? Aim high, shoot low. Fucked and fellated. Hell. She evaluated a Popsicle stick and wrapper ensemble on the coffee-table, sat full lotus, breathing having the sonance of a book's pages turning, shrugging like she was doing barbell-shrugs at a gym, mouth a batshit moth, broad belly soaked as an overused bathmat. Moon bulged herniatically, had this Day-Glo red. Zephyrean eddies. Foody aromas. Rain crackled not unlike leaves underfoot. Hills recalled papal hats. A true twilight insinuated itself before plowing as a pig's snout into a trough. Her breasts were missiles in the silos of her bra-cups prepared to launch, tits she wanted to bring to bear, or bare, my blinders beelining upon them, her thick thighs as loofa sponges. Automobiles' horns blasted. Her stomach's rumbling sounded thelassic. She made a chore out of preening the brambly thicket of her mane. And I could only imagine her yin-yang's probably-flax boscage. We were warmupping already. Setting the mood here. Atmosphere's wicked essential. I knew my sub knock-knock jokes were place-holders for real jokes. Then out of the blue she had asked prior what I had up my sleeve and I answered in this Bullwinkle-ish voice, "Presto!" Every bean's been spilled.

I'M DONE.

We Are Me

In the aftermath of an apocalyptical bash with its American armies of avid partiers drinking and drugging and accompanying vocalic white-noise, boom of bass and throb of treble, people moving like in a silent movie or some such shit, pink-cheeked and plastered, Staley Sweezy, with a pubertal, beaky, gawky, gooney look to her and gladiatorial gait and lest we forget cute-camel visage, stringy strands flaxen and yarnish, archer-squinting from sobbing, psychic being unwell, feeling as melting butter in the perishingly searing heat, anger deepening like an ocean's water and clad in an onyx leotard that smacks of dominatrix costume, slams the bedroom door of the musty crow's nest attic belonging to her igloo-shaped, doom-gray home, the house a horror-show, beside a level-headed, apple-red garage, a puce volleyball centered along with beach-um-brella and scooter behind a bumper-stickered jalopy in the driveway sporadically motor-oil-puddled and needing paving, in these slummy suburbs, the sullen sun an aura-lithiated bulb in a low, limpid sky. Drapes flap as flags. Plants accrete pollen. Chain-link fence quivers and trills in mewing winds. Hangman's noose of a rope round her chicken-neck. Bannery boyband posters Scotch-taped to the shabby wainscot. There was a barn-raising brouhaha in the crazed kitchen involving her mother, the wraithy, strawberry blond professional designated-driver for intoxicatedly incapacitated people who see a single street as double, Swann, and step-father, Orphey Bundage, a moody asshole of an asbestos miner, their verbalizations issued in terms of trajection. Staley had picked up the pace, sedulously sewing, tolerant. He, a musclebound madman, resembled an Eskimoid mannequinish fella, arms out cruciform during the argument, expression incongruously pleasant, strides strangely dancerly, making, adamantly, an antifashion statement, considering the Adidas sweats and Nike hightops age-inappropriate, and wearing a knee-brace for his notoriously and chronically dicky knee, acting like his life was dead, a citizen of the world historically tardy to each event and who cannot hold his tongue. Guns to him are toys. Crohn's Disease doesn't help one bit with his overall odiousness. Staley could never warm to him. So she stays cold. He's a hapless dipstick, toy-soldier stepping, gnat-annoying. His paraboloid dome covered by a McCartney-mop, hairline certainly recessing. He always gazes at her as if he could sure eat her for lunch. She'd stare at him as though he was the subject of an experiment she was conducting. What's

darn weird is he could occasionally offer these myste-
riously touching gestures, emotionally kind, behind the
scenes at least, buddies certainly not present, behaving
upbeat and lighthearted, which clashed with his generally cantankerous personality. He's profoundly perverse.
And his jargony bullcrap drives her bats. For her,
hearing the intense quarrel, it was a case of eavesdrop-
ping tourism, whereupon she plunged headlong into
the familial fallout. They spent huge amounts of energy
fighting. Thence the adolescent grownups coupled. The
slap-happy sex, with its grunts and groans, cork-popping
pocks and thwocks and sneak-squeaks, sounded not
unlike a lunatical, lusty tennis match, with really aggressive rapid-fire serves and volleys. She wanted them to
cut it out. During the intercourse she heard the news:
she, Staley, is a clone. Born in a beaker, a damn lab. Big
picture taken in here. She had an out-of-mind experience, occupying a pregnable space of the parlor. Makes
sense - Kidsy Chavis, a scrawny law-enforcement officer
(at the bottom of the totem pole), a Gomer Pylean
deputy, or Enos-esque, for a 'Dukes of Hazzard'-ian
agency, who by the way has a serious crush on Staley,
arresting the wonky, balding, baby-whale-ish Zerblis
Ladipo, a renowned scientist, who stuck out as a sore
thumb amongst the younger crowd earlier. Explains
everything. Orphey never could hold his tongue. He and
Swann battled over a credit-card bill. Spat left carnage.
Roman and lion. He called her a clueless cunt and she
returned he was a lowlife cocksucker. Staley noticed for
the first time he had a pair of little-gal-small-and-soft
hands. Warning signs about this brusque and humorless

guy were put up akin to Post-It notes from the get-go. Staley dreads a great deal the purgatorial destiny of the conflict awaiting her, thinking either she's gonna clean their clocks or the other way around. Her will nosedives and drowns. The fart of confidence is vac-sucked out of her. Freaky trees have the D.T.-shakes, bluejays, tweets sounding as athletic whistles, ratcheted out of them by a rodentine animal. Her verve with velocity has veered off-course. The seniorest highschooler in her cliquey inner circle (presently the college-studenty (apparel and attitude) bunch, at one time the brainwashy, cultish tribe thick as thieves, from blue-collar, downscale backgrounds, is on hiatus due to personality conflicts), her spandexed self in enforced solitude. She is a mediocre student, however, her academic scores aren't embarrassing. College, looming like the frigging Death Star, is a reality-avoidance topic. She surveys herself in the Alice-mirror. She is a cruel juvenescent caricature of an El Greco, she thinks. With all due respect she's right. Zephyrous stage-whispers. Sun winks in cloudlets as a smoke-alarm's red light. Lonely vista. Lavender refulgence. Crew-cut hill. Illumination's lurider. Her falcate fingers and toes. The netherworld neighborhood's environment's gauzily enshrouded by fog.

THE PRECIP VISUALLY CORRESPONDS to staticky, wiggly stripes on a TV screen from a VCR's iffy tracking. Chemically-slash-Crayonish crepuscular dusk oozes as a cat, lambency an autumnal orange, making everyone present, Staley, staid and sober, and Swann and Orphey, not so much, secretly nostalgic for the silentiously deadly dawn. Crescentic clipped nails and fetal butts in an ashtray on the antique coffee-table along with tenpinned beerbottles. Tension hangs in the heavy oxygen like humidity. A stain on the carpet describes a muttonchop. Time passes with sharp edges. A particularly nasty scene following the Wendy's megameal takeout. A heart-attack-serious meeting. Lots of psychological and physical rag-dolling. Caboose on tracks with loud clang and clank. Crickets sound as items hitting an electrified fence. Moon's a nystagmic eye rolled up in the socket of celestial sphere in its elongated ebony, possessing the darkness of an interstatish blacktop. 'The Brawl Guy' with Lee Majors is on the boob tube. Artsy high-contrasty chiaroscuro. Orgy of emotions occurring. A septuagenaric, always-yawning, craggy and corpulent neighbor's nonstop shrilly operatic singing frays the nerves. Staley, discipline in remaining completely restrained unbelievable, wonders whether they'll overstep parental bounds, the parameters rather pushable, or will the two simply keep their own counsel? Swann, a ravaged revenant, absolutely academically impoverished, is quite a clumsy contortionist on the dingy duvet, contained in her customary summery ensemble of halter top and Daisy Dukes. Her navel reminds you of a beer-can's pull-outable pop-tab, stretch-marked belly sagging as a hammock, drooping tits, with their fabric-poking, cornucopic-conoid nipples, like summer squash, chops bunny-pink, chiclets as Yahtzee-dice. And her pterodactyloid feet, soles the shade of red-skinned peanuts, have seen better days indeed, ostensibly Atomic-Bombed. Her lips are pursed, nostrils flared, peepers narrowed, and those rouged wrists would peg her as a falconer, only it is really because of being tied up. Her messed-up make-up on her ruined rictus (complexion waxy from smoke from her beloved Benson & Hedges; she is a hard-core nicotine-addict) is a spatterpainting. She reeks of cabbage. Her hourglass physique. She has on a broadcaster-headsetiferous band on to dam her bangs. Orphey starts pounding down foamers and Swann commences cursing. Plastic-mesh laundry-baskets substitute as recycle tubs. The place is a veritable disaster area, a virtual household debacle, a legitimate dump, and she has long since given up on endeavoring to keep the joint clean. She'd bet her bottom dollar evil elves break-and-enter and destroy it after her fiendish housekeeping. Behemoth bus. Synaptic lightning in the temporal lobes of the heavens. Stars sparkle like repeatedly flicked spent lighters. Her tacky pumps ride shotgun beside his toe-tagged-angled, wan loafers. Her formerly flowing patience is at its ebb. She trembles as if she has Parkinsonian tremors. Starboard-listing, knobby-elbowed, wheeze-choking, catcher-crouching, emphysemic, spectral Swann alternately sucks oxygen from its tank and puffs as a chimney on a cancer-stick, which is disturbing to behold by anybody's standards. Orphey has heretofore made a successful transition from tobacco to weed. Drizzle like powdery ground glass. Root-white effulgence. Mosquitoes arationally zip. Pigeons in the park disperse, are airborne as though barmy bats. A couple tow trucks with phone #s and catchy noms de guerre flashily scribbled on the doors parallel park, create a megatonnage of racket in the process. The city is way like nowhere else on planet Earth. Robins fly as balloons undone. Steel-mill sparkles of lit showers. Tactical-artillery roaches deployed. Orphey the yutz futzes with his phone, swiping and swearing. He is mentally sluggish, irrepressible and immature. The schmuck has the calming powers of a prisoner assailant. He puts a plug of chew into the raveling maw of his oral cavity. She accepts he's a groove in the LP record of her life. Her existence is a belt with a missed loop. She calls him an icky wacko, a smug turd, and he replies she's a lethal, unit-vicing bitch from hell, acts like he's emitting something sage. Happiness-wise, he is her Achilles' heel. Eyebrowless and runny-nosed he strip-mines a can of tuna. She refuses to respond. Swann interjects with a frosty cool your collective jets remark, harried-and-narcotized-appearing, her tone the nerve-racked, stress-heightened one, blackly blasted on brew. Staley gives her the best wiseacre Whatever shoulder-shrug. Both women neck-craningly glance at him, as if for an independent ruling, despite the damaging implications. Staley gives him a score-settling, chilled-revenge glare. To be able to disassociate herself from them ... Protracted cussing and complaining. Staley, tingles on her scalp insectival pincer-bites, to distract herself, imagines Kidsy, F Troop's Finest, with his squashed and smeared countenance, smushed skull, and smunched body, his wiring wrong, the dude not wrapped tight at all, who enjoys swallowing sedatives with barleywine and suspiciously freebases solo (never

ever on the job), and a Frankie Avalon fan, looking like a younger version of Don Knotts if vehicularly assaulted in a horrible auto accident, who drives a beige dune buggy. Once he confided in her that he often felt as though a scab on the skin of the universe and should be peeled off at some point down the road. Orphey stonefaced announces he's gotta piss like a racehorse and his stomach's acidy and he's gonna bake cookies and his dick's a leaking spigot. He is a bur under Staley's saddle. His whining peters out. With her he feels like a lowbrow knucklehead in the presence of a princess. Unbeknownst to her he talismanically carries a photo in his faux leather wallet her realer dad (biological paterfamilias, rabidly religious, retarded from massive quantities of opiates and alky, practically catatonic, anatomically atrophied, so horridly transformed he's a block of somatic cheese, a nightmarish submammalian fellow, progressively protozoan, dyed-tawny tresses overmoussed, stagnant, psychotic-seeming, with a permanent facial expression of reverent revulsion, articulate as a mud-bug, with a wardrobe mainly consisting of bathrobes, johnnies and slippers, in his malformed malleability stuck in a collapsible wheelchair, his private reserved room's walls collaged in thumbtacked pictures of Gandhi and Oprah, in this brooding nursing home in a nother county) took several years ago where she is pretend-provocatively posed in a skimpy maroon bikini, undressed to impress, on a verdant riverbank. His libidinous arrow points at her. She now shuts her map, sits and slouches on the spring-shot, mustard-hued sofa, apprehension so utter she yens to scram. She, feeling ganged up on, a scapegoat in a puppet state, decides to demonstratively, angrily kick a cream-colored upholstered chair, fed up. She's an angelic, acneous-pitted living lightbeam with a conchoid honker and seashell ears, optically comparable to an aqueous creature. She just needs the webbed hands, foots. She says Orphey is a parlor-tanned, tail-chasing, spin-doctory, cut-rate coke-dealer with the strut of a swaggery MP. From the itsy-bitsy bathroom, donning non-unique, technicolor, polyesterish clothes, he declares, in an eerily soothing grandparentish voice, his feces are a Black Mass, his pee barf-white. He is an infamous throne-splatterer. Jaysus! She's in a cage and he's the bars. She moves to the acrylic couch. Swann, whacked-out, slipping on prostie-stockings, and subsequently doffing them, existing in her own substance-induced galaxy, mien a death-mask, snaps, with a chain-smoker's froggy croak, she's got, Staley does, a geologic amount of statuesque nads for talking such smack, full of piss and vinegar. Staley snorts he's a boozing, ballsy bastard, an amoeba with a pulse, and chills in a trice. The sun is a yellow smiley-face circle without the smiling face. Checkerboard flooring. They discuss in detail this dweeby Zerblis guy getting busted and hauled away in the middle of the undeniably hopping shindig like he was a streaker at a sporting event, screaming he lost his Yes-Doze pills, how Kidsy initially flashed his shield as if he was starring in a 'Dragnet' knockoff. Major-league altercation before Swann steps up to the plate to inform her she gave birth to herself. Yes. True. See, years ago Swann got extremely sick and was in the hospital for months, with suppurating sores, severely heaving and writhing not unlike a tired (in a bad way) dog, diagnosed with a strain of virus that was a close relative of H.I.V., Progerius, which was then pretty much determined to be incurable, her integument scrambled eggs-puffy and violently twilight-purple. With cosmetics she was a truly scary clown. She had just weeks to live. Zerblis, a maverick director of a eugenics company with cloak-and-dagger operations, with a Saluki's physiognomy, hands and feet as shoeboxes, and a lecture-level inflection, intervened and made her an offer she wouldn't refuse. As per her request she was impregnated with an embryo with her DNA (there was no chance whatsoever of the disease being hereditary), but, lo and behold, a cure was found and Swann, pregnant, ultimately delivered Staley and raised, essentially, herself. To Zerblis it was taking advantage of nature, not violating it. Staley, weeping, rises and races, grabbing the car keys on the counter. In the junky Kia she burns rubber, the hideous hoosegow her destination. An institutional lightbulb flickers on above her head and becomes strobically fluttery. She must confront Zerblis, who is directly responsible for the mess. She heads right for it in a hurry, a huff.

AT THE HEINOUS CLINK, KIDSY, in his Mountiesque uni, the only one working, has desk duty, attempting to discern exactly what shade of brown pigment the ceiling and floor actually share if you put a pistol to his temple to make him try, when Staley arrives. Burnt sienna? Terra cotta? His boredom is brutal. A shiny ant is caught in a cobweb in the corner. AC is broken and it's wicked muggy. She finds out Zerblis posted bail and was released. In this town news travels Flash-fast, the grape vine stretches far and wide, and Zerblis got many different death threats, attributed to his sci-fi exploits. For his safety Kidsy took the initiative and him to a shed out in the woods on his folks' property to hide out for a while. Within an hour Kidsy is relieved and he takes her to Zerblis in his police cruiser, which is cool because he loves her company. Rainbow's 'Since You've Been Gone' plays on the radio's classic rock station. He's brain-locked, cleft-chinned, fish-lipped, HD-pied, a burned-out, withered husk, weak-kneed, and salivaless, rail-thin body sisboombaing, being with this transhumanly terrific, attractive and unattainable teenager, her extra-natural peach-tan perfect, so alien-avianly adorable he wouldn't be the least bit surprised to learn she has been shunned by her insanely envious fellow pupils, exiled for a scholastic eternity. He realizes under normal circumstances she wouldn't urinate on him if he were on fire on the sidewalk, he wouldn't have a snowball's chance, and he appreciates the opportunity of them tagging together. He feels decapitated and truncated, left a somatic stump, his high-caliber infatuation vascular-grade, schoolboy-smitten, canted as an umpire, wayward in a paralytic cognitive nexus. Her resonant, breathy, monovocal modulation. She stinks of rotting pear and graham cracker. Her long flipflopped feet smell of sugary sweet char. This is a-happening! Ruby-amber luminosity. Amniotic humectation. Branches dope-slap gutters in hot rushes of gusts, make ominous, ossein-cracking sounds. Hesitant raindrops are hitting and starring the Tootsie-Roll-tincted yards. Sock-shaped, nickel-silver cirrus coast ceremoniously. Rainwater merges on the oogly pavement, composes the cement. Leaves fall, rotate like propellers on beanies. She says the decent weather is more meteorological loan than sustainable present and he smirks in agreement. She's fed up with the daily shit-storm. Rugby-scrum of crows picking at a squirrel that was run over in the road trian-gulate their feeding in uncannily choreographed chaos. Cartilaginous wads of cumulus. Once there, out in the blighted bowels of the boonies, she convinces Kidsy to take a hike and/or fly a kite and he is sent packing. Leave. Swelter is very intense. Breezes bring relief. A weatherstained, aluminum trailer near generous woods. Birds ring more than chirp and soar in wobbled circles. Zerblis thoroughly explains the entire procedure, glancing askance at the clefs of her narrow ankles, from start to finish, clone creation and artificial insemination, all that wild jazz, to her. He has a gently demeanor, porpoise-teeth, and fat face stippled with rash-pimples, most notably on his wattled chin, derma vaguely dino-saurian, slack, strand-intensive, oleaginous hair over a neural-grey yarmulke of scalp, hanging thinly lank in a ladylike filamental flap, and these leather patches on his professorial blazer's elbows, a shy savant with a lurchy lush's lean-to amble, pitching himself forward; or a canter as a leashed pet. He reminds one of a squat shot-putter who let himself go, a jumbo jockey, with rims like those X-Ray Specs you mail-order from comic-books. Last evening he got trashed almost into a cerebral hemorrhage. He's ensconced in a patio-chair. Windowshades are lazylids of a person. Scintillation's cords of sinew. Sky blank of clouds. Staley impulsively, inexplicably, makes a pass at him, confesses she wishes to rub him raw, and he immediately rejects her, admits he's gay. Devastated, bum repelled, she instantly hastens to leave. When Kidsy hears about what went down, Staley coming onto Zerblis, from the man himself, over Denny's, Kidsy, a drama queen to the nth degree, pathologically insecure, ends up committing suicide. You'll be spared the specifics, but suffice it to say he napalmed his noodle in the oven, with the help of roofing insulation material, cooking at a numerically high number as a Thanksgiving turducken. Perhaps the details are important: The way he had the complicatedly rigged contraption (inescapable) his poor scallycapped coconut, in total turkeyfication, was undislodgeable. One can imagine his noggin inflating humongously, cranium squeaking like a squeegee, skull Amityville-stairs-creaking, brain blooming behind his High-Def blinkers, belfry an airy dirigible floating and exploding as a star in the Kenmore Orion, sparks not unlike from a braking train. He imbibed joe and ingested doughnuts beforehand. Things get more gross. And nuts. At the Sweezy residence Staley discovers Swann has passed out upstairs, practically in a narcoleptic coma from Old Ruffian, so comatose she barely has vital signs, with that sourpuss expression as she sleeps, and Orphey, not so much in her doghouse as the gulag, dressed in a 'Great Minds Drink Alike' tee and boxers, is watching 'Har to Har' starring Robert Wagner on cable in the storm-cellar of a basement, mesmerized, polishing his fingerprinty skeet rifle (costing mucho $), the fucker munching on buttered popcorn and guzzling Australian ale, his gut a deflated bladder, 1970s-news-anchor-toupee-hairdo combed and/or brushed maybe with maniacal verve. Spuds supper on the cafeterian dinnertable. She's livid and upset, for Kidsy has killed himself and Zerblis rebuffed her, booted her bottom, wants to hurt him, Zerblis, where it matters, her shouting auditorily reminiscent of sealish barking. Drencher's plucked strings of an imperceptible instrument. Grainy celluloid spate. Clouds unfold as video's time-lapsing carnations. She is exquisite and invokes an image of a hominal ornithoid. The wienie says he wishes to oink her and she returns he can pork her in any orifice of his choosing, only if he brings her the penis of Zerblis. A prime example of jail-bait carrot-dangling - you've got to pay the price for a piece. A swallowable pill for him, yet it is a bizarre, disgusting and schizoid request. He is bombed and lecherous and horny enough to pull it off. Should he take the deal and drop what he's doing like a rock and dash off? Is it possible this is a trap she is setting, and is he the booby traipsing into it? Holy mackerel, does he have the prerequisite spine for murder? His piratical earring glistens. Schlepping robotically to the portable fridge. Should he forsake common sense? Chrissakes, is he flummoxed! He assesses her with a palsied, hazy suspicion, like a gorilla in the jungle given a shaving kit by some lawyerly bozo on safari. She's a priceless pearl, a hitherto missing piece in his personal jigsaw. He's an organism unblinded by her brilliancy. His keister like a sack of meal, a cut of beef usually reserved for the butcher's hook. Her role is to maintain order. He has a hypertensive blush and goofy, lobotomized moue, paces around her as if he's a predator and she's the prey, glimpses her taut heinie, tight stomach. She ponders the extent of his persuadability, acknowledges it's disorienting and deranged. Situation is dicey. The identical inducements of her hard-boiled-egg-breasts and flat-buttock transactions and precise weight-transfers when she treads are more than enough motivation. He strategizes a podiatric feeling-out process, endures the high-impact Rockette-kicking of his heart in his chest. He fondles her bony hips. Her orgasmic intonation has the quality of being used in a soundproof studio. Her cardiac-stopping, eye-popping, squooshy tummy, divine, tight rump-cheeks vying for prominence. He schemes on the baptismal seduction of her. He will, assuredly, get the ball rolling. Molesting her vagina. No problem on that front. Would she be a killjoy? To him she is an Orphey-resistant odd duck who has the elderly's selective hearing and heroinely lissome proportions. She's a gangling goddess. He has a rapacious fetish for lithe girls. In the dentition-recliner he ritualistically chews Kodiak and spits into a janitorial-bucket-sized styrofoam cup. She is stricken with the soaking sweats when he mentions her rodent-nosed rectum, it's time to take the training wheels off, sexually speaking. She gobbles Planters and glugs Bud beer, has to evacuate. Remote control's Verizon-emblazoned and answering-machine large. His chortles sound as champagne corks, flatus like a tuba, cramming artery-unfriendly fries and clams, has a hypnotized aspect. He cannot resist the temptation of the fatal fruit. Fireflies' razzle-dazzle of circular flourish. Nacreous mist. Hail has the sonancy of Jiffy Pop popping in a microwave. Her arms are chicken-winged, poised in a diver's stance, when he tries to hug her, his arms out straight like imitating the blind. She allows this, erecting a defensive anatomic fortification, and pulls back when he puts her extraterrestrial's hands on his gluteal Valentine, kept in vile cottony material, and the action gets her chuffing and laterally bursting and yearning to sprint, dredging an excuse she has to blast over to Brooks Pharmacy for cough syrup. He has crossed the line. She peels his from hers as though tongues from metal in Arctic temps. He is cruising for an incarceration bruising. He attempts to embrace her and she skitters sideways as a crab. His existence til this point is the equivalent of perpetually plunging out of an airplane and Staley is his parachute to save his sorry candyass. Her tootsie-wootsies recollective of defib paddles. The firmament, once iron, is currently falcon-blackish. Goopy precipitation. Column of militaristic gleaming cockroaches in the grim pantry. Glow flies coruscate the sultry air, wave not unlike matches being put out. The vault is violaceously vivider. Scab-tinctured fakewood walls. Membrane-panes lashed benignly by onionlight. She writes out directions to the shack where

Zerblis is holed up on a Dunkin' napkin and Orphey bounces. Bloodied and disheveled, he returns hours later and presents the sanguineous, molluskan prick of Zerblis to Staley in a Ziploc bag. The castration took mere minutes. He brags he kicked ass and took names. It is tomb-quiet until he adds Zerblis resembled a mortified child, although thoroughly, brilliantly bald and baggily bodied, wet his pajamas when he finished carving him as an Easter ham. She's queasy, bone-chilled, a dead-ringer for the lean, wiggly subject in the Munch lithograph, gets a whiff of his underarms' ambient odor, looks at him like she's studying the teeny-weeny fine-print text of a manufacturer's speci-fications. He's a vulgate, steroidic Mr. Rogers-semblant jerkoff. His numero uno hobby is rathskeller fisti-cuffery and he's got a sergeantly authoritative-figure radiance about him. Like a dream he senselessly makes surrealistic sense somehow. His psychobabbly catch-phrasing riffing. As in a trance she takes the dink out and puts it in her pussy. Repulsed, insulted and infuri-ated, Orphey pulls out his blunt-barreled Glock 17 Wild West-drawingly from a cell-ish holster and shoots her in the throat. Swann abruptly materializes, discalceated, Rubensian figure and melon-knockers exhibited, wearing a tank top and scant panties, her adrenaline spiking, and stabs him twice in the back with a steak-knife. He nibbles on his pallid knuckles, bullet-hole eyes blinking at a radio-tower's rate, stag-gers, curtsies, whitens as a callus in Epsom-salt-water, his canine-whimpers with dimensions, sounding like pipes demanding plumbing, a hambone ladling it on, bug-eyed, mouth open as if for a root canal, his involuntary reaction leaving him seemingly conflicted, apparently dying with a knight's dignity. He appears as though he's a villainous character in 'The Six Million Dollar Man,' stumbling in slo-mo in the dank, forniciform room. He flops down spectacularly like a sack of flour, sprawled prone, makes distressed noises, larynx flattened-sonanced. Glossy beetles, unbidden and unexplainable, formiculate up and down the threshold's framework. Pin-drop silence. His death is seemingly unintended comic relief, proximal to the StairMaster. Crying, chin descending kneeward, Swann holds her probably dying daughter, ribcage feeling as a playpen, vascular organ a young 'un smacking its bars with a mallet (building or wrecking?), and describes the ordeal of the difficult pregnancy, including the morning vomiting, horrendous hemorrhoids, terrible hunching, woundedly bent, paling in pain from killer contractions, sinking into a hurting curl on the maple steps, in an unsparing heatwave, Staley scooped out of her womb by a stranger similar to ice-cream from a bin. Staley visualizes it, in a light like she's Artemesia, the Italian painter. Her falsetto flatulence crisp, rich and raunchy. They share a strong laugh. Tipsy from her libations she swaddles Staley in a Woolworth's plaid blanket. Orphey is definitely dispatched, blood with the rust tone of liquid excrement. Proof positive you can kill what is already dead. Swann has the urge to skedaddle ASAP with her daughter. She upchucks her breakfast and lunch which is remindful of afterbirth material, the redolence reelingly gawdawful, olfactorily overwhelming. Cloudlets in the presence of a litmus paper-blue empyrean. Lemon-and-lime slivers of sun and mount respectively. Gurgly, glottal sounds of the stream cascading into the sewers. Clouds not dissimilar to boat-wake water. Coruscation congregates. A rainbow is refracted in a sprinkler's plume, the squiggling spray of spritz a luminescent waterfall, variegated antennae, with an antiperspirant hissing soggifying a forest-green lawn. This diffracted spectrum is lovely. A hummingbird in the bright flowers is a flight acrobat, an avian artiste, the figure-eight motion of its wings key to its phenomenal ability to hover, thus staying still.

END.

Circus In The Sky

NOCTAMBULOUS FELLINI-FOLK. SUN'S A MASSIVE mouth silently screaming in a faceless firmament. On cardinal cloud-cliffs, in a horrid event horizon, is this Baroque, epical chapel, a rococo, churchy palace plucked from an obscure, fucked-up fairy-tale, with these blossoming, rainbow-colored fiery creepers climbing up the sides of volcanic brick towers akin to sooty industrial chimneys, alongside fire-escape scaffolding, incandescent curtains on wide, wild windows, a luminous, chimerical garden, variegated, blooming flame-bushes, their growth flourishing in blazing fashion, lava walkway, molten moat under a broken bridge of baby-bones, blackhole whirlpool, conflagrant waterfall cascading in a sluggardly slimy ooze over human-heinie rocks, the place like a Grotesk, gleaming, behemothic bunker, imbathed in ignited inferno-illumination, spreading as a conspicuous cancer (during the day; at night there's the illusion of radiant remission), with its paranormal (partial) possession of the amazing anatomical empyrean, a 'No Soliciting' sign, written in spidery scrawl, hanging on the gigantean metalline door, the osseous railing with intertwined visceral decorations fly-smothered. Here is Hades in Heaven, created by some inventive pyromaniac, a firebug fruitcake, an artistic arsonist in a febrile fit of insane inspiration. Burning buzzards screech and fly high. Insectival embers flit and hum. Lacteous light turns raindrops into Skittles. A (last) stand of Gordian Knotted, licorice Twizzlers-twisted trees lining an amorphous avenue. Vomitous vault. Sputum-soaker. The water-alarm shrieks. A jaundiced rubber ducky floats in a florid kiddie cesspool. Corpses of bicycles and scooters on a browned, barren field. Sewage-stream seeps. Rubble of ruins. Stunning force of the fulgor. Rocking-chair on a technicolor veranda. Silhouettes glissade like paper boats on a brook. Below the Purgatory Paradise, a miraculous city, a Shangri-L.A., BabyLondon.

A MEDUSAN MOON DRIFTS ON THE SURFACE of a scintillant, sickly sea of welkin, darkening as an unfathomable iris, from deep within, expands and contracts like a very large lung, and a planetary, prismatic procession of tattered tents glows as gigantesque birthday cakes and an astonishing, astronomical arcade established on uterine-hued cumuli-crags neon-nictates in phantoms of fog. This is the crazy candyland called the Circus in the Sky, a lit dream in the blackness of sleep, strange

slathered Fluffernutter sandwiched in between slices of
Wonder Bread. The joint's water under waves - active,
yet invisible. Porcupine-needle precip. In this limitless,
loony bin laboratory, testifying to weird medieval/futur-
istic experiments, on the third story of a magnificent,
bejeweled, glaucous mosque covered with Boschian pictures and networked in stutters of arterial chiaroscuro,
Slug, a cormous, Cab Calloway-voiced, acrome-
galic, albinal dwarf scientist with dandruff-intensive
Rasta-dreads, cross-hatched wrinkles, bat-pinched
countenance, veinal, vulpecular nose, villose nostrils,
Elvish-ish shaggy sideburns, bloodshot eyes rolling as
a slot-machine's cherries, and hayrick beard festooned
with pablum particles and rubber bands, clad in a snug
leather bondage suit and unbuckled Harley biker-boots,
his temper shorter than a Rottweiler's tail, leans forward,
a runty Faust, and surf-sighs, belt-strapped, contained
in a complex contraption that is a tentacle-booth connected to a titanium tendril of an octopus-semblant
carousel machine. His complicated, surreal science on
display. His blasting fart sounding not unlike the trum-
pet of doom. The clammy, crepuscular chamber has a
peeling, pasty ceiling with a big copper-and-brass bell
and sumptuous Caravaggean paintings of centaurs,
naiads, cherubs, cyclopes, angels, and dagger-stabbed
roses on it, supported by bent beams and deformed pillars with Michelangelo mathematics scribbled on them.
His minions, a phalanx of freaks, these abnormal acolytes, lurk predatorily, and are distorted in the muculent
magnifying glasses of his spectacles: the ample-arsed,
slack-shouldered, shrewy, bulbiform, doughy midget

wife, Minikins, flesh like dried soil, wearing kabuki makeup, kimono and Sears slippers, with vibratory quartziferous dentures, dirt-filled-duffelbag figure, ginger-dyed, roostery coiffure, she recalling a pallid Yoda in drag, and pungent with perfume; Pinhead, Nosferatuic, tendony, a galumphing gump garbed in an immaculate ivory clinical coat, purple velour shirt, green vinyl slacks and beige American Indian moccasins, spike-skulled, wretchedly wigged (made prolixly long), swan-necked (scrawny and fragile), celluloid-skinned, Kaplan-as-Kotter-mustached, and arthritically angular, having the muttonchops of an esteemed English lord, crocodilian mouth, and eagle-talons on flexuous fingers, flushed as if he lost the war of wits in his eminent element; Bunny, an achingly adorable, acneous, foam-white, gangling, bosomy, hippy teenaged girl, an eccentric temptress, a goofy, garrulous gamine with pestilential body-odor, dragon's breath (she doesn't bathe or brush), fat fanny, confection-inflection, a pair of pink felt rabbit ears on her pretty brunette head and wearing Dr. Seuss panties and athletic ankle-socks; Lyle the learned fetus, rheumy, gummatous and apparently composed of clay, mural'd with prison-ink (he actually served time in jail, incarcerated in a concrete cloudlet-clink, convicted for stashing contraband in his elephantine, Aframerican mom's womb), the standout being the 'I Heart Billy Mumy' tattoo, and a face like Wayland Flowers's Madame puppet (a waxen/putty/pimply version) with a deranged dental smile showing micaceous teeth and appareled in Victoria's Secret boyshorts and ordinary sandals, his mucilaginous umbilical cord quivering as a dowsing rod, and quite nervously, intonation comparable to Katharine Hepburn's if she were on a serious dose of quaaludes; Vindice an insomnious, aristocratic, intellectual, heliotrope-tinged intestine in a contraceptive cap and coiled yogic in spandex in a pickle jar filled with formalin, modulation Sylvester Stallone on Valium, getting around on a modified, motorized, psychedelic skateboard. They are quixotic Crusoes marooned on an incredible island in an ocean in its vastitude. There's a susurrous constellation of conversation, with star-spangling sentences, galactic grammar, the confab a quirky collage of refracting phrases, and sonances of beetle-bustling. Outside, glistening golden showers. Inside, outlandish Marshall-stack-sized stereo speakers unleash unusual Muzak adaptations of 'Annie' and, subsequently, 'Miss Saigon.' Spermatozoa sleet splats on grungy panes, sliding like snot. Stagnant air. Bunny sits in an olivaceous alligator-armchair as a zombie getting back into its grave, mango-stone nipples erect, salmon appendix scar on her flabby, sprawling stomach (reminiscent of puréed potatoes) looking like a heartbeat blip on a hospital's thingamajig, visible, butterflies in there, a lepidopteran lamenting, her poison ivy infection, not unlike water-balloons, bothering her, in proximity to a tungsten lamp. She's discalceated at this juncture. Viscoid humectation. A hominid fish, a scallop-eared Sturgeon Surgeon, dressed in an impeccably pressed Moroccan robe, putting on gooey goggles, a seraphical, aquatic doctor, works, meticulously, this outrageous blinkinglikemad, great gadget, his mutant colleagues spreading as a hemorrhaging pyre. Hail spermic, whisperous. Slug neighs and his cohorts whinny when an aluminum tray ejects from his flocculent, pendulous chest as if from a computer and the Sturgeon Surgeon uses forceps to remove a pounding heart from it, whereupon he holds it up rather cautiously, like an expensive item exhibited at an auction. The cardiac organ boomba doombas as a bass drum. Everyone studies it as though through a microscope, stiff as posts, until it stops beating. Gelatinous swelter. Griping mosquitos. Maniacally cawing crows.

"How long did it last?" Slug asks. His scrotally scrunched physiognomy, awful apocalyptic flatulence.

"Approximately five minutes," The Sturgeon Surgeon answers.

"An improvement at least!" Lyle says, sing-song-coughy, proud as a peacock, a Mexican jumping-bean, imbibing sugarcane soda and ingesting potato chips, sticky funicular lasso attempting to catch Vindice's container.

Slug stares at him like a bird unsure of whether or not to tolerate a squirrel on its bough, Lyle cringing. "You're as irritating as a wasp at a picnic." He grunts, winces in discomfort. "Goddamn neddy, you prick me as a thorn." The drencher is drumstickrimshotclickyclacky. Apoplectic winds yell epileptoidally. He glares at his sidekicks like a teacher at disruptive students in the classroom. His puerile grimace is comical.

"Sir, we're making strides," Pinhead, the second fiddle, with a kind of nectarean lisp, his tone as an MD questioning a patient where it hurts, and he speaks really slowly; a 45 played at 33. He shuffles flat-footedly.

"Hardly acceptable," Slug, scowling, his reply sort of visual, not audible, like it was meant to be seen, not heard. Sucking on his mitt (in excruciating agony) as a calf at mama cow's teat. His thoughts, together, are a window, articulations shattering glass. "There is jig to your jag. Why the fuck to these vascular organs shit the bed so darn quickly? Makes no sense." Mythological shapes of shadows on the commercial billboard wallpaper of the dome. Laminated mirror. Marijuana plants. Asthmatoid gusts. Lyle wrestles with his Stretch Armstrong, giving him a decent drubbing, and suddenly he poses and flexes as Hulk Hogan. Meanwhile, Vindice serpentoidally slinks out and slithers into a bell-jar brimming with formaldehyde, snorts and gargles, in the vicinity of wood-paneling and a bookshelf with rotting volumes, ashen crumbs and damaged doohickeys. He snake-sisses, gurgles.

"I am uncertain, although I might have a theory ..." The Sturgeon Surgeon responds.

"I'm listening." Slug moans, stitched by dryadic nurses in teddies, and groans, thoroughly bandaged. The procedure was evidently extremely painful. He gulps syrupy medicine out of a generic bottle and swallows a battery of tablets. A winking raven leers from its cage.

"Perhaps your system is resistant -"

"Meaning maybe it's my fault, you ganoid galoot? I'm tempted to turn you into caviar, or isinglass for that matter."

"I am merely guessing."

"I made you to conclude! I should gill-screw you and filet your inept keister and -"

"Sluggy!" Minikins snaps. "No tantrums!" Her feminine gesticulations.

"Bah!" And Slug, slumped, storms away, in anguish, throwing a hissy fit, hollering, "When I pass, the universe will be bedding bearing my bodily imprint! I'm a misinterpreted metaphor!" He doesn't notice Lyle flipping him off behind his back, thence micturating into his Evel Knievel chamber pot and manducating on strawberry Hubba Bubba bubblegum. Mangy jackals trot through the cobblestone courtyard and into a pumpkin patch. Children galore attired in kurta-jamas and clodhopper-shoes walk down the hothouse hall like they're on a pilgrimage to Mecca, having reached important points in their lives, cabals of cliques carrying umbrellas for protection against the pouring plaster and buzzing as bumblebees in summer, maneuvering around the stripped silver Mercedes-Benz inexplicably parked smack dab in the middle of the creamy, commodious corridor. The moon deflates as a punctured inner tube. Creatural claws of branches. Operatic orphans. Educated horses. Rain in the breezes passes for long Cher-hair being methodically combed. Severe monsoon. Resinous, stale oxygen. Telephonic ringing. Several rooks on the ledge.

BEAUTIFUL BRUNE IS A WHEAT-COMPLECTED, streetsmartslashtough Circe-enchantress with cynical, cerulean oculi practically popping on stalks, melanoid mane and baccate-mouth, an illogically gorgeous adolescent with this smoky, opaque vox and the poise of a visionary prophetess who issues like air filling a vacuum, her "afterlife" limbo (dysfunctional family) a bruise which never fades. She's in her favorite chameleon-clothes, changing colors depending on her ever-changing moods, magic woven into the fabulous fabric, metamorphosing material. Her best friends, partners-in-crime, are these juvenile, statuesque (by Phidias) sisters, slim, anemic, goth-chick mimes Anais and Aurelia. Drizzle scented as sandalwood shavings. Dusk descends.

Dawn ascends. Dust-motes in the luminescent lances are minuscular matches in muted melodies of mobility, orchestrated without a conductor. Purulent lambency suppurates through wholly peculiar Venetian blinds. The especially spacious and snazzy study has the fullness of a functional, mausolean den. Luxuriant Persian carpeting. Deliberately dated, abstract furniture … Flesh and bone … The elegant upholstery essential integument … It's a museumlike sanctum with its myriad avant-garde artifacts. Stillness seethes until Slug, slumbersome, stressed, pregnantly waddles in, drunkenly wobbles, with the lethargic pace of an elderly tortoise, trying to afford a modicum neatness to his dreadlocks and goatee, his cogitations rising like poisoned aqueous life in a lake. He struts as a chicken in the coop. His whips of words sting. Abrasional pouches under his lobster-peepers, probably because of cerebral exertion. He yawns like a lion, furrows on his brow a load of logs.

Accompanying him are Geeks, a gang of them, creepy, canted, gaunt grotesques with jerky gaits, gutturally babbling. Their prattle is a chorus of complaints in an untranslatable, curiously foreign dialect. Membranous atmosphere. Slug, the silly Satan, rips off this rude gaseous tweet, a non-lethal pewie, lights a schwag, and scarlets not unlike a waitress goosed by a patron. A disgusting stench of agriculture; artificial dung. A nasty follow-up (reverberating) raspberry, the stink horrendous. Pinhead, anticipating his boss's arrival, grandly gestures to a malevolent masculine genitalic Rube Goldberg thingamabob on the curvaceous desk situated on a Bengali rug. Slug, roach-clipping his reefer, feels as luminosity lured through cirrus, but remains smooth, like a stream over rocks. He is frustrated, as a vampire slurping blood from a victim and never being satisfied. With his expression he looks like a constipated person with conjunctivitis. He is a sob bereft of sound. He's a synapse of the brain of this uncanny community, linking stimulus and response, a nerve impulse transmitting control from the axon to the neuron, himself, to the dendrite of another, his (collective) cronies, causing the effect of everything. He is regarded as ruling with an iron fist in a comfy glove. The environment is on par with James Joyce's 'Finnegan's Wake', where the dead guy who won't die refuses to let the living live it up. Frowning, there are battlelines drawn on his forehead. Thunder rumbles. Levin's pulse-jaggedness on the monitor screen of sky. The aberrant apostles' respirations have the sonancy of bubbles pushing up in molasses and popping. They grumble and gabble.

Pinhead says, "I've interesting news." His incision-pies glitter like slantwise icicles.

Slug retorts, "You're as useful as a lantern in the daytime," fixing his gonads, "My pipsqueak Minikins was ready for enema-rastling." He belches.

"Please look into the crystal testicular balls," Pinhead, disregarding the insult, lingering as indigestion.

Dubiously Slug does, mumbles "Human animals," adjusting the pale penial lever, and he witnesses pedestrians spilling into labyrinthine troughs of streets of the Saint Petersburg-ish metropolis in mucoid mist, some moving like products on a conveyor belt, the view fuzzy in the pilose scrotum, his skepticism rising as the smell of herbs from tea, and he focuses on resplendent ragamuffin Brune, her beguiling riot of sheep's-wool curls (its part a path through a thicket), planate proboscis and plump-petal lips. Stealthily she squats, as a sniper; or like she's about to piss and/or crap on a lunarly cratered curb beside this Ford Mustang GT. Slug is stirred as a youth at Christmas, jolted, as if from electroshock therapy, cackle-crackling as though static, shivers locomoting on his spinal rail. Oh, he yearns to crawl on her like an inchworm on a pear, yens to be in her as a worm in an apple, lying on her like a revery on the mind ... "She's lovely, Pin, charming as a Baudelaire poem. Christ, she is exquisite. Glorious." He plunks on a vintage violet couch and sparks a cigar-sized joint, inspects it. "Lousy rolling job." He ventures into his own private Idaho, thanks to Puff the Magic Dragon. He burps.

"I have been surveilling her extensively."

"And you neglected to notify me?"

"I admit I was reluctant to inform you on account of the regrettable fact that you've endured many disappointments lately."

"Huh."

"Her data is off the charts."

"Hmmm."

"Rates off the Richter scale."

"Bring her to me immediately."

THE MEGALOPOLIS IS AN ADVANCED-ANTIQUATED, grimy-glistery Depression-era Coney Island in mushrooming miasma, or a Victorian Venice dreamt up by fantasist Jules Verne. Buildings could be mistaken for skyscraping tombstones. Moon alighted. Sappy the clown balances on a unicycle as a baboon in a vermilion vest juggles peaches. His blond go-go-dancer-goddess assistant blends in with the assembling audience. The crowd claps. A glabrous, ridiculously muscular strongman in a loincloth practices a radical, remarkable routine with a contortionist cutey with pert knockers and porcelain bowl-buttocks in an alley. A pack of tamed hyenas spectate on a carmine sofa. Zephyrean murmurs. Terrible downpour starts. Crimson vista mirrors a russety river. Preliminary sketches of savins, junipers and cedars encumbered by leafage engravings. Hawthorn hedges. Narrow, hideous and hellacious road with extraterrestrial Gates of Hell. Brune, in pathological peril, stubborn as a mule, in a plain striped dress, ratty plaid unlaced tennis sneakers, and a beret, is endeavoring to pop a cinereal car's ignition. Anais and Aurelia, in similar civvies, only in checkers, both all shine with no polish, bubbly as springs, with coltish grace, curtsey as in a parody of gastric distress on the trashy sidewalk with its Polyphemoid puddles. An alarm begins to wail in banshie dolor. Dogs bark, people shout, lights lightning-flash on.

"Hurry the heck up!" Anais mutters.

"The whole neighborhood's on to us!" Aurelia hisses.

Brune shushes them, feeling not unlike a bovine in a pasture pestered by flies, and totally applies herself to the task at hand, increasing the tempo, suppressing her scruples, on her tummy in the passenger seat, thick triathlete's thighs and taut ballerina's bum (covered in Bugs Bunny undies) exposed. "Knock it off! You two are distracting me!" And she croakily laughs, sounds as a male. "Tomorrow is Easter Sunday!" She huskily titters. The gas-guzzling vehicle roars. The gals pile in. Aurelia accidentally knees Brune in the groin region and Brune slaps her rump. Anais pinches Brune's posterior. They peel rubber, spinning out, skidding slightly, almost nicking a cobalt Jeep Wrangler, and speed off, Brune driving, obviously apprehensive at the wheel, the young ladies whooping it up, racing through the center of town, smoking pot and slamming whiskey. Cranked to deafening decibels on the radio is this psychotic jazz. Aurelia steers for a moment whilst Brune fervently French-kisses Anais, who is in the rear. The sportscar barrels through a busy intersection, recklessly burns round the rotary, bombs through the red-light district at the height of rush-hour, Brune and Anais still passionately making out, weaves in and out of gridlocked traffic, and eventually swirls out of control and crashes into a shallow ditch.

Vaginate flowers. Frost-feathered chlorophyll-grass. Penile trees. Lachrymose leaves. The Sagrada Familia violatively fingers a gilded stucco sky. Clouds cap an ancient frontier. Scummy pond. Lavender frogs on tobaccojuice lilypads with fulgent eyes. Hugeous Easter egg dirigibles, a couple tinfoil-wrapped. Topsy-turvy sanguiniferous river-bed. Nudie girly personages, Jock Sturges-esque, robustiously gallopade, move as waves, goggle with cruel curiosity and hum a Schumann song. The pulchritudinous tweens are alabastrine plants scattering their perceptible pollen of peals. Their ill-natured, malicious utterances are annoying, the kibitzing separated by the illusion of intervals. Acid rain. Brune feels half conscious and half unconscious, restrains her impulse to run, enraptured by the sights. Her breathing sounds like stones taken by the riptide and with a sepulchral resonance. Torrents of her locks in the inaudible draughts. Her intellect impaired. Upside-down striking phenomena. Row of languorous maples. Inconsolable seagulls. Butt-boulders touched improperly by digital branchlets. Fake flora and fauna swathed in scarves of smog. Images of storks. An au naturel female in a funny-bunny Halloween mask carefully approaches a wicker basket, stepping not unlike a boozer off a sidewalk after a binge; or, for that matter, someone awakening to awareness. Drafts are coarse-throat-clearing-sonanced. The naked woman peers in and beholds bald rabbits with papier-mâché Lee Van Cleef-frontages suffocating in writhing maggots. Brune cries, and it's out of sync, as bad film dubbing. It is her nightmare.

Brune's room in a ludicrously garish, unkempt house is Europeanly appealing, with an absolutely unique aesthetic. Numerous antiques. Blistered puppets and disheveled dolls make a most bizarre bacchanalian scenario on the sill. Popstar posters on the rubberized Day-Glo walls. The vertebral rusted radiator is a platform for more toys and trinkets. Play-Doh animalian sculptures on an oak dresser. Nanga Parbats of toggery and K2s of footwear on the mahogany floor. In her Santa-sleigh bed she rouses. A group of Geeks glower at her. Abruptly they attack her, binding and gagging her. They drag her, fighting wickedly, onto the roof and toss her into a special sonde, throw their equipment in, hurdle on board, and off they float into the bluing yonder.

Brune comes to, in an ebullient ensemble consisting of a sinfully heavenly burgundy rayon chemise, coral lace tanga, and matching suede fluffy pumps, on a pagoda of pillows in a cell as limpid as a cadaver in a translucent bag in a creek, and chock full of wacky whatchamacallits. Alchemically Minikins materializes, says hello to her, gawks at her like a hungry tiger in captivity about to be fed a chunk of meat, the look, an envoy of the eyes, boring into her breasts as an executrix's tool; or like a poodle contemplating mounting a much bigger bitch. She imagines glimpsing the teen's bits and pieces, pictures them vividly, and is abyssally ashamed. The bellybutton and tits will suffice. For now. Brune's heart shrinks as a pupil when struck with a change of light; or like a snowbank in an unseasonably warm early spring. She feels embarrassed in the kinky, degrading outfit. Her vagaries course in the subconscious (earth), instead of the conscious (clouds), and ultimately drift as stuff in a flood. She is completely shaken, as if on a Daytona-level cab ride. Goosebumps sprout on her. It's as though she's a defiant daughter expecting a paternal reprimand. She experiences the sensation that she fell while skating and is sliding on the ice, at the mercy of momentum; a land critter finding itself in aquapura; a chalk outline at a homicide scene; a drawing without detail. Her brain is a body inoculating itself, injecting sensibility to protect against the virus of insensibility. She stretches, revealing for a second the perky rosette of her navel, she appearingly crucified, nails of effulgence in her palms and feet, and she rises, like a thermometer's mercury when it hottens. She adapts quickly to this state, as super-starched garments softening over a brief period of time. It is a moist evening in its mucosity. Refulgent stars. She fools herself into believing she has confidence, like a shot-putter thinking he's going to hurl a pebble in competition. Sweat leaks from her pores as from faulty taps. She can customarily see trouble coming, like peeking into a psychical telescope. She's suspended betwixt strengthened and weakened. Interiorly she is a doodle, exteriorly a portrait. Vermiform nauseation squirms into her gut. She is discalced at this point. The situation is as disquieting as turbulence on a hitherto frictionless plane flight. She's un/yielding; a sail met by a squall. Is she sleeping, experiencing this reality "as if" she is experiencing it? Belief and disbelief (fluid and fleeting) are vocalizations in a responsory. Fountain burbling. It's as though she's diving towards water, but the onrushing reflection is the actual her. Odd. She feels like she is a Xerox copy of herself somehow; moltenore gushing into a brandnew mold; a belt in loops, keeping up the pants; brewing to a boil. She's borne by the automatism usually associated with somnambulism. It is as if events are happening to her in lieu of her participating in them. Geeks' gobbledygook.

Minikins, heavily, humorously maquillaged, offers her a styrofoam cup of steamysomething. "Cocoa. Swiss Mess, my comely klepto. Delicious. Mmm ... Cute crook ... You're barefoot." Fixating on her villiform venter, its optical nombril. Fantasizing her insectile thumb arriving on Brune's clitoral calyx of her pudendal flower. Fastening scrutiny. "Gosh, those succulent tootsie-wootsies ..."

Reluctantly Brune takes it. "Thanks," sipping hesitantly. "It's like I'm a train on tracks, the signals failing to operate properly." A meaningful glance cast.

"Call me Mini for short."

"Not for long!"

Lyle in dungaree overalls and Birkenstocks skips rope with his umbilical cord, aggravating as a pet wanting desperately to please its master, pausing to see if its owner is watching. They are like members of a madcap theater troupe. "Bowel-bud!" A respite.

"You've kidnapped me," Brune says. "False imprisonment."

"Golly, judging by your illegal activities below, my farty floret -"

"Hey! Enough!" Brune interrupts Minikins, miffed already with the insulting nicknames; unwanted social intimacy without the necessary acquaintance period. And the fucking air-raid modulation! Swept-flour cumuli. Shooting stars are torched witches soaring on broomsticks at warpspeed.

"You deserve to be in the penitentiary," Minikins rejoins, making a tipsy teepee with her blanched paws. "With your unlawful shenanigans." She brushes Lyle off. "Sinning is spiritual. Spontaneous rebellious behavior is an echo of sincere emotion. Consequences are derived from circumstances. The soles of the feet of lies often stomp up the dust of truth. Your vices are our virtues. Here is a tranquil meadow where we cultivate our principles. There's disorder in our order: a pharmacy where pills, though accurately arranged, are not stickered; a directory beginning at Z and ending in A. The me transforms into we. The world down there is a business gone frigging bankrupt, the one up here a shop opening with the potential for profit."

Lyle prances. "Brune, cookie, you hit rock bottom and don't bust!"

Minikins sniggers. "And what a bottom you got!"

Brune is out on a limb and it's breaking. Her heart thumps as sneaks in a dryer. She attracts problems to herself not unlike staples to a magnet. This is a representation of reality. Before, she was color-blind, currently she is not. Here's a caricature of there. Being up here is a simile for being down there. In the past she was an annual bent by a gale. In the present she is a perennial lifted by nice weather. She's feeling like she has a correspondence with perception, perceiving an object at different angles at once; she has lost and found something simultaneously; she felt a sentiment when awake and nurtured it in slumber. It's as if a wedge between fact and fiction has fallen out. She has lived a life 'tween heartbeats. She is restless like a shark in an aquarium. This asylum's a sneeze - involuntarily convulsive. Her equilibrium is effectively engaging with its ambience. Episodes occurring without occurrences. Her gray matter dim as a negative. Here, she's a butterfly. There, she was a caterpillar. She is an ice queen gradually thawing. The candelabrum's lucent tongues. Brune clasps her stubbly, compact calves with their grids of varices. "I wanna lawyer."

"No, you don't." Minikins diligently picks her nares, nates.

"My destiny …"

"What is that? Fate? In the middle of a head and headache."

"A hollow concept."

"It's all so comprehendible, my devious darling."

Lyle capers. "Death has a higher octave than life."

Minikins shoos him away. "Your existence to this minute … Erm … Endless ennui."

Lyle not to be deterred, "You subsisted in squalor, honey."

BRUNE IS CLEVER WHEN IT COMES TO AVOIDING difficulties (instincts are life's luggage for the trip), only this is indeed a toughie. Chrissakes! She is numb and yet aware, as though anesthetically sedated and the effect is wearing off, the surface sensations dulled, the underneath ones sharp. Lyle and Vindice chat, verbalisations sounding like Charlie Brown adult articulations. "Gross! Those things are yucky!" Her beefy, unshaven legs sway like sturdy boughs monkeys just relinquished.

"Lyle is an effervescent, educated homunculus," Minikins says, ogling her, "Who, um, as Vindice, is a product of a botched cloning exploration," she explicates, and gambols with the fetus. Meat bambinos with ketchup-and-mustard diapers.

"Yeah!" Lyle bobs as an apple in a barrel. "I'm a pussy

connoisseur ... Minikins ... Uh ... Her quim is my crib. She climaxes ... The orgasm ..."

"Vindice communicates telepathically," Minikins explains, frolics with Lyle. "His utterances ... These enunciations, oft erudite and exultant, exude into your noggin as ideas."

"Hello, Brune," Vindice says, tone rebounding in her noodle. "Later we shall commune. You may rub my rectum and -"

"Anais and Aurelia!" Brune exclaims. "My pals ... Buddies ..." She endures a piercing sorrow, her innards feeling like they're hulled by a foot-worked mortar and pestle. Sweets and fruits are brought in by a Negritic Sturgeon Surgeon in leisure suit livery and the lovesome, twenty-something lady, BJ, with a 1960s beehive hairdo, in a sporadically cat-furred poncho, the realdeal proofreader of the Circus in the Sky newspaper.

"Don't worry about them, dear," Minikins. "The sisters."

"They were, are, two with one inside," Brune. "Or, it is the opposite." She feels altered, as water leaving a mill. "What do you want from me?"

"Your heart, lass." Minikins' blinders are apparently widened, like by a hallucinogen, rubbernecking her inveigling omphalos. Lyle and Vindice's heinous hullabaloo cuts as knives. Eagerness for both parties facilitates the discourse.

BRUNE IS A PILOT IN AN AIRCRAFT in expectancy of a
(forecast) hurricane and is shaky in spite of the clear
calm. She feels like the embodiment of an injury that
could be healing, but a treated trauma can still leave a
limp. She senses a problem as a migratory bird senses
direction. She thinks: 'This mental institution is scare-
crowish! I will pull out the straw to see what remains
of it!' The Circus in the Sky, a vaudevillian funhouse,
has the moodiness of a boozer, wavering in and out of
sentimentality and brawling. Is it made of rock? It can
be chiseled out! She's determined to leave her mark -
a canine peeing on a hydrant. Its denizens will topple
like dominoes. She should chill too, as a pig wallowing
in mud; or a patient under the pleasing pressure of a
massage, only any promise of attaining relaxation degenerates akin to dying tissue. Her trepidation is transparent
as glass. Brune pops mescaline, snorts lines of cocaine,
swigs absinthe (making her heart grow fonder), smokes
opium, and swills JD.

MINIKINS, SOUNDING AS EVA GABOR SPEAKING in
tongues, blurts, "Make concessions to our customs. You
can stay gleeful, playing, being productive, obliging your
spanking-new cardiac organ, the sun, letting it distrib-
ute a gentle light throughout your entirety, and ensconce
your delectable derrière in our wonderland where miracles manifest like citizenry. It's a life/death role reversal
... You were, now you are. This is land devoid of boundaries, a sea without a shore, a plum without a pit. Enter

us, as eagerly as the wrapping of an Xmas present. Never ever again dwell in that earthly decay, the hellhole of disease and debris. We stress rectitude ... A regulation of conduct within a society -"

Brune cuts her off, "Do I have a choice?"

Lyle interjects, "Aren't you tired of that miserablistic snivelization?"

Minikins scratches an itch on her powdery wattles. "There's plenty of rope, lamb. You can either hang on or hang yourself." Phlegm rattles in her throat, as some sinister, schizoid, tiny troglodyte talking to itself in a cave.

"Hold on as a grape!" Lyle squeals, words chipped out of wooden sentences.

"Yes, and be picked, squashed, gobbled!" Brune rejoinders.

"Lassie," Vindice breaks in, "You are in definite danger."

"What did the colonic sonofabitch say? I felt the vibration," Minikins pules.

"He suggested I lend him a lullaby -"

"Flapdoodle!" Minikins digs out and flicks a scabrous booger. "Poppycock."

"Horsetwaddle!" Lyle, tenderly tugging at his teeny-weeny, cartilaginous cock. "Positive balderdash," caressing the li'l prick, hawking a loogie.

"I'm wicked baffled." Brune hugs a cushion for comfort.

"Lyle will tell all," Minikins, applying, sedulously, pancake. "You've transitioned over the threshold, crossed the Rubicon."

THUS CUED, THE ITSY-BITSY FETUS, stroking his genitalial gristle, lunges like a hitter in baseball charging into home plate, onto Brune, his Eskimoid eyes clam-ish, the lids shells, opening and closing in a teary beck, and Brune tilts her head, as if a swimmer unclogging an ear. Lyle'd left a snail-slimy streak in his wake on her denuded shoulder. Saffron haze. Melon-slice moon. Her visage a wave affected by wind. Clouds burgeon as though a bouquet from a magician's hat. Intervening, awkward silence. Brune's confusion ceases, like in a blind alley.

"This nuthouse is overwhelming ... Too much ... Way overdone ... Cooked ... Processed ... It's as a little graffiti on a wall ... You can make it all out ... When there's a lot ... You can't because there is so much!" Brune sniffles. Incense fragrance. "It is too trippy. Am I on acid?"

Minikins and her painstaking cosmetics application. "You've been a heretofore wandering Jew, a nymphean Ahasuerus, with an Egmont-esque freedom-fighter's mentality, and lonely and isolated as Julius Caesar."

GAUMLESS, GAUPING MINIKINS, derma layer resembling a puffy omelet, advertising herself, seeking the attention she believes she deserves from everyone she encounters, combs her Woody Woodpecker coif and ploddingly escorts Brune, in buttoned blouse and BVDs, slogging measuredly, as if struggling through a liquid medium, high on heroin, down the jam-packed, kaleidoscopic, hieroglyphical hallway. An anthropoid ape quadra-amputee in a straitjacket somersaults, a test tube clamped in his stained incisors, skrieking "It's a man's world!" continually, like a chant. His equine hinny. An anthropomorphic, obedient ostrich and grizzly bear tag along. Bonkers Brothers Quay stop-motion animation, interactive, plays continuously on the milky tiling. Brune swoons, as though from vertigo. Soon, however, she relaxes, not dissimilar to an agoraphobic finding relief in a shelter. She's an adventuress on a voyage of discovery. They are buoys bouncing on the briny deep. Catawampus crab-shadows scuttle. She muses on if sleep is a more fervid phase than wake. Are they separate extremes? One in the same? Are they, combined, another condition? A state to be referenced as a real irreality? She's inside-out, foreign to herself, like somebody else is experiencing everything instead of her. In the past her existence was a room with modest acoustics, whereas in the present it is one with satisfactory resonance. Before, her introspections were cuckoos, grounded, wings clipped, and now they fly. She builds cities of ideations on her cerebellum and her anatomic asphalt commences crumbling. The tide of her resistance to this sanatorium surges to the beach of realization, which leaves behind flotsam and jetsam of acquiescence. The gilly and its goobers and gimcrackery is so adequately equipped it's as a public restroom. To wit, the fixtures are accessible you barely budge to purge and wash! It is a jigsaw puzzle, in that the mind forms the picture and the body fits the pieces together. She feels like she's in an electrical storm. Her vascular organ is an umbrella opening. Below, she was under water. Above, she is on solid ground. Her smile is unsteady, as if it's on stilts. Next to Minikins, her tour guide, she is the anonymous in the company of the famous. The difference between here and there: sloshing brewskies at a dive bar and sipping champagne at a refined function. Excitement is hoovered out of her as fat from a liposuction hose. They hasten like they are fillies relieved of saddles and harnesses. Her prior life was flame burning in a defunct stove. She's confounded, like she's a convicted criminal of rape and the victim's parents show up at the parole hearing to plead for her imminent release. King Crimson's, 'Larks' Tongues in Aspic Pt. 2' is on an ovaloid radio. Through diaphanous drapes on filthy windowpanes she appreciates the whey-welkin, curdled canal, admirable abodes, chromatic rainbeads maturating on bounteous foliage on the pastel countryside, and this gathering of gallant cranes arabesqued by mizzle on a forget-me-not-bluish hillock. Cattle, stationary, in showers, on a fulgurously patina'd pasturage (out of a Normandy farm) remind her of Chinese women from way back when sprinkling water on just-caught fish. Skyline a marvel of sapphirine iridescence. Flotilla of ferries on a gambogian lagoon. Minikins treats Brune not unlike a headmistress a prize pupil, language "coming up" as numbers in a lottery, admitting her husband is a "cantankerous character dedicated to depravity," and also confesses she has a "secret taste for the nymphic, preferably supple and gawkily slender." Is Minikins flirting? Seducing her? Brune's gut is bloated, breadbasket a billowy ocean, an umbilicus vessel on it. Was it mis/fortune's wheel spinning why she wound up on this parallel plane? Minikins takes her medicinal morphine, canters as a cockatoo pacing its cage. Brune notices she has the side-whiskers of a butler, caked, cracked foundation, Japanese chrysanthemum in her fraudulent tresses: ornithological plumage. Lithium disco. Cavalcade of a collection of pen-and-ink illustrations, masterpieces of the art form, against the wainscot with its vignettes drawn in crayon, in the unnatural phosphorescence of a smoking-room, a capacious receptacle for nicotine, taken lock, stock and barrel from an early twentieth-century novel, its occupants with complete distinction, performers and rubes mingling. Brune feels like a hysteric who is hypnotized; or as a respectable lady in a disreputable haunt she frequents, a habitué from habit, worried about bumping into a familiar face and becoming mortified. Minikins hobnobs with hobbledehoys. Hydrangeas, rhododendrons, fugu, figs, mousse, sardines and cider on a luxurious table. Unsettled weather.

Minikins' stammered narrative unfurls. "This residence is necessitous to me as shade to light." She genuflects as in mocking a urinary emergency, diminutive being jiggling as currant jelly, crustal countenance like a flaky pastry. Screamingmeemie of her stinky-quaker. "The burg below is meaningless to me as Sanskrit." Her orientoid lamps, blood-reddish choppers, absurd grease-paint, ham-hocks. Enigmatic apparatuses. Adipose, apricot-pigmented sibling acrobats cartwheel in unison with a gorillian, ursoid, antelopian, hippopotamic, vulturous, rhinocerine entourage. Brune is awestruck, expectorates a "Wow." Her soul coruscates in its undefined depths, her surface drowning in scintillation. She is a midge, flittering into an immeasurable orchard, and is instantly absorbed by it, her perception increasing in proportion, the exceptional environment intensifying, the extraordinary impressions so enlarged they are misshapen, like encountering an optic screen - the closer you get, the more expanded the surroundings become. It is as if her individuality is diminishing. She feels as though she has stumbled upon a solution when the equation itself is unclear. Minikins' anguine palaver slips into the shrubbery of silentiousness, staring at Brune, bent over at the bubbler, like she's a vacuum about to suck her, Brune, in. The spectacle apparently starts and ends nowhere. It's a pompon opening before her, a symphony of stentorian sonority. She's blown away, knocked out by these manifold wonders, only belief can be brief, and it is reduced to fabrication influenced by fancy. They traipse. Fatigued and famished, she doesn't miss her middle-class parents. Nature's enforced bond was too tight, too taxing. Her spirit is a substance evaporating. Mom and Dad were planning to divorce, his innumerable infidelities ineffective bandaids for the marital conflicts. Conjugal catastrophe! And she blames her anarchistic behavior squarely on them, that toxic domestic climate. She and Minikins trudge. On the vortexical staircase their shadows unravel in reptiloid rhythm, converging and diverging in coal roots, their exaggerated silhouetted selves ebony eels hooked on intangible lines. An ogress and a madwoman serve chili and chocolate in a Duval-esque soup-kitchen in a dazzling cathedran structure. Polychrome statues are smashed to bits. Suddenly, llamas, geese, kangaroos, cheetahs, gazelles, emus, buffalos and giraffes stampede, skedaddling as cockroaches out of the woodwork in fumigatory fumes. Busty Bunny in her boxsies does a flirtatious flyby, pomaceous titties and pomegranate hind waggling. Mulatto trapezists swing not unlike chimpanzees, washing the grungy baywindows in riverine irradiation. In the cavernous kitchen androgynous cooks command unconventional ovens. Hermaphroditic waiters hither-thither come-hitherly. Minikins, Max Factored, pomaded and on pep-pills, toing and froing, is paged on the intercom in the psychoactive cafeteria, departs, and Brune is left to her devices. Is she a dove among the hawks? She's riveted to the risible. It is like she read an article on a familiar subject in a popular magazine and is incapable of changing the fiction into fact where it belongs! She has the sensation she is at once punished and pardoned, unhealthy and healthy, disconnected and connected. The sphere of what's what is warped. The nuts 'n' bolts're insecure. Validity is vaporous. An emaciated, effeminate lad, so sallow, wasted by fasting mayhaps, his chops a trapdoor, breathes flame and lifts weights in the gymnasium. A buxom, carrot-topped dominatrix in stilettos ululates, cracking her cat-o'-nine-tails, gaze pouncing on Brune as a feline on a mouse. Brune's look bangs into Bunny like a hammer a nail. Bunny is soft and spicy as an altar's candle, pretend-mopping, staring at her like someone accustomed to the light adapting to the dark.

"The Circus in the Sky comes across as a haven, but it could be a thornbush!" Brune says.

"It's like carousing with a cougar at a zoo: at first it's friendly, then it mauls you!" Bunny returns in a screech-owl voice.

"My thoughts are as babybirdies falling from the nest."

"You'll be ok."

"I'm Brune."

"Bunny."

"I think I was captured."

"Jeepers, that's original."

"How do you ..."

"Get here?" Bunny nudges the bucket with her satiny shin. "I heard only Vindice knows." Her cheeser is an artillery cannonade. "Ewww ... I apologize ... Sorry ..."

"You can break enough wind to turn a weathervane!" Brune, mustering a meager muffled poof.

"You can't even blow out a candle!"

They cachinnate-cluck like hens. Bible-blackish, starless twilight. They share a hookah pipe given to them by larval entities in bodices and tutus levitating over a pantyhose trampoline and embroiled in a savvy philosophical discussion and getting baked on powerful cannabis, making mallow-cirri, L'eggshells everywhere on the varnished parquet. Infantine valets in crepe bonnets umbrageously crepitate. Medical staff with tall turbans and Egyptian tunics and skirts helter-skelter. Disembodied Caucasoid Heads of State roll as bowling balls in Leonardesque effulgence into a 'Partridge Family' jukebox, whereupon they hold an impromptu meeting. Sinuous surfboards with wheels at skeletal parking meters. These are visions a sufferer of herpes would see! Callants in kilts eat callaloo, and with bally-hoo get into tomfoolery.

"Is Slug a sot, a Dostoyevskian scoundrel?" Brune asks, changing into a muslin dress and galoshes in a Renaissance stall with chiffon curtains, smelling the hollyhock and jasmine in a vase on the bench covered with cashmere, in Renoir-refulgence.

"He's a storyteller at bedtime, basically," Bunny answers, stepping into silken flipflops.

"I assumed you'd praise him to the skies. Is he a lion amid lambs? Am I barking up the wrong tree? I'm experiencing a sensation where I'm an actress playing a part in a defeatist drama and he's the director."

"The small fry is a distinguished, delusional dummy. Before there was banality, now there is beauty. We owe it all to the shrimp, in spite of his cock and bull stories. I'm Prometheus chained to his rock. I feel out of place, wrong, not right whatsoever, like I'm language spoken by a foreigner and the expression emerges as an entirely different emotion that is intended, and manipulated, as a literary writer coerced by a publisher to pen slang." Ventilator device and lissome tarts and their jacked pimps seen through a sizable key-hole. "I am revolving in a vicious circle."

"Well, an individual's smooth chest can seem fine on the outside, but inside only a physician can detect an illness, however insignificant." Brune puts on a Vermeer-ish pearl necklace. "He is a waterbug with a sparkplug physique." Her brain is like a geometer, removes the surface qualities of the conscious, to observe the linear substratum beneath them, the co-conscious. "I wanna discover the truth of this carnival." She's a Caliph Harun al-Rashid cutie-pie on a batsoid side-street in a bananas Baghdad out of 'Arabian Nights.' She has an incurable desire for Bunny. Lust is a crafty drug, bought at any price.

"It's there you'll find the false." Bunny picks a scab on her cuspate elbow, scrutinizing her toe-ring, anklet, sagging boobs, midsection, its limpet-depression, wishing she had a bra, a shirt, and appraises her callose soles. A steroidal lift-boy with an orangey toupee and porcine snout lugs employees up the hierogrammatic stairwell, the captivating cage out of order, a paunchy hall-porter, an old fogy allianced to him, scanning a yellow paper and puffing on peyote. Sequin stars over an excremental Seine in a breathless noon. An obelisk-shed. Oriental signs of the spate. Transvestic negroes in greatcoats close pterodactylid-wing shutters in the lavatory, scraps of convo littering the soaked atmosphere, expound shooting-party and dice-game theories, glance askance at a hotel's bell-board, take pot-shots at each other.

"I'm not gonna form some coalition and besiege the soil of this funny farm -"

"We should go."

Napoleonic, luscious library permeated by superb taste in literature. The ropy, mucousy Vindice with a 'Bionic Woman' bib and condom-stockinghat on (he could easily pass for a headless Sir Hiss from Disney's 'Robin

Hood' cartoon) sinuates into this 'Charlie's Angels' baby-chair and Brune flips the crisp pages of a vintage copy of 'Time Regained' for him to peruse. Chemical tang. A trollesque, morbidly obese nudist librarian with multiple chins and hellaceous howitzers snoozes in the tabloid ragazine section. Charo and Brundlefly, in astronaut suits and Chuck Taylors, sing a cuchi cuchi ole ole-ish duet of Blondie's 'Rapture,' Charo on lead vocals and playing flamenco guitar and Brundlefly doing the rap section, Devo as their backup band. Searchlights scour the overcast sky. Blowtorches protrude from the burntsienna ceiling where watersprinklers should be.

"You want departure, Brune. That is categorically sane."

"Fiddlesticks. Tell me. How do I get outta here?"

"Knead my anus, punkin, and I shall."

"Ugh! Gawd!"

FULIGINOUS GLOAM. BRUNE'S quaint, dank (not altogether disagreeable) quarters are furnished with garden-variety decor, including rustic ceramics, picture-books, novelty banners, and new-fangled toppers on a bridge-table. In the vestigial, somber gloom she rests, exhausted from the tea-parties in private suites (with brownsugar strippers), a social Homeric Odyssey, feeling as if she saw these receptions at a distance (not participating in them) and monumentally misconstruing everything, not unlike mistaking a mesa for a cloud, a yacht for a duck, an airplane for a dragonfly, zonked in a cotton tank-top and V-string thong. In the damp vastness of her modified closet the Russian Ballet puts on a supposedly brilliant performance of genius composer Ivan Ibitchacockov's 'In Search of Lost Time: Swann's Lake.' Lyle surreptitiously enters through the ajar door, wearing a hoodie and hoops trousers, a chick egressing from an egg, rising as though an embryoid efflorescence, a sickening surprise in a Yuletide stocking. He sports a hardon and his funiculus throbs. His head lolls Stevie Wonderishly; or like a flower, too weighty for its stem. Stealthily he uses a 'High Voltage Co.' pencil to pole-vault onto the Crate And Barrel junior-bed. His erection's a divining-rod. With his roseate, sandpapery tongue he licks her discalceated foot, focusing on the callused heel, lapping it as a lollipop, humping it, and he scrubs his caruncular scalp and starts to masturbate, licking his chapped non-lips. Slumbering soundly, she shifts and soughs, flat on her back. He straddles her vaginous navel and begins to simulate intercourse, wormily wriggling, thrusting with gusto, wiggling on her tanned middle as Billy Squier on the floor in that 'Rock Me Tonite' video, imagining he's riding the bucking bronco of her belly. It's like they're integral parts of a sexual trombone: she's the cylindrical tube and he's the metal slide. She wakes and smacks the homunculus, who splats on the AC unit. Wounded, whining, he exits, scrabbling for safety. "Jesus!" She bellows, hears his bawling, her booty-boom.

THE RECENTLY DISINFECTED antechamber-bathroom (clean as a whistle!) with monochromatic Saharan desert and mosaic motifs. Brune utilizes scissors to cut papers into pieces. Desperation for emancipation makes the water level of her plan rise. With a marker she scribbles messages on them. She endeavors to block out thoughts of massaging Vindice, to no avail. A waif whimpers, taps plaintively on the door. "Get lost!" Brune snarls. "I'm taking a dump and tinkle!" A futile effort. The foundling raps again.

BRUNE HAS TURNED into a reservoir of receptivity, dealing with the ebbing and flowing regiment, as an athlete adapts to a coach's routine, submitting herself to it, hook, line and sinker. Happenings arise like red herrings in a whodunnit. If coasting in dream, will she dock in wake? She's feeling as an item transported in another person's travel-bag because of some mistake. Pubescents, pre-and-post, are always arranged congruous to flowerets for a nebulous pageant. Their trouble-making never-ending. It is like being susceptible to scorching sun without the benefit of shade. Her goal is to escape, acting as if the ambition, a personal inclination, is a biological evolution - a tadpole metamorphosing into a frog. Her cogitations are congruent to bullets lodged in flesh. She broods on Vicks DayQuil ... It soothes you, yet the flu goes away on its own.

Snatch-stench of the harbor. Hemoid heavens. Soup of mixed monoxides and mugginess. Anais and Aurelia are raimented in sweaters, jeans and workboots, getting stoned and soused in a stolen sable Maserati proximal to a dino-dumpster. Gulls clamor. Fishermen knuckledown. Argenteous azure. Pelagic panting. Shawl of sparks spitting from a cargo ship. Boats bob. Horns honk. Claybank, clathrate precipitation.

Aurelia drags. "I miss Brune."

Anais glugs. "Our fearless leader ..."

Confetti spritzes on the filmy windshield. Brune's strategy coming to fruition. Billiards: sooner or later the ball will drop into the right hole.

"Hey! It's snowing!" Anais.

"Nitwit!" Aurelia, poking her sister in the ribs. "Read! What a twat!"

A scrap has this written (calligraphically) on it - 'Anais and Aurelia help me! I was abducted, am being held against my will! Clamber to the tippity-top of Moose Mountain at forenoon and look due north and you'll see a ladder of cloud. Climb it and come to my rescue in the Circus in the Sky! I'm relying on you, my double-edged weapon. And bring tons of explosives! Love, me, B.'

Anais and Aurelia gape and gawp at each other, resume smoking and drinking.

It is a typical YMCA-type pool. Euphoric, euphonious sounds of kids carrying-on. They shrill, swim, splash and scamper on deck. Such din! Minikins, crammed into a tangerine maillot, sashays, is the vigilant lifeguard on duty. She's recollective of a stumpy, gynecoid Joker in a onepiece bathingsuit. She chastises an egretic dweeb with a cuke-sniffer for an ambiguous transgression. A lithe, tech-twerpy brogrammer is a bystander. She castigates him too. Gigolos and their clientry. Bunny brazenly skinny-dips, has on her rabbit-ears, vitreous dildo-snorkel (with seamonkeys ordered from comic-books natating inside) and 'Planet-of-the-Apes'-feet flippers. Ted Koppel-toupee-water-lilies buoyant. Ligers unleashed. Brune, in a daring amethyst bikini, secures a towel around her waist, has had enough with the racket. Showering, she reaches for the Head & Boulders shampoo in the caskety tub when, without warning, Lyle swings, a homunculine Tarzan, on his umbilicoid vine (attached to the spout) from the soap dish, targeting her rosy sphincteric whorl, as though searching for salvation, a tampon perversely headed for the wrong orifice, and Brune dodges him at the last sec, and he collides full-force with the gastropodal toilet. He flounders for a mo, skitters off, blubbering, holding his hematic head. His Horton hears a poo brays not unlike a donkey.

IT IS AN OBJET D'ART-LADEN, obpyriform office. Brune, in jockeys and a tee, and Slug, dressed in a plaid amylaceous zoot-suit, are seated at the idiosyncratic, obliquitous King Arthur's Round Table, set with cutlery and crockery, the fuchsia napkins intricately folded into flamingoes. Phallic posts. Flames in the fireplace fling their mantis-shadows on the heartshaped hearth. Brune's showdown with Slug. An elevator-music rendition of the 'Ghostbusters' tune is on over the loudspeaker. In the Pompeian place cheerleader naturalists frenziedly put on a program, in dishabille anglaising, amusive, amuck, allowing their frippery-suffocated bodies to breathe, blotched like drunkards, sexy symmetries revealed, beauty displayed, presented to Brune's vision, and she is a prurient Prometheus, nailed by libido's Force to the rock of their Pure Matter. Their energized performance is pleasanter than Slug's company for sure. Attributable to her being obliterated on shrooms and meth, he sounds as Mushmouth from 'Fat Albert' on PCP while swishing sand. Cloudlets are a succession of vague, discernible dreams belonging to deviant broccoli, linked, and long-lived. Punch and Judy waitstaff slaving.

"Your advice is AS HELPFUL AS PROPOSING to a tightrope-walker that he should keep his balance above an abysm, and insulting as a millionaire offering a bum a plug nickel," growls Brune. "It's as if you expect me to embrace the positives of your proposition and shake off the negatives like water off a duck's back." Her amygdalate oculuses distend.

"Listen to me," replies Slug, the livid Lorax, pulley-lips creaking, noticing her cellulitic dimples.

"This funfair is a few keys short of a piano. It is an axis of evil where suspension of disbelief is drawn and quartered. You're a ferocious germ, in its virility, spreading victoriously."

"Your former sorrow now has the flapping wings of joy."

"You are the soil preserving the plant of this joint, an instrumentalist playing your own score."

He reconciles his disassociated testes on the sly, blazes dope. "Wait -"

"You're a military leader ..."

"The Salvation Army doesn't wear uniforms."

"What does that mean? Whatever. You are a dictator. The foolery flourishes under your control."

"You're taking this too far." A bombardment of his freeping unloosed.

"You want my unconditional surrender."

"I'm not unsympathetic to your plight." His Valkyrie-yelp of afflatus.

"You're tipping your hat."

"You sit where you stand."

"Dirk wears white socks."

"You spin me round like a record."

"I'm strong on my skates."

"You're a hard needle to move."

"Gotta find the groove first. This is a Divine Comedy. Har-har."

"You are Dante's Beatrice."

"I feel as a traitress who should be shot, or Marie-Antoinette condemned to the chopping-block."

"That's like comparing Watteau and Diderot."

"Wha? Your pitch is false, doesn't hit the true note. You need a tuning-fork. You wanna keep your side of the seesaw up. You're a malformed, bipolar jewel in the crown that's a false idol. The eventized onion is peeling itself."

"You've got pluck."

"I want peace."

"This is an even playing field."

"You're running up the score."

"You are a serpent." His floof is insane in the methane.

"And you're the charmer."

"To exist cheek by jowl? You are as perplexing as the pedantry of a scholar."

"You have got tricks up your sleeve."

"My calling card." He hiccups. "You're the conjuress ..." A fizzler follows. "You don't plant flags, you burn 'em."

"Sure enough." She pauses. "This is a breeding-ground for balderdash. You are the beast with your claptrap. You unload verbiage as an airman does bombs. This place is like some ingenious stage production with supernumerary thespians. I feel born again, as a phoenix. Mary, mother of God." She coughs.

"We sing from the same songbook. Our fires burn brightly." A cessation. "There are rumors you want to murder me as Rasputin."

"Should I spill the beans? Drop a dime? Sing like a canary or wind up in the slammer? You don't scare me! This is a lunatical Lusitania, sinking. And you are panic-stricken." She dips a croissant in coffee occupying a Whistler-mug. "The concentration camp with your marvelous motley and their sodomist scandals -"

"Hold the phone!" Blood boils in his veins like the juice of grapes in a winery. He's an utter wreck. "Your dead past is an alive present. Brune the black sheep. The underdog urchin."

"Oral fertilizer for your flowery lingua franca." An ear-splitting bugle-call. Zeppelins on a Monet-esque tapestry. Wagnerian sirens. A fair-haired butcher-boy in an ensanguined bath-robe. Satelloid moths. "The irrational renders the rational null and void." The panorama, at ground-level, with cumuli, is an oceanic expanse with glaciers. A robot Andre-the-Giant-as-Sasquatch and its simious swagger. "You're a body and we're the cells. We are words in accord with your thoughts. You are an Earth with your own revolutions. To me, you're a writer of some symbolist play, with its sublime passages, its plot with potential, and I'm a character that came along and blocked you, and you had to deviate from your plan, chart a new course. I changed your clock's time, the dates on your calendar."

"I want your heart." His jack-o'-lantern smirk.

"It's mine, not yours, mister. Heavens above!" Her sateened hackle hurts.

"You don't appreciate it. I swear I will replace it with a mechanical one that will last virtually forever. Trust me. We have the technology. I promise to move heaven and earth to make it happen. Your vital core is a connection to -"

"Your high-tech science is a blatant penetrative violation of nature. In my humble opinion. I can experience
love in its purest -"

"Love! Ha-ha! What is that? A honeybee which stings
once and it dies!"

"Take a hike. Child's play. Phony baloney. You are a
vicious villain in this opulent burlesque. Your Big Apple
is rotten. What a pathetic P.T. Barnum."

"Yours is mightier than any other -"

"Without it you're a George Romero."

"Excuse me?" He's exasperated, smokes his stubby mota.

"Living Dead." She harrumphs. "Why, what happened
to yours?"

"I was a mere mortal ... Eons ago ... It broke ..." He
tokes, passes the J bar to her.

"Make another. You and your unheard-of, far-out
inventions." She receives it, takes a hit off the spliff,
the buttend starring. "Good fuckin' ganja." Brume of
pakalolo.

"I must comprehend your -"

"Screw yourself."

"Bratty ... Bitchy ... Nincompoop ... You're a contagion
infecting the universe ... You could conceivably manure,
mulch our land, plant the seed of revolt ..."

"Cool idea! I'll keep it in mind! Tee-hee! The ABCs ..."

"Eh?"

"Always Be Cuntish."

"There haven't been many, but those who've rebelled remain in the Wing of Sad, contrasting, sharply, this Wing of Glad, for an eternity, conical craniums tatted with 'DUNCE' in broad letters."

"I'm shaking in my boots. What's with this Circus in the Sky shit anyway?"

"An enticing package."

In the lambdoid lounge, at night, Bunny saunters in, twisting quite a fatty, rigged in a dinner-jacket and Hanes briefs, and crash-lands on Brune's lap in a lageniform recliner, in laniary light, and says, "Okay, Slug is a tick, sucking us dry."

"He is a leech! His approach is confounding, like being in combat, and you can't understand the enemy strategist's tactics," Brune responds, inhaling and exhaling from the doobie. Her attraction for Bunny is a day attaining its apex: precise, pure. "He's a Shakespearian King Leer ... Heh-heh ... Who looks at us as a conductor at his orchestra that made a mistake during a concert." Stained-glass windows. "He is a country club tool box."

"War engenders bravery. Without conflict there's only materialism. Emotion is the foundation of action."

"This is an excessive empire."

"If legit, love lasts, as a species."

Brune's mouth transmogrifies into a sun in the rain of Bunny's hair, tongue tied not unlike a ribbon, raveled on the spool of her. The brightness of this rapturous romance outshines its darker aspects. Circumspect tactions, caring osculations. Their ardor is a fermenting wine. Brune feels like she's rising down, or plummeting up. Her infatuation has the impact of an avalanche - the snow is rather powdery, yet it packs a punch! To deny herself of Bunny would be as depriving herself of food: deliberate starvation. And the craving itself serves as nourishing sustenance. The tissue of uncertainty tears. Her resistance snaps like a violin's string. She is the sea, very much wanting to give and receive. They swap spit. Tonsil hockey. She ponders same-gender relationships as opposed to separate-gender relationships: it is permissible for crabgrass to grow in a yard, but when they develop in a patio's crevices they are brutally dug up! Bunny, fondled, titters, gives Brune a can of Pepsi. Muzak'd 'Fiddler on the Roof.' " I pray I'm not getting scammed." Brune's eyes feed on the ripe fruits of Bunny's hurdies. Their somatic eclipse. Love-making molestations. Yakking turds in the corner. Bong given, taken.

"Our friendship is free. Socrates didn't charge for his lessons. My life is an Open Sesame for you." Bunny remarks these perambulating peg-legged piratical exercise guru Richard Simmons clones, their shoulder-perched parrots squawking 'Secret Agent Man' in the caliginous catacombs. She is posed like a model for a painter, gazes at her as an anatomist an etching of an anatomy in a note-book; or like at a person profiting from a profanation. Guests, large and small, young and old, bombilate 'Peter Gunn Theme' in the Mandelbrot Set study with its

Sierpinski Carpeting, begrudging the eyesight.

"An enemy aircraft illumines the area where it wants to drop a bomb." Is Brune's an illusory, non-existent life? Unreal incidents are a crop of weeds torn up by reality. The rational is not compatible with the irrational. She adores Bunny. Her attraction is water in an artesian well, the height of lust in proportion to the depth of love.

"The scale of fantasy doesn't always correspond with the fact which inspired it."

Cythera, the lanky laundry-girl, puts quilts away in the Koch Snowflake closet. Vindice in a ribbed Trojan pro-phylactic conductor's cap cruises on his trippy skateboard through the orbicular, hippodromic living-and-dining rooms. Commotion in the fractal'd corridor.

"Disappointment pursues me like a perpetual tidal wave a surfer. I'm a ship at sea in a tempest with a scenic back-ground," Brune pouts. "Lyle was a nocturnal visitant."

"Don't sulk, sweetheart. He's vile. Vulgar. With his intravenous injections of semen-seltzer ... Forget it ... He's his own amative recruiting-agent who goes out to sign up desirable teenagers to copulate with." Hillbillies and hippogriffs on the wacky tobacky.

"With you I'm a memory coinciding with the impression, a mnemonic interpretation, that inspired it, me." Brune hiccoughs. "You are an optical instrument enabling me to see clearer."

Bunny hops as Chief Jay Strongbow on the warpath in the ring, yodeling Donovan's 'Sunshine Superman.' La Tour effulgence. "Nah ... I dunno ... I am a cloudy lens!"

Brune suspires. "I feel as a meaning, lost there and found here; a seed whose nutritional substance is feeding the plant of this rubber room; a cell undergoing chemical changes; a grain ripening. I'm venting. This booby hatch is a photographic darkroom where negatives of human beings are developed. The gondola of my grey matter is unmoored. I'm really on a roll. My life is a stream that cannot find a channel. This psycho ward's zaniness is precise as an altimeter's markings. It's a drawing with zig-zaggy outlines with no perspective. I am a sound imposed 'pon quietude. In the carnivale my existence has been extracted from life."

"Kosher." Bunny dips and dabs, fires the ack gun. "Chasing the dragon ..." And she boots up 'Third Stone from the Sun' on the boxy Bose.

BRUNE, DRESSED IN A JONQUIL JOHNNY, currently bound to an aluminumal slab in the Frankensteinian lab, was sedated by Bunny. The beverage was spiked, per Pinhead's instructions. Beside her is a drugged Slug in a grody gown. His respirings sound like Steve Perry's breathing from the intro of that 'Oh Sherrie' golden oldie. She strains, as if demented, pantomiming a manic fit, fingers flexing as though a gal of diminished mental capacity attempting to count. It occurs to her she's going under the knife. They're preparing to operate on her! Amoeban automata actuate molluscoidally. Rembrandtine refulgence. Freemason Latinists wearing boilersuits, bowlerhats and combatboots take a break and altercate over Virgil and Plato. A parade of marching mechanoid syringes with plasticine limbs goose-stepping, tributary-flowing. Minikins, the stocky succubus, powdered viper, and her high-priestess air, smug self-importance, Patty-Smyth-in-'The-Warrior'-vid-resemblant, keeps close tabs on the proceedings. Senegalese Sturgeon Surgeons, enamored of their profession, argue about Schopenhauer and the Stock Exchange. Raphael-ish emanation, light as souls, lay outpoured on the sensational jade floor. Odoriferous saccharoid sulfur in the saturated oxygen. Lyle, fly in Raybans, retro Adidas sweatsuit and Nike slides, gets a gander at Brune's nether regions, his right arm in a sling and left leg in a (signed) cast. At the flying-saucer boombox he plays air-guitar to 'Stranglehold.' She covers her privates with a sheet. Sturgeon Surgeons scurry back and forth with these disturbing implements. In the willy-nilly hubbub, Bunny charges in and unties Brune, announces, "I've had a change of heart!" Pinhead attacks her, heaves a left haymaker and Bunny throws a roundhouse that connects with his jaw, an incident not lost on his nervous system, his piece falling off, and he collapses, kayo'd. Minikins assaults them, pitches esoteric bric-a-brac and grandiose appliances at them. A brouhaha ensues. Michael Jackson's 'Bad' is at a loud volume on the ghetto-blaster. Brune scrambles and Slug tackles her. They clinch, sock one another. Dirty boxing with laser beam accuracy. Punches in bunches. A frenetic Keatonesque-slapstick strife. Brune's elbow-strike misses. Slug counters with a cross which lights up her schnozzola. She reacts with an uppercut that grazes his chin and he drills a superman punch into her solar plexus. Her axe-kick to his knee buckles him. Pratfall pugilism.

Mayhem. His jab and her hook land: cheek and abdomen respectively. Whereupon Slug shoots and gets the takedown. His ground and pound busts her face, tenderizes her body. Their backsides are bared. Her scarabaceous sphincter. His lumpen behind. They sprawl. Grappling. She bears the brunt of his hammerfists. "A coward living in a heroic age doesn't stop being a chicken-shit," he warbles as a thrush, thumping her, giving her a thrashing beyond belief. "You're a stink brought to us by a breeze, an unsightly sentence in an otherwise wonderfully written memoir." Then he mounts her, sweeps, gets side control, passes guard (and gas) in balletic skillful classic MMA choreography. She rocks not unlike a babe in the cradle. He cannot pull off an arm-bar successfully; they are too perspiry. She's crushed as a sugar cube under a truck's tires. His guillotine fails spectacularly. Unexpectedly, she retaliates with a triangle, transitions into a rear-naked choke and he taps out. It is all over! Vindice becomes a boa constrictor, wrapping round Brune's neck, strangulating her (he and Slug different arrows aimed at the same bull's-eye), until Bunny cuts him in half with a scalpel, and she spins and stabs Minikins in her turkey-throat. Blood squirts through her bratwurst-digits. She appears shocked, keeling over, limp as a wet rag. Bunny clutches Brune's hand and they beat a hasty retreat, run for the fantastic foyer via the Menger Sponge parlor, wheeze like bagpipes. Chaos erupts. Slug shouts, "There's no meat on the bones of your escape connivance!"

Anais frantically waves them on at the edge of an edifice of saw-toothed, terra-cotta, salt-and-pepper shaker spires. "We gotta scram! This kooky kermis is gonna blow to smithereens! We hid explosives everywhere! Aurelia has the remote to detonate and she's waiting for us! Move those tubby tuchases!"

Brune squeezes Anais. "Squishing ya ... The young 'uns..."

"... Are coming too!" Anais bites her earlobe. "We need to haul ass with promptitude!"

Treetops are frondescent parasols, or islets in an earthly sea, as Brune, Bunny, Anais, Aurelia and the youngsters scale down the cirri-ladder. Resolute sun. Country tranquil as the ocean after a storm. Mournful morningdoves. Ferns in humid gusts are kelp in a sylvan sea. Algal skeeters. Avian milky ways shimmer like reflections. Laurels remind one of jets of water. Eiffelish towers at a Parislike port. A lighthouse's lambency is as the luminosity of magnesium flares. On the terra firma of a marshy forest, Aurelia flips a switch on the doodad and the Circus in the Sky, Slug's Pompeii, his Vesuvius, an accursed city from the Bible, explodes not unlike countless costly Roman candles. It looks as cheesy CGI special-effects of a low-budgeted Hollywood movie.

Nerval luster. A traditional hospital ward. Nurses of diversiform ethnicity come and go. Brune is swollen, bruised and cut, constrained in this orthopedic corset beneath an afghan - a pommeled piñata. Her yap and whiffer seem melded together, eyes raccooned, strands geysered on pillows. Her Mike-and-Carol-Brady-dull parents are at her sarcophagus-bedside.

"Lord Almighty," says Father.

"We prayed ..." adds Mother.

"The accident ..." soughs Brune.

"Your heart never quit," Mother. "You were out cold. In a coma."

"I remember the accident ... Jeez ... Anais and Aurelia..." Brune weeps. Drip feed Morse code.

"They didn't survive," Father, "We are so sorry."

"You're wrong, Mom and Dad ... They didn't die ..." Brune touches her chest with a palm. "They will live in here." The fondness for her friends is heat gathering up in a gamut of feelings to become light and the electricity of her passion in a lightning flash creates a picture of devotion. It hits her like a brick off the ole coconut: Slug was Death. This realization has the effect of a douche of frigid aqua pura upon her. Her memories are fragmented, not unlike milk split up into digestible portions for an infant.

THE FIRMAMENT IS carnival-chromatic. She takes cognisance of these colors. An unruly ray of this recognition flickers, corresponds to a re-awakening, begotten of reality, which is decanted from the vessel of irreality.

FINIS OPERIS.

Vaginate Ceiling

From the swollen sore of summer seeps a muculent humidity. Sun's a peek-hole into purgatory. Its sailing voyage ends and it slowly sinks into the oceanic, glaucous sky. It disappears like a wraith. Evening plummets, slams with a thud. The moon is engorged. Horizon's pink-and-ebony like a Gila monster. The azure with stars is a hundred-eyed Argus. The villose, vaginate ceiling of the decayed, sooty smokestack, out-of-business, unmaintained, nuclear-storm-scarred, shrugging its slumping shoulders, a death-row-drab dump resembling a gigantic Wurlitzer with a sculptural suggestive shape, the place a slime-smothered sob, in proximity to a toxic waste site, purses its pussy lips as if to pucker up, then sticks out its clitoral tongue petulantly at teenaged Katinka, an eye-poppingly pretty (modelesque) Russian immigrant and former ballerina (torn ACL and no insurance and her career went kaput), a brunette, brawny, busty beauty, her bristling brown mustache lending a masculine note to her femininity, who has fallen on really hard times. Her brother, sideshow strongman tower of power buzzcut badboy Vadim, is currently out running errands. Windows, huge and rectangular, weep with condensation. The composed sun's a yolky zero committed to diurnally resolve in its place in the violet firmament like something pressed neatly into cooperating material. Arachnidan light. Rain jingles as pocket-change fiddled with. Tennis court parking lot with puddles that recall dark dipsomaniacal prints of a giant, abstract alphabets of metalline wreckage, wild, mangled and discarded, litter mating in shaggy leonine shrubs. The balding lawn has these webs of loamy mottle. Empyrean is an expression emptying itself. Tepees of canvas over bushes. This is an industrialized reservation. There's a definite digestive stink in the sterile oxygen. Hot air shimmers as water. Capillary vinage on facial structures. Illumination insigniates the warmish cement. Wads of wrappers vortexing in wind smelling subnormally of fabric-softener and dog-shit. The kekulean knot of Katinka's navel has lint in it. A mosquito bite in the tendony trench of her left leg. She has a Native-American-measured gait, pincered fingers clutching a Popsicle stick with its upper quarter-portion having this syrupy, rose flush, in incandescent ideograms on the oyster-colored, cool floor. Sallow paneling. Sparking dust-motes apparently stirred by some invisible force. AC unit not cutting the mustard whatsoever. The vaginal ceiling sports a presbyopic squinch. She I.D.s it. Is the cunt a creatus, manufactured in her mind? Freckles of stormclouds on the scalp of the skyline. Precip makes noises not unlike high-heel-shoes clicking on institutional marble. The stars are parasitic fungal specks in a moldy welkin. Discoid moon's blank stare. 'I am here,' she thinks. It squirts, the creature does.

"Okay, that is not necessary," Katinka says in struggling English, in her husky, thick accent. She paces back and forth leadenly, as though wearing deep-sea diver's shoes, dressed in candycane spandex tights, top and bottom, burgeoning belly bared, and jogging sneakers.

"Oh, indeed it is," the pileous pudendal creature replies in a raspy, Jack Webboid, world-wise-weary, drawling voice, apparently softened and solemn. It sighs dramatically. "You're behaving like a spoiled brat." Its pubic bush is salt-and-pepper in color. An awkward silence ensues.

"I feel as a character actress adapting to a new and difficult role, and I've finished my final line in the last scene -"

"And there is an uncomfortable quietness because you are anticipating the audience's applause." A second protracted sough of extreme exasperation from the penis flytrap. "Time to get with the program." It somehow alters its weird ocular character into a curiously haughty cuntal countenance, and, subsequently, prodigiously transforming itself into an expression of grinning idiocy, the transmogrification into smiling senility almost an art. These are successive states of very strange spectacle into a singular one all at once. The snatch changes, twitches and convulses as in a kind of epileptic seizure, creates a ridiculous caricature of its twatty self in an exaggerated fashion out of some ludicrous farcical production, an exceptional vision nonetheless presented to Katinka's lamps, offered only to her. The stench trench thing can be inoffensive and overbearing. It undergoes another remarkable metamorphosis (insectivally intensive), looking vaguely crustacean in chrysalid coruscation. The enfeebled furniture continually cringes.

"Take off the disguise. The party's over," Katinka, removing her sterling navel-ring from her stinging nombril. "The masquerade makes intriguing identities ..." She puts pink socks on her gnarled, callused feet.

"What, I'm on stage in a play and the curtain has already fallen?" Oscillations of its "facial" features with rhythmic significance, profoundly unpredictable. "Come on in, the womb is warm."

"You've managed to pass through an extraordinary philosophical, scientific, physical and psychological refractor to distort yourself to get me discombobulated," shaking abruptly as a manipulated marionette. Her stocky form rocks. There is a veritable smorgasbord of stimulants in her system.

"Whatever." The wizard's sleeve's cast suddenly compresses. Puppet-performances of shadows interiorize and exteriorize the meaning of human existence in the room that is not unlike a massive magic lantern. "Oral ballet of bloodletting beginning."

"This is a prolonged peepshow of reality and irreality, past and present, reason and unreason, the rational and irrational." She hugs herself closely, blood fucking frozen. "Shit am I confused." Dopesick, she needs to cop, heart a chainsaw in her chest, wanting to tear-ass for greener pastures. Irishized by cornsilk coruscation, looking collapsed as a capsized tent in a frosted-glass cubicle. And she sips her cappuccino out of a shot-glass-sized cup, not feeling hale or hearty, vindicative of her existence. It's hot out and her sizzling is bacon-in-frying-pan caliber. She is nail-tough. Oily puddles shimmy as spilled gas. Lightning bugs make Pollockian spatter-paintings with their light on the canvas of the air. "I'm nonplussed, like I'm this mismade Frankensteinian monster of a combined cardboard cutout of a beach's beefcake and bathingbabe waiting for someone else's head to be placed on my neck-stump."

"If it floats your boat, baby! What a thumpingly whacko thing to say!" Its trajectory into deformation, in a separate, sole space, the dimensions inconceivable, an apprehensible abstraction, a definitive aberration rather striking out of a surrealistic theatrical pageant entertainment with its fair share of incredibly imaginative and intelligent images. "With you, it's always a tablespoon when a dab will do." Bangkok-gone-bonkers, seasidescape city where industrial production is a powerful process. It is sort of cerebral. Buildings are convoluted paragraphs punctuated by filth. Architecture hallucinatorily hypnotic. Citizens fly akin to bats in a vast cave. The metropolis is a kind of sizable snare of spectacular scale. Pedestrians moving as quicksilver. Day was a dying match. Traffic serpentoidally slithers, asthmatically wheezes. Dusk's a dirty drape. Megalopolis is gloomy as an abandoned well. People are variegated smears of identities, drift like lost leaves, trudge as if entranced. "I'm smartly switching the subject."

"You're persistent as the press." Empyrean, overcast, oozes as though spilled oatmeal. "Your excuses are weeds woven into a nest of denial." She holds her being like she's liquid that will leak. She's so drunk and stoned and tired she could be blown over by a breath.

"You gulp the truth and gag."

"Hey, a boulder doesn't roll down the hill like a pebble."

"You sure can clip the wings of flightiness."

"You are wrong as a fifty-dollar bill in a change purse."

"Shed the pounds of me and be uplifted."

"Sure!"

MATHEMATICAL MAYHEM OF PIPING. Vacant lots. Nut-brown housing projects. Scuzzy, hackle-raisingly mean streets with municipal neglect. Unrelieved and withered leafage spronging in neural spasms of winds. Frondescent scythes. Her crescentoid-bill-reversed ball-cap. Illegal substances of differing potency dealt with due care. Warmth roils. Welder's eye of sun. She jumps up like she is shot out of a cannon or something, whip-lashingly airborne, slipping on a beach-blanket in the trailer-sized lavatory. She is poetry in motion, with an even distribution of mass, crustal ass-cleft disclosed. Bug-bits on a busted-up, bitten-lip-reddish

Chevy's headlights. It's on blocks on gravel and has window-webbing of fissures. Overtall weeds tight like strained tendons. Barbershop spirals of rubbish in snicking breezes. She ambles in a cape of coruscation as if God had caught her chin with a fishhook and began reeling her in only she resisted and he gave up the ghost. She's gonna rain-check going into town. Scraggly trees waver as though windshield wipers in indecisive irradiation. Her head beats as a heart pounds. She shifts with minimum economy and maximum effort, and yet she is feeling wooden. Perspiration purls on her. Silence is like the whole wide world is holding its breath. Rogue hornets fly suicidally. Pilot-light blue sky. Mongoloid-cranium moon. Precip smells of suede. Denuded trochal hillock. Vendors with carts. She puts on a tent of a top. Her physique as a stevedore's, Coke-bottle limbs feeling like logs, rock-solid abdomen with a migrainous ache. She's wasted on Percocets. Icky goo, laguna-green, of a flabby, pileous, bulbaceous, vascularly hued, squished arachnid. The gynecological creature's pubic filament is remindful of a parka's fake-fur fringe. It's sphincter-looseningly scary and stinks as a skunk. She moves toward it like a plant to light, her head cocked caninely, hearing a dog-whistle. Her basilisk-body-odor. A pink garage is laryngeally lined with intervals of interstices managing to merge into a meaningful confluence of cracks. An artery-red depository with pasty-gray windows and florid-purple, latex roof in the lithiumish brilliancy is a colossal cerebral cortex of concrete, glass and steel. Skull-colored skyline. Waftage with the sonance of a nebulizer.

"What you're doing with Vadim -"

"Without him I'm incomplete, as when a woman has a cancerous breast removed; she is more intact with less, when the source of pain is gone, and yet misses what was surgically taken. He's a juvenile in his favorite hiding spot - me. I, uh, put out the product of me like a manufacturer does goods in response to the market, um, him." Her heart beats like a kettle drum. She is exhausted, as though an explorer encountering an island inhabited by natives and has to contend with them. She is wary, like being in a vehicle driving on an unstable bridge. The villous, vaginous ceiling is her discovery without Vadim: a movie director chancing upon a possible starlet. And she feels like a rat in an anaconda's stomach; or, for that matter, having narrowly avoided an accident; sorrow ceased by a sedative. She's troglodytically dwelling in an elephant-grey, spherical-cuboid segment of the plant. Copterish fan-blades spin and it sounds unendurably as a Meemie screaming, toes smashed with a sledgehammer. When it's off and still it looks like a massive, metalliferous spider bolted into grilles in an ovaline chamber in webs of aluminumal, curvaceous ducts. "Your assholery ... This Iron Curtainish environment ..."

"Be responsible. It is critical to regulate your output. Your conscience is a rep from the board of directors of your person, an executive committee of one ignoring the majority of shareholders, that is, society." Juice squirts from the bajingo as pus from a squeezed pimple.

"To deprive myself of him it'd be on par with denying a blossom the opportunity to bloom. Love is, to me, a satisfied hunger. A thirst quenched. Corny, I know." Her words pour as morphine into a syringe. "We're harmonic chords struck in a tempest."

"The sick sexual tag with him is absolutely appalling. This prurient peek-a-boo ... It needs to stop. Soon."

Katinka gravidly grunts, stressed like a drawn bow, or tendons tightened before leaping. "Incest is best!" She farts, giggles. "I've gotta shave my armpits." She has the uppity attitude of a student explaining an intricate lesson to the teacher. "His legs are long as stilts, or steeples." She trembles like a leaf. Her flatus sounds as a bell's pealing. "His unit is a Druidic monument, a summit for me to perch upon. Vertigo would seize me." Rain from the sky is a cerebral hemorrhage. "A kiss or a touch from him is all it takes to get me riled, like when an arm of a clock teaches a number on its dial and a spring's released in the mechanism and makes the hour strike."

Mucous suppurates from the tampon tunnel like from a lanced boil. "Let him tickle your middle as if you are a puppy. That's far as it should go. Any twinges of guilt? A scintilla of regret? God Almighty!"

"Venting your vexation," toing and froing as though a target duck at a shooting range. It haunts her like night's ghost in the morning. "My brain is a fortress besieged by your bunkum." A bunch of unhidden, nonlethal landmines of small, Dr. Caligari-esque, Raid-and-Terminix-endorsed traps set to catch the nightmarish,

Tiger-tank cockroaches, critters to give you the hee-bie-jeebies, and these flak-jacketedly furred mice, feral chihuahua-hugeous, rodentine buggers so large the verminous bastards would give you night-terrors/sweats fucking 24/7 live and in living color permeating the place. Ember-reddened heavens. Coconut-fuzz on the freaky pudendum. Stoic trees in tortured shapes in the merciless, bloody shafts. Her phylacterish Stetson at an angle. Honking glide of geese. Humidity's wrinkly like fuel-fumes. Her fists tighten as scrotums in an Antarctic freezathon, freckled like flapjacks, peepers palsied, hiking herself up onto her tailbone to the little libraryish lamp. She nods as wheat, in a tit for tat, mano-to-muff Q&A. She toots from the rear, sitting Indian-style, gets cross-legged, taps idly on the bongodrums of her kneecaps. It has a hangdog, its pubes like Jack Lord's toupee. It whizzes in a great niagaran gush into this vat, and Katinka strategically places buckets for the post-pee drips. In the most remarkablest way the welkin is gingival. Her tiles of teeth twinge-ring as ears sometimes do. She wishes it ill. Are there chinks in its armor? Her pressurized belch.

"I'm a mirror reflecting you."

"Pull! You're skeet-shooting my clay-pigeons of rejoinders!"

"I'm playing my aces is all."

"You switch sides as a record-changer." Flannel shirt around her waist as a kilt, lying morguely and toad-tummy off-white, contact-sport-athletic, hooded in humid heat and chaotic chiaroscuro, piss-pigmented and highlighting anything at random, her quiescence contemplative, under the pussified ceiling. Arid blur of the air. Tentative tinkle, trickle of viscose spate, empyrean a soundless explosion, bloated sun the tangerine bloom of a cig-butt. She visors her brow with a hand to salute, or see it. Gespenst-umbrage enlargening and elongating could stand in as well-fed figures. Asterisks of spritz. Mammoth factories, chimneys of tan brick with creepers reminding one of hosiery with runs. Sky complements sea. Watery chalk from childrens' games on the curb's cement's whorish makeup running. Wind is congested. Atramentous agnate shade. Drops, loogie-like, dribble as from showerheads. Gusts have a locomotival roar and vegetablish odor. Locationless voices, accents ethnically vague. Gigantean hairballs of bushes with digitate thorns. Sienna dirt. Fireflies' electric twinkles. She is slumberously stunned, protrusive otter-oculi's lids going up and down like drawbridges, irises the color of weak coffee and shimmering as if behind plane engines. Crash-landed flying-saucerly Tupperware's uncomplex reflections in the metalloid cabinet are cubist, her image there an unbeautiful Plastic Man stretching like a rubber band, her movement making a visual, not audible, boing, her spectation saddening. Osteoporotically bent she has the comical flexibility of a cartoon character, Mary Lou Retton-muscular-and-compact, splayed on a velourish shag carpet in a textbook cheerleader split, effortless and no-nonsense, showing off for the vaginated ceiling. Gibbous moon is a spit-bubble protruding in slo-mo in anachronistic achromic clouds. Electrolysistic rash on the firmament's desiccated flesh. Stale oxygen with this mild creosote redolence. Bleached, embryonic brilliancy. She gets into a ruminative defecatory position over a chamber pot, her patience in the ballpark of religious, as though in expectancy of an epiphany.

"Tempest in a teapot here," she blurts.

"For you it's R & R's and bumping uglies," it returns.

"Let's be good to each other." It is a tawny, lanate blossom opening and closing.

"You live a vegetal existence"

"I could be a corn of wheat, falling to the ground and dying, and bringing forth fruit." Its clit vibrates like a tuning fork. "My idleness … Lassitude from indigestion."

"Your thoughts and words are Protozoa attached to their polyparies."

"The threads of our dialogue are crossing and doubling, a thin web thickening."

"My mind's a basin of rock rich in ores of ideations."

"Nature is molding you into a masterpiece of maturity."

"You're building me up as a church."

"To worship in."

"Spare me! Cosseting me as a kid!" She is heart-poundingly, chest-hairingly, engine-revvingly, circuit-blowingly, tooth-grindingly, rewiringly, neurologically-kick-startingly high, on customarily low-volt Ritalin, a doctored/designer/dependable steroidically-enhanced version, chemistry-influenced Xanax, and varietal tranqs, the complete caboodle costing serious $ (pinched on a solo B & E from a classy, upscale, gangrenous home, its lock so laughably easy to pick she could've sworn at it and it would've gladly unlocked itself without fuss, the burgling smart, sneaky and on a borderline semiprofessional level, the job free of bungle, save for the itty-bitty mistake of letting one loose, the raspberry sounding wickedly adenoidal, but luckily it didn't cost her, karma being the keester she kissed on a regular basis, the blood in her skull vaporizer-seething, her pulses adrenalised high-filter flashbulb-flashes, she scared shitless, rigor mortis-rigid, nerves twined and quailing quietly, stealing, en route to the ole oak door, a stick of Old Spice, a bottle of NyQuil, and a box of Kleenex for good measure. And she hit the pseudo-rural road running, cardiac organ champagne-cork-popping, with a lava-flow of energy and a pillowcase full of pawnable merchandise and money, feeling right as rain, optimism of a clean getaway skyrocketing, and to cap it off she flipped the bird at cold-dish-serving kismet, cosmic retributions delayed for the nonce on her victory lap), covertly purchased in the town's lowest of intestines, in terms of sections, a place so vile even the vagrants and vermin had packed up and moved, in a recession of an onionskin-yellow doorway with almost advertorial graffiti spraypainted on it, in horridly blond noonlight cascading as a creek's course, wearing an OJ-colored jumpsuit, from this standup stereotypic aged African American dealer, Jim Brown-jacked, a rap/jock ghetto-centric Grandmaster Flashy bro-in-the-hood sort who proceeded to supervisorily instruct her on the correct approach to usage, and threw in on the sly extra radically nuclear-grade opioids as incentive for a return visit from his spanking-brand-new clientry to boost profits for his booming business, and fessed he had Everestic loads on his familial plate, these are troubled times stress-fraught. He was like some crim sage, a lawless Svengali, dispensing major-league drugs and avuncular advice in equal doses. His force was positively irresistible. He sounded like he was giving a liaisonal lecture, transition-easing, ropes-showing her, and she attritively nodded, needing to get blasted like nobody's business. Her body was gnawed on by twitches, brain in a fugue-state, gunk in her eyes as Krazy-Glue. Sun'd gleamed palely in the flame-blue sky. It was snuff-white, trembled, as if reflected in water only wasn't. Either that or it shivered like a struck snare. Snot-clotted tissue-paper grid of clouds. Grackles cried.

 "Time's universality, its dimension, I can elucidate -" it continues.

"I'm gonna block my ears." She cuts it off.

"Hell, your indecent relationship is as unsafe as skating on thin ice in late winter, early spring."

"Throwing manhole covers like Frisbees!"

"He's slinkingly reptilian, knuckle-draggingly simian."

Both cast criticisms as farmers do seed, hoping they'll produce a healthy harvest. Slapstick silhouettes. Broomy trees spastically sweep the pollinic air. Gray pallor of the firmament. A crowd is a bouquet coming apart. Children race as chickens from the fox in a coop. The blackness is distanceless and Katinka strips swiftly and quickly subsides in the bubble bath. She thinks of Vadim. Where the heck is he? Her concern is a rock rising in a regressing stream, sap draining from a maple, worry washing over her like surf the shore. Arousal is a bow stroking her violinic venter. Her brain is a bowl containing ripe fruit of thoughts. She melts as wax. She grabs her big bosoms like kittens by the scruffs. Life to her is a recruit you train, a rebellious kid you must put to rights. It is a perpetual fencing match of issues to deal with, a youngster you raise with dedication. Her cogitations are complex patterns of a carpet not ontop but underneath, and, comprised, oxygen in a miraculous meadow. She scrubs soap on a washcloth and commences rubbing her torso, whereupon she starts fingering herself. The bearded oyster beleaguers her. She calls it a "Baby cannon."

"We're diametrically opposed."

"Your canned insights are from a fortune cookie."

"Use that mop-handle as a dildo on me," it says.

"Ew ... Disgusting ... What a cum bucket ..."

"You're a me-firster."

"... Reaching like Mr. Fantastic ..."

"Your cute tootsies as breadloaves ... Stumpy athletic legs ... Whalewide hips ... Acneous arse ... Strapping physique ... Muscular arms ... Gorillian hands ... Monkey mug ... Ribaldly rubiginose mistletoe berry mouth ... Stub nose..."

"Gawd, you are gross! What a lesbianic chatterbox!" She acknowledges the aesthetic artifices of the archaic sink and toilet, completely contrasting the rest of the crappy furnishings in the manufactory. "Can't I masturbate in peace? Christ, can't even bathe myself without you nagging or bitching -"

The cock socket has the characteristics of a crone's clam. "Your moral cells aren't composed correctly." Its customarily animated fold-movements cease not unlike a piece of clockwork.

"Shut up, meat flap," examining her devil-red soles. "Your attributes are alien to me."

The labial lips smirk. "Lady, you could be a criminal or a queen and I'd adore you." Its tone is as a Last Judgment-type pronouncement. The organ blinks. "You are not cognizant -"

Katinka's throat throttled by junk necklaces Vadim gave her as gifts. "Consciousness is a mind aware of a sand particle landing in an eyeball. Subconsciousness is a body unaware that its gut is infected by a parasite. I am alert, foo-foo." She is rosily complected, drugged. "Time is tyrannical." Embranching shadows on a decay-colored yard which is wreathed in fog like it is sent from a perfume-spritzer. Beastly swelter. Her perspiry penumbra on the sodden sheet. She's plenty comfy, ginormous bum (her buttocks convexical, overall ass with a Valentine-heart aspect) inserted into the armchair's cushion dented, no, cratered with the fossilized impression of her posterior from tons of sitting sessions, the sweat-soaked fanny-outline like a crackpot Keith Haring drawing. The neutron-blue sky with overlapping clouds is a timed exposure. Her full belly bulges as a recently risen loaf in the oven from a communal KFC dinner with Vadim. She remembers them doing the nasty, chugging, funneling and froth-ing like a Jacuzzi. They barrel-rolled too. Then they fetally curled. Her ghastly optical mucus. She is more or less dyed-in-the-wool damaged, dysfunctional and undelusional, paralytically alert from eye-boggling, unquantifiable amounts of nicotine and caffeine.

"Fist me," the vagoo says. "I wanna climax ... I haven't orgasmed in eons ..."

"This conversation is inappropriate, French fry dip."

"You're cruel ... And clever." It mutters. The hoo-hee offends her blinders. It speaks to her as a spirit sum-moned at a seance by a medium, modulation like it is issued by a gramophone. Fuchsia-red heavens. Nacreous sea. Feeble light.

"The conscious is an image. The co-conscious is the idea behind it."

"You are on the proper path leading to the solution to your problem," it mumbles. "Tidal waves of frustration have dredged up obstacles from the depths -"

"Tra-la-la," Katinka with a sing-song inflection. Her pallid flesh flushed.

"I'm trying to take the temperature of the environment." Vulval activity. Its coarse pubic hairs are appearingly from the vegetable kingdom, such as lichen, moss, et cetera, with a carroty-orange tinge in the golden corn of effulgence. It grants a reprieve. It is wrinkled as an over-used tablecloth, giantess genitals in an advanced state of age, and withered like a flower.

"You're polishing a turd," she murmurs, reflects on the

operatic mystery of her relationship with Vadim, a mountain whose promontory is of great altitude, who could easily pass for a pugnacious prophet, always behind her as a tail, or, according to the quim-ceiling, he's a spider spinning his scheming web on her. If he's a steeple she's a dome. They are a couple of contradictory conclusions to a single subject. She floats freely, like the anchor of difficulty has been hauled in. She considers herself to be a cutting curse caught in an atramentous abyss. Her shark-simper flickers as a candle-flame. In the whisky-hued light she glows not unlike a dazzling dawn. His potter's prints of bruises on the clay of her pale skin. Her back and bum are prickled, as if she leaned into a porcupine. Damp asphalt shines as though a just-Zamboni'd hockey rink. Funeral-ish filing of folks on the sidewalk. Rain's a sardine run. The rusty, steel-bladed fan clangily rotates, reminding her of his intoxicated circular-swaggering gait. She serves her bladder and bowels. He looks at her constantly like a doctor who knows he can procure a remedy to alleviate a patient's affliction; in essence, with confidence. His severe, velvety intonation soothes her. She remembers, however, flinching as a plant when touched, her serious panic for some reason pulsing, reveries roaming like clouds following a storm. Vagaries dissolve as Alka-Seltzer tablets in water. His fondling was risky business. She went coin-cold. And she bears the burden of beholding the mirage of him. He read her like Braille. More of his unwelcome molestations. His limbs were branches on the trunk of her. She'd swallowed his penile pride. His retainer-induced lisp. She was inebriated, shellshocked in a mindfield.

Humectation was wet-woolly. In seducing her he was a butcher sharpening his knives for slaughter. He laughed that her genitalial slit was so tight it was akin to a finger endeavoring to fit into a piggybank's slot to claw out some change. He said without her he was an alcoholic denied his liquor. She returned she's not a new recipe which cannot be cooked with old ingredients. Precip dripped like a defective tap. She fantasizes their silken visages are formed and deformed by the ochroid lambency, their satin beings, newborn-naked, merging, fusing into a mangled mythical figure, a dual-headed demon with a singular god-body, burning into ecstatic extinction. He was a lovely Lothario, a steroidic matinee-idol during an interminable intermission (after intercourse) and waiting for his cue. Occasionally with him she feels as a deer wanting to cross the road only instinct informs her a car is oncoming. His peepers had hunted her like a hawk. "Infatuation is a cheap trick," he chuckled. She assessed his greyhound's ribcage. He stood erect at the piano-key staircase. Genie-ish cirri. A penial train ejaculated semen-steam in a vaginal tunnel. The amalgamation of their apparel on the cool floor, Islamic in the cinereal phosphorescence. Her thoughts are checker-pieces on the board of her brain. Her conscience has a crack; where she can't locate. Reminiscences are snapshots projected on the screen panel of her skull. She's cerebrally enclosed in an acoustical emptiness of echoing calmness. Showers pit-a-pat. Attributed to the illegal drugs it is like a loose thread of her pubes is tugged, and the fabric of who she is unravels. Hours are a chain creating their own links; or snails making gooey tracks. Woeful welkin weeps profusely. Afro cumuli. Her musings are a confluence of currents. Vainly she attempts to suppress her hankering for him - moisture kept in a cloud. An arthritic ache for him. An expected longing. Not dissimilar to a prostie anticipating aggression towards her from a pimp; hazard of the biz. His feathery penis was a cherubic wing. He'd pursued her as a mountaineer a splendid summit. Above her he was a peak gazing down at a brook at its base. It is all about perspective: to the young the slaying of a lamb is murder, to an adult it is a process to provide food. Vadim was a bull at the matador of Katinka. Usually he is licentiously offensive, she is defensive. He kissed the Chinese eyelet of her omphalos, thumbed an excrementitious orifice, whispered, "Civilization is so damned pleased with itself when it accomplishes any objective. They don't grab the rest of what remains." He prodded her like cattle, wreathed her as ivy a chimney. They moved similar to smoke. "And they remain unfulfilled," he added, "like leaving a little of your meal on the plate despite the abiding appetite." He playfully slapped her abdominal flab, smacked her robust rump. "Living in a tent when you have a house." He reveled in reviving her insecurities. They were two orchids on one stem. Cockroaches as dates stuck on the tiles. He had roid-raged. She was twisted like rope. He was libidinously off the rails. Pine wood partitions were stacked willy-nilly.

"You were once white snow ... Now you're certainly dingy, insusceptible of change." The furburger is seemingly a sealing eyelid of an individual who'd suffered a stroke and is left semi-paralyzed, emitting a last prayer on the death-bed.

Katinka's blush-blotched. She ties a towel on herself, has an elephantine tread, the rubicund majesty of doomed royalty. "I feel like a subject, over time, sitting for a Michelangelan artist, and I'm being painted in these years, filled-in, embellished ... Or I'm a tree, appearance changed by the seasons ... I'm a swimmer out of sight and submerging ... A memory fading from a failing mind ..." Umbrageous geometrical shapes on the rotten wainscot. She puts on a concert tee, cotton panties, and flip-flops.

"In the geology of your buttocks I can survey the erosions of the edges of your butt-cheeks, in the mass of your derrière the dimply deposits that have developed over a period that has elapsed and -"

"Fancy way of telling me I'm fat. You are aneurysm-inducingly funny." The ingenue rummages in the refrigerator. "To be insecteanly angulose ..."

"You possess an adolescent arrogance, preserve this youthful vanity," the beaver snaps.

"You're a pussy in a phenomenal pantomime. A ball-breaker entire." She snarls and plunks on the carmine couch.

Teacups are hunched porcelain gulls on the sills of grungy, grated windows. "I'm a stride, backward and forward, in measured diligence."

"You are an itch that when you scratch you bleed. Pings 'n' pangs -"

"You and that lecherous scumbag Vadim are flotsam and jetsam. Your ethic is a wine cellar, your principles the beverages in the bottles, and gathering coats of dust. You're a wound he infects."

"With him, sexually, I'm a feather falling from a flying falcon, incandescence brightening the twilight. He is the key to my lock." The gamine stretches and yawns. "I'm inferior, he is superior."

"You're a slave to your master, at the mercy of your moods, impulses. You encourage this raunchy romance." The thing squinches.

"We're breath held in slumber, assonance in dissonance."

"Contemplating an edifice we discern its sturdiness from the outside, not inside."

"He and I are surfers swept by the same wave, desire, chemical combinations of a fantastic formula." Her lineaments are livid; mist conveyed on a brilliant beach. She plops on the saffron sofa and gesticulates sarcastically.

"You're an officer collecting the troops together and forgetting exactly who the enemy is. You guys should be water divided by a levee. You are a dry hand fit into a wet glove with him." It squints. "The remembrance of what happened with you ... It's like a rapist returning to further violate the victim ..." The vagine regains its composure. "The dismal despair -"

"What I wish to confess to him is stuck to my palate as peanut butter. He's our bone of contention. Plain and simple. He's like an actor who auditioned for a role I wanted and didn't get. I accept this and admire him.

What a pestiferous punani!"

"He is a maggot" The sugar notch winks.

"You are a Peeping Tom poon! You're like a passer-by viewing the awful aftermath of an auto accident."

"Do I even have a choice?"

"This is a war zone of clashing personalities." Katinka sedulously clips and polishes her toenails.

"You care about your outer hygiene but not your inner hygiene."

"I handle your badgering as a straw hut would a hurricane, a tissue a waterfall."

"You just dig up insults by the roots and plant them elsewhere. You crave hierarchical harmony when there's -"

"You're as a girl getting into trouble deliberately for paternal attention." She picks at cuticles, keister on a flat cushion.

"Life is a tyke, scared in the gloam. Death is the parent flicking the light on," the muff says. "You are napalming your system with those opioids." Fog makes momentary continents. "You're agent orange-ing yourself."

"I guess, hairy Manilow, I could, I suppose, live a squeakyclean Julie Andrews- 'Sound of Music'-like life only I'd prefer to die with the screechy nobility of Janis Joplin. You are envious of my terminal existence - lots of comings and goings." She ties with a rubber hose.

"Junkie Joan of Arc!" The sticky bun screams, has a mock-minstrel grimace.

"Yuri!" Katinka calls, and the domesticated mutant wasp,

buzzing, clinging to a screen, flits over to the capacious counter, wiggles out of its floss-leash, sticks its abnormally long stinger, scarifyingly turkey-baster sized, in a plastic container, siphoning some of the cocktail, and it flutters onto her wrist, skitters, searches for a vein, taps with its tiny legs, and syringely shoots her up. She slips on espadrilles. She is an anatomic autumn whitening with premature winter. "I am carmelized." Hideous firmament unalone and wide and sheer could cause a visual coronary.

"Puerile pincushion!" The velvet goldmine shouts, volcanically erupting. Molten lava of anger spurns it on. "Comfy, comatose? Enfant terrible!"

"Love, to me, Leave it to Beaver, is the equivalent of essaying to wipe tears while wearing a veil. The heart's an apple, cut in half, these halves shriveling, the seedy core turning. Sparks start a fire. He's a bug stuck in my nectar." Her plumate posterior and paunch. A pin of light is pulled and the grenade of the sun explodes. "I'm foopy ... Got to get gouched ... Cabbaged ... E-tarded ..."

"Oh, you travel the path of least resistance: luster onto a lawn."

"Unreality has gotten through the net of reality. I'm a stitch in material - once it's put there you don't notice it anymore. It is attributable to habit: a stray cat is brought to its death by a dog because of its routine, not by lack of luck." Although immobile, Katinka is mobile, due to the emanation and penumbrae. The scabs of her problems are peeled, revealing scraped delusions which won't heal properly. Hours flow into the ocean of days, and time swells.

"The cosmos, cutey, is a compromise of poetic veracity and volition," the cooch pipes up. "The surrender of will is societal suicide." The smog is a mortuary shroud.

"I'm steps taken. On stilts. Vadim sprays as a perfume."

"Or a skunk." REMs of the creatural ceiling. "Your heinous family history -"

"Your nonsense is a page of text ripped to shreds and haphazardly taped together."

"You belong to the Witless Protection Program."

"I'm the lab he experiments in. I am a knot loosened to a loop. I feel like I'm dreaming and deliquescing simultaneously."

"Give that bastard your pinkie and he'll take your whole hand. His head plays second fiddle to his heart. Or loins. People to him impede his progress. They're booby traps. With you he scrapes an instrument's string, muting the other ones."

"When high, my thoughts wobble as toddlers. When straight, they saunter like a film noir's femme fatale. I care for the welfare of my cerebrations, as a captain his company, but a man in charge must sacrifice some for the main objective."

"You've grown stouter, sweetie."

"And you're a manipulator, honey, honestly, able and masterful, with guile and spontaneity."

"You are Ulysses on a self-destructive Odyssey."

"Mmm ... Embracing my dead mother you mean?"

"Are you the spiritualist contacting a ghost?" The yahoo asks.

"Nope," Katinka answers and parks her heinie on the chaise longue.

"You and that prick Vadim should be different trains on parallel tracks traveling in opposite directions. A safety precaution."

"We are connected cabooses."

"Your integument has the pigment of yellowing paper ... Pages of an old book."

"I'm solid as marble!"

"You're gonna crumble like a statue." It suspires. "You study me as a zoologist a scientific discovery."

"Shouldn't I though?"

"Attempting to convince you to change your wicked ways is like trying to turn a vineyard into a river. Those delicate contours ..."

"Spare me. You're an oculist who wants me to see through a lens you prescribe." The vapor is a tinted optical glass in its vastity, the burg thus slightly blurred.

"You are a mechanical doll."

"I need to devalue myself, reduce the substance of my stature, become diminished, debased, in pumice stone?"

"I'm not talking reduction, darling, instead ... Renewal."

"Your verbiage is more flowery than a soldier cemetery." The vista has a severe case of rosacea.

"Your misdeeds will recede in time's mechanism. Vadim's

arms are prison bars."

"Go to hell."

"Ceilings are a precious, man-made species. Cosmically they cover humanity. I've misallied myself here. You are going to die in error with this self-indulgent narcotics-abuse."

"You're an inaccurate, lunatical interlocutress in my life. I enjoy living here. It isn't Buckingham Palace ... It's not the Ritz ... You're a harpy nest ... A creation that is the condensation of a woman's privates, with its whirling, whorling continuity." Katinka wonders whether the hot pocket is as an annual in a garden that would ultimately shrivel and be replaced by another perennial. She swallows a lemon lozenge. Her supple, beefy thighs. She fixes a ferocious glance.

"I have oracular foresight with Talmudic focus." The hairy Potter pauses. "I've taken to you as a medieval monk to scripture. I'm drawn to you by an irresistible force, like from some imperceptible suction-pump. You are a beauteous bull."

"Condescending to listen to you ... You are conferring upon me a cow's corpulence."

"A consequence of being chubby, dear."

"I'm not a damn doormat."

"I know. I won't show you the door, my darling."

"You've surfaced as an unaided abscess."

"You are absurdly hypersensitive. You have heart and head."

"I am a bundle of nerves."

"You're submersing in your esteem, laying down your dignity in groveling servility to your brother." Leaden grey sky. Fleecy wisps of cirri. Imminence of illumination in the somber mirk. "You're a queen in a Greek tragedy."

"I'm an islet with rough and ragged surfaces in passive resistance against lashing wrathful waves surrounding me and stuck in a buffeting gale."

"Your expansive body, inessential meat notwithstanding, has a sculptural quality."

"You are a trick or treat," her.

"You're a sum of your parts," it.

"With you I'm a savage in captivity and deluding myself I'm still free in the wilds …"

"These bonds are without shackles. Go on the straight and narrow."

"… The law governing my life …" She fastens an unflinching look upon it.

"These are incalculable, indiscriminate verbal thunderbolts."

"Could I be a sovereign subject in some stained-glass window of a church?"

"You are a Minerva statue."

"You lead and I follow, as if I'm a lower primate watching a chimp opening and closing a box during a test so I can imitate it," says Katinka.

"You're like that famous horse that had a diet of roses," replies the vaginoid thingie.

"I am a Homer heroine you mean."

"You look as though you're an imposing, voluptuous, Venetian vagabond, with a gravelled voce."

"There's an insurmountable barrier between us."

"But alas! Indissolubly bound."

"Not so," assuming a serious air amongst an array of leftover machinery. Her flatulence is a hoarse bellow. Cake-food spread on a tea-table like for a funerary feast rite. Her toothy Creststrips wintry whiteout.

"Leaving you would be as exiting a planet and entering another. You are adorable as a Victor Hugo poem, even behind that shellac of paint and powder."

"I'm a meagre Milky Way..." She huffs and puffs.

"With characteristics of nebulae," it responds.

"I am a star fading." She imagines Vadim's dick and testicles: a serpent, repressed and penetrating, sleeping 'tween two stones. He'd ejaculated with an exclamation. Hers was a decorous desire. A matrix of varicose ribbons running through her mineral-substance-solid calves. "There is a formulae to our personal protocol ... Signs of our situation susceptible to simulated incivility in flux and reflux -"

"You are stoned."

"I am."

"Your Dr. Feelgood's a belligerent benchboss ... We're not nations embroiled in conflict, dear Katinka." Its fur sticking out, it looks like it was electrocuted by a bored imp.

"You were shifty like a Shylock, waiting in the wings." She follows the stream of reflection in the region of memory. "You're the cement holding me together, a foreign element integral to my well-being, despite your mystifying origins, having incorporated yourself into this exalted existence of mine, assimilated yourself seamlessly into it, and cutting an abnormal figure. Your qualities radiate around me." The stomachic celestial sphere secretes an acidic gastric juice.

"We are different tributaries on divergent courses that'll end up in the same river of a situation." It has the stink of mingled rotting vegetables and faint fruitiness mixed with a barnyard stench. "In our conversation my words are like dead G.I.s you're stepping on in a sally."

"They are spoken with exaggerated emotion, common to the theatrical profession."

"You can re-become a person who is straight and sober, one with sharp-edged wit."

"It has survived intact!"

"You are a pudgy petit, a comely confection. I have saved you like Moses from those waters."

"Your rhetorical apparatus ... You aren't even here ..."

"I'm as evident as the vault above the earth, child. I am a paradise you are permitted to enter, only I can't chart your course on any map."

"Because I'm swimming in the submarine realm of the Nereids!"

"We're separate provinces with blockades to communication."

"You're a patroness of the art of flimflamming." A smile kindles her face. "Put a lid on your id!"

"Lord, I'm menstruating ... I'm having my period ..."

"Christ, gotta be kidding."

"I wish I were a fish."

Katinka rolls a beach towel and inserts it into the vagina like a makeshift tampon. There is a sudsy froth leaving a lacing on it. "Nothing to be embarrassed about. It's natural."

"Bless you." A pregnant cessation. "You secretly cook in a soul kitchen."

"You're officially on the rag."

"Unfunnyly hilarious."

"Where's my steak sub?"

"Vadim bounded as a hyena, hysterical, on meth, the translucency of his visage comparable to that of a jellyfish. You had the hair of an ambassadress, strands jets of water of a liquid mass of a French fountain-basin in the winds." Its pendent parts wriggle obscenely. Vexed keens of cranes.

"With him I'm a word, he's the etymology. I'm a statistic. He is a statistician." Her hawthorn-colored heels. Will it become something of legend, in an odd Olympian mythology?

"Your personality has diversiform threads woven to make a multitude of patterns in a fabric of form and -"

"Shhh ..." She shines like a comet. Her mellifluous moue stirs as dust, or aqua pura, compelling the petticoat lane's admiration. Heart pounding, her chest sounds as a shooting-range. Her muddy pies. Candies strewn not unlike the breadcrumbs of Hansel and Gretel. Irrationality restricts the view of rationality that resides in her essence.

"You make everything difficult, as an invalid seeking out a cure for her malady by reading the lines of a physician's face, when it's easier to listen to his verbalized diagnosis. Your behavior is like a planted seed which sprouts into something that was impossible to predict."

Katinka remembers Vadim in an orgy with Arbus-esque freaks. He was a billiard-ball, hit by the cue of carnality and rolling, in a calculated carom-shot, strik-ing an anorexic drag queen in a gown and high-heels, ricocheting off a Jesus homo in kamikaze goggles and dental retractor, deviating from the initial trajectory course, and winding up in the wrong hole - hers. It was a sad scene. Their moans and groans in the concupis-cent conundrum were musical, amplified humming harps, drowning out all other melodies on earth. It was athletic sodomy and she was a spoilsport. The other oddities watched intently. He grunted in her ear, "Our Unpleasantville ... They yen for something sweet to be soured."

SCHIZOPHRENIC WEATHER. KATINKA, MANE plaited in a ponytail and gleaming with gynic brilliantine, 'stache suppressed by pancake makeup, formidable glasses tee-ter-tottering on the bridge of her Jewish proboscis, tummy with its tumescence, wears a purple dress and sandals, panda-eyed with runny mascara, somnambulantly unsteady on the rickety fire escape, ticker tocking loudly, a gorgeous librarianish presence installed in a standing position at the corroded railing. The atmosphere with the flap dragon has gone automatically into a new phase, has changed, like a political climate instigated by a revolution. It heaves as a bust. Their differences unbridgeable. Gaga at the artificial apparition, a corporeal cunny, an unvarying, immemorial, imaginary vajayjay, grotesque, preserving its coochie pop constitution, however, and having an aspect of a dubious, rare, poignant novelty, her speech is described to it in a mute language expressed in extravagant gestures. She feels like her life is a jigsaw puzzle and can't fit a particular piece into her existence. Due to an encroaching cold she has a nasal twang. Hectic hail. Macaw-chromatic rainbow. Obsidian ocular puddles in concrete sockets on the macerated curb. Pedestrians are plodding, palsied sheep. The city is a stentorian symphony of horns, shouts, engines, jackhammers, and so forth. She opines she's cruising through life, concludes a plane without a pilot (ejected) will still assume its flight before eventually crashing. Melancholia swells in her like the moon in a sea. She has a (forbidden) planet's revolutions in the beanbag chair. She digitally fucks herself so fast her libido can't keep up. She has a bobblehead coconut, is parous with the creation of pleasure. Thence she falls asleep and has a nightmare where countless umbilical cords lash out of her vagina as the tentacles of an octopus, transforming her into a genitalic Medusa. She awakens. Ah, to be parenthesized with Vadim on the moldy mattress ... Kissing him is as smooching a stick of butter. Their Kama Sutra of flirty mannerisms. Drug paraphernalia on the polished pine table. He arises like a cat when the cabinet-door containing the kitty snacks squeaks open and gives her a Heimlich of a hug. His Mountie's jutting jaw. She stares catatonically ahead as in an anxiety attack. She catches the fragrance of his citrus-scented deodorant. His laughter has a flushing-toilet roar. Not for nothing he whispers in her ear, "Buckeroo, you've got pizzazz out the bazoo." Clouds coasting appear as if video time-lapsed. Light's stabbing sabers. The thing has an impassioned neutrality between them. Ferns, hairstrands blowing, list starboard in the snappy winds suety with summer's heat. A frankly ballsy Japanese motorcycle's a scalpel cutting the wettened asphalt, leaving a long slice in its wake, cinereal gristle exposed and left unstitched. Sprinkles hush. Gnats flit like floaters before your eyes like when a lightbulb is abruptly flicked on. Nonarchaic contraptions. Smeary sky. Pepto-Bismol-pink cirri. Visine-clear pools on smooth blacktop. Unusually dull steel girders. His firm grip on the cantaloupes of her tits, grasp of her loggy legs. She yearns for him to plug his cable into her electrical outlet, slide into her casually as into a pair of pants, but an event's end must be emphasized, whether it's musicians finishing an instrumental with a virtuosic flourish or brutes brawling in a bar: mallets on a timpani or knuckles on a jaw. They are blast furnaces, wire-walkers. He was shopping for groceries. She wants him badly! Time is a target missed by an inept archer. She's a

mango he devours; not in slivers either, but the totality
of her. Ammonial aroma of sprinkles of sleet. Her horsy
haunches when she trots! She gallops with a sense of
self. He is a robot who programmed himself. They are a
species of bird, singing the same song. When one slacks
off the other compensates, like the religious rowed in
pews in church, several nodding off during a sermon,
and a few atone, vocally, for them. The siblings are aliens
on their own native soil, so intuitive, immune to civilization's prejudices. She is stock he invests in, a tome whose
cover he cannot manage to close until the last word is
read. He's a survivor, a scrapper, loyal to a private (not
public) good. She is a positive effect on the negative
Vadim, the whole of his parts, frame of his canvas. He
appreciates her importance, as a swimmer does a life
jacket, a skydiver a parachute. She pictures them, brother
and sister, nude after nutsoid coition (they were metallic
fragments on a magnet of sex), wrapped as presents in a
Turkish blanket (given to her by her high-strung folks
who were successful sandwich-bag entrepreneurs and
part-time Method-Acting instructors) and throw-rug
on the lubricious linoleum in the commodious kitchen.
Doughy calescence of the day with its distillation of
clamminess. It was acrobatic copulation. They'd had
Seven-up, Pepperidge Farm cake, and Oreos, fresh sup-
plies for a necessitous junk-food debauch for relief, a
release in a behavioral modification routine, for she was
crashing and rapaciously hankered for a sugar-high in
the worst way. It was a non-narcotic dependence for
pete's sake! Mist seems sprayed by a mister. Yuri'd gone
into hiding, being plain rude. Their moist osculations

and dry tactions. Autumnal orange heaven. Obliquitous splendor. Insectile whirrings of winds, sheeny and reverberating as adrenaline in the system. The pair come together in a big balloon of primary-pigmented prurience. Parallelograms of shade established in the spacious, dim room. Her saliva is sticky, like it's pop. A pond is Ralston-resemblant. Grass looks as veal. He gives her the keys to the carnal car. She could go for staggering amounts of chemical aides and distilled spirits. Her dandruff detritus driving her bats, physical being succumbing in an undeft fashion to gravity by visible degrees onto the sumptuous recumbent recliner, broad bottom fitted nicely into its butt-imprint, eclipsing it, yeast infection yammering soundlessly. Its instructional manual is so cryptographically complicated she cannot bother with it because it's not invitingly informative. She unwinds near the wastecan, is preliminarily irritated by this not-irrelevant fact. Showers shush. She is frighteningly, fatally pretty in a womanly-slash-manly way no dope-smoking and beer-drinking could make unserious. Fate's lying in state. She has a toothy smile of illegal wattage, ample bosom, low-slung as a car. "I have a migraine, and it feels like I'm that plastic bear's head and someone's crushing it, me, to get the honey out," she says. Intersecting illumination's queerly unbright Xs. The creepy honey pot ceiling sounds like a crazy combo of Hal from Kubrick's film '2001' and a castrati choir, insists she'd shrunk in height, gained in weight, why she is apparently squat. There creeps into her smirk the appropriate aspect of amiability. She's cosmetically embalmed, with a lilac-pallor, barefoot, puts on a mauve maillot to beat the heat, and eats a raspberry tart. Her stellar opalescent eyes gaze blankly. Vadim's piercing glare and bird-beak offer themselves to her contemplation. If she is out of Dostoyevsky, he is out of Molière. The gross pecan patty vanishes as war, and leaving no trace behind it. Has it gone into oblivion? Or merely withdrawn? The bear trap was ill-placed, in its specific gravity. It appeared and disappeared randomly, the stack a port from which to embark and disembark, as a bizarre Bassorah out of 'Arabian Nights.' She feels like she has known it for donkey's years, immersed in the melodramatic misalliance, both timepieces hardly synchronised. The last thing she said to it was "I feel stupid, as a book-keeper who fails to balance the books." Her abdominous astronomical clock carved out of a lardaceous block tells her it is time to chow. Eventide falls with an expiring echo of un-sound. She ministered to Vadim's pleasure, fellated his ivory tower. She was like a tragic defrocked priestess with a glint in her eyes and had a Sarah Bernhardt aura about her. She was turkeycock-reddened, spell-bound and muddle-headed, in an aqueous murk.

"I wish you had a cock," he said.

"I wish you had a cunt," she said.

"Adam."

"Eve."

She took a gun out of her sequin purse, a glistening pistol, and shot him twice. Pop goes the weasel, she thought.

HUMAN REMAINS, HERMAPHRODITIC, were found in a

defunct smokestack, brooding and massive, by a hoid-
enly hiker.

363

Finis Operis.

A.I.: Automatous Infanta

M'YELLOW, YOU LISTENING? Yes and okay so it was one of those sneaky setup situations right outta that Chris Hansen American television show, um, a 'To Catch a Predator'-type deal where those sicko kiddie-diddlers think they're gonna pick up some ten-year-old staggeringly cute-as-a-button honey-pie on a street corner in an off-the-map-remote town in Nowheresville US of A and they find out the real hard way they've been badly bamboozled because law enforcement and a truth be told terrifyingly creepily blandly handsome guy with doll's hair looking heroic and accusatory at the same time's there to greet them and the excrement hits the proverbial fan, y'know? But in this case it's the police and scientists who've hoodwinked a pedophilic sap into believing he's meeting a stunning jail-bait teenaged dear only here she, the girl, is an artificial intelligence, uh, a synthetic being or whatever. No, not android, fuckface.

Different altogether. Trust me. Reason being they wanna see if the thing, the robot, erm, we'll call her Al, appearingly Greek and charmingly chubby and dressed in a flamenco-dancer costume, an ultra-adorable infanta I suppose, can rationalize I guess with the pervert, reason with the sonofabitch, can't use his Christian name, oh, we will name him Sabiston, for the sake of argument, to gauge whether or not she has the natural, innate, developmental aptitude to acquire these human instincts noninherent to get her own fake nuts 'n' bolts synthetic sweetie self out of a lousy and scary scenario. I'll have another, bartender. Straight no chaser. And peanuts. Please. Huh? Stupid. I mean, golly, what a dumbass question from a douchebag. Are you out to lunch? One can short of a six-pack? Gosh almighty. Of course she had an organ. And budding breasts. Bubble-butt. The whole anatomic shebang. Lemme frigging finish for Christ's sake! I figured you of all people would want to hear this shit, being abyssally and spirally head-long into sci-fi and stuff. Because it's wild and true. I'm not fibbing or lying altogether. You cannot make this crap up I'm telling you. Descriptions of 'em? He recalled a rabid, balding, homonine Baby Huey in a Gap getup and she resembled I'd have to say Herve Villachez in drag. The story was very visual when it was verbalized to me. Have you ever experienced total terror? Devouring dismay that grips your gut and won't let go? The kind that sucks your soul into a horrible vacuum? Had the plain awful awareness that you were going to die a dragged-out-for-the-freaky-killer's-evil-entertainment sort of death? It ain't anecdotal embellishment either.

Well, picture being a young lady who knows in spite of her robotic origins she's about to be raped repeatedly and ruthlessly and brutishly bludgeoned with a blunt object and left for weekend backpackers to quote unquote stumble on her bloody and bashed remains scattered as wadded picnic litter off the beaten path in shiny shrubbery of a mountain range rarely visited except by collegial hikers who pretty much invariably chance upon pummeled-beyond-recognition corpses. Naturally, because she's not natural, she's not consciously thinking of her dire circumstances and really grim and wickedly grave and potentially grisly situation, rationalizing on any authentic-kid level way whatsoever, only instead is actually feeling it, living it, smelling it, tasting it, with a dreamy accentuation of senses, complete hallucinatory clarity, suffering unendurably with an acute certainty she'll be brutalized and slaughtered with exotic instruments. I'm not fence-straddling here. I am not politically correct. By all accounts Sabiston was like a shark, swimming in circles through the city. Al was easy pickings, mocha-skinned, long-haired, a stone in a shimmering stream of light, playing hopscotch by herself in the seething hiss of Summer's drizzle, near a cracked gray cement wall that was apparently a waterfall, in this warehouse district that was as an Egyptian necropolis, these grabbing-hand leaves on maimed-arm branches, flies flittering ashen eyes disembodied, under an absolutely monstrous monk's head of a sun. Sorry ... She was programmed to believe her mom was home watching soap operas and her dad was MIA. Sabiston pulled up not quite hesitatingly in his dented, sable Saab looking at this juncture to've been an exhumed creepy bulbous male with shaggy, thinning mop, shifty not-alive pies and disturbingly deranged smile showing his dental disadvantage, and was compelled to inform the greener-than-Gumby gal in a demented movie-dubbed-sounding intonation he was in fact her bonafide biological father and the heartless dirtbag who was no-maybes-about-it a clever imposter always AWOL anyhow and who should be shot immediately and buried in a depthless grave for possessing the unmitigated audacity to pretend to be the genuine pops and in the process did the dark and devious character with utterly no hope of achieving decency in the world had the nerve to make her trust that he truly cared about her made him, Sabiston, ripping mad. The dimpled door was ajar. Reluctantly she climbed into the probably stolen vehicle and they drove off. She immediately caught on to his agenda. His ulterior motives were obvious. The main clues, and they were air-clear, was the Gorshin-as-the-Riddler-on-mesc-like laugh, mescal-fueled drinking session, Pat Boone-crooning. He was a freewheeling motormouth. You've got to remember too when an individual is subjected to perhaps pure, plummeting, spine-tingling, scalp-chilling dread, she/he mentally retains every last traumatizing second of the ordeal, the surviving person does. Being thoroughly specific, it's on a nightmare-level where everything is enlarged, spike-sharp, each detail alarmingly vivid. I'm endeavoring to remain removed from psuedo-Freudian, pompous-ass, recondite mumbo-jumbo. See, Al knew something was rotten in Denmark from the git-go when Sabiston was

grinning ghoulishly and dementedly ranting and sali-
vating while listening to saddening seventies stuff that
coaxes you into slipping your neck into a noose pronto
and he was leering menacingly and raving manically, his
vociferous vocalizations, like clockwork, going over as
bladder and bowel evacuations at the Vatican with the
Pope present as far as she was concerned. Instinctively
she was externally calm. Internally she was a basket case.
She instantly intuitively decided to play-act. To be that
immature and innocent and unreal, to have the instinc-
tive ability to realize she was more or less sizzling in the
frying pan is amazing to me, and to rationalize, in the
plunging timelessness of duress, to consider what was
occurring, what would happen to her sooner or later ...
Jesus. Think of it: Al sitting in the passenger seat of this
car speeding down the illimitable interstate with a
drooling lunatic at the steering wheel singing a Terry
Jacksian song at the top of his lungs and the crazy man
frothing at the maw was already planning exactly how
he was gonna get his jollies with her and discard her as
a broken toy in the woods many miles from civilization.
To precisely perceive the impending danger. To have the
capacity to handle a foaming screwball who is disgorging
a disquieting lingual storm. Extraordinary. To be
convinced in a matter of minutes, give or take, or hours
at most, you'll wind up as insect-covered leftovers in an
isolated area, casualty of some sex-slaying, is unequivo-
cally miserable. To encounter that class of anxiety,
endure it, and to claim the cerebral wherewithal to
analyze your plight and attempt to figure out a solution
to the problem is impressive. However, jumping out of a

junkbox traveling Speed Racerly fast on the highway isn't a valid option I assure you. Psychotic pedophiles by their nature are hypersensitive. He'd take the drastic action personally, that she'd prefer to lunge out and hit the pavement and lose flesh and get a body rash and passing for living roadkill and crawl broken-boned into profuse bushes rather than hang with him during a scenic ride cross country might float as a metalline dirigible. The idea of it ... I dunno ... Crying would backfire, accomplish nothing. If she screeched who the hell would hear her? Besides, he'd become extremely agitated. Would not be good. Crackpot child-molesters hate being shrieked on in the middle of things. Zero tale-enhancements here. Zilch. She knew she was up the creek without a paddle, but she was bound and determined to not be found mutilated, personal pieces strewn in a vast forest region by Green Peace-donating, Nature Valley-granola-chewing, redwood-embracing, L.L. Beanified, amateur adventurists. Not on her nonlife. His Grinch-smirk. Yes. Right. The entire drama was being monitored by the powers that be. Essentially her peepers were cameras and her ears were speakers. She turned actressy. Pretended. He cupped her knee with his palm, then stroked her thigh. She touched his hand, caressed it. Whereupon she slapped his shoulder gently and giggled. She became his daughter to put him on a guilt-trip. He babbled, fussed with the radio's volume/treble/bass knobs nervously. She kept up her thesping. He yenned for them to melt and merge and she yearned to abscond ASAP. They'd run outta racetrack. His inflection possessed a steely crackly staticky loudspeakerish quality, voice acquiring an animated vocal volume, in a gridlock clusterfuck, a battalion of road-crews in safari-hattish helmets and lurid-orange vests and work-boots paving a pot-holed exit-ramp flat, the workers making a tanned-and-dirty tableau. Then Al Hasidically genuflected, head rolled Ray Charlesly, poreless and perfect, fat feet barely reaching the floor, mane antennaed with the window open, keenly observant, in a trancelike state, a contrived coma, as though Sominexed into sleepiness, bovinic placidity approximating parodic. Sabiston meanwhile was a mummified man in denim jeans, sleeveless shirt and boat shoes without socks, reeking of B.O., disinfectant and singed dust on a portable heater, respiration cranked, glaring full-frontal at her, showing his disregard of oral hygiene, typical of many paranoid schizophrenics, classic sign actually, scratching his pock-marked visage, emptying its expression, as a poison oak itch, agitation ambient, popping prescription pills as gummy bears, and smoking turbo-charged weed. Their interactions, instigated by her, were turning intimate. She sparked the conversation. Momentumized it. She'd rallied, gotten a second wind in her sails, roulette-gam-bled, perspirational placenta soaking her akin to a newborn, methodologically staring flirtatiously at him, come-hitherlyly. Smart cookie. This was a crucial moment, a critical juncture to elicit his compassion and she was not gonna foul it up. He was not futzing around. He was thoroughly unipolar. Homework was done. On Zoloft and Prozac. Urinose, ammoniac showers. Painting a picture. Oxygen was yeasty-sulphury. His sweat was musky, eyes startled and virile, derma-layer sheet-white, plosivity of his prolixity gray matter-loos-eningly maddening, lingua franca grand-scale shoots off the bough of indulgent insanity, ostensibly saying he wished to be on her as white on rice. He knew he was indeed lousy at communicating. To her he was basically alien. He gave her the screaming meemies for sure. She hung in there, was humanly controlled and contained. She was his ticket to transcend. He had forsaken his scruples, punted his principles, succumbing instead to an individualistic imperative, a dense and multiform appetence, stuck in a moral storm. Enfolding and gauzy and tricolored distance. Sea and sky had the same silver shade. Rosily backlit trees' branches, mysterious and skeletal, belonging to a school's playground, made these filmed-witch-you-are-being-hypnotized-over-the-top gestures. Glowing-ghostly clouds billowed not unlike curtains. Sun had a hepatitis-jaundiced pigment. It was an orgasmic, tragic and chaotic tango and he wanted her as his partner. She had a false frown of focus. A titanic strain to maintain. Her ears rang as elevator bings. His countenance was a configuration of anxiety. The Saab had a nauseating stench of something unidentifiably sour, along with Lysol, a uremic odor. They took a detour at Mr. Burger and burned rubber out of the parking lot, hauling. He was weeping. She said she was glad as heck they were together again, relieved they were reac-quainted, put on the pressure tactics, a smart strategy, making Sabiston feel like a grade-A asshole for contem-plating violating her with abysmal apparatuses and leaving her for dead in thick vegetation for she was unquestionably a darling who made an emotional connection to him and affected him in a profound and downright poignant manner he had never before experienced in his pathetically deviant existence and he was a total jerk for his nutsoid considerations. This created a special angelic aura about her, set her apart from the rest of the pubescent pack he'd abducted and assaulted and used esoteric equipment on. Put her on another plane. She verbally soothed him when he sobbed, slowed into the breakdown lane. She hugged and kissed him, patted his shoulder, told him to stay safe. He shouted something and shoved her out into a patch of foliage and skidded off. It was a test drive, a radical experiment that thankfully didn't go haywire. Okey-dokey, pardner, you got me dead to rights. Busted. Saw through me like tracing paper. I lied. Sue me. I'm a cocksucker. It was him, not her. Imagine it. Just you.

THE END.

Infant

My life is amazed to find me alive. I'm Jeanne, an attractive, maybe Francis Bacon-modelesque, (mucronate) blade-thin (with admittedly thick butt), long-limbed drug-addict with a Rita Hayworth hairdo (if she came in from a hellaceous hurricane), overlush Betty Pagean body, and pond-scum green-and-night-sky blue peepers so filmy they appear to be under the surface of a murky pool, wearing pajamas 24/7/365, trying to take care of my sexless, seal-shaped, Down Syndromed, malodorous, malformed, papular, cross-eyed, pigeon-toed, carbuncular, typhlotic, hearing-impaired, snaggle-toothed, saurian-skinned, palate-clefted, rodential-faced, humped, hunched, noseless, unblinking, twisted and 'It's Alive'-teratoid toddler, a floppy, basically boneless baby I shall call "The Infant," on the second-story of this dead planet of a place, the unrepaired building looking frankly closed and cordoned, dumped than built, and resembling a brick brain with these ugly protuberant bay-windows and slate roof, a hideous complex that's whitewashed graymatter, with a skeletal fire escape, scabrous fence, pitiful, balding lawn, unpruned shrubbery, Medusoid silver maples with shiny bark, densely wooded area out back you couldn't short-cut through because there's no sanctioned trail to speak of, nothing but deciduous trees and thorny bushes and stuff, rutted road, useless train tracks, and steep eroding ravine. This is an abstract abode, a sum of its parts, a warped square containing intricately filthy furniture unexceptionally experimental, origins forgotten. I'm a horrific slob for sure, insistently zoned-out in an under-the-influence magic-spell. An elbow of an edifice, parabolic and plane-hangarish, the Archdiocese headquarters, winks with lights and nudges the ribs of double-and-triple-deckers, lined complexly, with abrupt, depilated yards, chain-link fencery buckled and bowed from unbelievably ferocious territorial dogs, the driveways invariably with oily camel-bumps. Someone's a female trailer-trash stick-figure symbol out front of a Greek pizza parlor. Enslaved to substances, my existence is an in-joke I'm alone and in on. Welkin's clouded curvature of a chin has a razor-burn. Moon is as if someone took a good bite out of it. Horizon's becoming hallucinatory. Hyperemic steeple gets flaccid in the fog. Strange sodiumish light. The Infant's shrieky, glass-shattering cry (Oskar Matzerath couldn't hope to compete) can be queerly compelling and could raise hair. Its heartbeat whumps like an applause kinda clapping with mittens on and its mouth sorta visually corresponds to a play production's buccaneer sword held sideways, either up or down, depending on whether it's happy or sad. When hungry the infantile thing would go absolutely apeshit, sweat-sheened, making a godawful racket, vanilla-pale, Jell-O flesh jiggling, and eat as a wild animal. Cosgrove, my lumberjackish, bad-news, business-meaning on-off boyfriend, big and dim both, with walrus mustache and whiskered dewlaps, Haystacks Calhoun-large, who could very easily pass for a retired collegiate-level football guard gone to pot, literally, his abdomen accordionizing while he avalanchely ambled, wearing an expression usually reserved for the strangulated, seemingly pissed-and-stand-offish, customarily dressed in a de-sleeved Eddie Vedder-esque flannel shirt, camouflage cargos and work boots, a chain-smoking speed-freak, and bearded biker-type whose Harley ride is his pride and joy (his anatomic hog too), a bruising brawler who happens to be a pool hall habitue, usually intent on the bar. Our nookie was an athletic event; he pecked and probed, his offense his defense, capitalized on my mistakes, and intuitionally anticipated anatomical angles to be available to him to exploit. Naturally, I won't lie here, the Infant scared the ever-living crap out of him, the completely creepy, cutting wail (with the sonancy of a cat meowing in heat) and cheap-vacuum-cleaner-screech coming from the nauseous excrement-colored crib totally wigging him out, but eventually he went with the flow, you know? Gotta confess its mesomorphic cranium and pallid derma wiggling as a motel's mattress when repeatedly kangaroo-hopped on courtesy of numerous young-dinosaur-sized juveniles didn't help things in my burgeoning relationship with him one iota. It was acceptance and/or tolerance more than understanding and/or compassion on Cosgrove's part. Which was fine. No problem. In fact, truth be told, he was more frightened of the mutant, Kafka-esque, scarabaceous roaches infesting the joint than scared of the chillingly monstrous child with a penetrative, piercing, blood-curdling scream. He realized the Infant was no regular kettle of fish, in terms of situation. The firmament with levin is apparently a vast forehead pulsing in extreme effort. I imagine interior lineman-lumpen Cosgrove's penis vibrating like a diving-board relinquished, remember the farts arpeggio-ing out of his ample ass. He, appearingly agitated, whipped out his cellphone when I sawed the spit and snot off the Infant using a damp paper towel. Its stink comparable to the sick sweet-sour stench of Athlete's Foot. He said his recent bowel movement was borderline balletic. My not-quite-steady BF, a beefy demon with nubbly chiclets, a meaty hombre with blood-pressure blush and ham-hands. I told him, breaking the ice, I was getting clip-on nipple-and-navel rings, had gotten plastic surgery, get anxiety attacks fairly often, perform occasional charity work at the soup kitchen, and win bread by professionally panhandling, yours truly being an integral part of this cliquey club, the members skilled and practiced and with technique up the wazoo in begging with the bowl. His hyphenated pies squinted severely, otherwise wasn't fazed. After he banged me hither and yon he left and the Infant had his, Cosgrove's, countenance, which bugged me the hell out. I went bananas. Cosgrove porked and hosed me. The

Infant is mine. I made it. Nameless, I gave birth to it, squeezed it out like a stubborn turd. And it was conceived in a moment of inebriated amorous impulse, with a mountainous, rattily goateed, tatted (one man tattoo convention), hirsute guy of my social stratum, in a leather vest, dirty tee and ripped jeans, Minshew, massively powerful and with the physique of a Gatorade barrel, stoic, yet self-conscious and clinically depressed (he had the stones and juice to say so during sex), who at one point in the decayed, low-budget luminosity lost his frigging mind when I started to read aloud the instructional manualish scripture quote written in Gothic script in sanguineous ink on framed vellum on the rotting pinewood wall above the oak dresser. When he departed he had the expression of a person on the verge of suffering a stroke. Minshew never darkened my door again. The empyrean with the lightning's cords bulging out of a strained and limitless neck. Steel wool cumuli. Crows hang congruous to little black boys in the 'hood. They hurtle themselves into the apocalyptic vault, plum-pigmented and heartbreakingly beautiful, their droppings the creamy color of willows' rinds. Mizzle an immeasurable mesh, sounding as something singed. Franciscan-bald sun. Radical harlequin patches from a rainbow. I swallow saliva. Dimples in my thighs congruent to dents in dough. I am encaged by my cravings. A pubic-black African American young lady fit as a fiddle (from my particular Heideggerian perspective) in a sailorish suit and wildly ordinary sandals with a poor posture obviously wrecked and self-obsessed orbits a parliament of jaundice-yellow cabs and summons instead of hails a taxi. She articulates in a monotone, like she's reading from a prompter. Her dun silhouette insectivally skitters on the guano-dappled pavement, bathed in parentheses and parallelograms of stuttering Magic Markerish fluorescence from honeycombed stores' neon, her baggy clothing billowing as though curtains over windows. Bridal veil of sprinkles. Leven's spikes in the graph of the azure. Beastly humidity. The spate reeks of dry rot and has the viscosity of stress-diarrhea. Thunder has the sonance of a giant's stomach grumbling. A tissue is a small kite. I partake of the cheese, caviar and cannabis a Haitian John, anorexially emaciated, gave to me for my services provided. Clouds spitting showers are those comic-book-joke flower-squirters. Robin's-egg blue heavens. My misshapen mouth ellipsed by lipstick, bug-eyes eclipsed by mascara. My cardiac organ chops like a helicopter. Pollen with the texture of talc. Crepitant creepage of the Infant's emergent birdie squawk is an audible/optical cue for Motrinish tablets. It projectile-burps, the stream as a whale's spout. Another belch. It is all right. Happens. Tampons and pantyhose on and in the seriously stained sink. My reflection held in the grungy medicine cabinet's mirror. Blunts in an ashtray. Cookbook volume with cracked vertebrae. Tubular currency utilized for sniffing pharmaceutical-grade gutter-glitter. Baglets of seeds. Chunklets of aluminum foil. Wretched weather. I untie the stupid damn gift-wrappish ribbon in my pixied 'do. Soaker sounds not unlike lit matches continually tossed into water. Grocery receipts the size of playing cards. Funnels of bills ya could siphon gas with. Drencher's needles are the tiny legs of disembodied wasps climbing downward. The Infant's eyes are colorless buds that continuously open and close. It breathes as a savvy swimmer preparing for a long-distance natation, integument like starchy cotton steam-softened, turning elephant-tincted (from a peach-pigment), tongue mercuric red, Ove Glove-handed and catcher's mitt-footed, swaddled in a washcloth-baby-blanket, it too darn creatural for words. Things got a whole lot weirder. To wit: when I met the verily dweeby and improbably named Dunkelberger, fishy-white, nerdly to no end, a Harvard grad, not too cool for school, flapping his gums and with ants in his pants, wardrobe, thoroughgoingly tweedy, hardly withit, cautious gait as a film-noir's gumshoe, the character really tripping on incredibly potent acid, a think-tank-and-Au Bon Pain-frequenter, senses unprecedentedly perhaps permanently distorted, putting me in my discomfort zone when he sat on the drum-tight bedside's stool, knee-bumping the wicker hamper and otiose ottoman, handling these Saran-Wrapped, Sierpinski gasket-shaped, shamrock-greenish brownies with the precise care a jeweler gives to precious diamonds, arranging them with Zen-like accuracy on his lap, mumbling sounding as Ethel Merman murmuring, only understand for a second I was desperate for money and pills and food and as a result I was certainly a willing participant in doing the nasty in exchange for a decent and fair reward. He was a humanistic exhibition of self-absorption, a performance artist parodying a narcissistic individual, sitting in prox-imity to the heinous mullioned pane inundated with ale-amberous lambency, commenting on the aesthetics of decoration in the apt., considering its artifacts of furnishings, promoted, okay, pinched from another person's pad, the room institutional, as an insane asylum, predominantly khaki not unlike a G.I.'s helmet, his hatchet-face dramatically profiled. We didn't discuss the Infant in any way or form. I wore a pine-hued poncho, pretty skirt and clogs, felt sponge-wrung-out, at the end of my rope and ready for a severe hanging. The sill's ledge, halated in shadow, was piebald from pigeon-poop. He stood in the exact middle of the lurid kitchen, noninsecure, overconfident mayhaps, on the polished hardwood floor in striated scintillation, telling me he was hardening, his prick was a county-fair corn-dog, sipping wicked weak wine (I grabbed at the supermarket while locomoting down an empty-yet-product- concentrated aisle prior to trundling into the checkout-lane with racks of candy and magazines with celebrious-and-human-disinterest stories aplenty, rotating as a Lazy Susan to see who was behind me), obliquely glancing at me. His stride was formal, footfalls staccato-sounding, kiss impersonal. I listened to the precip's serpentine hiss. Sidewalk was sable. Busy businesses had coronal canvas awnings. Ghastly-whitened crowd flowed similar to waste. Street was an opalescent seam. Rhythmless downpour psssted and looked not dissimilar to grainy hand-held 16mm projected on a screen of air. Claret coruscation on the cinereous curb was a half-healed cut on a palm. Chiaroscuro choreography. The celestial sphere was underwater-bluish. Our passionless, substanceless coition was like a mock-St. Vitus's dance in the sheets. Dunkelberger absconded unceremoniously. The vista had this garish afterglow in the wake of an LSD-fest. Milky, sheepy cirri. The Infant adapted his physiognomy and I went crazy. A while later I was screwed into submission by the Colonel Sandersiferous (immaculate ivory suit, bow-tie, the entire kit 'n' kaboodle) Harkless, a semi-successful, follicle-and-neurologically-challenged southerner real estate agent. I def didn't dodge the bullet with this bozo. Following the lusty rocking copulation he told me, his breath warm and stale as a dryer's, voice uncannily heliated, he had respirational difficulties and periodic gland swells pos treatable with the proper medications. He filled me in on the fact he wanted to bash my brains in with a Louisville Sluggerine bat and Chikara-knife-hack me into uncountable pieces and store me in baggies in the fridge next to the yogurt and cola. I panicked and tasted the coppery flavor of pennies. His psycho-philosophical horsetwaddle was nerve-racking. I managed to get rid of him by introducing him to the Infant. Harkless, the dirtydog nutjob, went all ghostly, facial expression possessed a narcotized opacity, the Infant's arachnodactylic digits wriggling in an undeliberate toodleoo gesture, the two of us in curious cooperation in getting rid of the jerk. He fumbled with his fly, reminding me of an adolescent nabbed by his hyper-religious parents for chain (and other such)-yanking, and bailed in a jiff. Whereupon I searched on all-fours the oriental rug for something to snort and in the process of weeping. Cerebroid sea. I sobbed copiously. The Infant I noticed had the lineaments of Harkless. Jesus Christ, I have the rather clear memory of the terrible ripple effects of contractions, pregnant with the Infant, in the late stage. I'd rolled on my side on the clean carpet in the 'Partridge Family' parlor belonging to the wealthy, generic, pudgy Pugh, on vacation in Tahiti at the time with his Wall Street buddies, akin to a wounded cow and cutting, clumsily, cocaine on the Cosmopolitan cover for sniffing. The city at an overall lit-fuse pace was like a nest that was whacked by a stick piñata-fashion by a bored preteen and the buzzing bees, or citizenry, went utterly ballistic. Classical music, a neighbor's, went from minor to major. I was discalced and dressed in a florid maternity blouse and black tights. I applied myself to the (surreally sad) doctor-suggested inhalation/exhalation exercises. Pain stabbed my stomach. My teeth were unbrushed and my feet were still bare. Fiendishly I freebased. My water burst instead of broke. I went into hard labor. The agony was intense, the anguish excruciating, and the Infant, with a sickening plunger-going-at-a-toilet sucking sound, sluiced out of me. It visibly smacked of a Big Mac (with double-dash lips) walloped by an MLB home run masher by way of the brotherly thing in the 'Basketcase' movie. Chills were on my spine. My mouth for a sec was a reddish smear - A holy mackerel mo. It was toastily warm. No more turning tricks. I swore to myself. And I breast-fed it. I'd decided to follow the arrow of responsibility pointing to the bambino. A DJ on the radio was verbally quick on the draw. The station played a cruel version of a Spice Girls song, the slickly produced/programmed instrumentation removed so the listeners could judge the vocal talent, or lack thereof, of the Fab Four. Tormenting. It slept on cushions surrounded by pet fencing. The Infant had a throaty, phlegmy rattle. Mucous leaked from its orifices. A porcine pule was unleashed when it woke. Pus seeped. Needle of my inner compass brought me to it. Dusk dangled like a quintillion spiders all at once. Creaks sounded haunted house-ish. If I were a clock I would've been twelve on the dot. I had disregarded dietary rules and was paying the piper. I should have been, health-wise, a finely-tuned Stradivarius. Its moaning had the sonancies of Charlie Brown parental patter. I missed my folks. Mom and Dad ... I had hepatitis. Abscesses. Collapsed veins. Cellulitis. Bacterial infections. The Infant automatically, inexplicably, would "acquire" the aspect of everyone I fucked, then, with an inaudible cartoonish twang, its own mangled mien would return in a matter of minutes.

My pulse recedes as the tide. I'm a beanpole-skinny, bubblegum-snapping, humanoid stork with a fair share of user-unfriendly boo boos on my bod having flown into reality on the red-eye, workless-related, with zero straight-and/or-sobriety-claims and in dire need of purge and detox, in established space and with the slightest mass in our sepulchral rat-hole with its waterstained wainscot. Mucoidal gunk on the anklebiter's parox-ysmic, reptilian oculi. My nightmare is a dream. Sheer schmaltz. Sorry. Dreadfulness of its earsplitting skriek. It is ringworm redolent and physically is recollective of a mutated infantine peeled Idaho spud, delicate as a shell, talking fragile here, with jonquil-yellow horns sprouting out of an egg-shaped skull, mint-green talons, lizardine nostrils, chiclets the shade of ripe grannysmith apples, and a kitty's tail; or it looks like a pinkening bladdery sac with four stumps. Its complexion has this seasickened pallor. Feces in its diaper on par with a chocolate donut nuked in a microwave. I brace for a crash-landing. I take off my nautical cap and platform shoes. And let's not get into the unconvincing wig either. I've got an aboriginal acumen when it comes to choosing members of the male species. Reservoir has the bilious tincture of Russian salad dressing with vomitous remains on top. Now I smoke an eight-ball and shoot heroin, ignore the bold-font STOP-sign warning of my instincts. My lids flutter like reckless REMs, and are lashless; a common 'basing hazard. Spectatorial ooohs and aaahs from a proximal stadium sounding as survivors of an accident. Storm's like a flock of ravens that've had sudden and simultaneous embolisms and are plummeting to earth from the heavens; or it's ambitiously conceptual Super-8. Guilt grips me as a Gila monster. I am haggard and hypertensive, unfazable and street-credentialed. I deal with mental issues and dispense foul language. The Infant "borrows" my face. Its features blur, and brightly, glowing celestially, and it gaaas excitedly, drooling, dropping its bottle. I've injected a pure triple-dose of Witch Hazel, supine on the settee. We will get better. Times'll improve. Perhaps. No quantumish leaps. The Infant, my angel, has my visage. I have indeed Xed myself. Ask it. It won't answer though. We smile together. I die with love for it. For the life of me I can. The single sky and solitary

shore of the same vivid violet are currently farther away,
drifting toward the day, haloed in haze, and lo.

385

Later.

Lion-Tamer

The path, the warmth. Belt desecrate by drought calls upon God for a soaker in some silentious enterprise man hasn't heretofore partaken of. Sunfaded, sawtoothed promontory where herons harangue one another, clamber hither and yon with dignity and grace. Dirtroads like dragmarks, wretched trails divergent, tracks lookin come an gone. Gusts in abstracts of arroyos, jutted rocks mute and mindless, sound as cooing doves. Cookfire from an encampment. Miners like militants. Smoke on the divide as breath plumed from flared, wore, equine nostrils. Bones of trees, savins and junipers mayhaps, a blighted clutch, throw up their ossein branches in a cognate of fanning motion, as in dismissal. Sun's brilliance of eye, clouded, Polyphemic, apportions indifference with its illumination. These crows are creedless heretics, avian disputants with no true consequence, stake their claim on pollenical plains with pollards terminated at last by a racing river by their own cautionary coordinates, them with the assurance of the arrival of a bevy of their brethren, whereupon they take their leave. Unknowable configurations of acacias and cypresses she'd quit sink in shade, distant and devoid of dimension. Villatic scenery. Vines not unlike catchrope. Gaunted, rich-smellen cows crop better tallowcolored grass mid the slouched and wasted and ill-joined cottonwoods yonder, at the sharpen edge of a grand glade, its great ground as the billyhide of cheapboots. Her silhouette, pitoven-pitch, lurches like a drunken squatter. Brickhued brook, blacken near to onyx. This here equipage in marketbaskets abandoned. Irrigation ditch almost as an abysm. Whitewashed clapboards over there on the dusty pasturage yeller an vast. Confused grid of soiled, ragged cumuli in cosmical consanguinity. Carcass of a gaudy caravan wagon. Showers stinkin of aluminum, have the sonance of somebody tapping their teeth. The countryside has the apparency of haven been scorched alive. A wrinkled, withered, becrazed, footsore, gypsean fortune-teller, his belly kinda like a blanket roll, doublehobbled by a ratty backpack, with articulate anatomic angulosities, an unholy schizoid incubus outa some backwoods boondocks carnivale, the sumbuck prophet under a canopy of leaves and on the shadeless shortcut, says he foresees somethin bad, the sonofabitch does. She stumbles, thence staggers by a gauntlet of sitting and sleeping straydogs, the mongrel motley payen her little mind. Vulturine carousel clumsily swooping in a deepening empyrean. Gambogian boscage. Pikeside brittle plantage proximal to a recentploughed creosote meadow. Those furrows exact filled with stale standingwater, dark of night, and scintillant as crowbars in coruscation. These flocks of geese waddling, wading, the afternoon paling, following an elephant-gray morning and its stagnant air, glass paperweight of sun receding over them serrate triptych of ridges, given off fugitive fulgor, into a grove of beeches and birches in a warp of humectation. Her canine panting, lumpen strides steady. Windmill sited on tilled, umberous earth. There is an awkward merry-go-round of terra cotta buzzards soarin above. Cadaverous pickup truck stripped clean. Stacked haybales. Adobe buildings with wainscoting oldfashioned. Breezes speak in an alien tongue. A bell tolls forebodingly. The vermiform moon in mescal cloudcover's conveying to the storybook range in inken infinitude. Viscose starlight. Laserbeam lambency from a low-budgeted sci-fi film. Smudges of shrubs. Ravens diving from the vellumly vault - illegible script, the ink running on the page. Stand of youngern evergreens and eldern redwoods, scrawny to Ethiopic emaciation, critters in 'em stayin hid. Bombinating bumblebees, flower-infatuates, dart to and fro. Drifters are roguen this windless day, negotiate thew a shallow canyon's cragged countenance, requisite reincarnations of them resurrecting in shadow form, becoming more 'n what they is, and vagabonding. Thunder and lightning rip through the maroon, endless-appearing firmament. Hugeous cliffs. Aberrants of vegetation elicit referent geometries of boundaries. A sadsack chatterbox whippersnapper stiff as a drawing board, smoke slipping out of his Camel cigarette not unlike a handkerchief'd from a magician's sleeve. A matrix of gulls flying overhead done empanel certain sections of the slatey welkin, it shorn of cirri. Petrol-pigmented lake. Gigantesque crags. Robustious rooks, robins. Sand as silica. Pines are petrified penitents in a fairytale obscure. Numerable avenues corrugate in the luminosity lay slurred and illimitable. Pitched tents from a shabby, impoverished pageantry. A miscellany of riffraff freckled by raindrops tramp through the rude, verdant brake, backlit, as the eventide encroaches. O Lordy canst thou, you an yourn, see her? Kinneret: an imperfect Pocahontas lookalike, a subtile barbare, all tattooing and scarring, so beautiful, albeit bulbaceous and burned (she caught in the crossfire duren warfare 'tween the stripes and squares), with her Medusa-serpentoid, crepuscular curls, bladdered breasts, punkin nates, a horsy hind yessir, who wandereth there, discal-ceate, as is her custom, reader, through the gorgeous, golden sand, contain in her burnsuit, worn under unctuous overalls, amongst the virgate, olden oaks yand, her quite natural pulchritude immaculate to any marring, indeed sanctified to untouchable, lummoxly lumbering towards a nebulous reckoning. Chirruping crickets bestir themselves, new-leapt from the pictur-esque panorama in its vastity and with its fair share of luxuriant profusion of brush enhanced by effulgence. Insectean snarls. The skeeters stang as if commissioned to. An affair of precipitation; drencher with indigotic inclinations received to the violaceous terra firma. Thunderous aftercrack o'er the lightless country, dimin-ished in its desolation, the levin nictitant. Longwalled compound and cobblestoned courtyard. Hoi polloi herd, impecunious, sally forth, yond, with facial expressions comparable to theater masks and shouldering agrarian implements and maybe could be misconstrued as though refugees from a Eurocentrically surreal play production. The shifting refulgence in a damned display of indelicacy in lascivious sashay. A smattering of pitter-pattering 'n' spattering spermoid sprinkles. Realshitty plankbridge. Donkeys plod, encumbered with much gear. Noon's calescent plumsun labors congruent to a humanheart. A hoop of muculent spatespray through the beaconbleached, verdigris verdure; midday's abrupt holywater blessing. Hellish clay hacienda. Saffron bonds of weeds in zephyrs visible. Mules whelmed by the provisions trundle, beasts allbut brokedown. A sudden propagation of transitory turkeys spastically strut in some strange freeform on sepia grass and raw mud. A sheetiron skyline. The dawning's fulgent talons claw thru the bedewed, tranquil spinney, the dense thicket congruous to splayed fans mismade. Clucking chickens helter-skeltering in a very bizarre drama like epileptoid, feathern clowens plucked from a backland circus. Insectival trills. Pooches balk-bark beneath a weird awning of these osteal boughs. An antique Victrola subsiding in a canvas hammock. Her broad feet, those heels strapleatheryn, ratherish filthy beyond description, always discalced justabout, a reminder, soles perhaps more akin to rawhide, she headen yonway. A stygian sparrow unexpectedly descends into a crisp clearing, an enduring expanse, then ascends as its soul sure would if its demise had come to pass in the dusk's peaceful hottened humidified sable solitude in some recondite history or other. Piercing notes of a chinook in cantillate. The world is a dream in anticipation of sleepers entering into it. Abiding celadon and rotten crabgrass invasive an rotten. Cello oxygen and its rooty odor. Heat's the legacy of summer. Barren, bronze bluffs. Her untendedto mane streams as seaweed. She shambles. The celestial sphere, cerulean, fraughtfull of evening cloudlets in rearrangement; riven revenants madden. A cavernous, sepulchral sanctuary for a demented, haggard, beanpole pensioner with an erroneous posture wayward in the insanity of its instancing, imperiled for want of sanity, questioning the answer of accountability of his deranged brain, in a surcease of divestiture gazing into his consciousness in a manner of counsel, and the rawboned retiree prepares his reedgrown deathbed. That vista is a suture in elongate. Squash patch. Starlings get crosswise of it by wing. She'd had a breakfast of canned pears, sardines and crackers, lunch of stewed tomatoes and bacon, and dinner of peaches and croissants. Her piceous locks like springcoils you would find in a mattress. Pertinacity in hiking. Horizon, ceramically a-gleam. Taking herself a productive leak and crap amidst flourishing shrubbery. Tussocks of esparto in the terrain are as reeves in a dun brine. Migrant jumbles of tumbleweeds. Brevity of enbrowned brightness ... Almightysent. Vinaceous rocks lanate with lichen in a crystalline creek are stony dishings in an anfractuous sink. Bistort. Ruminants. Serous pools. Kinneret clumps, believes the bunching goats and entrained buffalo four abreast pret near on gullied soiland in fogbanked pollendust are fixen to skedaddle to the farthern swale in the diurnal swoll, the interim sorted calves' skewed umbraged selves, false versions, in the process of metamorphose, manifesting hesitantly, and she wonders on the possibles of them gulching theirselves without supervision proper. Maneyed varmint, seratine-faced, sericate-skinned, in this serotinal time. Midges communicate their (unwelcome) animosity to her on their terms with rancorous roilings. Trudging with tenacity. Chipmunks skitter in the sloughing cutis condensation, hazed off by her. An assembly of pauperate onlookers, male an female, mong the pallidachromatic rangecattle. She, vervet-visaged, is cussin while eatin in a void. A piebalding feline chouses several livid lizards and no idjit trying not to faller off the gigantean escarpment, the grail of sun aglow and longdown. Vespid chitter on flathat knolls. Augments and amazements of florae and faunae. Ducks singlefile on the pewter placidity of a silken lagune. A few wheel and swing upwards. She plunks on satin plantleaves, the crushed cap on her bulbiform cranium belled in gritty mistrals. An owl's screech shrill-sings and lags. A secondary shriek gets lost in space. This angulous treebranch a hairsbreadth from her moled temple. Frantic and careening gnats ... sporadic. Copper coin of sun. Sienna sierras, seen allstark at daybreak. Grim and grungy Hispanic farmemployees stippled with sweat crowded on roughboards on a flatbed rubberneck her, the junkbox a profound and pathetic prodigy embarking on an ambiguous adventure, the rattletrap a vehicular vision took from a child's nightmare in prolongation after a poignant apocalypse. Alabastrine sand like salt rime. Roaming folks. A weather-lined, cave-cheeked,, stool leg-skinny, tanned codger of no determinate age, born of humble origins, poised as if for a dumbass daily dress rehearsal, the fossil dizened with diaphoresis, parasitic pain lodged in his gut, he as though in a conspicuous condition of curse, a deputy of despair in the encompassing estrangement of torrid, desiccant desert without a badge of honor, a feller of unalterable selfabsorption preoccupied by problems, ones not reckoned with atall, his person, with bunodont dentistry, aware of wrongs which cannot be righted, calamities that had befallen him Gawdswill you'd conjecture, perspiration now like coaloil, a silverchain yolkwise on his narrow neck, afore a lowceilinged hovel, swearing oaths to hisself, being incommensurable with these environs. Ebon eyecup of rodenthole in the sentient earth. Sightless moon. Impassive light on brackish puddles of promise in the taut terrene. Sun had been a paperskull in deathly declamation. Atmosphere's cohesion. Apples and grapes hanging from branches are as disembodied eyes dangling on stringy, slimy cords after they were sucked out of sockets by savage madmen in a disassembled, doomed, medieval universe, its evils, sins and soforth therein kept more or less, humanity the adroit architects of its perishing, the dryheat bearing life away further into the estate of eternity. A rubiginose pond in paste-pigmented glitter is a supine, liquescent djinn, an illusory, glimmering mirage recumbent and not vanishing, the water's movements like ones within a womb. Wildfloret worshippers in rumored roseate radiation. Bluen sky elaborates a sapphirine sea in an infantine forenoon's feverdream. Galumphing and besorced by transmogrifying, phantasmagoric phosphorescence, Kinneret is a glorious gorgon. Wicked gales press 'pon her granulate particles, such grainy slashings, and for a bit she forbears to resist, composing her operculums, lids protective, closed. She feels as a dull tool requiring sharpening, barging on the lineage of landscape foreign to her barefeet, in incarnations of illumination that indemnifies its life in death, gone to the late hour. Her celia shut, in a trice, for the nonce. Sorrowful cemetery on the outskirts of the sticks enshadowed. Stupefied Mexicans standing enfiled next to an enfilade of cratewood caskets like witless workers wrenched from their normal occupations. Chimleysootobsidian channel. Here, somewheres South, vice shuns virtue. More is revealed than concealed. Nothin swore to secrecy. Starting-points and destinations knowed. Beginnings an endings familiarized. The sombrero of woven straw crammed into a muslin sack she had alighted on fits practically perfect. An aggregate of yahoos. Cranes quarrel anew. A porcine tween nymphet, bottleblond, in a malachite twopiece swimsuit and matchen flipflops, in abeyance at a jade rindle. Creatural crying as in bereavement occurring about her. Poultry stalking seeds indiscriminately on a lawn flaxen. She revels in her squirt, relishes her dump, in propinquity to a clarion rill. Topaz light. Petaliferous constellations, glistery ignitions in a nameless, ordinate cosmos. Tootsies gauging, gouging the powdery gravel. Yardfowls sound like women wailing, their families murdered in executional procedure by ritual assassins, sobs commended to the Upstairs. Association of yokels cloistered. Weak garnet nightfall longin coming, the moon as a feastday offering for deities. In the crepuscle's commencement the deluge slacks, made partial by sheaves of leaves. She has a worried physog, wears it, essays to ascertain the severity of it, putting herself forward, padding on an aqueous embankment. Dim domicilios. Figurines artsycraftsy in basketry. Crumbling coral cantina. Strong humus volunteers itself to her filly's nares. Sallow, halfgrown kids, a dozen perchance, clad in skimpy bathing costumes, battle barbaric for a tireswing, not unlike jackals over freshbeef, at a polluted swimminghole, evincing, effortlessly, import, as if they're adolescent icons extant, shadows outsized mimicking 'em. She recalls, visually, her phizz, a deer in conical headbeams, feeling as though she is a juvenescent immigrant imported to a faraway nation. Stars are blazen bovinic oculars whilst they feed. Porcelained glint, waxing and waning, unwillingly, a sacrosanct inquiry feasible, sectors of the atramentous area, enameling it. Sampling darklooking wellwater ... Tastes funny ... She sighs shallowly. Rain reeks of iodine. The sun, lonesome, yawns yellowly, with its rigor risen to its meridian, the region below with reverence. Conchoidal rocks cauterized by lapsing coruscation where hayseeds are enisled. Burros dillydally at a row of huge, slumpen habitations, the umpteen shacks composing the uncoiling riverside route with its oodles of senseless palmettos, the sashless panes with butcherparchments stapled to the frames, visceral stains recollective of mapped quarters, localities longago since forgot. A bullmoose halts. Scorpions scuddle.

Napped moths orbit satellite. Damselflies do figure-eights around compost piles. Sedate sky with discolorations of clouds. Emanation exhorts the earth to expand. An outrageous metalline mechanoid of choochootrain barrels and whistles downcountry. She breathes akin to fire in wind. Plenteous pigs pule. Sod opaque with the dampness. A mangy, tawney tabbycat laidup in parch foliage. Church's spire's a middle finger recalcitrantly and blasphemously erectile in a ruinous town depopulate. Hectoring hawks on high. A spritz possesses an antiseptic aroma. Hoofing operose. Swifts spew in a seemingly inane venture. A hirsute hermit, heeling about the peat moss, arrect, at his own ordinance, nodding like some freaking sage, silhouette titubate, he windowed by a vitreous torrent, brings in a kayak, it as a mutate, deaden snake, out of a charcoal millpond, making her privy to a practice she can't comprehend, an action she can unveil no signification to ascribe from all that is patent. She takes stock of it nonetheless. Micaceous cipherings of cirri. Skeins of blackbirds commensurate to writing on the cyanic stationary skyline. Echelons of elms are agnations of sentries in which bluebirds flute. An enormous elk. Herders drive lambs upcountry wheres livestock mill. Sheepbleats. Insectile spores spring over archaic acres inameliorate and settlements shoddy. Lagunas analogous to liquidtables alltold. She makes the acquaintances of a trilogy of girls her teenage - sexual pardners, a cute lesbian couple, vulpecular, sultrystunner Nicola, nerdybirdy, rangy Selina, with her Scotchtaped wonkyrims, and adorable, awesome, racehorse-lithe, lengthy, loquacious and androgynous Roarie with her boy-styled pixie-cut. Kinneret takes a shine to her right off the durn bat. Hellos and goodbyes exchanged. And at her Ark-shapen home, she actuates to her ablutions, deems herself abdominous. Out, out brief candle! JimBob, the big ol' aged lion on his lastlegs, gnaws on the remaints of his deermeat on the frontporch in its decided decrepitude.

EN VOYAGE TO HER CUSTODIAL JOB in the populous borough, JimBob copping z's, shuteye necessitous, at the house on the uglyrug and rubbermat combo on the algum floor, Kinneret's ample, Armenoid arms are pendular in the mephitic murk. Gearteeth of pinnacles, atypical aiguilles, in figments of fog. Her algetic feet. A russet nighthawk fords the irrestorable obscurity, disappears like an acherontic scream in the rippling nighttide, a sign, to her, of ill omen, on this leafy, dusty boulevard, its resounding squawk ratcheting o'er miter-buttes, in deliberate acceleration. After-redolence of ripened rot in a tenuous twilight where these fading figures of sequestered Aframerican peons in burialsuits forage in the substantial forest as the chanting condolent in an antecedent commemoration. Mounts stenciled by sprinkles, ordained into wraiths of mist. Fulgurous headlong falling. Chaparral islanded in waxen an ironore pools. Elvish encirclement of ferns in reprieves of soup, an abyssal substrate to the dusk of some inscrutable, eccentric election. A parasol asplay on twin sawhorses. Eve not unlike a sibylline enactment, with its smack of hail, muted a tad by the wilderness. Velutinous moss on those boulders. Improbable surroundings. Trip-wirings of spider-threads. Leafage left as tawdry lace. For grits, ham, biscuits and beer! Waterfowl in allright plight in the soggy marshlands. She sloshes thew. An idling orange Dodge Coupe, an autofact salvaged from an older time. Equinic nickering. Glowflies go to their demises when the sun rises, redly, them plunging mistaken into the breaking lambency. She hurtles on. Reservoir lying sanguinary. A wary and haunted Injin fella examines his pack of Lucky Strikes cigs and a gorilloid galoot reads a beatup bible at a paintflaken Rexall drugstore jus off the blacktop highway. Pretty Kinneret on strick pastureland in oscillations of random luminosity. Straitness thataway. Lit sweat shoots off her like sparks from a catherine wheel. Brazen bootleggers glower, overtly into outlawry, in the bonedry coppice. Cotton-white cumulus. Hillbillies virile and predatory in the chartreuse copse. Leadslag lightning, and good 'ns; trinity of stigmata bedazzling. Apron on a rocker at a halcyon pond. Acreage in ornate luminescence in its jaundice glare. She remembers the curvaceous worm of previous moon, oddly restored by its reduction, moonshiners, aligned, malevolent in their morbidities, these goddamn varmints staring at her gams as players in a chessmatch, waiting for her to move her piece on the board in a prescribed fashion, one gallused, gargantuan, bearded joker, cormous head meticulously cocked and folding an encrusted quadrant of his flannel collar, gazing at her. Forge fire in her tumid tummy. Hydraulic toil of her planetoid haunches. Planarians of cirrus. A methodically ruining ballcourt, graffiti writ, where youths'd play yet. Public premises in a negligible precinct. Sun's this broke egg gawp. Nonbelligerent light allembracing. Bending and sissing of cane. Tolerable temperatures. Animalian racket. An unreasonable roadway, trod, shadebanded. Lads, bucknaked, swim and splash in the glaucous stream. She peruses their starknudity. Animalic noises ampin on up. Incandescence leaches away the wanness it made at first. Jays chatter wayup in the towering sycamores, close to touching the hemic heavens. A province, undisturbed, in rumination of a brandspankingnew sunrise. Morn troubled by eerie vapor and spotted by unfenced, illsorted oxen, moaning and groaning, the riders calling. Bedlam of bonkers birds. Mead proffers sparse fare. Showers jangle. Mesas majestic. Lumber piled evensteven on the siding of a stuccoed, tinrooven warehouse. She shoos pesky sibilating mosquitos, aswirl. Uncountable sullen steers. Ghostblanched overcast with its chaos of cloud. Her tolling hurdies. Wet an warm day. Shiftwhines of winds. Motorsmoke mizzle. A hamlet left in the wake of an undocumented plague. Drag ain't been rode much, she surmises. Leantos in intense incalescence. Alps looken masoned up by professionals skilled. Vulturous veering. Hellaceous mugginess. A dirigible-boar budges like a bloated dignitary. Kinneret thinks of a swarm of stars. Her micamib-eyes. Environed waftage, suspirant and sonorous alternate, rich and resonant, in tentative suspension. Arid hinterland harbors a grudge gainst mankind, who manages to roll on. Whisks sound as an irate Pantagruel sucking at his gnashers. She stamps, trots thru the anhydrous boonies. Shanties in quantity bevel. Sleet in a slant. Puffing on a Marlboro and popping rimationed, hemispheroid shelled nuts in simultaneity, her core burning like the earth's would. The firmament, anil-hued, in an ungraspable formality, fulgurate with afterflashes of levin. Mud-walled cabins anear, in variant states of disrepair, annectant, and annealing, their days numbered. Yawing gaps of the colossal cairns of scarps, rockface residuum of an aftermath from a nuclear fallout. Bursiform sun. Empyrean greyed over with cumuli in an excellent metamorphosis. Her feet harry through oozy muck of the classic land, gravy mirk, her blood in a flood, in the mental world's wacky weather, in a scene of a quintessential enclave. Vireo-olivaceous, soften lea. Luciferian light, the Devil's digits carven the wilds. Makeshift coffeemill. Jerrybuilt factory. She has a penchant for gal-pegging, moves cylindroidally, carrying her haversack as a soldier would her slain comrade, in times fabled, ere long. Plethoric puddles with lube properties. Misanthropes caper not unlike mechanical monkeys. Lindens gesticulant. This littleshit farmboy in dungarees wrote on yells to her from wavy wheat, thar she blows, and mimes, the undeveloped prick, retardedly, hurling a harpoon. And she vaults as if a jumbo javelin. Livelong nightfall in its tarry tenebrousness. A shed's a disastrous shrine of a consecrate broken clan, it deprived of sufficing whatchamacallits, the crummy windows, triangulose, permitting irradiational contrivances of astral inauguration. She has a sensation of being the condemned on the verge of confronting her wouldbe executioner, having profaned the place. Brighten moon's a brilliant punch-bowl. The ground has a tendinous substance to it. Here is where the weak suffer and the strong thrive. Fishy stars snagged in a seanet of cirri. Her melon hurts. Gnarls of fireflies chock-a-blocken's an homage of a constellatory sacrament. Denuded kindergartens lick-ety-split into muddled sedge. Kinneret, in addition to being a janitress, is a lion-tamer, financially scraping by, earning a decent living. More kiddies divested. She has performed with JimBob at joints such as nursing home, loony bin, high school, and clubs for veterans. She is generally well-received by her meager audiences, making so-so money. Serpent's tongue of somebody's fire. Loco lolitas, underage smartasses, pieces of work, bunnies respiten off the disreputable ranch, get a liquor load on, putting on rollerskates. An awkward albatross fitfully flies according to the fair winds' vicissitudes, cures itself of its struggles in an intolerable flight, plungingly landing, instincts, a species of inestimable reason, it does hearken to. It breathest outbellyingly at having not downed itself into doom. Breezes undeviate. Welkin in its turquoise crucible. Gusts with their oblique energies. Garter snakes with their vivacity, sparkling scales, slip, slink away. Greatwhite-colored clouds, spinnin in quiet riots, cruisin sidelong, from her angle anyways. Satanic cerise aqua pura. Birds' wings impatient of any beating. A barn stuck in woe's technical degeneracy everlasting, the entire shebang sad, a logged scorn to glad, in the receptive rays. Moody mosquitoes with the sonancy of harp strings. Cloudlets smooth the seam of skyline.

Intertwisting ivy on treetrunks. Unmeaningly melancholic tributary of baptismal blood in brilliancy unresting in an interlude of time. Cattish purrings of those oceanic swells. She respites as though a tigress tuckered out. Nonstop rain. Tantalising trailertrash. These gravestones like mammoth sharkteeth. Vainglorious Barbiedolls, inebriate jailbait, in revelry. Barbarian-drumming thunder. The lightning draws in the bittersweet vault. Blackmen swig rotgut after the hideous moil of harvesting. Darkness quickens with its imminglings of umbrageousness an animate beings. Stars suckled by the horizon. Her shadow chafes the loam. A backwoods boogeyman, a grotesque hick Grendel ... Amateurish three-ring gilly goin on. Anguishings of the area, agonies of them natives, panoplied in poverty, torments prayers are powerless to assuage, direr dread unappeasable and millennial. Sun looms outa the cloud which lay as a canvas-cover unbounded. Phallic rockyheight rising erect out of a pubic bush. A jeep grouses, grinds up a brambly grade. Not much left of the light, saturate at this juncture. Lunatic foxes barken. A bus gripes, tires rumpling on the soggy bracken of the acclivity, the declivity. Wigeons and shovelers, indifferent demoniacs, sounding wrong, loophole in the foliate dressage of hemlock, their shrouded forms on the sodden, caven terrain, roots imprinted in it, like a feeble skeleton in the skin of the sick. Lousy clamminess, as if it's sanguine-sogged or something. Kermis succubus. She trowels the perspiration off her beetling brow with a gorillian mitt. Filthstained wreckage of an outhouse amiss in integuments of mahogany plants. Mobile mannequin. Bailiwick's a desperate nightmare of the world whole. Stars as though embers from a bonfire. Stewed-rhubarb-tinged topography pumicing. A reptile like rope ashore of a greentea basin. Scalpriform grassblades. Implausibility of the temps. Drovers take a breather by a composed tarn. Accordion compression of time. Gesturing maples with austere attitudes. Trees' stumps as gravestones for the hastily buried following battle. Vegas ... volcanic. A stringy seeress, an arthritic saurian, unconstrained wanderer, softball-sized dome agoggle, attempts to cajole Kinneret into hiring her for sooth-saying services, and Kinneret tells the sorceress, wearing a stetson and dungy dress, she holding it tailorwise, she wants none of it thank ye. Grosbeak and warbler spirals in chimeless chinooks. Rapids like a solvent locomotive thew the gorge. The bombastic fart sunders her rectum and rind of her rump. A nother flatulent explosion. She scratches her itchy keester and anus, indexer socketed in that pelagial sphincter. She hops like a beleaguered baboon. A hypnotic cataract. Tables of branches as a tangled trial. A select biplane, the symbol, summation of the sky, drones, its flight its ... property. In her anterior existence her cogitations contravene. Briny deep contradicts the vista, however, it doesn't run counter to it, evidence in the event. Winds are wordulations of the departed an dredge up wrappers in temporary tarriance. Tasajillo seclusive. Clothespins clipped on laundrylines in an encapture of effulgence. Life, she deduces, is a query to death. Attrition of the acres. She gobbles bland tortillas and goaty cheese, vilely rank sure. Nacreous splendor downriver where these squirrels sit swaged into the scrub, jabberin and subjugate. Antelopean activity. She watches intently, gets sidetracked by them evertime. Spits of a spate. Catclaws of sticks. Cacti in segregate. She espies a muscled, lissome mountainlion, is spotted by it. She suspicions it had tracked her. She leaves out of here. Rain like poured metal. Castoff hubcaps, just off the interstate's tarmac, a roadway repository. Clouds in the jus unexplainable azure look hacked, as if by a visionary vivisectionist. Composite of weather conditions at dusk's onset. She marches measuredly, as though a marionette manipulated. Alien aspens arch in the gusts. A steamboat saloon. Godmade aft comin to a boil. Territory baked brickhard. Clotted quizzical crows with reckless beady eyes. Her bread-basket breasts from her tramping. Domiciles in varietal states of dilapidation. Spruce's bark like bones drawn 'neath derma, with gravity and endued with ants. Smaze and its ubiquitous undulations. A podgy possum, kittenish an cagey. Spears of scintillation as continuous cosmical candles burning, deliquescing and guttering until, alas, they're gone. Hump of chips. A mayfly makes a miscue in trying to bite her elbow as she pinches snuff between thumb and forefinger from the generic box and puts the gooey chew in her lower lip like a nurse'd put a baby into its crib. Spine-joltingly traipsing through pools reminiscent of liquescent shimmying orifices, obscene and myriad. Her tongue twirls as a lick of flame, the soaker slashing down. Vines like lashes of whips in hiatus. Sun leechlike on the epidermal heaven. Scrotal scrunch of her snuffer. Cannonly report of thunder.

Levin, decorous, over the steeprock peakling thru the cirri. A gauche crane, awry-feathered, aghast into immobility, its courage palsied, verily, refulgence frailing it, assailed by ambivalence, pottering about the serried precipice. She mislikes the undecision! Fixen to drench, sho. Wackytobacky against her gingergums. Beacon arrives long and short. Kinneret conjures her maw, large and in charge, slaving day and night, rain or shine, to keep a roof above and victuals below on the table, retrospects pa's bludgeon-hammering and snore-sawing, the spindling bastard. It was all hands on deck to make ends meet in the household. Breath was constantly difficile to breathe with the smut and gilings, on that living land. Girning girlie gisant at a gilgai gilted. A travesty of a tyke, unhale and top-heavy, in torn Levis, saucery peepers portentous, he a brooden image, feeding hens and a-fanning hisself with an issue of dog-eared Penthouse magazine, in cinder-cloudlets, simultaneously a-moving betwixt 'em, doing a dopey dance, a fool's cavort, on human-growed grass with sulphurous pollen. Cumuli ribbons on the spool o' the sun. These lanes are lame limbs of a somatic meadow. A trifling ruffled rooster passeth ... she kin ketch it ... jest ... keen to do so ... cougar-quick ... shucks ... Implacable tenement, urgent and irredeemable, in an irrevocable cessation of disgruntled stability, illumined and engendered with its tenants. A lardy, bottlenecked bumpkin with leontiasis parleys with this rustic, muraenid-faced slut, their juxtaposed essences, corporeal precursors to their silhouetted selves, in competent mummery in appropinquity to a mure. Useless air in its bestirred sibilances. Gnurled mimosas, scarecrows a-tall, resolved out of their rigidity by continual light and shadow components, in shaping solution, travail 'pon the ownable property. Her paw scours her curly mop. Adumbration with penurious and perverse ubiquity. Her pores weep diaphoresis. Stones rubble down an altitudinous ledge where a zaftig hiram was. Her blouse blotched with perspiration, her pies semiclosed in loess granules. Mistrals stertorous. Sheet-lightning lucently stains the glabrating, pebbly, blind slope, the stifling, sticky evening crouching melanoid, and the habitat is drownded as she ets franks, cauliflowers and swigs perk java. It's aimin to storm. Her owl-oculi, outen the middle of nowhere, nigh toward a dandy daypeep, she moving not unlike a leopardess and wishing she were in her nice nightgownd and snuggled with JimBob on the floor with its smears of dirt and full of holes, those walls with soaring streaks of filth, by the cozy fireplace, she laying as a felled bull, the cuddling cat bolstering and sustraining her, a purring buttress, she hearing his rever-berations of respirations, he in rapt slumber, the penumbrae in repetition, created by fiery speech organs, in recovering elongation, congealing like in intolerable suspense and beyond ultimate time. A butch tomboy vagrant in a tankini and Keds lowtops does acteth annoyen, insulteth by her very existence, glares at Kinneret with malignant intent. Kinneret is resourceful, often relies on her guile to survive. She has a Nazi stride ... goosestepping. Avian aggravation. Her blinders unblinkingly cast aloft, centrally fixate on the oncoming overcast, celestial sphere aflame in solar fire. Swashing streamlet. Precipitation sieves through the frondescence. And she conducts herself into the uninspiring building, schlepps to the commodious elevator.

Imagining an inviting schtick with JimBob, something involving flaming hoops and balancing beam, Kinneret scrubs the bathrooms, vacuums the hallways, empties the bucketliners, and dwells on the paltry turn-out on an ecruing lawn of a derelict asylum, a week earlier, and the audience, comprisen patients and staff members, where the show, as it were, she put on wasn't a debacle, but borderline. It was more amusing and entertaining for the "crowd" what JimBob didn't do as opposed what he did do. Uprighted and bipedal, they performed a brief tango and waltz, provoking claps and cachinnations, only he refused to roll over and play dead. He merely dozed. He resisted "attacking" her too, wouldn't be lured by her junglebabe outfit. He just drowsed. A smattering of boos was interspersed with guffaws. She was paid two-hundred dollars cash by the ogress director. Grudgingly. Not paydirt. No jackpot. Money earned though. She raided the freezer, ripping off pork chops, chicken breasts, fish and steaks, loading up a pillowcase. Gig wasn't a total loss ... She notices that Roarie, knelt at the tarry edge of an edifice's roof, looking like she might be thinking of committing suicide ...

Kinneret opens the main bay winder and asks, "What're ya doin?"

Roarie expectorates a loogie. "Nothin you need know of."

"You're not gonna lunge there."

"I may."

"I don't wanna see you pancake yourself."

"Don't watch. Get outa here."

"Come on in. I've got chips and soda."

"Fuck me!"

"We can discuss it."

"I should die."

"You have options."

"I dunno ..."

"... Choices ..."

"I'm busted."

"We all need fixin."

In a stuffy office they slouch in vinyl swivel-chairs at disorganized desks. "What's it like, owning a lion?" Roarie, munching Wise.

"On par with havin a dog, but bigger," Kinneret, swilling Pepsi.

"I appreciate the goodies."

"Hey, be part of our act. Join us. You won't rake it in, only I suppose we'll get by ok."

"What will I do? I lack experience."

"Be you: sexy."

Pistoning chiaroscuro in illusional conviction,

fluctuant in the oil of oxygen. A barely-legal lass with a tallow shock, broke leg in a defaced cast, in a burlesque of boredom, has a kisser as if carved by a kooky caricaturist, hair like it was painted on for chrissakes, she done brushing it, in boxsies the color of cow's cud on her pole-physique, possessing no modesty on the emaciation of her figure, a fixture, harsh and precious, flouting itself, and rubberoid Croc clogs. She's wooden-backed, thick-nosed, thin-waisted, marble-eyed, and arch-necked, the outline on her ribcage similar to a watermark on a bridgepiling, steps slidingly, as though a sled on snow, appearing noctambulant, waiting to awaken. She is composed, debatably triumphal and tragic, ashen integument drum-tight. An inflatable pool with glycerinate contents, turgic and tralucent. She'd swum and lain and took care drying off with a Yogi Bear towel, apparently unwell, discommoded, like she has been rawhided, or bedrid. Her mammy, librarianoid, has on a commonplace maillot and wedge-platforms, is observant, holds a package, the parcel wrapped in newspaper as a bomb, claims "it's ourn," the caliper of her clock measuring her expression of concern, capitulating, questioning and intent, diminishing and disappearing altogether when a passel of pubescents, spokes of a universal rim, quicken paces for her and her (presumed) daughter, in their driving gait, a smart piece aways though, soil gouting, backflung beneath repudiant bare feet, the muck, uniferant of its compact density, soporifically whisperous on them, the young tootswoots, dreamy and dainty, footprints on the nickeliferous trail healed away by the seeping water, mended by that mud.

Kinneret and Roarie noodle, lax-bodied, hit the road running, JimBob swaying on his tailwagger's leash. The drafts quaver off, voices, vocal-chords strained, returned, in vocalic reversal, to the larynx, the volitional radiance in retrograde. Rubious scariation of sky. The Creator's cruel earth. He chastiseth. This detestable garage with an amalgamation of cars which sholy don't sell, entrails of engines strewed. A claret, hunkered, spraddlelegged goshawk on a telephone-wire. Pinpoints of Roarie's pupils. Levee looking riz somehow, foam and rubbish in there. Rinkydink fencing swagging along a bar of quick-sand, mid-sunk, Roarie's lamps blaring up, observing logs bob in a jam like she would circus animals, pallor suffused to pallidity, prissy, jawing and complaining bout the prospects of negotiating it, lingua franca fumbling, having a mind to digest the idea in her brain. Kinneret's mitts on her fat flanks. Brink of sedge. A rainbow's the prismatic arc of a hoe choppin. Trollesque hedgery, deaf, dumb and blind, hushful and hostile. Glowflies as little flames of soldering pipes. Bellowsed beercans. JimBob swaggering. Pollinical webs. A disabled doe lopes. Moon rises as told. JimBob chows his freshkill. A lone graywolf indexes the sights from its stony scar, devising a plan, puzzling in instruct with its intuition, behaven starved out. Kinneret sweats, like she laid in snowmelt. Roarie polishes off her eggs and franks. JimBob at his fill, kept a low profile, blinkers glazed over, engorged on liver. Intestines in a rabbet as serpents in a pit. Canadian geese yard theirselves in a fen. Lupine yowls hearkened for miles perchance. Ovine baaaing. Anuran croakin. Owlet hooting. JimBob is tethered.

Grub scrounged up on improvise and given to them by a grizzled, gabby oldtimer ranchowner. They thank him and tell him to take care and he replies "Roger that." The moon's an innoxious threat, vista sacred on it. An indigent pony tromps thew the bog skummed with flotsam and jetsam. The thicket trivial and subdued. Nighttime with its impermanent profundity. Spectral saplings with questing creepers, abashed and flagrant, monuments to the monotony of mournfulness that circumscribes the floorless forest, faltering in the beams. Calculant creeklet. Soothen succession of a dell's hillocks. An impromptu practice session has Roarie contracting a case of "Scarlett O'Hara fever," gussied in fancy frippery. She grabbles, with gusto, a leftover lock, blumps natural on the mushy bank, faults the waft taking it, in peremptory umbra, soughs, and snaps "fiddlesticks," dursn't know what else to say, misfortunately mixed up in the latent weald, and somersaults over a sphinxianly attitudinized JimBob, who wallops her ass with accuracy, and Kinneret chortles, to Roarie's chagrin. Her Dutchboy bowlcut is a plastered smear on her ivorine scalp chocked with dandruff. Omnipresent puddles dimpled by rainbeads. Clouds mold the empyrean. The moon seeks something, mammalianly striving, not unlike a mortal, and the ladies do not begrudge it. Valley is comparable to machinery which operates for a long duration on its own, a coulee with its infinitesimal ludicrosities, its salvation sought and found through its tribulations. Godly weather metes. Devil of nature. A zep-shoat scuttles. Froggy crowin.

The initial public performance with Roarie, with a
week of preparation under their belts, wasn't a smashing
success, nor was it an unmitigated disaster. Not even
close. The show was held for a crowd of codgers, retired
firefighters, on a defunct football field, where Kinneret
noticed the tangible rapport JimBob had with Roarie.
With her gymnastics background she allowed Kinneret
to invent some new and innovative choreography for
bold routines. It was Roarie's idea to wear negligee and
mules. Kinneret had no objection. JimBob was enkin-
dled, enlivened, roaring, gambading, wrestling and
boxing. It was beauty and the beast. Although sloppy,
the production went over fairly well. In the finale,
JimBob, defeated, wheezed, on his back, Roarie's foot
on his ribs, pounding her chest and flexing her muscles
as the audience of coots in unis applauded. The act took
in a thousand bucks! Neg firmament.

From a commonplace department store Kinneret
buys henna-hued work-boots and puts 'em on less
she want her feet to hurt from walken thru the incan-
desced badlands in the nooned effulgence. A dingle
of trees unique to one and all. The raspy showers have
the sonancy of vocalchords strummed by mucoid
respirings and is redolent of sourlaundry. Branches as
ropylimbs of oldmen. Bluebottles whirl like dustmotes
in the rhomboid refulgence. Brumal wisps search out
the wetted ground in hellaceous herbage. Cirri cored
outa the welkin. Poverty is the thread sewn through

the fabric of a patchwork quilt of community that lay under an improvident Maker who'd made it. Those stars coruscating in the ebonizing cumuli: bejeweled beard belonging to a Divine Being. Storm as wrath. Boughs waving reminiscent of a king's arms settling his subjects. Kinneret's nearest neighbor, Silverberry, resembling a cross between Denver Pyle and The Lorax, if he went to pot, a Melvillean madman in maculate cords and with an anvil-skull, is cleaning his shotgun in front of a succumbing fire. She, intimidated, takes Roarie's hand, feeling as deerskin. Mountains beheld, unknowable. The veridian sun making its traverse. Megamucho viridity. Vitriform sprinkling with its vitamine tang. Prolongate wake-tracks of a van. Kinneret's skull beats with blood - a fist on the casketlid of a person buried premature. JimBob's sides go in and out as a dudelsack, massive head holdin low, mane mussed. A violet hawk skates on an icy vault, wheels in the crazings of coruscation. Sodden air thick like the earth's crust. The humidity is horrendous and there's no relief for it. They can't get quit of it, both wringing soak with perspiration. Without any warning whatsoever Roarie pulls off a cartwheel and Kinneret claps, JimBob, lost in his leonine thoughts, startled, some slobberstrings of saliva swinging from his monstrous maw, and he squares hisself and grumbles. Roarie sprawls, mumbles, snubbed to a chainlink fence, and chuckles. JimBob moseys on over, sniffs her pelted axillae and laps her chin. Roarie snickers, hugs and smooches him. Kinneret experiences the pings and pangs of jealousy, for they are connecting, have chemistry. Contumacious soaker. Tresses, misconstrued in the blowing breezes, amended isochronously, sawing back and forth yonway. Whited sun in a bilged heaven with a custody of cloudlets in quietened pandemonium Kinneret speculatively observes occasionally. They take a needed break beneath a leafy baldacchin, shovel in burgers and fries, the greenbelt interpreted of the dusk swallowing everything like a diabolic phantasm, devouring and antic allaround. A butterballish badger freezes neutral as a taxidermy example. Obeliskboulders. Scud of stars. Rancho widereachen. Legging it. They run into Nicola, the sexpot firebreather, and Serina, an able acrobat. The talented ingenues come to the conclusion they should combine their efforts, have a doublebill, travel and play together.

The gifted gamines bring the house down, performing for a respectable gathering of law enforcement personnel in a precinct parking lot, the entertainment imaginative, exciting, innovatory, nuanced and unpredictable. They worked out the kinks during the gig, tweaking, and fine-tuning on the fly. Kinneret confesses she gets an erotic and electric charge out of sharing the stage with Roarie, who admits she is in agreement. Arachnidan wordage, perceptibly a-dangle, hanging harmless on webfloss, from salmon tonguebeams, talking the voiceless prattle, sounds made in significant solitude of recessional refrain, the beginning and ending, in their clandestine coming of slown silence, a quietus in secret sos it should be lawed for conspiracy. Dangers and difficulties of the act were surmounted with plenty of aplomb, albeit imperfect sure enough, credit, according to Kinneret anyway, given to the Ruler of all, her … "insignificance" encompassed by His environment, entire and firm, she swole up and on the lope, dankened tanktop licking planar to her fullflesh while she ambulates, looking like she waked, taking a chew of tobacco. Span of pigeons dickering. Murmurous gusts. Aspens shivering as if they got an aguer. Roarie has a hangdog, mumbling her mouf. Gulls set to fetching themselves fish in the peasea. Nicola, gait neat of foot, removes her hoodie, bolded by the alky in her system, as though ordered to do so, by Serina. The day'd befallen the damsels like misfortune. Rubes, they putter upriver, abnormalities in a Gehenna chasm, drift as wood. Window-washer rattles like chains. Language sounding scripted, read outloud, in conversate.

At this crummy, wilted Red Rose hotel, Kinneret and Roarie, pared to their skivvies and slippersocks, clash. Roarie made advances affectionate and Kinneret refused them, hence the heated argument. Feeling rejected, Roarie storms out, in a huff, and parties with Nicola in her tacky room, Selina out getting groceries. She returns to discover Nicola and Roarie French-kissing and bunny-hugging. Selina goes to Kinneret and they defiantly club-hop around town, JimBob snoozing on a rucksack. At dawn, trashed from carousing, Kinneret and Selina find Roarie and Nicola gone, a note left

behind: they are moving on without them. Selina osculates and tactions Kinneret, who lets her take advantage
of her. JimBob watches them making love on the bed.

KINNERET HOOKS UP WITH SELINA, however, they do
not have nearly the same connection as Kinneret and
JimBob had with Roarie. The land and its lack that
can never unvirgin, coerced in a resound of consecrate.
Tearing down the trail as a pair of cyclones, past droop-
branched, motile cypresses, beholden, recapitulant, fore
the Prime Mover, those bees wontedly bumbling, the
sun interrogatory, raveling out of the roiling clouds,
gaining its head, an opaline current bubbling, fuzzed
in haze, ostensibly made from tin, start to finish of the
glare's glazing in an unsounded fulmination of unbe-
lief, a shed like a cubistic beetle. Nimbuses of bushes,
bloomed as blossoms, light dappling on them, become
reaccruent in the unwinded, immotile daytime. Avians
ejaculant. Mungy negroes, taciturn, pieceways, with no
inference of movement, almost anticipant, isolate, from
reality and irreality. A gramophone in a chicken coop
the tinct of blotting paper, its incumbents distinctive and
daresome. "I'm fitten to build one myself." Hits what
Selina blazons, she with her duck's derrière, a charmen
stern, pretty as a picture, still like stone, and she belches,
a guttural burp, lays an egg, a cowlow sonance. The spray
has an odor of turpentine. Sand with the tincture and
texture of talc. Stars wink, nested in cirri. Mayflies churn.
Stacks smoked for eons, presumably. Bugwhirled polder.

Encarmined ravine. Spooklike vapor. Limpeared sheep in sustain of their steadfast fidelity to an anonymous vineyard. A big girl, preggers, ensembled in a shapeless sundress and waders, augments the atmosphere with her ample aura, on the creakseat of a squeakwheeled, brokespoked bike, on a ditchbank in the wood winey-piney, tremendous in its triviality, she limberlimbed and pleasantphysog'd, punctuating the prairie. Outraged halations of skeeters. Kinneret and Selina put on an act at a nudist colony. The matinee offering is a fiasco. A failure. Kinneret glances askance at these nekkid juvies, exhibitionists, as representations of a different race. They are noticed by her with neither warmth nor coldness. Her moray eel trap and enrapt eyes.

A HAZEL EAGLE, SHRILLING, GLIDES, PITILESS, potent and unrecking, sufficient in self-crucifixion on that Cross-sky. Drizzle sisses like cow's milk squirting into a pail. Popcorn cumuli. Countrybred bitch's singsong, distent-gutted-gluted, parturient as it may be, probably reportorially yapping saccharoid, blundering in the dewy scrubland, her tenor cranky in the fullborn moon's shine, stars flickering matches, Heaven in the smog achromatizing as an older billboard advert, her undergarments guttergrunged, purloined possibly, she glommed in the obsid oralcavity of darkness, a zephyrine tongue lapping her, cumuli crumbling not unlike moldy fungi. Reeds thigh-high, defined by primrose luster which can lay full upon 'em. The range turns clearer, as a photo in liquid, in the mist dissipate, faintly ammoniac in its smell, chilly cleanness, the clarity increasing. Semicircling clumpen weeds arch the ceaseless spring, sunshot, flowing like time. Shadowbrooded ave is an arrant arras. Drabby brush in a cove. A cocoa osprey strays off its ossicular branchlet and in stillwinged suspension exhumes a gristly worm. Bodiless fecund voxes stop midvoice, inbreath liquiform, an accrete from an environment compounding the cosmos, the imperceivable substance of it. The heartthudding thunder. Garbled manshaped cottonwoods. Brighten blurs of leven bulge. Shaggyhill as a beheaded mammoth. A quarry in Augustaurific aurora. Them penitentiary purlieus, besmirched with lachrymose soot, tears of coal, and adjacenting gating. A cloudbleakened swath of sky, strewnpacked with the cirri, toddler-trebling. By ordinary Kinneret would take interest - a chemist an her concoctions in a laboratory. Not now. Stormbrew's silent like a silhouette and surreptitious. Her heartbeats as footscuffing. Cloudlets in crepitate. Selina's icecold peepers brimmed with woman … sufferingsinning … bitchery instantaneous … looks like a flaccid protagonist with an idiot's flabby face, frustrate, in some simulation of a puppet production, of despoliation and ordeal, moving as a twig floating on water, with a heathenish eagering, her body suggestive of it being jellied. Dimunition of lipsize as she decisively forms her speech, ponderous, she laxen at a fence inyawned on playground realestate. An unsmokin chimney. Mizzle smacking of stable and crabapple. Kinneret dreams of her hunched, spartan bedroom backhome, with its sabbath summerfilled draughts, wanting to be there with her lion. The azure, abject, in abnegation of allcloud. Her roughplanked walls, pealing steep ceiling, sagging, biding door, phantasmoid somatic indentation in the soiled, pronetomb mattress, lying so, as a macabre monstrance. Whippoorwills a-whistle. A granitoid, graven, rugged farmer. Jessamine stars aburgeon in the galactic garden. Selina's b.o. like bread-dough and walnut, breath as citrus-candy, drifts consistent with an air-hockey puck above a game-table, pies potty like cracked marbles. Absinthian aqua pura. A humdinger hoopla is to happen in their special todo.

Fishhawk horizonward, flight of its own weight, making fast for the empyrean, vanishing in the clouds akin to a chalk etching being erased on a blackboard, with shady alacrity fluttering up to the deceptive, nacreous, somnambulant apex, this vertex impervious to time, a sentry, unbending and stiffbacked, to a necromantic portal, avianly overladen. Pensive babyblue of the moon, notseeing, backglared, imprisoned in a lid of cirrus, in the fretted frontage of the firmament. Unnumbered mares in a measured savannah, deathcoloured an plowed. Vomitous channel. The winds flatvoiced. Underwatery-wavy shadows, brunet as a raven's wing. A juggernaut negrite with a monklike rictus, straight as an arrow, next to a oneroom, kerosenelit millshack, chops wood on an umber grassbank in incipient lambency, his activeness an adjunct to inactivity; a theatring of movingpicture effort. Desisting not unlike in consultation. Rain retributive.

A blunt-cranium'd negress, mask-faced, turned out in a dahlia kimono, exists in this perpetuate sough of sluttishness, has the air of an absolved martyr, seashell mouth a hovel of jagged, yellow chiclets, drivels rigmarole, Afro, strobile and illclipped, invoking the heritage of her harlotry, in the infallibility of refracted fulgence, her heyday longgone ... For a sold-out assembly of recovering addicts, in a closed-school gymnasium, an accident occurs. To wit, JimBob, missing Roarie, and being uneasy with Selina, mauls her, Selina, and she is rushed to the hospital in an ambulance. JimBob is euthanized. He goes peaceful. Kinneret is with him at the vet's, holding him and sobbing. Her soul and spirit feel put down. She is banned immediate from the circuit, license revoked permanent. She walks, dead to the world. Bedlamite drencher.

THE LANECUT EXTENTBIT. Slaverous welkin. Brusque, inwardlistening birds, ascending and descending in the swift crossslanting luminosity. It's weeks later. Species of folks meandering, harnessed in serviceable, sweatfaden, rested raiment, dip snuff, have those irascible screw-features, secede from society you bet of their accord, and boondoggle in a barnlot, modulations - perseverative, jollifying, easy and quick, right kind. Slow-spittin sky, immanent with precipitation. They are liven effigies of themselves. On footgnawed dirt, boardflat, holden bandanna bundles, bleacheyed and overalled, in what is an inescapable environ. Unhurried cumulus solve the static vault. Battery of bow wows. A tubulose, middle aged, perspiry, hairy hobo, dressed in trousers, rootless in this universe, contrives to look fatal, have a decorum of gravity, an augur of his attitude, a lank cig contained in the corner of his foul chops at an arrogant angle, down on his luck with no upswing. Rattlesnake-sounding showers. Fierce stove of summersolstice with its baken regularity. Mendacious clouds sneer across the confounding countenance of skyline. Locusts malinger. Overlingering malodor of spoilt meat. Mesa monuments. Patinapolished vista with the anticipatory agitation of cloudcover. She is heavybodied, leaden-loined, tumescent-tummied, all alone, composed of sedentary zaftig, in her Homeric Odyssey. Unpaved roads spread with many myrtles. Bungaloid pads, cunningly carpentered, oblong and unobtrusive, in scin-tillation suspire. Loafers preach and pray, fatuous and sonorous, all wellmeant, in the bitten luminescence, harmonic chinooks. Floury sand. Insectoid pulses. Her whale-weighty build's congenerous to a sack of meal. Our Maker's sufferance. A corrupted countryside with demarcations of constructions. Primarily masculine population interrupted by intermittent feminine pres-ences. Attenuation of vivid celestial sphere is malleable metal. Jolly crackfellers swag on the saffroning esparto aslink with salamanders. Flies get foul of their beings. Bedeadened dogie. D'ye see? Foam-freighted surf dwelt upon the shore's detail, elucidating it. Seaside industri-alfield dustdry and enfolded in unceasingly unwearied shadow. Savage waves burst down on indefatigable, indestructible rocks. Mystic head of sun vital, held there, wondrous an haughty. Damocles-sword light. Salted sprays. Frond-fans. Whither blows the wind. Wherefore all the birdcries? Wilddogs woof. Cranes caterwaul habitatorily. Mastodon-mounts. Kinneret rechristens them hills leviathanic. Overcast blots out the empyrean's existence, its space a subtle chaos in its blacken eterni-ties, in this here humane age, wherein it done bequeath the moon's unmistaken shinen character. Fossiliferous boughs. Vesuvius-esque crater. Flinted firmament termi-nate in cirri, made by Divine Providence. It behoves one to describe. MittelEuropa megapolis bottled by bureau-cracy. Gales barbaric. Kinneret's gait like she's boozy in a boat on the rapids. Cumuli active, cruise on up there. Lordly coconut trees. Welkin engulphed in unextin-guishable flames. A disgraced and depressed Kinneret attends Roarie and Nicola's act at a cancer treatment center, the show going astray when Roarie, dancing in a teddy on the platform, loses concentration, gazing at Kinneret in the audience, and getting distracted, and misses her cue, getting burned by Nicola's spat flame. Mayhem ensues.

A Nordic, anthropoidal, lowbuilt, onearmed pulpiter, a revivalist with the boiled, bloodless religi-nose hellfire-and-brimstone, orally engulfs a corncake in this rectilinear of threshold of an orbiculate parish on a cedar knoll, he from Indianny and popping up as a bubble convinced on a beck, in soporific contem-plation currently, expression faraway, his alonginyears, hairslicked and runted pappy coasting like a canoe, him in his senility. Mosquito-netting of rasping downpour. Oftused, bottomless well. Symbolical, unwavering, well-nigh madglare of moon bulked round. Neversunned chocolate trogteen tubetopped and in scantshorts is an adolescent avatar of Kinneret's angst, within a stone's throw of townshaped diggings, solemnizing its pretension, even past its former glory, and which hasn't been painted in a stretch, pulpous lawn the allmother of extensity, a beaked girlie, unalarmed and approaching as that beetred light, who has had her victories and defeats. Kinneret had put on a solid striptease performance at an honorable college for these trustees, faculty and alumnae, in a scarceutilized, crudeclean meeting room on campus, for banknotes, where she was lit not unlike land in lightning, in abandon of her anatomy, burlybody bared. And she had cursory sandpapery intercourse with an impish teacher, then slept stringstraight and rigor-mortis in his cot, and woke to smoke ganja and longed for home, its sparse furnishings and worthless keep-sakes, boards and nails, those consonants of clouds and vowels of valleys in panoramic sentences in the para-graph of the cosmos, spoke in the language of her life ... her native tongue ... Pre-and-post-pubescent pigling and lionet in probability with nymphomaniacal-level promiscuity proclivities adorned in loungewear in an unvarying period of play and purposeful loiter in the vespers, imperious and insatiable, of a Biblical Hades of Hicksville, USA, fiddle with each other with convic-tion and the detached impersonal disinterest of trained nurses, at a hollowing fencepost, as a couple of things in throes, taking Kinneret unawares, the octopoid tentacles of her tress flailing in the overriding of winds, bugs in bumming paraphrase, the sun a dying coal of anticlimax. Flow of their especial experimentations, like the tide on a shore, flirtatious momentum bearing them, monotone inflections abnegant in sterile oxygen, on the spent terrain, behaving as volitionless sisters, and strangers too, flood of emotions damming, both impulsively tossing in a greytunnel of halfdeath and indirection, animalcreatures exchanging delights unmentionable. Upflare of finches from pollen-padded esparto. She reproaches herself, has regrets in self-pity. Someone sexless, noiseless and negrine, with a snakehead snoot. Her anime-eyes. Forward-lookin and back-shrunk trees 'neath a soft-hued azure with its summer-stars. A cannyskulled, wildhaired, outwore countrycousin in unwashed workclothes, reek overpowering, labor-hardened and tub-ish, a crusty cap'm nosey, the foetid southerner with yankee ancestry's attention solely on her, canvassing her like she is an outlander, a human agent foreigner, allied with aloneness, blumping about the motor-blatting Chevy shitbox in a pall of smoke engine-engendered, he fulltongued and moiling, with a momentary moue, waftage whupping, his bays, in baritone, longdrawn, when the car seizes. An avian exodus. Sourceless niggersniggers. She feels like an eggsucker, as if her senses are the elements, has drug herself on the plausible driedplains as though a bloodhound on a new scent, trompling breathless like the day itself, she odorous and obese, her leatherhard flab flyspecked, heat having a palpitant quality, morn's humidness a reiterant chiaroscuro, abrogating the assertive, accomplished air, her carriage changed in them interminable insects. Retching up to shield her Chinesed optics and hollering, at endurance's limit, yap shet, aft coming alive, aurously, in the yetlight. Her abdomen acquiescent for aspirin to relieve its ache. Fluxes of jonquil-hued rays. Wormriddled picketgate. Weather in its friggin fickle phases, its immutable rules she obeys, gusts calf-yellin an gwine. Her arteries as threshing hoses with serious pressure. Dampdirt not unlike unovened piecrust. Her armpits stench analogous to cave. Her shadow perishing and borning again. She moves snackward, craving pretzels and cookies ... A woodenfaced, puttypigmented fellow in beaten brogans, sulled and crazy in the clock, dialedup, seemingly could pop his cork at any minute, reads the funnypaper, propped by his tractor, wearing his Sunday bestest, in the vicinity of a benignant mulberry at a depot in appearing vanquishment, his port pontifical, glacierish, prophetlike, in sublimination, expression paradoxically mobile and immobile, evocative of something premonitory; a puppetpuss operated by faulty springwork. Them breezes sound as a needle on a phonographic record. His lip movements are out of sync with his vocalizations, like he's a dummy controlled by an invisible ventriloquist. A rock-visaged gent, charred-candlewick-semblant, at an alright post office, standen in a continual ebb of dust, with a weary grimace and clench-fisted chair-arms. Mom-and-popless foundlings frolicsome, orphans astink of vitamin, life a cost to pay, ravening devilings willynilly pellmell, befooled of the need for society by fate, in the mush. Sun in cloud is a failin street lamp. Paunched Kinneret's bearlike bod an bafflement abundant. So much sludge. She is testy. An illkept cur sounds querulous. Haziness is a repressed quiver. Generations of prolific peoples super-imposing an erosiongutted, tedious boardinghouse, it queershaped. Weazened, geriatric feller in front of a cryptic combine breathes deep, hams clasped behind his shaved head, a self-conscious hardware merchant and yellow-bellied ex-marine, uncomplex as a corridor, who went to war on blind faith for ole Uncle Sam, with his unsleepen eyes and daredevil cardiac organ. Diffident persimmon and sassafras. A hulking youth with a subterraneous profile, a moribund mask, loosejointed and hattermad, near this fringe of spinney, listens to terrifically cheeping birds. Undeviation of chimeran condensation, Confederate-gray. Heliographic flickers of fulgor ... leafbrown. That fellah, kept in his make-believe, a living landmark, diminished by distance, yon the realm of your seeing. She stares at him like a judge pronouncing a sentence on the convicted. Framed sign-board, vacant and prepped, regenerate and ramifying, will be the eventual recipient of an ad, as the recep-tacle of a vagina prepared to ultimately receive the seed from a penis, the prick in a cunt like a beast in its den. Oxygen's audible, abating in aspersion. Fogbank as cannonsmoke. Her blinders possess a gambler's calcu-lation. She is fanaticfaced and urgenthearted, tranquilly cantering, her being a barricade out of the middleages, feeling as a wheel in quicksand; or a fish in a bowl. A strappen hoyden, prolly desperated, holds a hymn-book and a yearling-sized youngun clammedup, them's riding the bumps of existence on welfare, speaks heresy, preempting Kinneret's ponder, hiatusing her fortitude in a privilege of forbearance, within flowers fragranced and fullsprung and composite of colors, those flies skirmishing thereabouts in contemplate.

Epilogue

A month passes and Kinneret winds up on a structure's zeneth, in considerate of killing herself, when she notices a disfigured Roarie, proximal. Both burned, deformed. Getting down together. Roarie tells Kinneret that Nicola, despondent over everything that had transpired, hanged herself, only not before donating her blood to save Selina's life. The ocean sounds not unlike leonine growling.

That's all.

Acknowledgments

Eric, Nina, Harriet, Paula, Sammy, Vic, Sue, Mary and Linda, for their sweetness and support and being loony extraterrestrials.

Photo by Jaymes Dickerson

Christopher S. Peterson has been seriously dreaming since he was fetaled, jumping the umbilical rope, as it were, immersing himself in Icarusian flights of fancy, such as imagining an indigotic, umbrageous populace alienating on gambogian ground in presentiments of palsy. He enjoys film, music, animals, working out, football, hockey, and living blissfully in nerdvana. He has been published in several lit mags very few people have actually read. He was properly educated at Wildwood Elementary School in Burlington, Massachusetts and currently lives in Atlanta, Georgia with his four kooky black cats.

Fomite

About Fomite

A fomite is a medium capable of transmitting infectious organisms from one individual to another.

"The activity of art is based on the capacity of people to be infected by the feelings of others." Tolstoy, *What Is Art?*

Writing a review on Amazon, Good Reads, Shelfari, Library Thing or other social media sites for readers will help the progress of independent publishing. To submit a review, go to the book page on any of the sites and follow the links for reviews. Books from independent presses rely on reader to reader communications.

For more information or to order any of our books, visit http://www.fomitepress.com/FOMITE/Our_Books.html

More Titles from Fomite...

Novels

Joshua Amses — *During This, Our Nadir*
Joshua Amses — *Ghats*
Joshua Amses — *Raven or Crow*
Joshua Amses — *The Moment Before an Injury*
Jaysinh Birjepatel — *Nothing Beside Remains*
Jaysinh Birjepatel — *The Good Muslim of Jackson Heights*
David Brizer — *Victor Rand*
Paula Closson Buck — *Summer on the Cold War Planet*
Dan Chodorkoff — *Loisaida*
David Adams Cleveland — *Time's Betrayal*
Jaimee Wriston Colbert — *Vanishing Acts*
Roger Coleman — *Skywreck Afternoons*
Marc Estrin — *Hyde*
Marc Estrin — *Kafka's Roach*
Marc Estrin — *Speckled Vanities*
Zdravka Evtimova — *In the Town of Joy and Peace*
Zdravka Evtimova — *Sinfonia Bulgarica*
Daniel Forbes — *Derail This Train Wreck*
Greg Guma — *Dons of Time*
Richard Hawley — *The Three Lives of Jonathan Force*
Lamar Herrin — *Father Figure*
Michael Horner — *Damage Control*
Ron Jacobs — *All the Sinners Saints*
Ron Jacobs — *Short Order Frame Up*
Ron Jacobs — *The Co-conspirator's Tale*
Scott Archer Jones — *And Throw Away the Skins*
Scott Archer Jones — *A Rising Tide of People Swept Away*
Julie Justicz — *Degrees of Difficulty*
Maggie Kast — *A Free Unsullied Land*
Darrell Kastin — *Shadowboxing with Bukowski*
Coleen Kearon — *#triggerwarning*
Coleen Kearon — *Feminist on Fire*

Fomite

Jan English Leary — *Thicker Than Blood*
Diane Lefer — *Confessions of a Carnivore*
Rob Lenihan — *Born Speaking Lies*
Douglas Milliken — *Our Shadow's Voice*
Colin Mitchell — *Roadman*
Ilan Mochari — *Zinsky the Obscure*
Peter Nash — *Parsimony*
Peter Nash — *The Perfection of Things*
George Ovitt — Stillpoint
George Ovitt — Tribunal
Gregory Papadoyiannis — *The Baby Jazz*
Pelham — *The Walking Poor*
Andy Potok — *My Father's Keeper*
Frederick Ramey — *Comes A Time*
Joseph Rathgeber — *Mixedbloods*
Kathryn Roberts — *Companion Plants*
Robert Rosenberg — *Isles of the Blind*
Fred Russell — *Rafi's World*
Ron Savage — *Voyeur in Tangier*
David Schein — *The Adoption*
Lynn Sloan — *Principles of Navigation*
L.E. Smith — *The Consequence of Gesture*
L.E. Smith — *Travers' Inferno*
L.E. Smith — *Untimely RIPped*
Bob Sommer — *A Great Fullness*
Tom Walker — *A Day in the Life*
Susan V. Weiss —*My God, What Have We Done?*
Peter M. Wheelwright — *As It Is On Earth*
Suzie Wizowaty — *The Return of Jason Green*

Poetry

Anna Blackmer — *Hexagrams*
Antonello Borra — *Alfabestiario*
Antonello Borra — *AlphaBetaBestiaro*
Antonello Borra — *Fabbrica delle idee/The Factory of Ideas*
L. Brown — *Loopholes*
Sue D. Burton — *Little Steel*
David Cavanagh— *Cycling in Plato's Cave*
James Connolly — *Picking Up the Bodies*
Greg Delanty — *Loosestrife*
Mason Drukman — *Drawing on Life*
J. C. Ellefson — *Foreign Tales of Exemplum and Woe*
Tina Escaja/Mark Eisner — *Caida Libre/Free Fall*
Anna Faktorovich — *Improvisational Arguments*
Barry Goldensohn — *Snake in the Spine, Wolf in the Heart*
Barry Goldensohn — *The Hundred Yard Dash Man*
Barry Goldensohn — *The Listener Aspires to the Condition of Music*
R. L. Green — *When You Remember Deir Yassin*
Gail Holst-Warhaft — *Lucky Country*
Raymond Luczak — *A Babble of Objects*
Kate Magill — *Roadworthy Creature, Roadworthy Craft*

Fomite

Tony Magistrale — *Entanglements*
Gary Mesick — *General Discharge*
Andreas Nolte — *Mascha: The Poems of Mascha Kaléko*
Sherry Olson — *Four-Way Stop*
Brett Ortler — *Lessons of the Dead*
Aristea Papalexandrou/Philip Ramp — □□□ ϖ□□□ϖ□□□á/*It's Overtaking Us*
Janice Miller Potter — *Meanwell*
Janice Miller Potter — *Thoreau's Umbrella*
Philip Ramp — *The Melancholy of a Life as the Joy of Living It Slowly Chills*
Joseph D. Reich — *A Case Study of Werewolves*
Joseph D. Reich — *Connecting the Dots to Shangrila*
Joseph D. Reich — *The Derivation of Cowboys and Indians*
Joseph D. Reich — *The Hole That Runs Through Utopia*
Joseph D. Reich — *The Housing Market*
Kenneth Rosen and Richard Wilson — *Gomorrah*
Fred Rosenblum — *Vietnumb*
David Schein — *My Murder and Other Local News*
Harold Schweizer — *Miriam's Book*
Scott T. Starbuck — *Carbonfish Blues*
Scott T. Starbuck — *Hawk on Wire*
Scott T. Starbuck — *Industrial Oz*
Seth Steinzor — *Among the Lost*
Seth Steinzor — *To Join the Lost*
Susan Thomas — *In the Sadness Museum*
Susan Thomas — *The Empty Notebook Interrogates Itself*
Paolo Valesio/Todd Portnowitz — *La Mezzanotte di Spoleto/Midnight in Spoleto*
Sharon Webster — *Everyone Lives Here*
Tony Whedon — *The Tres Riches Heures*
Tony Whedon — *The Falkland Quartet*
Claire Zoghb — *Dispatches from Everest*

Stories
Jay Boyer — *Flight*
L. M Brown — *Treading the Uneven Road*
Michael Cocchiarale — *Here Is Ware*
Michael Cocchiarale — *Still Time*
Neil Connelly — *In the Wake of Our Vows*
Catherine Zobal Dent — *Unfinished Stories of Girls*
Zdravka Evtimova —*Carts and Other Stories*
John Michael Flynn — *Off to the Next Wherever*
Derek Furr — *Semitones*
Derek Furr — *Suite for Three Voices*
Elizabeth Genovise — *Where There Are Two or More*
Andrei Guriuanu — *Body of Work*
Zeke Jarvis — *In A Family Way*
Arya Jenkins — *Blue Songs in an Open Key*
Jan English Leary — *Skating on the Vertical*
Marjorie Maddox — *What She Was Saying*
William Marquess — *Boom-shacka-lacka*
Gary Miller — *Museum of the Americas*

Fomite

Jennifer Anne Moses — *Visiting Hours*
Martin Ott — *Interrogations*
Christopher Peterson — *Amoebic Simulacra*
Jack Pulaski — *Love's Labours*
Charles Rafferty — *Saturday Night at Magellan's*
Ron Savage — *What We Do For Love*
Fred Skolnik— *Americans and Other Stories*
Lynn Sloan — *This Far Is Not Far Enough*
L.E. Smith — *Views Cost Extra*
Caitlin Hamilton Summie — *To Lay To Rest Our Ghosts*
Susan Thomas — *Among Angelic Orders*
Tom Walker — *Signed Confessions*
Silas Dent Zobal — *The Inconvenience of the Wings*

Odd Birds

William Benton — *Eye Contact: Writing on Art*
Micheal Breiner — *the way none of this happened*
J. C. Ellefson — *Under the Influence: Shouting Out to Walt*
David Ross Gunn — *Cautionary Chronicles*
Andrei Guriuanu and Teknari — *The Darkest City*
Gail Holst-Warhaft — *The Fall of Athens*
Roger Lebovitz — *A Guide to the Western Slopes and the Outlying Area*
Roger Lebovitz — *Twenty-two Instructions for Near Survival*
dug Nap— *Artsy Fartsy*
Delia Bell Robinson — *A Shirtwaist Story*
Peter Schumann — *Belligerent & Not So Belligerent Slogans from the Possibilitarian Arsenal*
Peter Schumann — *Bread & Sentences*
Peter Schumann — *Charlotte Salomon*
Peter Schumann — *Diagonal Man Theory & Praxis, Volumes One and Two*
Peter Schumann — *Faust 3*
Peter Schumann — *Planet Kasper, Volumes One and Two*
Peter Schumann — *We*

Plays

Stephen Goldberg — *Screwed and Other Plays*
Michele Markarian — *Unborn Children of America*

Essays

Robert Sommer — *Losing Francis: Essays on the Wars at Home*